# THE FAIRIES
# OF SADIEVILLE

# THE FAIRIES
# OF SADIEVILLE

## ALEX BLEDSOE

**TOR**

A TOM DOHERTY ASSOCIATES BOOK
NEW YORK

THE FAIRIES OF SADIEVILLE

Copyright © 2018 by Alex Bledsoe

A Tor Book
Published by Tom Doherty Associates
175 Fifth Avenue
New York, NY 10010

www.tor-forge.com

Tor® is a registered trademark of Macmillan Publishing Group, LLC.

The Library of Congress Cataloging-in-Publication Data is available upon request.

ISBN 978-0-7653-8336-5 (hardcover)
ISBN 978-1-4668-9156-2 (ebook)

Our books may be purchased in bulk for promotional, educational, or business use. Please contact your local bookseller or the Macmillan Corporate and Premium Sales Department at 1-800-221-7945, extension 5442, or by email at MacmillanSpecialMarkets@macmillan.com.

First Edition: April 2018

Printed in the United States of America

0  9  8  7  6  5  4  3  2  1

To Valette

*They say if you see a turtle on a fence post, you know it didn't get there by itself. Well, neither did I.*

## SPECIAL THANKS

Byron Ballard
Deborah Blake
Emily Carding
Kiki Dombrowski
Grammy-nominated James P. Leary
The staff of the Mount Horeb McDonald's,
    for being so nice while I wrote and revised
    great swaths of this book.
Janis Mirkle, Melissa Roelli, Linda Colby,
    Jessica Williams, and the rest of the staff of
    the Mount Horeb Public Library
Diana Pho
Signe Pike
Jay Rath
Adam Selzer
Everyone at Sjolind's Chocolate Shoppe
Bill Yeates
Nicole Youngerman

And extra-special thanks to Jennifer Goree,
    whose songs have provided the titles for all
    the Tufa novels, but who has never had a song
    actually used in one. *The Fairies of Sadieville*
    fixes that.

# I

# THIS IS REAL

## 1

The odor hit Justin first. It was mostly the aroma of old books, along with mustier, more organic smells: a touch of mildew, the accumulated reek of old-man sweat, and the whispery memory of tobacco from the days when professors could smoke in their offices. Not that it was ever a good idea for anyone to smoke in here, with all that flammable paper around.

He gazed silently into the darkness until he felt Veronica's hand on the small of his back. She asked quietly, "You okay? We don't have to do this right now."

"Yeah, I'm good," Justin Johnson said. "No point in putting it off. We have to start sometime."

He turned on the light, and bright fluorescent illumination flooded the room. The little office looked as though an entire big-city library had somehow been condensed and jammed into it. Books, papers, CDs, DVDs, VHS cassettes, vinyl albums, open-reel recordings, and even one lone eight-track tape lined the shelves and, once those were filled, rose in piles almost to the ceiling.

On the walls hung maps, posters, and old photographs, many in black-and-white. Pride of place was given to an eight-by-ten autographed photo of Woody Guthrie, signed with the trembling hand that was a symptom of the disease that eventually claimed his life.

*To Doc Adams,* it read. *Keep fighting!*

Justin recalled the first time he'd seen it, on the day he met the surprisingly named Dr. Dock Adams. The man had looked like a biker Santa, with a white beard and long snowy hair that dramatically swept back from his weathered face, his blue eyes perpetually atwinkle. But that first day, he had mainly looked puzzled at the sight of a black kid in a leather jacket waiting in his office, a guitar case at his feet.

"Hello," he said.

"Hi," Justin replied, and stood. "I'm early."

"I never am." They shook hands. "You must be Mr. Johnson. Well, have a seat. Before we start, I have to get my coffee. Would you like any?"

"No, thanks."

It took him three tries to hang up his windbreaker on the hook behind the door. While he went to the teacher's lounge for his coffee, Justin looked around at the kaleidoscope of items on the shelves. He was pleasantly surprised at the number of African-American books, recordings, and memorabilia.

Adams returned, picked his way carefully around the piles, and dropped into his desk chair. Justin sat as well.

"So," Adams said after his first sip. "You want to study folklore, specifically folk *music,* here at good ol' West Tennessee?"

"I want to study with you, Dr. Adams. Since you're here, I'd like to be as well."

"Call me 'Doc.' Spell it however you want. Just never 'Doctor Dock,' please."

"So noted."

"I see you brought your guitar." In his heavy drawl, it came out "GEE-tar." "You don't have to audition, you know."

"I take it everywhere."

"Let me see it."

Justin opened the case and passed him the instrument. "Takamine," Doc murmured. "Don't you like American?"

"I like the sound. Don't care where it comes from."

The old man put it across his lap and strummed a shimmering E-minor chord that sent echoes of the Beatles ringing through the small office. "Dreadnought body," he muttered. He inspected spots where the finish was worn. "And lots of use. By you?"

"Yes, sir. I got it new when I was sixteen."

Doc handed it back. "That's a pretty nice gift."

"I thought so."

"You play anywhere?"

"Sometimes at open mics. I've been in a couple of bands."

"Write your own songs?"

"Yeah, some."

For a heart-stopping moment he thought Doc would ask him to play one. But instead the old man picked up Justin's thesis proposal from the desk and peered down his nose, through his half-glasses. He would've already read it carefully, so this was just for drama's sake, but Justin felt a knot of nerves twist in his stomach anyway. "Justin, I don't mean this as a racial thing, but I can't see any other way to phrase it, so I'm apologizing in advance." He paused. "*Why* do you want to study folk music with me? Because my expertise is the Scotch-Irish diaspora to Appalachia, and that's just about the whitest subject in the world."

"It says in my proposal that I—"

"Forget the paperwork. Tell me. In words that don't sound like you've memorized them, please."

Justin thought for a moment. "Because I want to understand why some music lasts."

"Then why not go study music? You got your BA in it already."

"Because I don't want to be just an academic. I want to *make* music that lasts. So I figure, if I can understand where meaningful music comes from, and why certain songs resonate when others just fade away, maybe *I* can do it someday. Make music that lasts, that is."

"Like you are now?" Doc said.

Justin looked down in genuine surprise; he hadn't even realized he'd been strumming softly along with his words. "Sorry. Habit."

"A good one, as far as I'm concerned." Doc leaned back in his chair and put his feet up on the desk. "Well, welcome to the Department of English at West Tennessee University. Hopefully, you'll bring a new and valuable perspective to this. And remember . . ." And here Doc had really grinned, the first of thousands of times Justin would see that merry twinkle flare like a pinpoint spotlight in his bright blue eyes. "Folk music is supposed to be fun. So there's no reason studying about it can't be fun, too."

"I agree," Justin said.

And now he stood in that same office, two days after Doc's funeral, preparing to sort through a lifetime's accumulation of things that were both junk, and priceless.

"At least," his girlfriend Veronica Lopez said wryly, "he left something behind."

"Too much," Justin said.

"Well, nobody ever thinks they're really going to die, do they?"

"Especially Doc," Justin agreed.

"When you pass seventy-five, though, you ought to take some precautions," Veronica said. "Like maybe going to the doctor occasionally."

"He lived like he wanted. He died the same way." The police, called when Doc failed to show up for his office hours, found the old man on his couch, headphones on, a smile on his face. Justin had not been able to find out what he was listening to when he died, but whatever it was, he was glad it left the old man happy in his final moments.

The English department secretary, Mrs. Lundoff, said from behind them, "A little overwhelming, isn't it? I swear, in all the years I've worked here, I saw truckloads of stuff go in, but I never saw anything come out."

"It's not that bad," Justin said. "Once we get started, it'll shake out pretty quickly. He was organized, just not in any way that you'd recognize."

"Yes, the alphabet regularly vexed him," she said dryly. Then she turned wistful. "He smiled and wished me a good evening on his way out, and they say he was dead an hour later. I still expected to see him come shuffling in this morning and try three times to hang his coat up before he finally got it on the hook."

They all laughed a little at that.

"Well, I'll leave you two to your work," Mrs. Lundoff continued. "There's more empty boxes and garbage bags in the storeroom if you need them. Also rubber gloves and some of those respirator face masks like you use for painting or yard work."

"I don't think we'll need those," Veronica said.

"Don't be so sure. It wouldn't surprise me if there's a dozen different kinds of mold in here. And thank you, both of you, for being willing to help out. He thought the world of you, and I know wherever he is, he's glad to know you're the ones taking care of this."

When Mrs. Lundoff was out of earshot, Justin said quietly, "Wherever he is, he's laughing his ass off, she means."

Veronica smiled and threaded her fingers through Justin's. "Where do you want to start?"

Justin reverently took down the signed photo of Woody Guthrie. He looked into the legendary troubadour's black-and-white eyes, smiled, and put it facedown on the desk.

"We'll start here. That'll be the most recent stuff. Let's separate it into piles: originals, photocopies, and miscellaneous."

"I bet I can guess which will be the biggest pile."

"Me, too. But we can subsort that pile later."

Doc Adams had been one of a literally dying breed of academic, a man who created his own discipline out of a lifetime of interests, research, and publishing. Although he was technically part of West Tennessee University's English department, his expertise was in the way folklore from Great Britain and Ireland made its way to the Appalachian region. He'd written the definitive history of the dulcimer, conducted countless workshops at the Museum of Appalachia, and traveled the world as a noted scholar. And legend said he'd spent three weeks shacked up with Sandy Denny, during which he convinced her to form Fotheringay.

Why he'd remained at tiny little West Tennessee University was a mystery to most people, but not to Justin: Doc had not only tenure but carte blanche, since the prestige he brought the school more than made up for his occasional jaunts into less-than-scholarly fields. If he wanted to spend a year researching the imagery of rabbits in songs from northern Georgia, they were content to let him.

Justin had been his last graduate student, and after that initial interview, he never pulled rank again. Doc invited Justin and Veronica out for drinks at the local "members only" pub (due to the area's convoluted liquor laws, you could only get liquor by the drink at private clubs; so the "club" charged one dollar for a lifetime membership) and regaled them with stories of his trips to Ireland and the Scottish Highlands, where he'd sought both folkloric evidence and beautiful red-haired lasses with equal success. He flirted mercilessly with Veronica in terrible Spanish, which made all three of them laugh, and he helped Justin prepare academic articles for publication.

The papers on his desk were a cacophony of topics and

sources, in no particular order and to no obvious purpose. Doc believed in pursuing each and every tangent as far as it went, and for as long as it held his interest. Organizing this, Justin realized, was not going to be easy.

After three hours, Justin and Veronica had cleared about two-thirds of the desktop, and were coated in dust and book dander.

Justin sneezed. "Maybe we do need those masks."

"Look at this," Veronica said in wonder. She held an old three-ring binder, the ragged cover patched with duct tape and the pages faded to yellow. Veronica read aloud a note clipped to the cover:

> My mother loved music, but we could not afford a record player. So she sat beside the radio and each time a song she liked came on, she listened and wrote down as many lyrics as she could. Each time, she got a few more, until finally she had the whole song, and put it in a special notebook. My love of folk music started with these notebooks.

It was signed *Doc Adams, 1983*. The date marked on the first notebook page was *November 14, 1929*.

"That's so sweet," Veronica said, her eyes misting. She opened the notebook and sighed. "Oh, my God, look at this!"

On the page were carefully written lyrics in a beautiful cursive hand, faded but legible despite nearly a century having passed since they were recorded. The first song was "Wayfaring Stranger."

Justin put his arm around her shoulders. "It must've meant a lot to him, to have such a tangible way to remember her."

Veronica wiped her eyes. "I'm just so glad they won't be thrown away."

"Me, too," he agreed, and kissed her cheek.

"Excuse me," a new voice said behind them.

The English department chair, Dr. Coffin, stood in the door. He was in his sixties, dressed casually, and looked over the neat stacks Justin and Veronica had already sorted. "You've made some headway."

"A little," Justin agreed.

"I appreciate you doing this. If we'd had to pay an archivist to start from scratch, all this material might've sat uncatalogued for years. Just sorting it into basic piles saves us a great deal of time and money."

"It's a pleasure to do it," Justin said.

"Do you agree?" Coffin wryly asked Veronica.

"I do," she said. "I loved Doc Adams."

"We all did," he said sadly. "He'll be impossible to replace."

"Any word from the faculty search committee?" Justin asked.

"No, with the school's budget like it is, his position may stay empty long enough for you to claim it."

"Hopefully not. The students deserve better."

"The students always deserve better," Coffin said. "But the men who hold the purse strings over in Nashville don't see the profit in studying things like folklore. And to them, if there's no profit, there's no value. And that reminds me, Mr. Johnson: come see me tomorrow, so we can get you set up with another masters committee advisor. Does eight o'clock work for you?"

"Yes, sir."

"Then I'll leave you to your work. Thanks again."

When he'd gone, Veronica said, "Do you think that's true? That the only things that matter are ones that turn a profit?"

"I think he's right that the people who control the money think that way."

She shook her head. "Then you and I will never make a living."

"Sure we will," he said, and pulled her into a kiss. "Me with a degree in folklore, you with one in parapsychology, we'll be rolling in it."

"My degree is actually in psychology, you bum," she said against his lips. "So at least I'll be able to get a job."

"Then you can support me until my research makes us rich."

When they broke the kiss, she said, "I need a break," and looked for someplace to sit down. The desk chair was filled with a stack of papers, so she chose what looked like a solid pile of magazines. As soon as her weight settled on it, though, the slick covers slid out from under her and she fell to one side with a surprised yelp.

"Graceful," Justin said as he helped her up. "Been sitting long, or just reading about it?"

She looked down at the magazines, frowned a little, and said, "Hey, look."

From the very bottom of the pile she lifted a metal lockbox. It was gray and featureless except for touches of rust on the corners. She placed it on the desk and tried to open it.

"Locked," she said. "Wonder what's in it?"

"Probably something personal," Justin said, and turned back to his work.

"Wait, you're not curious?" Veronica said.

"Of course I'm curious, but I imagine we'll find a lot of curious things before we're done. We'll make that the start of the 'curious' pile."

Veronica looked down at the box. It was big enough to hold a stack of notebooks, and clearly had something inside, but that something was not heavy the way papers or text would be. And it rattled when she shook it.


"What do you think is in it?" Veronica asked. The humid spring night air blew through the curtains, drawn in by the fan that was all their combined student budget could afford. They didn't really mind. She lay naked on her back, while Justin sat on the edge of the bed, also naked except for his guitar. He strummed a few chords, then noted them on his laptop.

She saw that he hadn't heard. He could dive so deep into music that he lost track of everything around him.

She poked him and repeated, "What do you think is in it?"

Justin looked up. "What's that, Detective Mills?"

"Don't do it," she mock-warned.

"Are you asking me—"

"No!"

"What's in the baaax?" he finished, imitating Brad Pitt in *Seven*.

"You are awful," she said, and they both laughed.

He put the guitar aside and stretched out beside her. "Whatever it is, we can't just break it open. It might be private family stuff."

"He didn't have a family," she protested. "We're his family."

"We're his friends, watching out for his dignity."

She scooted closer and draped one leg across him. "Come on," she said teasingly, gently pressing her hips against him, "aren't you the least bit curious?"

He pushed her onto her back. "I'm very curious."

"So what do you think is in it?" she asked again, wrapping her legs around him.

"I don't have a clue," he said as he began to move more rhythmically.

"You worked with him every day," she said breathlessly, meeting his movements with her own.

"Only for the past year," he said, shifting his weight to free one hand to caress her breasts. "He's been at the school for thirty years, and who knows how much stuff he might've . . ."

For a few urgent moments neither of them spoke. Then, after

he rolled off, caught his breath, and kissed her deeply, he said, "We don't even know how long that box has been there."

"If the stack of magazines on top of it was any indication, quite a while," Veronica said, tucking hair behind her sweaty ear. "Some of them went back fifty years."

"Look, our job is just to organize and catalog it. It's all the property of the school."

"I know. It's just that I hate mysteries."

He chuckled. "You mean you love mysteries. You're a freaking ghost hunter."

"Parapsychologist."

"Po-TAY-to, po-TAH-to. Either way, you eat mysteries for breakfast."

She smiled and stretched with contentment. "I do indeed."

# 2

Dr. Coffin looked over Justin's folder. He was the kind of administrator who printed out hard copies of students' files so he could flip dramatically through them at moments like this. Except for the noise of rattling pages, the only sound was the droning air conditioner and Coffin's occasional, "Hm."

"Sir?" Justin finally prompted. He was dressed like a white frat boy, in khaki shorts and a polo shirt, but he dripped with nervous sweat. He hadn't even brought his guitar, so there was no tactile comfort to be had, and Coffin's tone didn't help.

At last the department head closed the file, leaned back in his chair, and said, "Well. I see where we are now."

"Where is that?" Justin asked, hoping he sounded polite.

"Doc wasn't the most rigorous advisor, was he?"

"I don't have much to compare him to," Justin said with a little chuckle that died in his throat. "I mean, Veronica has Dr. Tully in psychology, and that's the only other masters advisor I've really heard about in any detail."

"Hm. Dr. Tully, I suspect, requires a little more . . . organization, we'll say, than Doc did."

The suspense was getting to him. "I don't mean to be impertinent, Dr. Coffin, but should I be worried? Because I am."

"Hm? Oh, no, I'm not criticizing your work, you've done exactly what Doc required. It's just that without his advocacy, I'm not sure the rest of your committee will be . . . satisfied."

Justin's stomach dropped. "Oh."

"But it's not too late for you to graduate on time. It will just require a lot of work."

"Can you define 'a lot'?"

Coffin closed the folder. "As in 'starting from scratch.'"

Justin's stomach dropped. "Sir—"

"Justin, your thesis is 'Contemporary Folk Music Performance and its Connection to European Sources.' In practice, that essentially means you get to go catch a lot of current acts, doesn't it?"

That was exactly the way Doc had described it, over a joint they'd shared on the older man's back porch. Justin said, "It's a little more than that . . . sir."

"Oh, that's right. At some of these concerts, you *are* the act."

"I learn things playing the songs live that I never would listening to recordings." It was true, but it sounded impossibly weak spoken aloud.

"I'm sure you do." Coffin tapped the closed folder. "Look, I'm not speaking ill of Doc, he was a friend and colleague for many years. But when you go forth into the world, you'll be taking the name of West Tennessee University with you, especially as one of our few minority graduate students. So it's my job to make sure you don't embarrass us. And truthfully, giving you a degree for this would."

Justin's mouth was so dry he almost couldn't speak. He managed to croak out, "So what should I do?"

"Well, first, I'll be your new advisor and committee chair.

I'll help you as much as I can, because I like you and I do want you to succeed."

"Thank you, sir."

"But I simply won't accept some of the nonsense that Doc accepted. He was a brilliant man and a top-notch scholar, but as a teacher and advisor he was, frankly, lazy. He was an old hippie, and he liked hanging out with students a whole lot more than he did holding them to standards." He paused and leaned his elbows on his desk. "I need a better idea from you, Justin. For your thesis. And not to put too fine a point on it, I need it yesterday."

Justin was numb as he walked the short distance from Coffin's office down to Doc's. Veronica had left a note on the door: *Back after class. Love you!* He got a cup of coffee from the teachers' lounge, went into Doc's office and closed the door. He sat down behind his desk and surveyed the mess that had been Doc's domain.

He couldn't believe all this had come down on him. Two weeks ago, his academic future was assured. Now he was adrift, tumbling without the parachute he hadn't even realized Doc represented.

Justin wasn't exactly afraid of hard work, but he hadn't done much of it in his life, either physically or academically. Most things came easily for him, and he'd gotten used to that. Doc had been the perfect advisor for him, steering him toward the biggest rewards with the least possible effort. He suspected, though he'd never asked, that he was mimicking Doc's own career. But Doc was gone now, and he was on his own.

That, he realized, was a first.

When Veronica arrived, she took one look at him and said, "You're dressed like you're pledging one of those fraternities that beats up guys like you."

"I met with Dr. Coffin."

"And?"

He went to her and sagged into her arms. "I'll tell you about it, but not right now, okay?"

"Okay," she said, and kissed him. "What do you want to do?"

He gestured around them. "Work at something where I can at least see the progress."

"Okay."

They continued sorting and organizing Doc's office, arranging things in silence unless one of them had a work-related question. Then, as he went through one of the desk drawers, Justin suddenly said, "Aha."

"What?" Veronica said, looking up from a stack of old chapbooks.

He held up a key ring with a single key. "I think it's the answer to your prayers."

"*You're* the answer to my prayers, hot stuff, but if that's the key to the lockbox—"

"Let's see," he said.

The key did indeed fit the lock, and with a little effort, it turned. The hinges squeaked as the lid rose.

Inside rested a metal film can. Protected for so long, its finish was still a shiny silver. Black electrical tape wound around the edge, sealing the two halves together.

A wide paper label was affixed to the center, and on it were written three words in Doc's distinctive, often unintelligible handwriting. These words, though, were clear.

*This is real.*

Justin carefully lifted out the can and turned it in his hands.

"Is it an audio tape?" Veronica asked. They'd already started a stack of reel-to-reel recordings.

"No, it's a movie." The can's width told him it was sixteen millimeters, and if the reel was full, it was a film of about fifteen to twenty minutes.

"What's it about?"

He tapped the label. "A documentary, according to Doc."

"Can we watch it?"

"Watch it?"

"Come on. You know you want to." She put her chin on his shoulder, and whispered, "Your devilish girlfriend might get all hot for you if she saw it." Then she switched to his other shoulder and said, "On the other hand, your angelic sweetie might give herself over to chastity."

He turned the can over in his hands. Technically it was sealed and should probably stay that way, but like Veronica, he was now dying to see what it was. Doc had countless other media that they'd sorted through, but this was the only actual, physical *film* they'd found. And everything else was labeled, identified, and often found together with Doc's copious notes. This was the first enigma.

At last he looked at her, grinned, and said, "Okay, come on." He took her hand, and they practically ran out of the office.

Steve the A/V librarian turned on the light in the windowless study room. He carried a huge old sixteen-millimeter projector in one hand and a toolbox in the other. He put the projector on the table and unwound the cord, which held its shape despite being off its holder.

"This thing hasn't been used in years," Steve said. "I think the last time was some sorority 'silent movie' night, when they wanted a real cinema experience. I don't even know if it works."

"So you keep saying," Veronica said. Steve was young for staff, and cultivated friendships with students who shared his love for obscure movies. After his first conversation with her about Werner Herzog, Veronica became one of his favorites.

"The real test will be if the bulb holds out," he said as he continued to set up the projector. "If it doesn't, I don't know if I can even find a spare."

"We'll cross our fingers, then," Justin said. He carried his guitar, and Veronica held the film can tightly, as if afraid it might somehow vanish before they could see it.

"One of old Doc Adams's treasures, eh?" Steve said. "He helped write the grant request that got us our digital transfer equipment a couple of years ago. Thought we'd already put everything he had out on YouTube."

"He may have forgotten about it," Justin said. "Found it in a locked box, with the key tucked away in his desk."

Steve looked at him skeptically. "Doc Adams forget? He was sharp as a tack right up until the day he died. He might've hidden it, but he wouldn't forget it."

Justin and Veronica exchanged a look. The idea that Doc had deliberately buried the film hadn't occurred to them.

Steve saw it. "Having second thoughts?"

"No," Justin said.

Steve flipped the switch, and the bulb flared to life. He quickly switched it off. "Whew. Looks good."

Justin handed the can to Steve, who found the end of the sealing tape and unwound it. Then he wrestled to get the two can halves apart. At last, with a metal scraping sound like a sword being drawn in a video game, he pulled it open and took out the mostly full reel inside. He pulled out the white leader until he got to the actual film. He held it up to the light.

"Looks vintage," he said. "It's been sealed up in that can, so there hasn't been much disintegration."

"Is it safe to watch it?" Justin asked. "I don't want it to burn up or anything."

"Should be."

As Steve threaded the film through the gears, Justin and Veronica sat on opposite sides of the table so they'd have a clear view. When it was ready, Steve turned off the light and switched on the projector. On the bare white wall, they watched the blank leader, then the first images.

The title card read:

*Spectacular Motion Pictures presents*
**THE FAIRIES OF SADIEVILLE**

No writer or director was credited. And there was no sound, not even music.

"Is it silent?" Justin asked.

"Looks like it."

The image faded in, from a reverse iris, to show a slow tracking shot of rounded, forested mountains. Then it cut to the busy street of a small town, filled with people, horses, and one early-model car. In the foreground a covered stone bridge provided a natural frame. A title card immediately afterward identified it as *Sadieville, a Smoky Mountain coal town.*

A man carrying a tin lunchbox and wearing a miner's helmet strode down the street and across the bridge. A cut, and this same man walked through the forest. He was identified as *Litt Larkin, an honest coal miner.*

Another man, bearded and wearing a fedora, waved to him from up the trail. The two men met, and the angle changed to a medium two-shot. A title card read *Litt meets his friend Dallas Walters, a moonshiner.* The two talked in silence for a long moment, Litt mostly shaking his head, Dallas clearly entreating. Finally Litt nodded, and Dallas clapped him on the back.

A title card read *Litt agrees to carry moonshine for Dallas.*

Then there was a cut to a man hiding in the undergrowth, watching the other two. He was identified as *Jim Barton, a young revenue agent sent to apprehend the moonshiner.*

Justin took out his guitar and began to noodle along with

the film, trying to absorb its atmosphere. It didn't seem to be a comedy, so it must be a melodrama. He played dramatic minor chords and slow notes.

When Litt and Dallas parted, Barton followed Litt. A short distance away, he accosted him. Litt shook his head, but Houston was adamant. A title card explained *Barton forces Litt to show him where Dallas's still is located.*

Then the film cut to show a girl from behind as she watched Litt and Barton. After Barton departed, Litt stood with his head down, clearly dejected. The girl, still shown from the back, emerged and approached him.

A title card read *"Don't be afraid, Litt Larkin. Come with me."*

Litt looked up, and mimicked surprise with such an over-the-top pantomime that Veronica snorted a laugh. "Sorry," she muttered, and covered her mouth to hide her giggles.

*So it's a romance,* Justin thought. He changed his playing to accommodate this new direction.

The girl wore a long dress with a lace collar. She took Litt by the hand and led him offscreen. Three long shots followed, of the girl leading Litt along a high ridge that showed off the scenery behind them. Finally they emerged into a sunlit clearing.

"That's not the same girl," Veronica said.

"What?" Justin said.

"That's not the same girl from earlier. This girl is taller and skinnier. And look how she's dressed."

Justin hadn't noticed. But he did notice that "Litt" was also dressed very differently, and played by a noticeably different actor. "What's that about?" he said.

Now the girl turned to Litt and finally revealed her face. She was beautiful, clad in a flowing summer dress, a completely different outfit from the prim one she'd worn moments before. Her hair was dark, and she had the cheekbones of a Native American. The new Litt stood casually, without a care in the world, nothing like the worried character he'd been before.

A title card read *"Litt Larkin, do not be afraid. I can save you with my magic."*

The next shot was clearly a continuation of the first. The girl stepped back, lowered her head, and held her arms out to her sides. The film went momentarily out of focus. When the image cleared, the girl stood in the same spot, except . . .

She now had *wings.*

Justin froze in mid-note. The only sound now was the projector's clicking.

The girl's clothes were gone as well, replaced by a white, to-galike wrap that shimmered as she moved. Her sparkling wings made one slow, graceful flap, and she rose from the ground and hovered a couple of feet in the air.

The shot held as Litt stepped closer and slowly put out a hand. She took it, and her wings moved until she rose even higher and her body turned to hover horizontally, parallel to the ground. She and Litt kissed.

"Great effects," Steve murmured.

A title card appeared: *Dallas burst in on them.*

If the earlier acting of the first Litt had been over-the-top, then Dallas's look of surprise was even more ridiculous. There was a cut, and Dallas ran into the center of a totally different clearing, one that might've been an indoor set. He looked around, mimicking surprise, and they saw that this, too, was a new actor, with a fake beard and different hat.

A title card read: *"Where did you go? Litt Larkin, you betrayed me!"*

The film returned to a few more seconds of the second Dallas pacing the fake clearing, then cut to a sunset—or rise, it was impossible to tell—over the mountains. A title card explained, *The fairy took Litt to her magical land, and they were never seen again in Sadieville.*

This was quickly followed by *The End.*

The film slapped against itself until Steve turned off the projector and turned on the room lights. For a moment all three were silent.

"Wow," Steve said at last.

"I thought this was supposed to be a documentary," Veronica said. "I mean, the sticker said it was real."

"Maybe he meant something else by that," Justin said as he put his guitar away. His mind turned over various possibilities but kept ending up with only one, and he didn't dare say that one aloud.

"Why did they switch actors?" Veronica asked.

"It almost looked like they combined two different films," Steve mused. "And I wonder how they did the fairy effects? I mean, they were pretty sophisticated about special effects back then, which is not generally known. But that sure looked real."

Justin looked down at the can lid, with Doc's comment stuck to it: *This is real.*

"But, I mean, it can't be, can it?" Steve finished.

"I don't see how," Justin said, but he didn't sound convinced. "I mean, it had title cards, and a story."

Steve picked up the can's bottom half and turned it over. "Wonder where this film came from?"

"It said 'Spectacular Motion Pictures' at the beginning," Veronica said.

"That doesn't help. There were hundreds of film companies back then, some on the East Coast, some in California. I don't suppose you've found anything in Doc's papers about it?"

"No," Justin said. "We've basically just gotten started on them."

"Too bad." He set the film up to rewind onto its original reel. "Well, if it's okay, I'll take this down and digitize it. I'll burn you a copy onto DVD."

"Thanks," Justin said, suddenly nervous about letting it out of his sight. "Is that a safe thing to do? For the film, I mean."

"Totally. We scan each frame individually. Doesn't hurt the film at all."

"How long will it take?"

"As long as it takes to watch."

"So you could have it by tomorrow?"

"If it runs as smoothly as it did just now. If it starts breaking and I have to piece things together, it'll be longer."

"Justin," Veronica said quietly. "Steve knows what he's doing."

Justin nodded, smiled as if everything was fine, and made small talk as Steve packed up the projector. But inside, all he could think about was what he'd seen, and the message Doc had left:

*This is real.*

# 3

As they walked across campus, Veronica finally asked, "Are you ready to tell me how your meeting went this morning?"

He put his free arm across her shoulders. "You're the psychic."

She poked him in the ribs. "And you're the guy who's about to sleep on the couch."

"The bed *is* the couch."

"I didn't say *our* couch."

He took a deep breath and said, "Coffin's my new advisor. He doesn't accept my thesis. I have to start over."

"Completely over?"

"Completely. Nothing I did for Doc will pass muster. I need a new idea, and I need it fast."

"Shit," she said.

"Ah, don't worry, I'll think of something."

"Stop that. You can't fool me. I know you're scared. I would be, too."

He pulled her closer and squeezed the handle of his guitar case, holding on to the two things in his life that he could always count on to be there. "I think I know what I need right now."

"I bet you do, too."

"No, not that. Well, actually, yes that. But also, I need Cadillac's."

She scowled. "Really?"

"Yes."

"That place makes me nervous."

"You'll be fine. I'll be with you."

"You're not as intimidating as you think you are, hot stuff."

"Then I'll bring this." He raised the guitar case. "Nobody would dare fuck with a black guitar player's girl."

"Uh-huh. When's the last time you got in a fight?"

"Second grade," he admitted.

"And you wonder why I worry."

"But I won."

"My hero," she said wryly.


Cadillac's pool hall was full that night with undergraduates on their last fling before spring break. All the tables were active, all the bar stools were taken, and watching over it all was the man himself, Cadillac. He was indeterminately old, and had been old as long as anyone could remember, but like Doc, he always had an easy rapport with the kids, and everyone loved him.

The clientele was a mix of college students and town folk. Justin had changed back to his normal clothes and left his guitar at home, since the only music allowed in Cadillac's was the jukebox. Justin felt the locals' eyes on him, and even more on Veronica; they didn't like students, and they especially disliked minority students. But unlike some places in town, no one here dared make a scene. Among other things, old man Cadillac was tight with the town's police, who were a whole lot more serious than the campus cops.

They made their way to a table, where another couple, Adrian and Lydia, sat with a pitcher of beer. Like Justin, Adrian was a graduate student in the English department, although his path was significantly more traditional. Lydia was an undergraduate in foreign languages, specifically Spanish and Portuguese.

"Dude, I heard the bad news," Adrian said. "You're in the grave with Coffin now."

"Yeah," Justin said. "And he tossed out my thesis. I have to get him a new proposal ASAP."

"Shit. Any ideas?"

Justin lifted his beer. "I'm here to research it right now."

"Write drunk, edit sober," Adrian said, and they touched glasses.

"Oh, come on, you two," Lydia said. "I didn't come here to be depressed."

Justin took a long drink. "I'm not depressed. I'm just . . ."

"He's depressed," Veronica said.

"I would be," Adrian said.

"Stop it!" Lydia said. "Veronica, maybe we need boyfriends who don't mope around all the time."

"Maybe we just need to date each other," Veronica said, and mock-kissed her friend on the lips.

Justin and Adrian froze in mid-drink, their eyes wide.

After a long moment of silence, Justin said, "Don't stop on our account."

"I'll get my camera," Adrian added.


By the time the bar closed at twelve, Justin was drunk, Veronica was lit, and they stumbled the three blocks to their apartment. Once inside, they sloppily kissed and made their way to the bed. As they fumbled with each other's clothes in the darkness, Veronica said, "You're completely missing the obvious, you know."

"Oh! Sorry," he said, and bent to kiss her breasts.

She pulled his head up. "Not those. Although hold that thought. Your new thesis."

"What?"

"That movie. Fairies in Appalachia. The whole concept."

He forced his beer-fogged brain to consider this. "You think?"

"I do. I think it's fascinating. And so do you."

He sat down, his boxers around his ankles as he thought. "You know, you're right. It's been bouncing around in my head all night. Where did it come from? How did they do those effects? Why did Doc say it was real?" He smiled at her. "Damn, girl. That psychic stuff comes in handy."

Veronica slipped off her panties and threw them across the room. "Got nothing to do with being psychic. I just know you."

"Oh, yeah? Then what am I thinking right now?"

With a sly grin, she lowered her head to his lap. He lay back and said, "You read me like a book, babe."


Veronica stood in the doorway of Doc Adams's office. Her hair was sleep-tousled, and she'd pulled on one of Justin's faux-ancient concert T-shirts, which hung almost to her knees. She said, "I figured this is where you'd run off to."

It was two in the morning, and Justin sat on Doc's office floor methodically going through papers. "I sobered up, and I couldn't sleep."

"You mean I didn't relax you enough?"

He grinned. "I never said I wasn't relaxed. I just couldn't get to sleep. A problem that you didn't have."

"I *do not* snore."

"And I can't play a G6 chord." He carefully put a newspaper article on top of a pile of other yellowing, fragile clippings. "But anyway, rather than just stare at the ceiling, I thought I'd come down here and be useful."

"How's it going?"

"Not great."

Veronica asked guardedly, "So have you found any mention of it?"

"Not a one. No mention of the movie, Spectacular Pictures, or a town called Sadieville. Certainly no mention of fairies in Appalachia. If Doc knew about it, it's buried even deeper."

"Have you looked online?"

He gestured at his laptop, open at the cleared center of Doc's desk. "That was the first place I did look. All I found were crumbs."

She picked her way past the piles and sat down cross-legged on the floor beside him. "Like what?"

"I found mention of a Sadieville in Kentucky. And there was a coal town named Sadieville in Tennessee that suffered some kind of mining disaster in the early nineteen hundreds and disappeared."

"The whole town?"

"Apparently. The sources were kind of vague. And Spectacular Motion Pictures existed from 1912 to 1917 in Fort Lee, New Jersey. In that time it put out between four hundred and five hundred movies, most of which are lost."

"That's a lot of movies to lose."

"Most were about the length of the one we saw, and shot in less than a week. Quality didn't seem to be a goal. But there was no mention of one of them being *The Fairies of Sadieville*."

" 'Scuse me, folks," a new, deep voice said.

They looked up. And up. Campus security Officer Hall, six feet seven inches tall, loomed in the door. His voice was as deep as his size implied, giving him the campus nickname "Lurch."

"Evening, Officer Hall," Veronica said.

"I saw the lights on, and for a minute I thought Doc Adams had returned from the dead."

"If anyone could, it'd be him," Justin agreed.

Hall expertly scanned the room. Alcohol was forbidden on campus, and he was always vigilant. When he saw none, he said, "You're working late."

"He couldn't sleep," Veronica said, "and that meant I couldn't sleep."

"Just be sure and lock up when you leave," Hall said. He looked around at the office: half neat stacks, half chaotic piles. "Doc never did get the hang of filing, did he?"

"No, he was more into piling," Justin said.

When Hall's clicking footsteps had faded down the hall, Veronica said, "I have a suggestion."

"What's that?" he said, continuing to look through papers.

She took his chin and turned his face toward her. "I need your full attention."

"Okay," he said.

"I want you to be honest with me. When you saw that girl turn into a fairy, you thought the same thing I did, didn't you?"

"What's that?"

"That it was no special effect. That it was what Doc meant by that sticker. You thought it was real."

"Maybe for a second."

"Do you know anything about fairy lore?"

"I binge-watched *Lost Girl* once. Does that count?"

"No."

"Then no, I don't know much."

"And you call yourself a folklorist."

"Not until Coffin says I can," he said wryly.

Veronica ignored him. "Did you know that people still claim to see fairies?"

"They can afford better drugs than I can."

"I'm serious."

"I can tell. Where are you going with it?"

"Maybe the answer isn't in folklore."

"Then where is it?"

"In *my* area. I think we should talk to my advisor, Dr. Tully."

"The witch?"

"She's a Wiccan priestess," Veronica corrected. "But she's also a parapsychologist, and if fairies really exist, or did when that film was made, it's a lot more her area than Doc's."

"Maybe you're right," Justin said. Then, despite himself, he yawned.

"Come on," Veronica said, and got to her feet. "Get your laptop. You need sleep. Tomorrow I'll call her and make an appointment."

"Okay, but just what do we tell her?"

"The truth. That we have a movie that may show an actual fairy, and we want to know if it's real or not."

"That sounds crazy."

"I know. But trust me, she won't hold that against us."


Once again, the first thing Justin noticed was the smell. Unlike Doc's office, Dr. Tully's smelled fresh and spicy, like patchouli incense mixed with the homey aroma of dried flowers. Instead of the piles of clutter organized in a way only Doc could navigate, Dr. Tully's floor was clear and her shelves were neat. The only strange thing was that she sat behind her desk with all the lights out, silhouetted against the window and listening to her laptop through earbuds.

Dr. Tanna Tully was the youngest tenured faculty member at West Tennessee University, and one of its most notable. Although technically she, like Veronica, studied psychology, she'd written three enormously popular books on her specialty, parapsychology, and countless scholarly articles. She was a pagan living and working in the heart of the Bible Belt, and yet she managed to navigate it with grace and panache.

Veronica reached past Justin and turned on the lights. "Hey, Tanna. It's Veronica and Justin."

She looked up suddenly and said, "Oh, hey! Sorry about the lights, y'all. Come on in." She took out the earbuds and closed her laptop. Then she stood up. "Hi, Justin. Nice to meet you. I've heard a lot about you."

Justin was a bit taken aback. Veronica had told him lots of things about her advisor, including that she was blind, but hadn't mentioned that the woman was also gorgeous. She had a wild mane of wavy red hair, and big blue eyes that, even if they didn't work, were certainly striking.

"Pleasure to meet you," Justin said, and held out his hand. Veronica nudged him sharply.

Dr. Tully smiled. "You're holding out your hand for me to shake it, aren't you?"

"Yes," he admitted. "I'm not very smart."

"But he's cute," Veronica said.

"So you've told me. Don't worry about it, Justin, that happens more often than you can imagine. Please sit down." They all did, and she added, "So, what can I do for you?"

"We've been cataloging everything in Doc Adams's office," Veronica said. "He was Justin's advisor, and they were really close."

"I'm so sorry for your loss," she said. "Doc was a good man and a fine scholar. I couldn't believe it when I heard he was gone. But you're not here to commiserate, are you?"

Veronica nudged Justin. "Tell her."

"We found an old movie in Doc's office," Justin said, and gave a quick rundown of the film's contents and the note Doc left on it. Dr. Tully listened silently until he finished, then said thoughtfully, "Sadieville."

"I found mention of two," Justin said. "One's in Kentucky. The other was the site of a coal town that closed down about the same time this film was made."

"I've heard about that one," Dr. Tully said. "The town vanished overnight. A cavern beneath it collapsed, I believe. So this movie was filmed before that, then."

"If it was really filmed in Sadieville," Justin said. "Some of the scenery looks genuine, some not. The movie is a bit . . . haphazardly put together."

"But you think it shows a real fairy?"

"I . . . I suppose I'm open to the possibility." Until he said it out loud, he hadn't realized that it was true. "Tell me, did Doc ever talk to you about it?"

"No, unfortunately. Doc and I tended to meet only socially, and neither of us wanted to talk shop then. I really knew nothing about what he was working on until he published it. Still . . ." Dr. Tully sat back and tapped a pen against her lips as she thought. "Veronica, look something up for me online. See what county Sadieville, the one that disappeared, was in."

Veronica took out her phone and began to search. It took a bit, because the mentions were pretty light on details, but finally she said, "Cloud County. Never heard of that one."

"I thought so."

"What's so special about Cloud County?" Justin asked.

Dr. Tully said, "Justin, would you please close the door?"

Justin got up and did so. Immediately the room seemed to grow closer, and suddenly felt more like a temple than an office.

"Have either of you," Dr. Tully said quietly, "ever heard of the Tufa?"

Justin said, "No."

"That sounds familiar," Veronica said. "But I can't place it."

"That's not a surprise. They keep to themselves, and don't like it when outsiders come poking around."

"Who are they?" Justin asked.

"The conventional wisdom is that they're what's known as 'triracial isolates': a mixture of white, black, and Native Americans. The Brass Ankles of South Carolina are another group, and so are the Dominickers of Florida. The Tufa have black hair, dusky skin, and bright white teeth; that last is where it's said their name comes from, 'Tufa' as a corruption of 'tooth.'"

"And?" Veronica prompted.

Dr. Tully's voice, casual and easy moments before, took on a weight that surprised them both when she said, "There are others who think 'Tufa' is a corruption of 'Tuatha.' As in 'Tuatha de Danaan.' As in the original fairy folk."

"That's interesting," Justin said. "But how does it apply to this?"

"Pretty much all the Tufa live in Cloud County. Where your fairy film is set, and was possibly made."

"Are you saying," Justin asked slowly, "that the Tufa are actually fairies?"

"Descended from them, at least. Some say that when the first Scotch-Irish settlers moved into the mountains, the Tufa were already there. A few say they were already there when the Native Americans came."

"What do *they* say?" Veronica asked.

"Nothing. The few stories anyone's gotten out of them all contradict each other."

"That sounds a little. . . ."

"Outlandish?" Dr. Tully chuckled. "Yes, it does." She picked up a small electronic device from her desk. "See this? It's an EMF meter. Do you know what it's for, Justin?"

Veronica had occasionally brought them home, so he recognized it. "To determine the presence of ghosts."

"Wrong. It determines the presence of electromagnetic fields. Those may or may not be ghosts; that has yet to be proven." She put down the meter. "So when you have a story about a group of people that might be fairies, all that story tells you is what the storyteller thinks. It doesn't tell you objectively whether or not those people are fairies. And what did Carl Sagan say, Veronica?"

" 'Extraordinary claims require extraordinary evidence,' " Veronica said.

"Exactly. And we don't have that, for either ghosts *or* fairies."

While Justin tried to absorb all this, Veronica said, "But you believe, if that movie was filmed in a place where there are stories of people descended from fairies, that she might be a real fairy?"

"I don't 'believe' anything. That conclusion is, frankly, ridiculous. But then, what else would a fairy tale be?"

"So what should we do?" Justin asked.

"I don't know what you mean."

"Well, I mean, we've got this film, and—"

"Justin's considering making it the topic of his thesis," Veronica said.

"I can answer for myself," he deadpanned to her.

"Yes, but it's so much faster if I do it."

Dr. Tully laughed. "You two are adorable. And that's a fantastic idea."

"You think so?" Justin asked.

"Oh, yeah. If you can find out the history of that movie, and in the process tie it in to Cloud County and the Tufa, that'll be fascinating." She sighed wistfully. "I wish I could see the movie."

"Me, too," Veronica said. "Thanks for your time, Tanna."

"Of course. And a pleasure to meet you, Justin. I hope to hear you play sometime as well."

"Exactly what have you told her about me?" Justin asked Veronica.

"Only good things, I promise," Dr. Tully said. "But Justin?"

"Yes?"

"A word of advice. You may already know this, and I apologize if I sound pedantic, but . . . remember, the Tufa are real people. They have jobs, and families, and lives, just like you do. They *exist*, just like you do. And they'll no doubt read whatever you say about them. Keep that in mind."

Justin gazed into those blank blue eyes, and for a moment thought he saw tiny swirling points of light, like fireflies. Then she blinked and it was gone. "I will. Thank you."

"Justin, I need to talk to Dr. Tully for a minute alone," Veronica said. "I'll catch up with you downstairs."

When they were alone and the door had closed, Veronica said to Dr. Tully, "Would you do a tarot reading for me?"

"I've got a class in fifteen minutes."

"Not a full reading, then. Just a three-card past-present-future."

"Why?"

"Just to settle my mind."

"You know a tarot reading doesn't really predict the future, it's—"

" 'A meditation tool best used as a way to understand your own subconscious, or that of the person you might do a reading for.' I know, I did read your book. But please. Seriously."

Dr. Tully thought a moment, then nodded. She took a wooden box from a desk drawer, opened it and spread a soft cloth on top of her desk blotter. Then she pulled out her tarot deck.

It was a standard Rider-Waite-Smith deck, worn with years of use, which Dr. Tully had brailled herself so that her fingers could read it. She shuffled them once and handed them to Veronica, who also shuffled and then cut the deck three times. Dr. Tully took back the cards, sat still and quiet for a moment, then placed the first three cards in a row on the cloth.

The first card was a two of wands. Veronica frowned; it represented travel combined with study or work, and she had no plans to go anywhere. Was she about to be offered a chance to pursue her studies somewhere else? Maybe even abroad?

The center card was the High Priestess. As a card from the major arcana, the ones with names as well as numbers, this carried a lot of symbolic weight. She smiled a little; in her own readings it often came up as the one that represented her, and in its second position, it told her that she would be an important part of the trip.

The third card was the five of cups, but it was upside down, or "reversed," as the guides called it. In that position it meant acceptance, moving on, and forgiveness.

That made her pause. What would she need to forgive? Or be forgiven *for*?

Dr. Tully ran her fingertips over the cards, reading them. "Interesting. Does it answer your question?"

"I'm not sure," Veronica said honestly.

"I assume it has something to do with Justin's mystery."

Veronica looked up. "Why would you say that?"

"Because you sounded more excited than he was about it."

Veronica was glad Tanna couldn't see the blush on her cheeks. "Okay, you got me. I *am* excited. I saw that film, and it really put its hooks in me."

"What about it affected you so strongly?"

She thought a moment. "The implication."

"The idea that 'this is real,' like Doc said?"

"Yes. Doc was many things, but he wasn't gullible. He wouldn't be taken in by a prank."

"That's true. But what if the label means something else? What if you're taking literally what he only meant as a metaphor?"

"Do *you* believe in fairies?" Veronica asked.

She chuckled. "I *believe* in possibility. I *act* based on facts."

"I'll try to remember that."

"Oh, and one more thing."

"What?"

"Turn the lights out when you leave. Have to save money where we can, if we want to keep the university open."

———

Justin waited on the first floor when she came out of the stairwell. "Why is it," he asked, "that my advisors look like old manuscripts with legs, and yours look like her?"

"You study the past, hot stuff. I study the future."

# 4

"*Now* why are you up?" Veronica said through a yawn as she raised her head from the pillow. The clock read 1:16 A.M. "You used to sleep like a rock after sex. I'd ask if I was doing something wrong, but I know it *can't* be that." When he ignored her joke, she said in a drawl, "Breaker one nine, this is Sexy Mama calling Space Cadet, what's your twenty? Come back."

Justin sat at the table, the only light coming from his laptop screen. "Oh, hi. Sorry. Steve sent me the file of that movie. I've been rewatching it."

Veronica sat up and pulled on a T-shirt. "Justin, it's after midnight. Again." She got out of bed and came over to him.

"Before you say anything, just look at this." He scooted over so she could have half of the chair. "Remember the part where she changes into a fairy?"

"Yes."

"Okay, it goes out of focus right when she changes, right? Watch." He played the moment for her. "So I just assumed that they'd gone blurry to hide the costume change. But look."

He played it again, and paused in the middle.

Veronica yawned and shook her head to clear it. "It's nearly one thirty in the morning, Justin, what am I supposed to be seeing?"

"Right here. This is a tree in the foreground. The out-of-focus bit doesn't affect it. And look at the guy."

He pointed to the figure of "Litt." The blurry effect did not change his outline, either. He stayed sharp.

"And?" Veronica prompted.

"And, this blurry effect comes from the girl. It's not a camera trick. It's like . . . the air is rippling from some kind of power surge, created by—"

"Her really turning into a fairy? Justin, can we talk about this tomorrow?"

But Justin was already hyped with excitement. "Do you know what glamour is?"

"My freshman roommate read it like the Bible."

"Not the magazine. It's a power that fairies have to make people see what they want them to see."

"Yes, I know, I was being facetious."

"Can't you be satisfied with being Hispanic?"

She lightly smacked the back of his head. "You're about to be satisfied with your right hand, smart guy. So you think that's a fairy putting on her glamour?"

"Or taking it off."

Veronica wanted to go back to sleep, but the thought took hold in her brain and wouldn't let go. "Run it for me again," she said quietly.

He started the video, and she quickly reached up to pause it. The image captured the woman in mid-hover as she drifted from vertical to horizontal.

"Okay, they had stage-flying rigs back then," she said, more to herself than Justin. "They did *Peter Pan* onstage, right? So this isn't impossible."

"They had those rigs," Justin agreed, "but where is it? Where is it attached to her? She's barely wearing a sheet, for God's sake.

And how could she change position like that? Wires have to go in a straight line, and the wings are so big, they cross any path the wires might take."

"I don't suppose they put it in during post?" she said dryly.

"Back then, I think 'post' consisted of rewinding the film."

She reached past him to the touch pad and scanned the video backward and forward, looking for a telltale moment of clunkiness that would assure her she watched something manufactured, a trick done with mechanics and perspective.

Justin stretched and yawned. "Well, I've had it for tonight. I'm going to bed." She heard him hit the mattress with a loud, limp thump. But now she was wide awake, scanning the video back and forth, looking for some clue that she was seeing a story, and not a fact.

The next morning found Justin and Veronica at a library study table nestled in a corner, with printouts of old newspapers scattered around them. Justin looked down at the few notes he'd made. "That's not a lot of information."

"How," Veronica said, "can such a major disaster be almost entirely forgotten? It's almost like somebody's come along and deliberately erased it. Did they have the NSA back then?"

With no luck researching the film itself, and the fairy aspect being questionable at best, they'd decided to look for news about the lost coal town of Sadieville. The Nashville *Tennessean* had a small story that mentioned the Sadieville disaster, noting its "extreme" loss of life, with a death toll of "over 400." It told of the permanent departure of the Prudence Coal and Coke Company from the area. But that was it; none of the scattered small local papers that might also have covered it still survived, and the news apparently didn't register even as close as Cincinnati or Atlanta. No books on coal mining history mentioned it.

Justin recalled the many, many detailed accounts they'd found for other disasters, like the Monongah mining disaster in 1907. It was repeatedly cited as the worst in American history, and that only cost 367 lives. So how could such an event as the Sadieville disaster happen and not make a ripple in history?

Just as disturbing to Justin, though, were the pictures of living miners going about their jobs back in the days before unions, or even basic safety regulations. Their white faces were smeared as black as their lungs with coal dust, a disturbingly similar look to old minstrel performers. But these dead-eyed, slumped-over miners had not chosen to blacken their skin. Their lives had done it to them.

He felt a jolt of entitlement at those thoughts. His father was a lawyer, and his mother a fund-raiser for various charities. He'd never done physical work that wasn't his choice; his time working at McDonald's, and for a groundskeeping firm, had been intended to build "character," not support a family. He'd never wondered about where his next meal was coming from or whether he'd have a place to sleep if he lost that job. He certainly never recalled his parents coming home physically beaten down by just getting through the day, with the mixture of defiance and defeat he saw in these photographs.

He flipped through the pages until he found a photograph of African-American coal miners. Three of them stood in a line, gazing at the camera with grim, sullen expressions. One had a pickax across his shoulders. The ironic thing was that their natural skin didn't look much different from that of the white miners darkened by coal dust. Were the mines some kind of great equalizer?

Then he read the caption: *Black workers were brought in as strikebreakers when miners attempted to unionize.* So even in holes hundreds of feet underground, when the environment itself was colorblind, there remained a color bar. Not only were miners in general treated as little more than pieces of machinery to be replaced when worn out, but black miners were doubly expendable: either killed while working, or fired when the strike was resolved.

"We need to find out where this town was," Justin said. "I mean, *exactly* where it was. It's got to be on maps, doesn't it?" He pounded the keys as he typed search terms into his laptop.

"Are you all right?" Veronica asked.

"I'm fine," he muttered without looking up.

She knew that when he got in this sort of mood, all she could do was let him ride it out. Besides, all the pictures of coal, rocks, and mines had given her an idea. "I'll be back in a little while," she said as she stood.


In one of the geography department's empty classrooms, Veronica unrolled the big topographical map on the teacher's desk.

This particular map was marked *Department of the Interior U.S. Geological Survey.* It was yellow with age and smelled of must and mold, two scents she now recognized instantly thanks to Doc. The two rubber bands that held it rolled up had snapped the instant she pulled on them. But luckily the image was still clear and sharp. She used her phone, keys, and two books to hold down the corners.

It showed the entire state of Tennessee. The date in the legend read *1915.*

"Aren't you in the wrong building, Ms. Lopez?" a new voice said. She looked up and saw Ryan, an undergrad she'd taught in her Intro to Psych class the previous semester.

"Hey, Ryan," she said. "I didn't know you were a geography major."

"Minor. Major's in business."

She gestured at the desk. "I needed to check something on one of the old topographical maps."

He looked over her shoulder. "This map's from a hundred years ago. What are you looking for?"

"A town that fell into a hole."

"Really?"

"So they say. It was a mining town, and the caves beneath it collapsed. If any map showed the town before it vanished, it would be this one."

She moved to the eastern end of the state, and found the list of counties. She located Cloud, which was so tiny it took her three times scanning the area to spot it. Within it, only one town was marked.

"So you're looking for this Needsville?" Ryan asked, pointing out the dot.

"No, the one I want is called Sadieville. But I don't see another town in the county."

Ryan put down his backpack and leaned close over the map beside her. "What about this?" he said, indicating a dot a short distance from Needsville. There had once been something printed beside it, but it looked like the name had been erased or scraped away.

"Is that meant to be a town?" Veronica asked.

"I think so."

"Why would they erase the name?"

"You said it fell into a hole. Maybe it was easier to do this than redraw the whole map for one tiny town. What was the name of this town again?"

"Sadieville."

"Does that look like 'V-I-L-L-E'?"

The scratch or erasure was imperfect, and tiny fragments of those letters could be pieced together. But she knew from her psych classes that it could also be apophenia, the term for seeing patterns where none existed.

He pointed out a hashed line that ran past the unidentified dot. "Then this makes sense. That's a railroad. You couldn't have a coal town without railroad access back then, or even now, for that matter."

She grinned at him. "You sure came by at the right time, Ryan. I'd have been looking over this thing for hours." Then she picked up her phone and made several photographs of the map, showing the relationship to Needsville, a town called Unicorn, and several other small communities.

When she returned to their table in the library, there was a note from Justin saying he was searching microfiche newspapers on the one ancient machine tucked in a far corner.

Veronica opened her laptop and called up an online map of Needsville. Google Maps, which had no trace of Sadieville, had no trouble finding the other Cloud County town. She used the images of the old map from her phone to locate the approximate position of Sadieville, then switched to a satellite view and zoomed in.

At first it showed only treetops. She scanned them methodically, looking for any indication of the former town peeking out. There was nothing: not a foundation, not a street, not even a sign of the railroad. In the century since the disaster, the mountains had apparently consumed every last trace.

She rubbed her already tired eyes and took a deep breath. This was ridiculous. Even if she found it, it wouldn't prove that the film was real, only that they'd used a real town's name in an old movie.

"All right, Veronica," she said softly to herself. "You have ten minutes, and that's it. If you don't find it by then, you'll give up and get back to your real life."

"Were you talking to me?" a girl said from a nearby book stack.

"No, myself. Sorry."

"Don't worry about it. I've had tests that made me talk to myself, too."

Veronica returned to her computer screen and began a systematic review of the area that once, if the map was right (and if her interpretation of the map was right), contained Sadieville. She zoomed in and still saw nothing but treetops and small clearings. Each time she thought she'd spotted something man-made, it turned out to be a false alarm.

Then a small gray patch with two visible, regular edges caught her eye. She clicked for more zoom, but she was at maximum. Was it a bridge? Was it the concrete remains of the covered bridge they'd seen in the movie?

She carefully noted the GPS coordinates of the thing, then incrementally zoomed out. She saw nothing else. But the more she looked at the partially visible gray area, the more certain she became.

"Well, hello, gorgeous," she whispered.

"Same to you, handsome," Justin said as he dropped an armload of bound magazine volumes onto the table with a loud thud.

"I might've found it," she said, trying not to shout.

"Found what?"

"Sadieville!" She let out a little titter of glee.

"Really?"

"Yes!" She turned her laptop so he could see.

He sat down beside her. "Honey, you know this is *my* project, not yours."

"I know, I know, but *look.*"

He gazed at the screen. "What exactly am I supposed to be seeing?"

"*This,* dummy!" she said, pointing. "It's what's left of the covered bridge from the first shot in the movie."

He tilted his head. "Are you sure?"

"I'm pretty sure."

"You were pretty sure Jon Snow was really dead, too."

"Technically, I was right."

He looked more closely. "It could just be the foundation of an old house."

"It could be, but the GPS coordinates match the map."

"What map? And what GPS?"

She told him about the geography department map, and how she'd located the same place on the satellite image.

He looked at the screen for a long moment. "It does look like it could be part of a bridge," he said at last.

"It does," she eagerly agreed.

He looked at her. "And you really do think this would make a good master's thesis?"

"I do. It's a cinch. Nobody's done anything like it."

"Yeah. Well, I guess I better get a proposal together."

Coffin sat back in his chair the way he'd done days earlier when he shattered Justin's world. "Interesting," he said in his flat way.

Justin had shown him the film, the article that mentioned the Sadieville disaster, and a screen grab from the satellite map. He'd explained the difficulty they'd had in finding any details about the disaster, despite the apparent scale of it. He made the case as stringently as he could, pointing out the connections with the Tufa, and the utter lack of any other scholarship about it. Now he waited.

"I thought," Coffin said at last, "that you intended to specialize in folk *music*. This is a silent film."

"I hope to find some forgotten songs written about the disaster."

"Hm. Perhaps you will. Have you ever met a Tufa?"

"Not that I know of."

"I have. I knew one when I was in the service during the Vietnam War. He had the best singing voice I've ever heard." He paused. "One night I was on guard duty. This wasn't in Vietnam, mind you, it was in California. I heard something above me, and when I looked up, there he was, on the roof. The thing is, there was no way for him to get there, short of a very long ladder. Yet there he was. I yelled at him, and he ducked out of my sight. When I got a spotlight and shone it up there, he was gone. He never mentioned it, and since I had no proof, neither did I. But I've always remembered it."

Justin had no idea where this was going.

"I remember thinking at the time," Coffin continued, "that the only way he could've gotten up there, or down from there, was by flying. But that made no sense. Until right now."

Coffin leaned forward. "I'm going to be very curious to read what you uncover about this. I expect actual scholarship, though, not just rumors and stories, no matter how compelling or copiously footnoted. Any songs you find, you have to document. I don't want any doubt that they're genuine." The implication that hung unspoken was, *You better not just make one up.*

"Yes, sir."

"And remember, too: the Tufa are real people. They're not just characters in old stories or legends. If you speak to any of them, as I'm assuming you plan to, treat them with the same respect you'd want someone to show you."

"Yes, sir."

When Justin got home, he told Veronica the good news. They had celebratory sex, and as they lay in bed afterward, she asked him, "So what's next?"

"I can go down on you."

She poked him. "No, not that! Although I'm not saying no. I mean for your thesis."

"Well . . . spring break is coming up. How do you feel about going to look for Sadieville?"

"You mean go out in the woods?"

"That seems to be where we'd find it."

"Sure. I haven't been camping since high school."

"You like camping?"

"You bet! You be Oscar Wilde, and I'll be Bette Midler."

"I imagine there's motels nearby that we can stay at," he said, reaching for his phone.

She slid her hand down his chest. "Ooh, you want to fuck me in a cheap motel."

"Or an expensive one. Or the bed department at Ikea."

"They caught Adrian and Lydia when they tried that."

"We're slicker than they are. And it sounds like fun. The trip, I mean. And the other stuff, too, but I don't think Dr. Coffin will give me credit for that."

"Probably not. *My* grading, however, is strictly pass/fail."

"Did I pass just now?"

"You did. Twice, in fact."

He put his phone aside, maneuvered over her and began to kiss down her stomach. "So can I get extra credit?"

"Ooh, you teacher's pet, you."

Eventually Veronica fell asleep, but Justin stayed awake, staring up at the ceiling as the afternoon sun lengthened and distorted the shadows of tree branches. The noise of traffic, thumping bass, and students calling out to their friends could barely be heard over the box fan's drone.

Spring break lasted a week, so he'd have that long to gather most of the firsthand information he needed for his thesis. Then he'd have to come back, sort it, transcribe it, and figure out how to present it first to Dr. Coffin, and then to his committee.

He'd have to focus, in a way he hadn't done in a long time. He'd have to think of himself as the black kid with something to prove again, even though he was pretty sure his race had nothing to do with this. Then again, he could never be sure, and that was the fucking bastard of it.

He glanced down at Veronica, her bare curves a delicious burnt umber in the reddish light of late afternoon. He knew he was lucky to have her, and that she would fuel his resolve as well. He didn't want to disappoint Coffin, or the memory of Doc; but most importantly, he didn't want to fail with Veronica watching.

At last he got up, dressed, and quietly took his guitar outside. It was hot and muggy, but he didn't want his playing to wake Veronica. He sat on the front steps of their building, watching the cars and students pass on nearby University Avenue. A few waved in his direction.

In the fading light, he strummed aimlessly, going through snippets of a half-dozen songs, until he realized he was playing a melody that he didn't quite recognize. Where had he heard this song before? *Had* he heard this song before?

There were words, too, ones that fit the tune with the inevitability of the best lyrics. He sang:

> *Can't go back, don't have the will*
> *Can never go back to my—"*

He stopped. The next word, the one that rhymed and fit so perfectly it *had* to be right, was: "Sadieville."

He sat, frozen in mid-strum, waiting to see if more of the song would come to him. But there was nothing, and even the fragment that he'd just sung faded rapidly. In moments, he couldn't remember it at all. All he knew was that it was no song he'd ever heard before, and it sounded nothing like his own feeble attempts at songwriting.

"What the fuck was that?" he whispered to himself.

# 5

Cloud County was the smallest county in Tennessee, so small it was occasionally left off maps entirely. That suited the residents of Needsville just fine.

Needsville itself had a population of 357 in the last census; roughly four hundred more lived scattered in the country around it, in isolated hillside dwellings or on farms tucked into small hollows. Virtually all had some measure of Tufa in their family, and most shared the common Tufa physical characteristics.

The most famous Cloud County resident was probably Bronwyn Chess, née Hyatt, who joined the army during the Iraq War and came home a war hero. Yet after just a few years she, now the wife of a minister and mother of a small girl, was mostly forgotten by the outside world. Which, of course, suited her just fine as well.

All the Tufa liked it that way. For many years they were on the wrong side of the South's color line, and suffered for it. Their secretive ways and legendary musical aptitude spawned rumor and legend, which in turn prompted more and more withdrawal.

But now the twenty-first century, with its pervasive

interconnectedness, pushed against this isolation. More and more Tufa risked the consequences of leaving and sought their way in the world. They all knew they would someday have to come back, since all Tufa were inextricably tied to Needsville. But they also knew that the seclusion of the past was no longer practical. Like it or not, the world now knocked on their door.

At the Catamount Corner Motel and Cafe, Cyrus Crow—known as C.C. to his friends—unlocked the front door. He was a big man, six feet four inches tall and a trim two hundred pounds, and he moved with surprising grace for his size. He'd purchased the motel almost two years ago, and opened the cafe when he renovated. He had kitchen and wait staff, but no one else came in this early. It was still an hour before his sunrise regulars arrived, so he also turned on the porch light.

"Dang!" the man who'd knocked said, holding up a hand to shield his eyes. "Trying to blind me, C.C.?"

"Sorry, Terry-Joe." He stepped back and let the other man enter.

Terry-Joe Gitterman carried a mandolin case, which he carefully placed on one of the cafe tables. He was in his early twenties, slender and of average height. Because of their shared heritage, they looked like relatives, but in fact were only distantly connected.

Terry-Joe asked quietly, "Anyone else here?"

"You don't have to whisper," C.C. said.

"This early, my voice ain't all the way awake." Terry-Joe took out his mandolin, fished a pick from his pocket, and looked up at the ceiling. "That where you hear them?"

"Yeah."

"Any place you can open up the ceiling?"

"The kitchen's got drop panels."

"Take one of 'em out. You got a garbage can ready?"

"About a third full of water, just like you said."

"Put it right under that hole." Then he smacked his forehead. "Damn. Forgot my mouse oil."

"What's 'mouse oil'?"

"Oh, you gotta have mouse oil."

"Why?"

Terry-Joe grinned. "In case they squeak."

C.C. groaned, then went into the kitchen and set up the ceiling and garbage can as Terry-Joe had instructed.

Terry-Joe took down one of the chairs propped upside down on a table and placed it on the floor. He sat down, feet spread, and began to play a quick, sprightly tune that had the sweet certainty of the best folk melodies. The heel of Terry-Joe's tennis shoe tapped softly against the floor, keeping time.

He sang, in a high clear voice:

> *See that rat, walking by*
> *See that rat, walking by*
> *If I kiss that rat, I might die*
> *See that rat, walking by . . .*

C.C. held the swinging kitchen door open, switching his attention from the open ceiling panel to Terry-Joe.

Terry-Joe continued:

> *See that rat, dancing by*
> *See that rat, dancing by*
> *If I hug that rat, I might die*
> *See that rat, dancing by . . .*

The first little whiskered nose poked out of the darkness in the ceiling, followed by at least a dozen more. In moments mice clustered around all four sides of the opening, peering down into the water below.

*See that rat, running by*
*See that rat, running by*
*If I love that rat, I might die*
*See that rat, running by . . .*

Now the little mice faces were on top of each other, as they rushed to get closer to the edge. C.C. was appalled: he had no idea there were so many of these vermin in his otherwise spotless kitchen. He'd left out traps and poison, but they hadn't worked, which is why he eventually asked around for someone who could sing the rats away.

"Get ready," Terry-Joe called out as he played, then sang:

*See that rat, falling down*
*See that rat, falling down*
*If that rat hears me, it might drown*
*See that rat, falling down!*

The mice began to leap from the hole and drop into the garbage can. The first few splashes quickly became a cacophony of frantic squeaks and desperate swimming, as the mice fought to get up the slick plastic sides of the can. A tesseract of gray bodies tumbled from the ceiling for a good two minutes, then finally dribbled to a stop. The last mouse managed to catch the edge with one tiny paw, dangling there for a long moment before he finally fell to join the others.

Terry-Joe finished playing with a flourish, and C.C. clapped in approval.

"Did it work?" Terry-Joe asked.

"It did," C.C. said.

They peered into the can. Already many mice were dead, drowned by the frantic weight of the others.

"That's a bunch, all right," Terry-Joe said. "You better look for how they're getting in."

"No kidding. Tell me something, though."

"Sure."

"How did you find out you could *do* that?"

They both laughed.

C.C. took two twenties from his wallet. "This cover it?"

"Oh, hell, C.C. Took me five minutes."

"And you saved me a couple of hundred for an exterminator, not to mention what the health inspector might make me do."

"All right, then." Terry-Joe pocketed the money.

C.C. let Terry-Joe out, locked the door behind him, and went to haul the garbage can out back. He'd let it sit for the rest of the day, to make sure all the mice were dead. Then he'd drain them and burn their little carcasses.

Thirty minutes later, with the kitchen fired up and cook Diamond Ike Hubbard standing over the hash browns, C.C. turned the sign on the front door to OPEN and prepared to start his day.

This was a Saturday, and it meant that in addition to his crew of regulars, he might snag some tourists. People you'd never expect were drawn to Cloud County and Needsville by a deep call that usually meant they had at least some Tufa blood in their family history.

C.C. was mostly Tufa, and it showed. Before he bought the motel from Peggy Goins, he'd been a jack-of-all-trades, repairing machinery and doing other odd jobs around the county to get by. Then he'd met Broadway actor Matt Johannsen, and everything changed. He found the nerve to strike out on his own, and so far the motel and cafe had been successful. Of course, the biggest success was that he and Matt were engaged to be married, despite their long-distance relationship.

He looked up as the bell over the door rang. A black-haired girl of about fifteen, with long gawky legs and the kind of eyes you couldn't look into for long, came in and said, "Hey, C.C."

He made a complex hand gesture of respect and fealty. The

Tufa community had its own internal structure, and those at the top were not always who you'd expect. "Good morning, Mandalay. Care for some breakfast?"

"No, just stopping by. How's Matt doing?"

"Fine. Still playing to sold-out houses. He's got two weeks off this summer, so he'll be coming down then."

"Good. I can't wait to see him again."

"Me, neither."

The bell over the door rang again, and an elderly couple came in. "Morning, C.C.," they said, then pulled up short when they saw Mandalay. They each made the same hand gesture C.C. had used earlier.

"Mr. Moss, Mrs. Moss, good morning," Mandalay said. "Don't mind me, I'm just here to talk to C.C."

The couple nodded and sat at the table farthest from the door, and the girl. They kept a discreet eye on her as they looked over the weekend specials.

"So you did need something?" C.C. asked Mandalay.

"Sort of. I think you may have some out-of-town visitors today. If you do, try to help them out."

"Sure," C.C. said. "What will they want?"

She shrugged, the way only a teenage girl can. "You know as much as I do now."

The Tufa believed that in this world, their gods rode the night winds, and that on certain nights and at certain times, if you stilled your mind and listened intently, you might hear them whisper. But for Mandalay, those voices came through as clear as hers did to C.C. right now, and there were rumors that she'd even seen those deities with her human eyes.

"Well," C.C. said.

"That's all. See you later." She turned and bounced out the door, momentarily no different than any other teen girl.

"What did *she* want?" Mrs. Moss asked when she was sure Mandalay was gone.

"Just to give me a tip about something," C.C. said. "I'll get your coffee out to you."

He went into the kitchen and took the carafe from the warmer. Diamond Ike asked, "What'd that Harris girl want?"

"Said some strangers would be stopping by, and we should help them out."

"Help them out with what?"

"You know as much as I do now."

Ike shivered. "That girl gives me the willies. I'd purely hate to be her."

"Why?"

"I wouldn't want everybody getting the willies every time they saw me." He bent back over his stove and stirred the scrambled eggs with his spatula.

As he took the coffee to the Mosses, the doorbell rang again and a woman of about thirty, with long wavy black hair, came in. "Hey, Bliss," C.C. said.

"Hey, C.C.," Bliss Overbay said. "Hey, Mr. and Mrs. Moss. Have any of you seen Mandalay this morning?"

"She was just here," C.C. said.

"Spreading more of her hush-hush," Mrs. Moss said.

Bliss Overbay looked surprised. In the Tufa hierarchy, Bliss was second only to Mandalay, and functioned as the girl's advisor, right hand, and messenger, at least until Mandalay reached adulthood. "Really? What did she say?"

"She said some people would be coming soon," C.C. said.

"Any details?"

"Not a one."

"Well, I guess we'll know when they get here. Did Mandalay say where she was going?"

"Nope. Sorry."

"No problem. I'll see you later. Next time you talk to Matt, tell him I said hi."

"I will."

It made C.C. prouder than he liked to admit to hear his friends accept his relationship with Matt. The Tufa, for the most part, were pretty tolerant in general, but C.C. had been, if not precisely closeted, certainly discreet about his queerness for most of his life. Now it, and he, were fully in the open, and it had gone better than he ever expected.

After Bliss departed, several more early-morning regulars came in and took their usual tables. C.C. adored that part of running a cafe, because it meant his establishment had been accepted by the community. That had not been a given; when Mrs. Goins sold the place, many predicted that he wouldn't be able to make a go of it, or that he'd turn it into an exclusively gay vacation spot for out-of-towners. But he'd tried to run it as Mrs. Goins had for so long, and it appeared to be paying off.

Except for the decor, of course. That had gone, and wouldn't be back. Mrs. Goins had stocked the place with exaggerated countrified knickknacks, edged with lace and painted with trompe l'oeil flowers. She said it was for the tourists, but given her own penchant for appliqué sweaters, he doubted that.

He looked out at the bright sunlight filtering through the last of the morning's mist. Visitors were on their way and he was supposed to help; that seemed simple enough. And fairly benign.

But, as he recalled from Matt's first visit, newcomers could, with very little intent or effort, also turn everything upside down.

## 6

"Oh, my God," Veronica said softly, leaning forward over the steering wheel.

They'd driven from Weakleyville to Nashville, spent the night in a nice hotel near the airport, and gotten up at sunrise to travel the rest of the way. Once they left the interstate, with Veronica driving since it was her car, the rolling landscape lulled them into silence, broken only by the plaintive music of Nickel Creek coming from Justin's iPod.

Veronica grew up in Meridian, Mississippi. From the delta to the Gulf of Mexico, the state rarely produced a real hill, and certainly no mountains. She'd flown over the Rockies a couple of times, but that was looking down; now she gazed up in wonder at the first rolling foothills that marked the Cumberland Plateau, with the Smoky Mountains rising in the distance.

"It's so beautiful," she added with a sigh.

"Watch the road, not the sky," Justin warned.

"I have two eyes."

"You want me to drive so you can look?"

"No, you think the white lines on the road are just

suggestions." She forced her attention back to the moment. "Don't you think it's beautiful?"

"I do. It's why the Scottish Highlanders chose to settle here. It reminded them of home."

"I know what you mean," she said wistfully.

Justin looked at her skeptically. "Your home is in Mississippi, and your people are from Puerto Rico."

"True, but don't you feel it?"

"Feel what?"

She wasn't sure how to describe it in words that didn't sound either trite, or lunatic. But looking up at those rounded slopes, she felt as if she drove toward a massive *embrace*, one that would both comfort and protect her. *Howdy, sister,* they seemed to say. *You may not be from here, but you're welcome just the same.*

"Never mind," she said.

"No, seriously, I won't make fun of you. What?"

"Like you're coming home to a place you've never been before."

He looked up at the mountains, and realized what she meant. "Yeah," he said. "*Sehnsucht.*"

"What?"

"*Sehnsucht.* C. S. Lewis talked about it. It's nostalgia for a place you've never actually been."

"What language is that?"

"German. The Germans have a word for everything."

"Yeah," she agreed softly. "Yeah, it's exactly that. *Sehnsucht.*"


A half hour later, Justin said, "I need to pee."

"Why didn't you go at the restaurant?" Veronica asked.

"Because I didn't need to pee then."

"It's from all that iced tea you drank."

"I like iced tea."

"Believe me, I know. How long until we get to Needsville?"

He checked the map on his phone. "Not long, but I really can't wait."

"All right." She pulled the car off onto the shoulder and turned on her emergency blinkers. "Hurry up, I don't want some good ol' boys to come along and offer to show me their piston rods."

He opened the door. "Do you even know what a piston rod is?"

"I can change my own oil; can *you?*"

"Then why don't you ever do it?"

"Because I am too fucking grand," she said with a dramatic eye bat.

He went a short distance into the woods and was soon out of sight. Veronica idly tapped on the edge of the window as she waited.

They had a vague plan to ask around for anyone who might know the location of what was left of Sadieville. Old people in small towns, at least according to Justin, tended to remember things at least one or two generations back. If that didn't work out, they had GPS coordinates and plenty of experience hiking. They'd find what remained and document that.

The one thing they hadn't discussed was the obvious: a Latina and her black boyfriend would certainly stand out. They'd both had their share of experiences with racism, but this was the first time, as a couple, they'd ventured into what they believed was the heartland of it.

She looked into the rearview mirror. The highway behind them remained empty. The last whispery traces of mist from the night hung low in the shadows; where the sunlight touched, it had burned away. Before long, the sun would be high enough that none would be left.

Then she jumped as Justin shrieked and ran from the trees. He slammed into the car. "I saw a dinosaur!" he gasped.

"A what?"

"A *dinosaur*! It looked right at me!"

She wanted to laugh, but he was clearly frightened. She looked past him into the woods, but saw nothing moving. She opened the car door, forcing him to stand back.

"Okay, okay, calm down," she said as she got out. "Tell me what you saw."

Between big gulps of air, he said, "I was standing there peeing, and something moved in the trees over to my right. I looked, and there was a dinosaur's head right there. It had red eyes and a long neck. I zipped up and ran."

"Show me."

"Show you?"

"Where you saw it."

"I'm not going back in there!"

She sighed. "Justin, whatever you saw, it wasn't a dinosaur."

"You didn't see it!"

"Let's just methodically look for some evidence of what it was. We're scientists, remember?"

Her reasonable tone calmed him down, and he took out his phone. When she looked at him, he said, "If I see it again, I don't want to just have my dick in my hand. I want proof."

They carefully approached the place where he'd seen the animal and surveyed the leafy forest floor. Veronica saw nothing, and was about to give up, when Justin whispered, "Here! Look at this!"

She joined him and peered down at a bare spot where the leaves had been pushed away. The ground, soft and muddy, bore the three-toed print of something that certainly looked like a dinosaur foot. It was as big as Justin's hand.

"See?" he said excitedly. *"See?"*

"You made that."

"With what? The spare dinosaur foot I carry in my pocket?"

She took his phone. "Put your hand down beside it for scale."

He did, and she took several photos. "Look around for some more."

They did, but they found nothing. As they made their way back to the car, both of them watched the woods for strange shapes.

When they were back safe inside, she said, "Okay, I don't know what you saw. Maybe a giant chicken or something."

"It was green and had a long neck, just like a velociraptor," Justin insisted. "Come on, aren't you supposed to know all about this sort of thing? You're a parapsychologist!"

"That's cryptozoology," she said with narrowed eyes. "Not parapsychology. And whatever it was, it's gone, and we might as well just file it away as one more weird thing. Unless you want to look for it?"

"No!"

"Yeah, me, neither. Let's get going, then." She started the car and pulled it back out on the highway. Justin turned and watched out the back window, but nothing emerged from the trees to chase them.


"So this is Needsville," Veronica said as they slowed down and crossed the city limit. She was careful to observe the posted speed, since so many small towns were speed traps. Even though there was no traffic in either direction, she let her car creep down the street.

She looked out at the small, decaying town through her sunglasses. "I didn't expect anything so . . ."

"Dead?" Justin offered.

"Yeah."

"Everything bad in the economy hits Appalachia the worst." He pronounced it "Apple-ATCHa."

"I thought it was 'Apple-LAYcha.'"

"Nope." He recalled the YouTube video that author Sharyn

McCrumb posted about why the pronunciation is important. "Apple-ATCHa means you're on the side that we trust," she'd said, and Justin understood that. Getting the trust of the locals was something every folklorist wanted.

"Where's the library?" Veronica asked. She'd been with Justin long enough to know that was always the first thing he sought.

"There isn't one. There's a bank, a school, a post office, a convenience store, a couple of garages, and a motel with a cafe, but no library or newspaper."

She looked at the many empty, boarded-up buildings along the main street. "Wonder what they used to do when all these places were open? Coal mining?"

"No, as near as I can tell, after the Sadieville mine disaster, there were no more coal mines in Cloud County. The people may have worked at other mines farther away, I guess." There was actually only slightly more information available on the history of Needsville than there was of Sadieville. An old bluegrass banjo player, Rockhouse Hicks, came from here, and an Iraq War hero, but otherwise there were no notable citizens.

She pulled their car into the row of parking spots in front of the Fast Grab convenience store. A sign on the door read, PRE-PAY FOR GAS AFTER DARK.

Those words were crossed out, and beneath them was written, ONLY CUSTOMERS THE CASHIER KNOWS DON'T HAVE TO PREPAY.

That, too, was marked out, and the final words were, MANAGER SAYS EVERYONE INCLUDING ELVIS MUST PREPAY.

"Trusting people," Veronica observed.

Inside, a young woman worked behind the counter. Her name tag said LASSA. She looked up and said, "Can I help you folks?"

"I hope so," Justin said. "We're looking for what's left of a town called Sadieville."

The girl looked blank. "Never heard of that."

"It's a coal town that used to be around here."

She thought hard, then shrugged. "Sorry."

"Are you sure?"

"Only town in this whole county is the one you're standing in right now. Nearest one is Unicorn, across the county line."

"Are there any old-timers around who might remember it?"

"I suppose you might find some down to the cafe."

"The one at the motel?"

"Yeah. There's a bunch that meet there every morning to drink coffee and solve all the world's problems. Here's a spoiler: it's the Democrats' fault."

"Thanks," Justin said.

"Buy something," Veronica whispered to him.

"Oh! Uh . . . I'll take these." He grabbed a couple of shopper newspapers from the counter.

"Those are free," Lassa pointed out.

"Here," Veronica said, putting two boxes of breath mints beside the shoppers.

"Is that a hint?" Justin asked.

"No, a 'hint' is when I leave them all over the apartment."

The girl giggled. Veronica stood on tiptoe and kissed Justin's cheek while he pretended mock offense. "Y'all come back and see us," Lassa said as she handed Veronica her change.

Veronica pulled the car back out onto the highway and drove—slowly—to the Catamount Corner motel. She parked at the end of a row of old cars and trucks, many of which sported homemade repairs to the body work.

"Look at that," Veronica said. "I haven't seen an El Camino anywhere but in my dad's old high school pictures."

"Which one is that?"

"You don't know what an El Camino is?"

"I'm not a car guy. This can't be news to you."

"It's the one that looks like the bastard child of a car and a truck."

"Ah. I can see why it didn't catch on."

"My dad says one time he walked into a parts store and asked the clerk, 'Can I get a gas cap for an El Camino?' The clerk said, 'Yeah, that sounds like a fair swap.'"

As they got out, Justin's phone dinged. He looked at the message and said, "Oh, boy. Steve put the movie on the English department's YouTube channel."

"Is that bad?"

"Probably not, but still, I wanted it to be something that didn't get noticed until my thesis got published."

Unlike the other buildings in town, the motel sported a recent paint job and new signage. On the door hung a neat sign that read, UNDER NEW MANAGEMENTSHIP. As they entered the little cafe, the bell over the door announced them.

The interior was as freshly decorated as the outside. Everything was tasteful and rustic. A pair of ceiling fans slowly turned, casting shadows thanks to the skylights above them.

Justin and Veronica stopped just inside the door. A dozen people sat there around two tables pushed together, and all twenty-four eyes turned to stare at them.

"Oh, that's right," Justin said through his fixed smile. "It's all white people here."

"They're not white, they're Tufa," Veronica murmured. "Remember what Dr. Tully said?" She stepped forward and said brightly, "Hi, y'all."

A chorus of "good mornings" responded.

She smiled, waved a little, and turned back to Justin. "See? That's how it's done. All you have to do is be friendly."

Over her shoulder, Justin saw every man in the room watching her ass as she walked. "Uh-huh," he said. "That's got to be it."

While they waited to be seated, Veronica noticed the framed pictures lining the wall. The nearest one showed a newspaper clipping featuring a young woman in an army uniform, and a headline that read, BRONWYN HYATT, NEEDSVILLE HERO, RE-TURNS HOME.

But the next one really held her attention. It appeared to be from a musical, and showed a handsome young man dancing. Something about it was extremely familiar, but she couldn't quite place it.

A big man emerged from the kitchen doors holding two menus. "Good morning," he said cheerfully. He wore a nice pressed shirt with the initials *C.C.* stitched over the pocket. "Welcome to the Catamount Corner. Just the two of you?"

"Yes," Justin said.

"Sit anywhere you'd like."

"Excuse me," Veronica said, indicating the dancer's photo. "Who is this?"

"That's my fiancé," C.C. said proudly. "Matt Johannsen. He's on Broadway in the show *Chapel of Ease.*"

Veronica's eyes opened wide. "That's it!"

"What's it?" Justin asked.

"I saw the touring version my freshman year, at the Orpheum in Memphis."

"Yep." The big man practically beamed. "I'll tell you something else: the show was about us. Well, not 'us' as in me and him, but 'us' as in our community."

"Really?" Veronica said, pretending surprise. "I had no idea."

"Congratulations on your engagement," Justin said. Now that gay marriage was legal, it popped up in the most surprising, for straight people at least, places.

"Thanks. We're holding off until Matt's run in the show is over."

"Will he move here," Veronica asked, "or will you move there?"

"We haven't decided yet. But we'll work it out."

Justin picked the table farthest from the locals. He held Veronica's chair for her, then sat himself.

"I'm Justin, by the way," he said. "This is Veronica."

"Nice to meet you. I'm Cyrus Crow, but everyone calls me C.C."

"Oh, I thought that stood for the name of the place. The Catamount Corner."

"Nope. Just a coincidence."

"So it's not for Cloud County, either?" Veronica asked.

He laughed. "Dang, I never even thought about that one."

One of the many things Justin had learned from Doc was to personalize encounters; a researcher seeking data didn't make it very far, but a friendly guy talking to another person could often get exactly what he needed. Doc boiled this down to, *Be polite, be honest, and be respectful. And be sincere about it.*

"Tell me," Justin asked, "have you by any chance ever heard of a place called Sadieville?"

"No," C.C. said. "Is it around here?"

"It was. It was a coal-mining town back at the turn of the last century."

"Needsville's the only town in the county. We don't even have any of those little unincorporated places."

"Sadieville supposedly disappeared a hundred years ago in a mining disaster," Veronica said.

C.C. thought it over and shook his head. "No, I don't recall anyone ever mentioning that. Coffee?"

"Iced tea," Veronica said politely. "For us both."

"Sweet or unsweet?"

"I'm from Mississippi, where we don't even know the meaning of 'unsweet,'" she said.

He smiled and nodded. "Coming right up."

After he was gone, Veronica leaned over the table and said in an urgent whisper, "*That's* where I'd heard of the Tufa before. Remember in Dr. Tully's office, I said I had some vague memory of them? It was from that musical. *Chapel of Ease.*"

"What was it about?"

"A ruined church haunted by ghosts from the Civil War, and a modern couple who kind of mirrored them. It would take too long to explain, but the important part is, all the characters were Tufa. I don't know why I didn't think of it before." She shook her head. "So you think it's really all been forgotten? Sadieville, I mean."

"I'd think something like that kind of sticks with you. Some places have whole museums for lesser disasters, or at least a roadside plaque."

"That's a good point," she agreed.

"So there's got to be *someone* around here who remembers."

As they looked over the menus, the group of old people began to talk again, their voices rising as they settled back into their normal rhythm. Then the bell over the door jingled, and a man entered with a little girl in his arms. He was clearly not a Tufa, as his sandy hair and pale skin testified, but the girl definitely looked like one.

"Hey, Reverend Chess!" one of the old men said. "Morning to you."

"Morning, Garnett," the newcomer said cheerily.

"How's little Miss Kell this morning?" Chester asked.

The girl, who looked about three, had big eyes and a serious set to her tiny face. When she saw that everyone watched her, she buried her face in her father's neck.

"She's fine," Craig Chess answered. "She's just got the shys. She's going with me up to Miss Mary Delia's place to deliver some groceries."

"You wanting some biscuits for her, then?" C.C. said as he emerged from the kitchen.

"If you've got any fresh," Craig said.

"All ready to go," C.C. said, and handed the paper bag over to the minister. As Craig reached for his wallet, C.C. said, "Your money's no good here, Reverend. At least not when you're doing such a nice thing."

"I appreciate it, C.C."

Kell looked up at the bigger man and raised her arms. C.C. obligingly took her, gave her a kiss on the cheek, and said, "Hi, there, Kell."

"Hi," Kell said.

"Are you helping your daddy out today?"

The girl nodded vigorously.

"Do you like visiting folks?"

Another nod.

"That is a sweet little girl," one of the old men said sincerely. "Y'all are mighty lucky."

"We're surely blessed," Craig agreed.

C.C. handed Kell back to her father. As he settled her in his free arm, she looked down at Justin. "Bye-bye," she said without smiling.

"Uh . . . bye-bye," Justin said.

Craig carried Kell and the biscuits out the door. The girl continued to look at Justin until she was out of sight.

"Now what," Justin said, "was that all about?"

"Oh, I wouldn't put any stock in it," C.C. said with what sounded like forced casualness. "She's just a baby. I'll be right back with y'all's drinks."

He was as good as his word. They each ordered scrambled eggs and hash browns. When the food arrived, it included two sausage patties.

"We didn't order the sausage," Justin said.

"Courtesy of Diamond Ike," C.C. said. "It's his extra touch for first-time diners. He claims the sausage is so good, you can't help coming back for more."

" 'Diamond Ike'?" Justin said.

"My cook. Well . . . that's not—"

"Yes it is," a voice called from the kitchen. "I'm a cook."

C.C. leaned down and said conspiratorially, "He went to the

Culinary Institute in Hyde Park, up in New York. But he doesn't like to brag about it, so we can't call him a 'chef.'"

"How did he end up here?" Veronica asked.

"My boyfriend met him, and when he said he wanted to get as far from New York City as possible, Matt said he knew just the place."

"Tell me, C.C.," Justin asked, "any idea where I might find out about Sadieville? Any kind of local historical society or anything?"

"I'm afraid not. Closest library is in Unicorn, and there's the special library in Cricket."

"What makes it special?"

"It's exactly like it was when the first settlers came to Cricket, back before the Civil War. You can't actually check anything out; it's kind of a museum."

"And the one in Unicorn?"

"Oh, that's a regular one. But if you're looking for information about that town you mentioned, the person to see is Miss Azure."

Justin caught movement in the corner of his eye. The other patrons, who had returned to their own conversations, turned and openly watched. If C.C. had broken some code of silence by mentioning that name, though, he seemed unbothered.

"Who is that?" Justin asked.

"She's a professor, specializing in folklore and local history. She lives by herself way out in the woods, but she knows everything about this area, all its history *and* mysteries." He said the last with a small smile.

"Do you have her number or e-mail?"

C.C. was about to answer, then realized the others were watching. "You know, now that I think about it, I might've spoken out of turn. Miss Azure lives all by herself out there for a reason. When she's not a guest professor at some college or other, she pretty much keeps to herself."

"Well . . . can *you* ask her if she'd talk to us?"

Before C.C. could answer, a new voice said, "I can take you out there."

One of the men across the room stood up. Justin could've sworn that they had all been older men and women, but this one looked about their age, and was dressed in jeans and a baseball cap.

He held up his phone. "I overheard you guys talking so I went ahead and texted her. Hope you don't mind. She asked me to show you the way out to her place." He smiled a wide, open grin. "Hi, I'm Tucker Carding."

"I'm Justin, and this is Veronica."

"Pleasure to meet you both."

"We appreciate the offer," Veronica said, "but if you could just give us directions—"

"You'd never find it," Tucker said. "Would they, C.C.?"

"No," C.C. agreed, although there was an odd tone in his voice. "She does live way out there."

"I know what you're thinking," Tucker said lightly, "but I won't take you out in the woods and skin you or anything."

They all laughed, but Veronica kicked Justin under the table.

"So what do you say?" Tucker continued. "Take about twenty minutes to get out there."

Justin and Veronica exchanged a look. "I guess . . ." he said.

"It's nothing personal," Veronica said. "It's just . . ."

"Here, take a picture with me." He squatted down beside her, and Justin, not seeing any way out of it, took the picture. "Send that to someone you trust. That way if anything does happen to you, they'll know who you were last seen with."

Justin saw no graceful way to refuse, so he sent it to Adrian with a quick explanation.

"Ready to go, then?" Tucker asked.

"Can we finish our breakfast?" Veronica said.

"Sure. Just holler when you're ready."

Tucker and C.C. walked back toward the kitchen doors. Ve-ronica watched them talk softly, with an occasional glance their way. She said quietly, "I do not like this, Sam I Am. I do not."

"We don't have to go," Justin said between mouthfuls of food.

"How can you eat now?"

"I'm hungry," he said, pausing to put the woman's name into his phone's search engine. "Look, if you really don't think it's safe—"

"No, I'm probably just being paranoid." She cut her eyes at C.C. and Tucker. "What are they talking about, I wonder?"

Justin looked up from his phone. "This must be her. Azure Kirby. Ph.D. in History, M.A. in English Literature. Currently on sabbatical after teaching at Appalachian State University. She's real."

"That doesn't mean they know her. Or that they *don't* intend to rape and murder us."

"No, but it does seem less likely."

"*Why* would he offer to help, though? What's in it for him?"

"Maybe he's just nice. Some people are."

"I guess you're right. Besides, we're here to find stuff out, aren't we?"

"We are. Now eat up."

"I'm not hungry," she said honestly, still watching C.C. and Tucker. Whatever they discussed, it certainly seemed intense. "So are you going to ask them about the dinosaur?"

"They'd think I was crazy, wouldn't they?"

"They would. First a disappearing town no one's heard of, and then a dinosaur in the woods."

"They're both real," he said seriously. The words immediately recalled Doc's words on the film can.

"I believe you," she agreed, still watching the two men talk.

# 7

At least the scenery was beautiful. But only Justin got to really enjoy it.

Veronica had to focus on driving. It was fine while they stayed on the highway, but once they left it, it was all she could do to keep Tucker's beat-up truck in sight through the dust it kicked up. The roads grew rougher and bouncier, and their guide showed no sign of slowing to make the passage easier for the newcomers.

"I get no signal," Justin said as he checked his phone.

"Can't help that," Veronica said through gritted teeth.

"Damn, honey. Shouldn't you slow down?"

"Tell *him*."

"Is he trying to lose us?"

She flexed her fingers on the steering wheel and said, "He'll have to try a lot harder if he is." She was the unofficial tailgating champion of Lauderdale County, perfectly willing to ride the ass of rednecks who drove forty-five on Interstate 20. She squinted through the dust and trusted her instincts to keep her from driving off the road into a ravine, where they might never be found.

"I'm getting worried," Justin said. "And I need to pee again."

"The time for both of those was back at the cafe," Veronica said.

"I didn't need to pee back at the cafe."

"Is your bladder the size of a thimble? Maybe you should see a doctor."

"I did. I told him I was having bladder-control issues."

"What'd he say?"

" 'In that case, get off my new carpet.' "

Tucker's truck descended into a small hollow. Up ahead, over the treetops, rose a thin column of smoke.

"Luke, I've got a bad feeling about this," Veronica said.

"Stay on target, Red Leader," Justin replied.

Tucker stopped so abruptly that Veronica almost skidded into his tailgate. Justin again checked his phone, but there was no signal, so his location app couldn't tell him where they were.

"Can you find your way back out of here?" he asked Veronica.

"I sure hope so," she said as she turned off the engine. "Do you see any sign of a house?"

He shook his head.

Tucker got out of his truck, stretched, and waved for them to join him. "C'mon, y'all. This is as far as the road goes."

As the dust from their passage settled, Justin and Veronica saw that the road dead-ended at a fence without a gate. A sign said PRIVATE, NO TRESPASSING. Beyond it was a clear grassy path between stands of thick woods. It disappeared over a low hill.

"Y'all just keep walking," Tucker said. "Stay on that path, and it'll take you right to her. She's waiting for you."

"You're not coming?" Justin said.

"No, I got to get back to town. People to do, things to see, you know? Today I've got to pull a four-wheeler out of the mud where somebody got it stuck. People think them things'll drive on water, you know? But they don't. They sink just like anything else."

"It says 'no trespassing,'" Veronica pointed out.

"Y'all ain't trespassing. You've been invited."

Veronica tried to catch Justin's eye, but he gazed off down the trail. He asked, "How far is it?"

"Not too far."

"Let's get our backpacks," Veronica said.

"What do we need—" Justin began.

*"Let's get our backpacks,"* Veronica said in her no-nonsense voice.

"We'll get our backpacks," Justin told Tucker.

Justin followed her to the back of their car. She opened the trunk and, when she was sure it hid them from Tucker, said softly, "I'm *really* not sure about this, Justin. What kind of college professor doesn't have a driveway?"

"One who values her privacy?" Justin said as he lifted her pack and passed it over.

"We only have this Tucker's word that this leads to her place. Hell, we only have his word that he actually texted her."

"It's a pretty elaborate setup for a trap, don't you think?"

"Is it? Have you watched no horror movies in your life?"

Justin shouldered his backpack. "You're not in a negligee, so I'm not worried."

She put a hand on his arm and said seriously, "I am."

He paused to meet her steady, grim gaze. "All right, if you really don't want to do this, we won't."

She scowled. "No, I don't want to be the reason you don't get what you need."

"Are you sure?"

"Yes. But I reserve the right to say 'I told you so.'"

"You wouldn't be you if you didn't."

They joined Tucker at the fence. He said, "Just climb on over. Won't take you ten minutes."

"Can we have your number in case we get lost?" Justin asked.

"And Professor Kirby's number," Veronica added.

He was already walking to his truck. "If you get lost, it's because you're walking backward with your eyes shut. Seriously, it's right over the hill. And don't call her 'Professor Kirby.' Here she's just 'Miss Azure.'" He got back in his car and started the engine. It was too loud for further conversation. He nimbly swung the vehicle around and drove off the way they'd come.

When the sound of his departure faded, Justin turned to Veronica. "Let's go."

They disturbed a flock of small butterflies feeding off a patch of wild yarrow just off the trail. Since the butterflies were as white as the blossoms, it seemed as if the flowers themselves launched into the sky and swirled around them before heading off into the woods. They reminded Veronica of the fluttering soul in *The Devil and Daniel Webster,* and so for a moment the bucolic scene took on faintly sinister overtones. After all, once she'd accepted the idea that the old movie might show a real fairy, then anything was possible. But her common sense reasserted itself, and forced her mind back to the moment; these were just insects drawn to the tiny flowers.

"There's a dinosaur," Veronica said suddenly.

Justin jumped. "Now that's just mean."

As they walked, Veronica felt her apprehension drain away. The rolling mountains could be seen in every direction above the trees, their distinctive blue slopes making the horizon a series of waves. She felt the antiquity of the place, the weight of time and patience that the land itself must have had for the passing of eras. Once these mountains had been tall and jagged; now they were not only smoothed down, they were covered with forests, like some great giant snuggled under a blanket. Only in rare places did bare rock present itself.

"Man, this place is gorgeous," Justin said.

"It is," she agreed. "I was just thinking that."

"Wonder what it's like to grow up here?"

"Different." She really couldn't imagine it.

"Not too many blacks or Latinos around, I bet."

"Not with no jobs to be had," she agreed. Then she pointed. "Hey. Look."

The wisp of gray smoke they'd glimpsed earlier rose straight up in the still air above the trees, only a short distance away.

"Where there's fire, there's civilization," Justin said.

"Joan of Arc would disagree," Veronica replied.

Before long they smelled the odor of something delicious cooking. At last they emerged into a clearing, with a small cottage at the center. The house's sides were made of round logs with some kind of white chinking between them, and the smoke rose from a tall stone chimney. The roof sported wooden slats and three solar panels. A small satellite dish was mounted in the corner. To one side was a garden filled with vegetables, and a Jeep parked in the shade of the trees.

As they approached they also heard music: fast bluegrass with mandolins and steel guitars. A cat walked up to greet them and pressed itself against Justin's legs.

"Hello, there," Veronica said, and knelt to pet it. "How are you? Aren't you pretty?"

They both looked up when the music stopped, and the front door opened. A woman stood there and watched them over the tops of her glasses. She wore a scarf tied tight around her forehead, with black hair falling down her back. She had crow's feet and smile lines, but they couldn't quite peg down her age. She was tall and slender, and when she saw them she said, "Hello. You must be the ones Tucker texted me about."

"Yes, ma'am. I'm Justin Johnson, and this is my girlfriend Veronica Lopez. I apologize for dropping by so unannounced."

"You were announced, you just didn't do the announcing," she said. "Come on in and have some tea."

They followed her inside. No lights were on; illumination came through the windows, casting the corners into shadows. Odors of flowers, cooking, and other, less identifiable smells

filled it with a not-unpleasant homey atmosphere. An open laptop rested on the dining table.

Veronica nudged Justin with her elbow and nodded at the
walls. Musical instruments hung from pegs; Justin recognized
most of them, but not all, and he was delighted to see that they
bore the wear of frequent use. "Doc would love this," he said
quietly.

"I beg your pardon?" Azure asked.

"I'm sorry, I was just saying that our friend Doc would love
seeing all these instruments, especially since they all look like
they get played a lot."

"Doc who?" Azure asked. "Watson? Turner?"

"Adams," Justin said. "From West Tennessee University."

"Oh, that Doc," she said with a smile. "He was a character.
Heard about his passing, too. Did you know him?"

"He was my thesis advisor. I was his last graduate student."

She put a kettle on the stove beside a simmering pot and
turned on the burner. A circle of blue flame leaped up under
it. "I always loved it when he and I were at the same conferences.
He'd been doing this longer than most of us had been alive, and
lordy, the stories he could tell. Well, I'm sure I don't have to
remind you, if you were his student." She wiped her hands on
a towel, then put them on her hips. "Did you have any trouble
finding the place?"

"No, Tucker led us right to you," Justin said.

"Well, good." She gestured at the table. "Please sit."

They did.

"Were you also Doc's student?" she asked Veronica.

"No, I'm in psychology."

"At West Tennessee U.? Who's your advisor?"

"Dr. Tanna Tully."

Her expression grew more mysterious. "Ah, the firefly witch.
I know her, too. Did you know they call her that because her
blindness goes away at night when the fireflies are out?"

"No, I didn't."

"It's not a secret, but it's not common knowledge, either. She's an extraordinary woman." Then her smile returned. "So it seems you both have acceptable bona fides from people I admire, but who evidently couldn't help you with whatever you're doing."

The kettle whistled. She got up and poured water into three cups, then dropped bags into them. She put them on the table. The cups were mismatched, and one was cracked in a way that made Veronica think of Chip from *Beauty and the Beast.* The tea, whatever it was, was sweet and smelled great.

"So," Azure said, "what brings you to my door?"

"I'm doing my thesis on the Sadieville disaster," Justin said.

"Sadieville," she repeated, turning the word slowly as if examining it from all sides. "And Doc was okay with that?"

"Doc didn't know about it. After he died, my new advisor insisted that I start over. Said my initial thesis wasn't rigorous enough."

She chuckled. "Doc was going to let you slide with something easy, eh?"

"He was," Justin admitted with a smile.

She sipped her tea. A different cat jumped up on the table and rubbed its cheek against her shoulder. "And how did you even learn about Sadieville?"

He explained how they'd found the film, and from there the few scraps about the vanished town. Azure listened intently, and when Justin finished she sat back thoughtfully. The cat wandered over to Veronica and purred as she scratched under its chin.

"That is some story," she said at last.

"I know," Justin agreed.

"I don't suppose there's any way I can see that film?"

"Actually, it's on YouTube now," Justin said. "Can I borrow your laptop?"

She passed him the computer. He quickly found the site, and

the video. He positioned the laptop so she could see, then he and Veronica moved to watch over her shoulders.

When it started, a blast of lively piano music burst out; Steve had evidently added a score from the library's collection. Justin hit mute, and said, "It's better without the cheesy music."

When the first wide shot of the town appeared, Miss Azure murmured, "Oh, Sadieville," with a wistfulness that positively ached. But she watched the rest of the movie in silence.

When it was over, she got up, took their cups and glasses to the sink and washed them out. Justin and Veronica exchanged a look; they'd barely touched theirs. Were they being dismissed?

At last she said, "Sadieville doesn't get talked about much, you're right. It was a terrible tragedy. Worst in Cloud County history."

"I'm surprised there wasn't a memorial sign in town," Justin said.

"Well, you have to understand, the Great Sadie Mine was opened in 1912, Sadieville was founded in 1913, and the disaster was in 1915. Not a lot of time to build up a community. And since most of them died when the mines collapsed, there weren't a lot of people left to spread stories." She tapped her fingers along the back of a chair. "Only the locals survived."

"Why only them?"

"Because there were so few of them. I don't imagine more than half a dozen Tufa worked in the mines."

"Why so few?" Veronica asked. "I'd think people around here would be glad to have jobs."

Azure brought back a plate of cookies. "I hope neither of you have a nut allergy." They shook their heads. "Good. I've been told my peanut butter cookies are the best this side of the Tennessee River."

Veronica took one, and nodded enthusiastically after her first bite. "This is wonderful. Try one, Justin."

He hesitated. Azure saw it, and smiled wryly. "I see that you've heard some of the *other* stories about the Tufa."

Veronica stopped in mid-bite.

"That we're descended from the fairy folk of old," Azure continued. "And so, if you accept food or drink from us, you'll be trapped with us forever."

"Dr. Tully mentioned something about it," Justin admitted. "Not the trapped part, but the fairy part. She didn't take it too seriously," he added quickly, "and she warned us not to."

Azure took a cookie and returned to her seat. "Did she also tell you anything about our history?"

"Not really. She said all the stories contradict each other."

"That's probably true. But I think you'll both understand." She chewed and swallowed the bite. "The Tufa, quite frankly, don't look entirely white. With our hair and skin, we look like we have some black or Native American blood in us. And for a long time, especially here in the South, that was enough. Because part black was full black as far as the law was concerned."

"The one drop rule," he said. Something he'd heard his grandfather talk about back before the old man passed away.

"That's right. One drop of black blood in your veins meant you were black, no matter how white you looked. And guess which state was the first to make that idea into law?"

"Tennessee," Justin said.

"Exactly. In 1910, two years before they discovered coal and founded Sadieville. So not only did not many Tufa want to work for the mines, they wouldn't hire many. Not unless they could totally pass for white."

Veronica cautiously took a nibble of her cookie.

"The reason you haven't heard much about Sadieville is that the only people left to tell about it were us, and we don't talk to outsiders," Azure said. "When the world considers you less than a person, it makes sense to keep to yourself. I'm not saying it's a good thing, especially now, but it *is* how it's always been done around here."

"You seem willing to talk about it," Veronica asked.

"I'm a historian." She got up again, went to a shelf and removed a heavy jug. "This is Cloud County Paint Thinner, and I wouldn't recommend it to anyone with a weak heart, bad liver, or who might be pregnant."

"I'll pass," Veronica said, and when Justin stared at her, said, "No, I'm not pregnant, dummy, I'm driving."

Justin accepted a glass of the clear liquid. "I'd recommend sipping," Azure said.

He did, but it still stung all the way down, and made his eyes water. "Thanks," he said, but it came out as a whisper.

"Proud of yourself?" Veronica teased.

Azure tossed her glass down in one swallow, and poured another before she sat. The cat crawled into her lap and settled there, one paw poking limply into space. "So. Sadieville."

Justin took out his phone. "Do you mind if I record this?"

She thought that over. "I'll be quoted in your thesis?"

"Yes. If you don't mind." Justin tried to sound casual, but inside his stomach knotted at the thought of having to take notes by hand, or worse, being denied permission to quote from it.

"Quoted on Sadieville," she mused. "Well, I suppose now that you've got that film online, it's more likely other folks will come sniffing around looking for it. So, yes, go right ahead. Let's get this on the record."

"Thank you."

She waited until he had the phone set up, then began. "The Sadieville coal seam was discovered in 1912, and the Prudence Coal and Coke Company bought the rights. They opened up the Great Sadie Mine Number One, based on the idea that this was an offshoot of the Cumberland Gap coal field, which had already made a lot of people rich. None of the company men were locals, of course. The money that came out of the ground left almost as soon as it was made. And that's still true. Like Larry Sparks said, 'They turned the hills and hollers upside down when they started digging in the ground.'"

"Why was it named the 'Sadie' mine?" Justin asked.

"After the owner's younger daughter. The company was named after his older daughter, Prudence."

"How big was the town?"

"At the time of the disaster, Sadieville employed 250 men and mined 130,000 tons of coal annually. It began as a drift mine, one that tunneled horizontally into the mountain, following a coal seam that was between six and eight feet thick."

"Is that big?" Veronica asked.

"Huge. Most seams are around four feet. The pick miners made sixty cents per ton of coal they extracted, paid in company scrip."

"What's that?" Justin asked.

"Company currency. Can only be spent at the company store, or at other company facilities."

"Is that legal?"

"It was then. Miners got paid once a month. They worked ten-hour days, and their coal was measured in what they called 'long tons,' which was 2,400 pounds. That came from British coal mining, but of course it meant that they had to work harder than if they'd used the standard American two-thousand-pound ton."

"Shit," Justin said.

"It was a hard life," Azure agreed. "But the Prudence Company played fair, so they never suffered a strike. In 1914, they worked 295 days out of the year, which around here was phenomenal. Usually the winter shuts down everything for weeks."

"So who were these miners, if they weren't locals?"

"A lot of them were professionals who came down from

Pennsylvania and Kentucky. They brought their families along, and the boys, when they got big enough to work, followed their fathers into the mines."

She poured another glass. She no longer seemed to be looking at them, but gazing past them into space, into a world that once existed.

"The company built their houses, and charged them $1.50 per room, per month. They got access to the company doctor for fifty cents a month. You could get a baby delivered for five dollars. There was a school, an amusement hall, several bars, and of course the company store. The only way in or out was the railroad; there were plans to cut a regular road, but they never had the chance." She took a sip. "The only law was a county sheriff on the company payroll, so he was more than happy to turn a blind eye unless things got really out of hand."

"Wait, the company paid the sheriff? Do you mean, like a bribe?" Justin said.

"No, they paid him up front. You see, the county was so small, and so quiet, that we didn't even *have* a sheriff until the mine came along. And after that, we've never had another."

"Was it a dangerous place, then?" Veronica said.

"Of course. Lots of people died, and lots of murders went uninvestigated and unpunished. If I remember right, in 1914 alone there were twenty-three unsolved killings, most of them drinking and gambling related. And then there's the Boardinghouse Massacre."

"That sounds exciting," Veronica said.

"It certainly was at the time. Seems there was a beautiful young girl staying at a boardinghouse, and three miners competed for her attention. Eventually the suitors shot it out, and all of them died. The poor girl was shot as well, but survived."

She was far away now, her eyes glazed with the look of distant memory. Then she blinked herself back to the moment. "I apologize. I think the moonshine's getting to me." She put the cork back in the bottle and slid it away down the table. "Where was I?"

"You'd told us a lot about the town and how dangerous it was," Justin said. "But how did the disaster actually happen?"

She thought for a moment. "Depends on who you ask. The most common explanation is that the miners broke into a subterranean river that no one knew about. It flooded the mine, and once the caverns that were previously filled with water had emptied, the weight of the rock and buildings above broke through and the town simply fell into the hole. The problem with that idea is that, like I said, the mine was a drift mine."

"So the mine went horizontally, not down to where the water was?" Justin asked tentatively.

"Right. If it had been a shaft mine that went down, or even a slope mine that went at a slant, then it would make more sense."

"Are you sure it was a drift mine, then?"

"I suppose I could be wrong about that. And there might have been other causes. I've heard more than once that one of them old hard-shell preachers in town might have used dynamite to blow up the underground river on purpose, and to open the cavern beneath it. He was a member of the White Caps, which was a vigilante gang like the Klan who went around thrashing people with hickory switches when they didn't live up to their ideas about morality. He plumb hated any miners who weren't one hundred percent white, including the Tufa. The only problem with that story is, how did he know about the river when even the company geologists didn't?"

They sat quietly for a few moments. Then Justin prompted, "How many died?"

"There are only round figures to work with. Some say three hundred, some say as many as five hundred. Remember, it wasn't just the miners, it was their families, and all the people who had businesses in town."

"And no one tried to rescue them?" Veronica asked.

"There was no one to do it, and by the time the word got out, it was too late."

"What about the Tufa who were there?"

"As I said, the Tufa who worked there had sense enough to leave before it happened."

"That sounds," Justin said carefully, "like maybe they knew it was coming."

"Or had a hand in it," Azure said. "You're not the first person to think that. But the company men couldn't find any of the surviving Tufa miners to ask them, and there was no physical evidence to back up the claim. So it was written off as an act of God, *force majeure* for insurance's sake, and the coal company left." She smiled. "And given the way the industry has behaved in other counties, tearing off mountaintops and polluting streams and groundwater, I'm very glad they did."

"So is anything left of the town?" Veronica asked.

"Nothing. The hole's all filled in and overgrown by now, and it would be very difficult to find. It's been over a century, you know. Mountain winters aren't kind to man-made things." She looked up at them and smiled. "And that's what I know. Was it helpful?"

"Very much," Justin said. "Thank you."

"Was there anything else you'd like to ask?"

Before Justin could speak, Veronica asked, "What did you think of the movie?"

Azure propped her arm on the table and rested her chin on her hand. It was either a studied casualness, or the effect of the moonshine. "I'd heard of this film. A company out of New Jersey made it, I believe, before the movie industry all relocated to the West Coast. Filmed part of it in Sadieville right before the disaster. But I'd assumed it was lost. Nitrate film doesn't age well, and it goes up at the slightest spark. It killed more than a few projectionists back then, when it overheated in the projection booth. Did you ever see a movie called *Cinema Paradiso*? There was a scene with that sort of fire." She paused, drummed her fingers on her chin, then asked, "How did Doc preserve this?"

"It was in a film can, at the bottom of a pile of magazines in his office," Justin said.

"It was taped up," Veronica added. "Seemed to be airtight."

"I guess that must be why it survived. I wonder where he found it?"

"And," Justin said, "it had a label on it, in Doc's handwriting."

"What did it say?"

"It said . . . 'This is real.'"

They sat in silence, broken only by the loud purring of one of the sleeping cats. Finally Justin added, "Do you know what he might've meant by that?"

"I suppose he meant that it showed a real fairy," Azure said.

Justin and Veronica exchanged a look.

"Did it?" Justin asked.

She laughed. "I'm not qualified to say."

"All stories come from somewhere," Justin said.

"That's a folklorist talking, all right," she said with a sly smile. "I'm a Tufa. All those people back at the cafe were Tufa. Do we seem like fairies to you?"

"I meant no disrespect," Justin said.

"It's not disrespectful," she said with a chuckle. "The original fairy folk, the Tuatha de Danaan, were mighty warriors, marvelous artists, beautiful musicians. They ruled for a thousand years, and if you believe the mythology, they still rule in a secret land called Tír na nÓg. If you want to think of us as creatures out of folklore, those are certainly acceptable ones."

"So it's *not* true?" Veronica pressed gently.

Azure's eyes narrowed, and the amusement left her voice. "Is that why you're really here? To find out the truth about the

Tufa? Is the whole thing about your thesis and Sadieville a smoke screen?"

"No," Justin said seriously. "Not at all."

"Because that's happened before. Back in the early two thousands, before they devolved to aliens and Bigfoot hunters, one of those cable history channels came here and made a documentary about us. They told us it was just about how handmade musical instruments were created, but when it aired, it was all about the 'mysterious' Tufa, and where they might have come from."

"I never heard of that," Justin said.

"That's because it aired once, and disappeared into their vaults after no one watched it. A lot like the way this movie disappeared."

"I swear, I truly want to find whatever remains of Sadieville."

Azure looked at him for a long moment, then said, "In that case, I hope you find it."

Justin picked up his phone and turned it off. "Thank you, Professor Kirby. We appreciate your time, and your honesty."

Azure stood, as did Justin and Veronica. "Oh, it was my pleasure," she said, back to her pleasant self. "I actually miss talking to students when I'm away from them. I appreciate you two trekking all the way out here."

"And thank you for the refreshments," Veronica said.

"Glad you enjoyed them. And I promise, no curse was involved." They all laughed at that.

Veronica nudged Justin. "Ask her about the dinosaur."

"I beg your pardon?" Azure said.

Justin glared sideways at Veronica, then said, "I saw something odd on the way here. Out just off the highway. I thought . . ."

"He thought it was a dinosaur," Veronica said.

Azure's eyebrows went up. "Really?"

"Show her the picture."

Exasperated, Justin took out his phone and pulled up the photo of the track. When she saw it, Azure smiled.

"That's not a dinosaur. It's an emu."

"The bird?" Justin said. "The one from Australia?"

"Yep. A few years ago, a fella tried to raise a flock of them for their meat, but somehow or other a bunch got loose, and now they're breeding. Damnedest thing. The males get cross in the spring when it's mating time, but otherwise they pretty much run away whenever they come across a person."

"There, you see?" Veronica said. "Perfectly reasonable explanation."

"Sorry to disappoint you," Azure said. "A dinosaur would've been a lot more interesting."

They shouldered their packs, made their good-byes, and departed. When they'd hiked out of sight of the house on the way back to their car, Veronica said, "So what did you think?"

"That was fascinating," Justin said, with real enthusiasm. "I can't wait to transcribe what she said."

"So you believed her?"

"You didn't?"

"I think there was enough truth in what she said that the lies blended right in. And when you listen to that recording, I bet you'll find she didn't actually tell you as much as you think."

"That's cynical."

"She didn't really answer the elephant-in-the-room question: how could all those people die with no mention of it surviving?"

"Yes, she did."

"She told us stories. Even she wasn't sure."

"That's not dishonest."

"Whatever, Justin. It's your damn thesis, not mine." Annoyed, she strode rapidly down the hill toward the car. Justin sighed in exasperation and rushed to catch up.

———

Azure watched the young couple until they disappeared down the trail. She was not the least bit surprised that, as soon as they were out of sight, Tucker Carding walked out of the woods on the opposite side of the cottage.

"How bad is it?" he asked without preliminaries.

"They know about Sadieville. They have a copy of that movie, *The Fairies of Sadieville.* I saw it."

For a moment his expression was one of almost infinite sadness and loss. "You saw Sophronie?"

"I did. It's on the Internet, if you want to see it."

He shook his head.

She paused, then asked, "Do you think it might be time?"

"I don't know. I haven't heard anything from . . . *her.*"

"The night winds have blown some strange things of late," Azure pointed out.

"Yeah." He looked down thoughtfully, and chewed his lower lip, until at last he decided. "I don't know if it's *time* time, but I do think it's time to let the rest of the Tufa know."

Azure nodded. "Then I'll contact the First Daughters."

"And I'll keep an eye on our friends," he said, and turned to go.

She put a hand on his arm. "Wait, Tucker. I know that you know where *it* is, and that it's near Sadieville. You're going to make sure they find it, aren't you? And then see if the passage is open to them. Am I right?"

"Maybe," he admitted. "They did sort of drop in our laps, almost like they were deliberately sent to us."

"But we don't know that."

"Are you not willing to sacrifice a couple of strangers for a chance to . . . ?" He trailed off, leaving unsaid what they both knew.

"I don't know that I am," Azure said. "And deep down, I don't know that you are, either."

"Well, we'll cross that when we come to it," he said.

They made complex hand gestures of respect to each other, and then Tucker went back into the woods. As soon as he was out of sight, Azure picked up her cell phone.

"Bliss," she said when the other end answered. "We have a situation. I need to meet with the First Daughters."

She listened for a moment, then said, "Yes, it's the full moon. I don't know if it's a coincidence; you know who to ask about *that*." Another pause, then, "Good. I'll see you there."

She hung up, picked up her cat and buried her face in the soft fur. She sang softly, with great feeling:

> *Never go back, don't have the will*
> *Can never go back to my Sadieville . . .*

# 8

As they settled in for the night at the Catamount Corner Motel, the only place to stay within at least an hour's drive, Veronica said, "I'm sorry for getting so snippy out there."

"No worries," Justin said. "It was all pretty weird."

"No, seriously," she said. She slid between him and the bed where he was unpacking, and put her arms around his neck. "I'm sorry. I know how important this is to you, and how little it has to do with me. I shouldn't get so emotionally involved."

He put his hands on her hips. "I actually kind of like that about you. The way you take what I do so seriously."

They kissed, and she teased, "So show me your thesis statement, big boy."

He put his arms around her. "I *do* feel like I should be working. Transcribing what Professor Kirby said. Figuring out where we're going to start looking for Sadieville tomorrow."

She put his hand on her breast. "What do you feel like now?"

He looked down at his hand, then up at her, and

with satisfaction she saw the shift in his gaze. "I don't have to do my homework right now, I guess."

"Mm, good guess."

He began to move his hand. "I think I have a take-home quiz I might work on. For extra credit."

"Just remember, the teacher doesn't grade on a curve."

"It's pass or fail?"

"The practicum sure is," she said, turned him and pushed him down on the bed.

Later, as she lay awake while Justin snored lightly beside her, something occurred to her. She had seen the play *Chapel of Ease,* and yet somehow forgot all about it. She loved that show, loved the music and the story and the sheer intensity of it, and it had entirely slipped her mind, in the same way the Sadieville disaster had slipped out of history.

And both involved the mysterious Tufa people.

She turned and looked at Justin's sleeping face. He looked impossibly young all of a sudden, like an innocent boy. She felt a surge of affection for him, and a desire to protect him that almost brought tears to her eyes.

She draped his arm over her and spooned backward into his embrace.

The First Daughters of the Tufa met irregularly, but always on the full moon. There was no arcane significance to this, only the practical: they convened deep in the forest and wanted to avoid flashlights or anything that might allow them to be followed and observed. There were those Tufa who resented the power of the First Daughters, especially among their opposite number in the Tufa clans led by Junior Damo.

The night was cool and damp. Fireflies drifted up into the higher tree branches, and patches of foxfire glowed from fallen trunks and limbs. Most Tufa gatherings, even the serious ones, were filled with music, but this one was silent and somber.

Around the circle, women who looked enough alike to be sisters, or mothers and daughters, waited expectantly. The First Daughters were exactly what the name implied: the firstborn female children of each generation who still maintained true Tufa bloodlines. These women had a special awareness of their new world, and they were respected because of it. They were the first to forge a relationship with the night winds, those spirits, or deities, or whatever they were, that guided the Tufa destiny here. They were the first to learn how music, in this world, could alter events and even the fabric of this reality, in a way totally different from their place of origin. Some of the women were part of lineages that went all the way back to those times. And some of them—because time doesn't work the same for every Tufa—remembered those times firsthand.

Many Tufa women were infuriated that a mere accident of birth kept them from being part of the group, but those in it knew that it was no simple honor. It carried a weight of responsibility none of them would wish on anyone else.

When they were all assembled, young Mandalay Harris said, "Thank you all for coming on such short notice. Azure has some important information she needs to share."

Azure stepped into the center of the circle, slowly turned and made hand signs of appropriate respect to those watching. As a sometimes professional storyteller as well as a part-time professor, she was usually at ease as the center of attention, but not here, and not now.

"Today, a couple of young people came to visit me," she said, her voice trembling. "They're college students from the other end of the state, and one of them is doing his master's thesis on . . ." She paused. "Sadieville."

The women looked blank.

"Where is that?" one asked.

"Sadieville was a coal town over near Black Creek," Azure said.

"What, *here*? In Cloud County?" said another incredulous voice.

"Yes."

"When was this?"

"At the beginning of the twentieth century. In 1915, the cavern beneath Sadieville collapsed, and the whole town— buildings, machinery, people—vanished overnight."

She saw the confused faces around her in the moonlight. No one could recall anything about this.

"There's a reason you've never heard of it," she said. "The Tufa leaders at the time decided that to keep more coal people from sniffing around here, they should sing the memory of the town and its people out of the world. That included our memories as well. Over time almost all trace of it has been lost."

"Then how did your visitors find out about it?" Bronwyn Chess asked.

"Luck and serendipity," Azure said. "They found an old silent movie that was filmed in Sadieville just before the disaster, one that I thought was surely lost by now, too. Somehow a late colleague of mine had a copy, and now it's been uploaded to You-Tube. It shows a pureblood Tufa, Sophronie Conlin, letting her glamour down."

"Who is Sophronie Conlin?" Carnelia Rector said.

"You don't remember Sophronie because her memory was sung out with the town's. The only reason *I* do is because Viney Conlin, her mother, was my great-grandmother, and she and the rest of the Conlin family were . . ." She searched for the right word. "Exempt. We were the keepers of this secret."

The group fell silent as they absorbed this information. It was one thing to sing up magic that helped keep them safe, or that brought good things to those who needed it. But something on this scale could've only been done by most of the Tufa singing together . . . which meant they'd agreed to sing it out of their own memories.

Finally Azure said, "I think the easiest thing to do would be to sing you the song we used to hide the memory. It should let it all come back to you."

Azure cleared her throat, then sang in a high, clear voice:

*As a girl I walked your hollers,*
*Down by the shallow, springtime creek,*
*But now where I walk, a shadow follows,*
*And I pray the Lord my soul will keep*

*Lost my baby, lost my son,*
*Lost my only, my only one,*
*Can't go back, don't have the will,*
*Can never go back to my Sadieville . . .*

The lightning bugs left lazy trails of light through the air, and the moon shone down like a spotlight. At first, there was no change. But one woman gasped, and then they all reacted as something inside their minds opened up, releasing memories and knowledge that had always been there but hidden behind a song spell of irresistible power. The story spilled forth, images and emotions that overpowered in their chaotic rush. Several broke out in sobs, some clung to friends or sisters, and the rest just stared into the darkness as the blinders fell away.

Azure continued to sing:

*In Sadieville, there's haunts in the trees*
*And theirs are the sighs moving the leaves*
*And the cold air that seeps*
*Through the cracks in the floor*
*Can never go back oh no, not anymore*

*Never go back, don't have the will*
*Can never go back to my Sadieville . . .*

And in all their minds, they saw a train arrive in a grimy little town, unknowingly bringing those who would precipitate the death and horror to follow.

# II

# SADIEVILLE

# 9

"'The country around Sadieville has a sort of half-civilized aspect,'" Ben Hubbard read from the newspaper, having to shout over the noise of the slowing train. "'Yet it is beautiful nevertheless, the work of nature in her happiest mood.'" He closed the paper and looked out the train window as the scenery changed from heavy forest to areas cleared for the town.

"And this," Ben added, "must be Sadieville." The screech of locomotive brakes cut through the air. Ben Hubbard was twenty-one, with unruly hair and a thick mustache waxed up at the tips. He was the epitome of a young man of his times, having seen in the new century as a child and now fully intending to enjoy it.

His boss, motion picture director Sean Lee, leaned over to share the view. Sean was twenty-nine, with receding hair and a dimpled chin. He had grown up hearing stories of the Civil War and the greatness of Abraham Lincoln, and of how his family's shame at their tenuous connection to the Confederate general prompted his male ancestors to heroic acts on behalf of the Union. Sean, though, had no such drive; he only sought out false conflict, safely brought to life by actors under his guidance. "Wow," he said.

"How do you mean that?" Ben asked. "It looks like just another dirty little coal town to me."

"I wasn't looking at the town," Sean replied. "I was looking at the mountains."

Ben turned to the man beside him. He wore a full suit despite the summer heat, and at the moment was asleep with his hat down over his face. "Richard," Ben said, and shook him lightly. "We're here."

Richard Arliss sat up slowly and yawned. He was ridiculously handsome, with a square jaw and a pencil-thin mustache so neat it almost looked drawn. His hair was parted along a razor-straight line, and slicked down to a lacquered shine. He was always referred to as "Mr. Arliss," or "Richard"; never, *ever* "Dick." He was twenty-six, and knew he was the best-looking man in the room. Any room.

"Ah, that explains the smell," Richard said, wrinkling his nose. "Not even the East River during the summer smells quite so rank. What causes it?"

"You get used to it," Ben said. "By tonight, you won't even notice it."

"And how," Richard said with his precise diction, "do you know that?"

"I grew up near a coal town," Ben said. "Went with my dad to deliver dry goods to the company store. Almost made me puke going in, but by the time we left, I wasn't even aware of it anymore."

"Mm," Richard said. He stood to his full five-foot-six height as the train slowed. Outside the windows, the platform and station building momentarily blocked the view.

"Grab the gear," Sean said. "Don't let it out of your sight." Ben nodded and left the car, jumping onto the platform before it came to a final stop and waiting as the porters unloaded the luggage.

"If young master Benjamin is gathering your toys," Richard asked, "who will carry my bags?"

"You will," Sean said.

"What sort of uncivilized wilderness is this?"

"It'll help your performance to do a little manual labor," Sean said with a grin.

"My performance needs no 'help,'" Richard said. "I'm a professional."

"So you keep saying."

Aside from the three movie people, the only other passengers were a young clerk who resisted conversation, and an overweight geologist who wouldn't shut up. Everyone in the car now knew he'd been brought in by the Prudence Coal and Coke Company, who'd opened the Great Sadie mine, to determine if this unexpected vein of coal eventually connected to the Cumberland Gap coal field to the west. If it did, then a lot of lawyers would get very rich sorting out the mineral rights. He scooted to the window beside his seat on the far side of the car and looked out.

Sean joined the geologist at the window. On the mountain slope above them was the mine itself, the Sadie Number One. A long wooden slide led from the mine down to the town.

"It's beautiful, isn't it?" the geologist said.

"Yes, indeed," Sean agreed. "What's that slide up there?"

"That's the tipple. They use it to slide coal down to the hopper, and from there it's loaded into waiting train cars."

"Isn't that something?" Sean said.

"The coal they're sending down is three hundred million years old, did you know that?"

"I did not."

"You've heard of dinosaurs?"

"Yes."

"Well, that's two hundred million years older than even the oldest dinosaur we know of. All these mountains? They actually formed the bottom of the ocean then."

"What happened?"

"Two pieces of the earth's crust ran into each other, and with nowhere to go but up, they went up. Then, over time, the elements wore them back down. Who knows, in another two hundred million years they might be at the bottom of the ocean again."

"And science told you all that?"

The geologist had the same gleam in his eye that Sean had seen in some of the raving street-corner evangelists in the city. "Science," the geologist said seriously, "tells us *everything*."

The geologist tottered off to collect his things. Sean took one last look at the mountains and let out a relieved sigh. His whole career depended on this place, and now he was certain he'd been right. Some things just couldn't be filmed on city rooftops, where sets were built to take advantage of the summer sun. That was fine for dramas that took place in small rooms, telling trivial tales of everyday trials. But he had something larger in mind, and it needed a bigger canvas. It needed what he now saw out the window.

"Hello, beautiful," he said to himself.

"Beg your pardon?" Richard said.

"Nothing. Let's go get settled and organized for auditions."

They quickly disembarked, grateful to be out of the hot car. Ben carried the tripod under his arm, the camera in its case across his back, and a bag containing rolls of raw film in his other hand. "Can someone grab my suitcase? I'm out of hands."

"I'll get it," Richard said. Beneath his haughty manner he was a decent man, and although he'd never admit it, he liked Sean and Ben immensely. Like him, they saw the future of this new art form called movies, and he'd much rather work with them on an interesting mistake than do yet another profitable but overwrought melodrama onstage.

Sean led them into the small station, past the shuffling people moving to board the train. He noticed that they all looked tired, with none of the excitement that he usually saw in travelers. Wherever they were going, they weren't looking forward to it, or they were too tired to care.

"Excuse me," Ben asked a well-dressed man checking his pocket watch. "Do you have the time?"

"Ten to," the man said without looking up.

"Ten to what?"

"Tend to your own damn business," the man said. He snapped the watch shut and went out the door toward the train.

Richard turned to Sean. "Is that typical Southern hospitality?"

"It's not a good omen," Ben said.

"Do you believe in omens?" Richard asked.

Ben smiled. "Sure. Omens, portents, and signs. Just like Madame Marie over in Asbury Park. She read the cards and told me I'd be taking a long trip with two friends."

"Did she say how that trip would end?"

"Her exact words were 'in revelation.'" He laughed.

Sean shook his head and walked over to the ticket window. A tall, rangy man in an ill-fitting shirt and visor cap looked out at him. When he spoke, Sean saw only two teeth, one in each gum. He said, "Can I help you, young man?"

"We're looking for Mrs. Delaney's boardinghouse."

He looked them over suspiciously. "You three more company Yankees?"

"We're not with the mining company."

"Then what's all that gear?" the old man said, nodding at Ben.

Sean leaned close. "Can you keep a secret? We're here to make a motion picture."

"A pitcher? Like at the pitcher show?"

"That's right. But don't tell anyone. It's a secret." He was pretty sure that word of their arrival would now spread like fire through a tenement.

"Now, the boardinghouse?" Sean asked again.

He pointed toward the exit. "You see that street out there?"

"Yes."

"That's the only street we have. So turn right, keep going, and look on the left. Three-story white house, tallest one on that end of the street. There's a big ole oak tree in the yard. If you reach the half-built church, then you've gone too far."

Outside the station, they stopped and took a moment to orient themselves. Richard looked around and held his handkerchief over his mouth and nose. "And you consider this picturesque?"

"No, I consider *that* picturesque." He gestured at the mountains. "This is just our base of operations."

"I might asphyxiate before we start filming."

"Then we'll just prop up your corpse. Wouldn't make any difference in your performance."

Richard threw back his head and roared with laughter, until the fumes sent him into a coughing fit.

Most people were on foot, and had the battered look of longtime miners. A few horse-drawn wagons made their way through, and at least one Dodge touring car skidded along the muddy thoroughfare, the driver shouting for people to get out of his way.

"How did that even get here?" Ben asked.

"On the train, like everything else," Sean said.

"The very definition of rustic charm," Richard observed dryly.

"Yeah, but look at the *faces*," Sean said, watching as the wave of tired miners filed past them. He loved their looks: all hard angles, sunken cheeks, and hollow eyes. They walked with a stooped, defeated air, except for a few who strode with raised chins and confident glances. This was exactly the authenticity he sought, and he felt the thrill of anticipation at getting it all on film. "Look at the history in them. You don't get that from actors."

"Indeed." Richard sniffed. "As a rule, we practice hygiene." He pointed up the street, at a building with a large sign proclaiming, THE GREAT SADIE HOTEL. "Why aren't we staying there?"

"I thought you'd prefer the personal touch of a boardinghouse," Sean said.

"Does 'personal' include a young lady's company?"

"You'll have to arrange that on your own. With your own money."

As they walked, Ben moved close and said quietly, "I hope this is all worth it, Sean."

"It will be," Sean said with certainty.

Mrs. Delaney's boardinghouse was the oldest building in town, and as promised, an enormous ancient oak shaded most of it. A recent paint job could not entirely disguise the way it had been repeatedly enlarged during its existence. It was now three stories high, with a wraparound porch and a kitchen that had once been detached as a fire precaution, but was now connected by a wooden hallway.

Two old men sat on the porch in rockers, their faces smeared with black coal dust. One sipped from a jug resting on the back of his forearm, his wrist bent to keep his index finger looped through the handle by the spout.

It was a movement that Sean had never seen before, and he discreetly pointed it out to Ben. "Look at how he's drinking."

"Heavily?"

"No, with his wrist bent like that."

Ben shrugged. "So?"

Sean shook his head. "That, my friend, is why you'll never be a filmmaker. You've got no eye for detail."

"Not when I'm lugging a ton of your stuff. Can we go inside so I can put it down?"

Instead of answering, Sean went over to the old men. "Hello. Do you live here in the boardinghouse?"

The nearest one said, "A-yewp."

Sean took out a business card and handed it to him. "I'm going to be looking for people to be in a motion picture in the next few days. I'd love to have you."

The man passed the card to his friend. His friend shrugged and handed it back. The first man returned it to Sean. "Cain't neither of us read a lick. But we'll either be here or up to the mine if you want us."

Sean took back the card, which was now smeared with black fingerprints. "Er . . . thank you. I'll be in touch."

"Bless your heart," the second man said, and then the two laughed.

Inside, Ben gratefully put down the tripod and bag of film. The entrance hall opened on a sitting room, filled with oddly opulent furniture. No one appeared to greet them, so Sean called out, "Hello?"

"I'll be right there," a woman said from upstairs.

"Charming," Richard said quietly as he looked around. "Decorated in early Old West whorehouse."

"Stop it," Sean said. "We need these people to like us."

"Most of them can't even understand us," Richard said.

"Then we have to learn to speak their language."

They fell silent when footsteps came down the stairs. A woman in her thirties, large-bosomed and with an impressive coif of dark red hair, stopped at the bottom and smiled. "Well, you must be the three boys from New Jersey. I'm Mrs. Delaney."

"I'm Sean, and this is Ben."

"And I am Richard Arliss," he said with a bow. "I am from New York City, unlike these two provincials."

She did a little half-curtsy to Richard, then daintily shook hands with Sean and Ben. "It's a pleasure to meet y'all."

"Don't get many Yankees here, I'll bet," Ben said.

"Actually, we get quite a few. All the company men are Yankees, and this is where they stay."

"Not the hotel?"

"Not if they're planning to be here a while. We've got one young couple who are waiting for their house to be finished. This town can't grow fast enough to keep up, I'm afraid."

"Well," Sean said, "it's a pleasure to meet you, and to stay in your fine establishment."

"Oh, please," she said with a laugh. "I got all my furniture from an estate sale at a Kansas City whorehouse."

"Told you," Richard muttered.

"But," Mrs. Delaney continued, "I do offer breakfast and dinner, along with clean linens and baths for a quarter. So let's get you moved in." She looked at the tripod. "Lordy, what is that gimcrack?"

"It's a tripod," Ben said. "It holds the camera steady when we're filming."

"Is that the camera on your back?"

"Yes, ma'am."

"And you can make a whole movie with just those two things?"

"There's at least one other essential component," Richard said. "You need someone to point that camera *at*."

"Are you an actor?"

"I am," he said with a proud little mock bow.

"My daddy always told me that actors were worse than Catholics."

"And he was entirely right."

They all laughed. Mrs. Delaney turned to Sean. "I don't know what you expect to find here that's worth putting in a motion picture. A full set of teeth is scarce, and an honest man is even scarcer."

"I'm sure I'll find what I'm looking for," Sean said.

"I hope so," Mrs. Delaney said. Then she led the three men up the stairs to their rooms.

## 10

The next day, Sean went up and down the street posting the following flyer anywhere he could:

WANTED:
Local people with interesting faces
Men, women, children
Good pay, potential for more
Come to Mrs. Delaney's boardinghouse
Tuesday at 9 A.M.

The man behind the counter at the company dry goods store took the flyer from Sean, looked it over, then said doubtfully, "You taken a good look at the people around here?"

"I have."

"We ain't pretty."

"I don't know if I'd go that far."

"I would. Most of us are so ugly, we have to sneak up on our mirrors to shave."

"Well, whether you're pretty or not, you're definitely interesting."

His eyes narrowed. "You planning to make fun of us, then?"

"No, not at all. I want to film things that nobody else has seen. To show the rest of the world how beautiful it is here."

"What's so beautiful about it?"

"The mountains, the sky, the way the mist hangs in the trees in the morning. You may not think about it because you see it all the time, but believe me, the rest of the world doesn't, and they'll be amazed."

He thought this over. "I reckon you can hang this, then."

"Thank you."

"You want interesting, you should film yourself some Tufa."

"What's that?"

He thought some more. "Ah, don't worry about it. Just stick your sign in the window, and I'll make sure people see it."

"Thank you."

As Sean continued up one side of the street, Ben made his way down the other. He stepped through the swinging doors of a saloon called the Lignite Lounge. He was a little surprised to find it open, and he waited for his eyes to adjust to the darkness.

"Come on over here, son," a man's gravelly voice said. "I ain't gonna bite ya."

"Don't want to trip over anything," he said as he carefully walked to the bar, where he fumbled his way onto a stool. He looked around, and saw that the rest of the bar was empty.

"What's yer poison?" the bartender said, in an accent Ben recognized.

"Are you from the Bronx?"

"Ya got a good ear. Most people here can only tell I'm from north of Maryland."

"I hear some Irish in there. You from Highbridge?"

"Goddamn, son, I'm starting to think you're a mind reader. What about you?"

"Baychester."

"Well, then, the first round's on the house."

He produced a jug identical to the one they'd seen the man on the porch drinking from, and poured a clear liquid into a glass. "They call this Cloud County Paint Thinner. Some say it'll make you go blind, then get your sight back, then go blind again."

Ben took a sip, then shuddered as it burned all the way down. "Holy shit!" he gasped.

"That'll put hair on the hairless, won't it?" the bartender said. "Reckon I should introduce myself. Everybody here calls me Quinn."

"Pleased to meet you," he choked out. "I'm Ben Hubbard." He indicated the bottle. "Why do you serve that, if you want people to come back?"

"Because I can get it a lot cheaper than I can real stuff brought in on the train." He poured himself a shot and downed it. "It gets smoother as you go," he croaked, and offered Ben another shot.

Ben shook his head. "I guess alcoholics will drink anything."

"Alcoholics? There's no alcoholics here. Do you know what an alcoholic is? It's someone you don't like, who drinks as much as you do. And, since I like everybody, none of my customers are alkies."

"How much do I owe you?" Ben asked.

"Like I said, it's on the house. I only take company scrip, anyway, and you don't look like a company man."

"Well, then, here's to the Prudence Company."

They tapped their shot glasses.

"So what brings you down here?" Quinn asked.

"I'm here with my boss. We're going to make a motion picture."

"A picture? Here?"

"Yeah. You might not believe it, but pictures about hillbillies are big business."

"Whoa, now, you don't want to be using that word around here."

"Business?"

"Hillbilly. These people may be from the hills, but they work harder than you or I ever will, and they don't complain nearly as much as we do. I've been down here among them for a year now, and they've earned my respect."

"Sorry. It's my first time here."

"I understand. And I know what it looks like at first. Blank eyes, dirty skin, slack jaws, old clothes. But these people raise their families and don't ask anyone for anything. They're good folks, and I'm proud to serve them." He paused. "Unless they're Tufa, that is."

"Tufa?"

"Yeah. There ain't too many here in Sadieville. Most of 'em live over in Needsville, and don't have anything to do with us. But the Prudence Company bought the land from one of them, and there's a few that come here for the work."

"What are the 'Tufa'?"

"Well, they're—"

He was interrupted by a half-dozen men who came loudly into the bar. Most wore overalls, although two wore surprisingly nice pressed shirts. They waved at Quinn and took a table in the darkest corner.

"Hold on, have to earn my keep," Quinn said, and left Ben to ponder the strange course of his life that brought two men from the Bronx together here.

By the time Quinn finished taking orders and delivering drinks, that first jolt of moonshine had settled, and Ben was light-headed. He burped a little as Quinn returned and said, "You know, you were telling me something really interesting, but I'm damned if I can remember what it was."

"It was about the Tufa."

"That's right. Who are they?"

"Like I said, most of them live over in Needsville. That was the only town in the county until Sadieville. Not that you'd find it; I can't tell you how many people say they've gone looking for it and claim it ain't there."

"What's so special about the Tufa?"

"They look different. They all have black hair, and kind of dark skin, and every one of them has a perfect set of teeth."

"That's a rarity."

"Around here, that's definitely the truth. But that isn't all. You better not ever turn your back on one, or they'll steal your wallet, your watch, and your firstborn."

"Really?"

"That's what I hear. 'When you cut a Tufa into ten pieces, you ain't killed him, you've just made ten Tufas,' is what the miners say."

"That's harsh. And . . . a little incomprehensible. What exactly does it mean?"

Quinn leaned close. "It means they aren't all the way human."

"Is that true?"

He shrugged. "They look human to me. They spend human money, that's for sure, and that's all I ask."

Ben's head began to clear, and he knew he was onto something. "What else do you know about them?"

Quinn thought for a moment. "They're all musicians. Some sing, some play instruments, but all of them are amazing at it. And . . ."

"What?"

"Well . . . and this is just pure gossip, so I can't swear to it, and I haven't ever seen it happen myself. But they say that if a man gets tangled up with a Tufa woman, then he's done for."

"Hell, that's true of women everywhere," Ben said with a laugh.

"Not like this," Quinn said seriously. "They say that if a Tufa girl gets tired of you, then you'll waste away to nothing within a month. She doesn't just break your heart, she takes a piece of your soul."

Ben was about to make another joke, but there was something in the bartender's voice that stopped him. "Well, damn, Quinn," he muttered at last. "Hope I don't run into one of them, then."

"Like I said, there aren't too many here, and I've only seen one Tufa girl in the year I've been here. As long as you stay away from Needsville, you should be all right."

"The town that nobody can find."

"I didn't say 'nobody' could find it. Just the people who went looking for it, intending to get into mischief."

"Were they usually drunk?"

"Probably."

"I've been known to lose my way in that condition, too."

"Ain't we all, my friend."

Ben stood, put a fist to his chest as he belched again, and said, "I better get back to work. We have to get started on this picture as soon as possible."

"How long does it take to make one?"

"A day or so, if everyone's on the ball. This one's kind of an experiment. My boss wants to see if he can make a good movie using just people who look right, instead of actors. Can you post this sign behind the bar?"

Quinn looked it over. "I don't see any harm. Can't imagine too many people will be interested, though."

"Thank you, Quinn. And I appreciate the drink."

After he left, Quinn used a hammer and tack to hang the poster. One of the miners who'd entered got up and walked over to look closely at it, then left. His friends continued drinking.


Mrs. Delaney started to enter the front parlor, then stopped in her tracks. She backed silently back into the foyer and peeked around the door frame.

One of her new Yankee guests, Mr. Arliss, strode around the parlor. He wore his waistcoat, trousers, and bowler hat. In one hand he carried a stack of paper, while with the other, he gestured grandly. Then he cowered, then raged, then laughed. All in absolute silence.

When he paused for a sip of his coffee, Mrs. Delaney entered with a cheery, "Good morning!"

"Good morning, Mrs. Delaney," Richard said cheerfully. "Marvelous coffee, by the way."

"Thank you."

He grinned knowingly. "I suppose you're wondering what I'm up to, pacing around like a maniac?"

"I beg your pardon?" she said, all innocence.

"I saw you watching."

She laughed at herself. "I suppose I'm not very good at sneaking."

"For your information, I was rehearsing."

"For a play?"

"For our motion picture. The camera doesn't record sound, only movement and expression. And it requires a different vocabulary than the stage."

"I don't understand what you mean."

He smiled at her. He was well aware of just how disarming his smile could be, especially with women. In many ways, it was his greatest talent. "When I perform onstage," he said patiently, "the audience is far away. The back row can often be hundreds of feet from the stage. So to make sure they know when my character is surprised, I have to project, like this."

He stepped back and made an exaggerated, full-body gasp of surprise. She started to laugh, then caught herself.

"No, it's quite all right, it *is* funny when it's right in front of you. And that, my dear, is where the camera is. So my performance has to be scaled down, like this."

He gave a start of surprise, so realistic that Mrs. Delaney looked behind her to see if someone else had entered the room.

"See? There's a difference. So rather than rehearsing my lines, as I would for the stage, I'm rehearsing my movements." He paused for another sip of coffee. "Once I worked for a motion picture director who had a chart of five expressions: happy, sad, angry, afraid, and in love. He would bellow, 'Number three!' and the actor would pull expression number three. Luckily for actors like myself, that approach never caught on."

"That's fascinating," she said sincerely. "I'm sorry for interrupting."

"Oh, that's quite all right, ma'am. Tell me, have you seen any of my pictures?"

"Unfortunately, no. They just opened a picture house here, and it's been playing *Judith of Bethulia* every Saturday night for the last six months. I don't suppose you're in that one?"

"No," he said through a forced smile.

"Well, I'm sure when this one is ready, it'll be a huge—"

The front door opened, and they both turned as a beautiful young woman with long, jet-black hair entered. She wore an old-fashioned high-necked dress that was tattered and patched in places, and at least a size too small for her, and carried a neatly folded stack of sheets. When she saw them, she stopped.

"Mrs. Delaney," she said.

"Hello, Sophronie. You can wait in the kitchen."

When the girl had gone, Richard asked with undisguised interest, "Who was that?"

"Sophronie Conlin. She does drop-off and pickup for the laundry."

"She's very attractive," he said, still gazing after her.

"Yes. But I wouldn't spend time with her if I were you."

"Oh?" He returned his attention to her. "And why not?"

Mrs. Delaney lowered her voice. "She's a Tufa."

Richard lowered his. "What's that?"

"It's like a nigger, except a little more white."

Richard frowned. He neither liked nor disliked Negroes; many of those he encountered were first-rate performers, and he always respected talent. The morality of the societal barriers that kept them separate never crossed his mind. "Really?"

"Yes. The coal company bought this land from her family. They cheated them, of course, and now her father is a miner, and she and her brothers and sisters work where they can."

"Goodness."

Mrs. Delaney, annoyed, said, "Well, I should return to work myself. Thank you for sharing your insights with me, Mr. Arliss."

"Please, 'Richard.'" He bowed, with a grand sweep of his hat.

She blushed a little as she left.


As Sean continued up the street, hanging notices wherever he could, he caught the unexpected, sprightly sound of a banjo. A crowd gathered around the front of a small building with a sign that said, SADIEVILLE JAIL. At first he feared it was a lynch mob, but as he drew closer, he realized they were happily clapping along.

When he reached the edge of the crowd, he heard someone singing:

> *Oh, I'm Sheriff Brag Bowden, and I sure do want your*
> *vote*
> *I'm a good man and an honest one, with trouble I can*
> *cope*
> *I'll knock some heads and jail some drunks if that's*
> *what is required*
> *And I'd appreciate your support so that I can be rehired*

Then the singer began to yodel.

Sean stood on tiptoe. A man stood on the porch of the little jail building, picking expertly at his banjo. He was short, portly, and about as intimidating as a beach pail even with the sheriff's badge pinned to his shirt. He rocked back and forth in time to his music, and his yodels filled the air with their ululating keen.

Sean worked his way closer. When he was almost at the front of the crowd, he saw a little girl dancing on a square piece of wood placed on the muddy ground. The fringe of her dress waved back and forth, and her hard black shoes raised a rapid tattoo of clacks from the board. Sean had seen many tap-dancing acts in Manhattan, but there was something serious and primitive about the way the girl moved, all her attention focused on her feet.

Sean evaluated her face. It was still smooth and plump, but the beginnings of lines were already there around her mouth. He knew what hard times did to attractive girls, and to see the first traces of it here was both powerful, and heartbreaking. He had to get that face on film.

And the sheriff! *If only movies could talk,* he thought bitterly for the millionth time. *And sing.*

The dancing girl and the banjo-playing sheriff finished together, and the crowd clapped its approval. The sheriff handed his banjo to a waiting deputy, and stepped down to shake hands like any other politician seeking office. When he got to Sean, he paused and said, "I don't believe I know you, son. You a newcomer to our fair town?"

"Yes, sir."

"A company man?"

"No, sir, I'm here to make a motion picture." He put a flyer in the sheriff's hand. "I'll be talking to people at Mrs. Delaney's boardinghouse first thing tomorrow morning, and I'd sure like to see you show up with your banjo."

The sheriff looked at the flyer, then at Sean, then back at the flyer. No one spoke. At last he said, "Well. Ain't that purely something. I'll think about it, young mister . . . ?"

"Lee. Sean Lee."

"Like the general?"

"Exactly like."

"Any relation?"

"I should be so lucky."

The sheriff threw back his head and laughed. The people around them did the same.

"Y'all come back tomorrow morning for a whole new song," Sheriff Bowden said to the crowd. "And don't forget to vote come next week!"

The crowd broke up, and Sean was about to leave as well when he felt a firm hand on his shoulder. "Y'all just hold up a minute, son," Bowden said. "I'd like a word with you."

Sean fought to keep the fear from his face. He'd had bad experiences with law enforcement thugs hired by the Motion Picture Patent Company, Thomas Edison's attempt to keep the technology of filmmaking under his personal control. He once saw an extra get his arm broken in two places by a group of duly deputized Pinkertons.

But the sheriff, he quickly realized, was not out to intimidate him; he was, in fact, star struck. "You know, young man, it's funny that you mention me being in a motion picture, because I've seen *Judith of Bethulia* every Saturday night for longer than I can reckon. That acting thing can't be that hard, can it?"

"Not at all," Sean assured him.

"And how much money are we talking about here?"

"Fifty cents a day."

"Well, ain't that something," Bowden said.

"Tell me something, Sheriff," Sean asked. "What's the best place to meet people, other than right here?"

"Hell, son, the same two places as everywhere else," Bowden said with a bighearted laugh. "The church and the saloon."

———

The clerk at the train station had been right. The church, nestled at the corner of the lone street and stream beneath a copse of pine trees, was a work in progress. The sides and roof were built, but braces still held up the porch roof, and the windows were just bare rectangles. A sign out front proclaimed it the BLACK CREEK PRIMITIVE BAPTIST CHURCH.

Sean gazed up at the open door. He'd been raised Catholic, and after narrowly avoiding the attention of his parish priest as a boy, had no use for any church now. Still, he had to assume the sheriff knew his town.

He climbed the steps and entered the vestibule. He waited while his eyes adjusted to the inner dimness. The pulpit and pews were already placed, but there was no piano or organ to provide music.

"May I help you, young man?"

Sean turned. A lean, tall woman stood between him and the door. Backlit against the brightness outside, her face remained hidden, but nothing about her felt friendly.

"Hi, ma'am, I'm Sean Lee. I'm here in Sadieville to make a motion picture, and I wondered if you'd mind posting one of these where your worshipers might see it, in case any of them are interested."

The woman took the poster with a quick, snapping gesture that reminded Sean of a snake striking out. "A motion picture?"

"That's right."

"No, I don't think so. I'm sorry."

She handed the poster back to him, then politely pushed past him and went through a door at the back of the sanctuary. He stared after her, then shook his head and left.

# 11

All the seats at the boardinghouse dinner table were filled that evening. In addition to Sean, Ben, and Richard, there was a young married couple dressed in proper East Coast fashion, the two old coal miners from the front porch with black dust still visible where their washcloths had missed their hairlines and ears, and a lone young man who looked unlike a miner, a store clerk, or management. At the head, near the kitchen entrance, sat Mrs. Delaney.

"So, Mr. Wortham," she said, "how's your house coming along? The company doing a good job for you?"

"According to the foreman, it should be ready in another two weeks," the young Easterner replied.

"That's wonderful. Although, of course, I'll be sorry to see you both go."

"We appreciate your hospitality," Wortham said. His wife added a polite nod.

One of the miners spoke up. "Miz Delaney, you got any bologna hid somewhere?"

"I'll get you a slice," she said, and went into the

kitchen. She returned moments later with a slice of bologna on a plate, which she served with a fork.

"Thank you, ma'am," the miner said. He pulled a set of false teeth from his pocket and expertly fitted the bologna into the grooves of his dentures. He popped them into his mouth, bit down, then worked his jaw experimentally. Satisfied, he looked around and saw Sean and Ben watching. "Cheaper'n that denture stuff they sell at the store," he said with a suddenly toothy grin.

"And disgusting to do at the dinner table," Wortham said. "I'll thank you not to do that again in front of my wife."

The miner's smile faded and he looked down at his plate like a chastened child.

"Whoa, take it easy," the odd man out said. His voice was low, melodic, and somehow commanding; suddenly he had everyone's attention. "If what he does really bothers you, maybe you should pay him more, so he wouldn't have to do it."

Wortham started to snap back, but the other man's steady, apparently neutral gaze stopped him in mid-word.

To break the tension, Mrs. Delaney said, "You skinny young Yankees need to eat up. I swan, I can't imagine how you get up enough energy to walk up and down the stairs on what you eat."

"I think we'll be considerably heavier by the time we leave," Sean said. Mrs. Delaney laughed.

"Yankees?" Wortham said with a loud, forced laugh, overcompensating for his earlier outburst. "But you're not with the Prudence Company, or I'd know you. Where are you two from?"

"New Jersey," Sean said. "Ben here grew up in the Bronx, in New York City. I'm from Maine originally."

"I understand you make motion pictures," Mrs. Wortham said. When her husband glanced at her disapprovingly, she said, "Mrs. Delaney told me." Then she withdrew into herself like a spooked turtle.

"Yes, ma'am, we do," Sean said. "I've directed eighteen. And Ben here is a very capable cameraman."

"That's a glorified term for a gofer," Ben said.

"'Gopher?'" Mrs. Wortham repeated. "Like the animal?"

"No, like 'go for' this, 'go for' that."

"Why don't all of y'all just go to hell," the miner with dentures muttered without looking up.

Wortham made the dishes jump with a slap to the table. "Whoever you are, sir, you will apologize right now. My wife and Mrs. Delaney are both present, and I will not tolerate language like that used in their presence."

Wortham's outrage was genuine, Sean knew, but he was picking the wrong battle. The company man was tall and slender, with the soft pale hands and narrow shoulders of someone who spent his time hunched over ledgers and reports. The miner, if so inclined, could probably snap every one of his bones with his bare hands.

But the miner, still not looking up, mumbled, "Sorry."

"What is your name, sir?" Wortham said, and pulled out a small notepad with a tiny pencil attached.

"I don't think that's necessary," the odd man said. "This gentleman's just tired from working all day."

"I have worked all day as well, and yet I can still control my tongue," Wortham snapped.

"Not to put too fine a point on it, but pushing a coal cart and pushing a pencil are fairly different things."

Sean tried to place the man's accent. It wasn't the local one, nor one from the northeast that he'd encountered before. If anything, it was a truly neutral, featureless tone that revealed nothing about its origins.

Wortham was not calming down. "I'll have *your* name, then, sir!"

"Carding. Tucker Carding." When Wortham started to write, Carding added, "That's C-A-R-D-I-N-G."

This made Wortham even angrier. "I am quite able to spell, sir! And I resent your implication that what I do is not 'work.'"

The miner stood up, tossed his napkin onto his plate, and glared at Wortham. Sean had never seen such contempt, and fear, in a man's eyes. The miner said, "Yeah, you work moving numbers around so all the money goes to people like you, who sit in padded chairs and smoke big cigars while people like me work ourselves to death." He began to cough, a deep-chested rattle that quickly got away from him, forcing him to lean on the chair back until the fit passed.

When it did, he stood back up and said, "You wouldn't last half a shift of real work, Mr. High-and-Mighty Company Man." Before the red-faced Wortham could respond, the miner strode out of the house. His friend got up and followed.

"Who was he? *Who?*" Wortham demanded of the remaining diners.

Mrs. Delaney turned to Wortham, her eyes flaring with anger. "Mr. Wortham," she said seriously, "you may in fact be a high power in the Prudence Company, but in this house, you are simply another guest. Those men pay to stay here just as you do, and if you can't be civil, then perhaps you should find other accommodations until your house is finished."

His wife reached over and took his hand. His face still red, Mr. Wortham choked out, "I beg your pardon, ma'am. It was bad manners of me to make a scene at your table."

"It certainly was," Mrs. Delaney agreed.

Wortham pulled his wife to her feet. "Come along, Phyllida." Without waiting for a reply, he led her out of the room and up the stairs, his feet loud on the wooden steps.

Mrs. Delaney shook her head. "Every time that happens, I swear I'm not going to take in another company man."

"Does this happen a lot?" Ben asked.

"Whenever management and labor get together." She sighed.

"I'm afraid it's mostly my fault," Carding said as he stood. "I'd hoped to calm things down, but I only made them worse."

"One man's rudeness is never another man's fault, Mr. Carding."

"That's kind of you to say, but I think I've done enough damage tonight. Thank you for a lovely dinner." He nodded at the others and headed for the door.

When he heard the front door close, Sean asked, "Who was that?"

"Mr. Carding? He eats dinner here a couple of times a week."

"What does he do the rest of the time?" Ben asked.

Mrs. Delaney frowned. "You know, I'm not sure he's ever mentioned it. I don't think he works for the company, but I'm honestly not sure."

"Isn't that odd?"

She shrugged. "It takes all kinds. Maybe he's a Pinkerton."

Sean's stomach plummeted. "They have Pinkertons here?"

"Who do you think keeps the miners in line when they talk about striking?"

When she'd gone into the kitchen, Ben said, "You look like you've seen a ghost."

"If the Pinkertons are here—"

"Oh, for God's sake, Sean, grow a backbone. The Pinkertons here work for the mining company, not Edison."

"But if they get word—"

"We'll be gone before they do."

Sean forced his panic down. He turned to Richard. "What do you think?"

"I think Ben is right," Richard said. "You should grow a backbone."

As they got ready for bed in the room they shared—Richard had insisted on a private one—Sean and Ben heard Wortham through the wall berating his wife. "Do you not recall your station before I married you? You were barely above these cretinous miners! I gave you status, position, and all the accouterments of society! In return, I expect your total obedience to me, and your support for my career."

"Wow," Ben said, fluffing the pillow on his narrow single bed. "What an asshole. If my dad talked to my mom like that, he'd have been singing soprano by the next morning."

In the pause, they heard Mrs. Wortham's soft voice, but could not make out the words. But they had no trouble making out the sound of the slap that followed.

"I don't like that man," Ben said.

"Neither do I," Sean agreed. His bed was near the open window, and the breeze was welcome. "But it's none of our business, remember. We're here to do our job quickly, and get out as soon as possible."

"Still worried about the Pinkertons?"

"If you'd ever had a run-in with them, Ben, you would be, too."

"I did, once. When I was a kid, I was a messenger between nickelodeons, and one guy paid me to bring the films to his lab so he could copy them before I delivered them. Somehow the Pinkertons got onto him, and I walked in on them while they were teaching him a lesson."

"What did you do?"

"I walked back out real fast. One of them tried to chase me, but I knew that part of the city too well."

The door slammed on the other room, and heavy feet stomped down the stairs. In the silence that followed, they heard soft sobs through the walls.

"Should we say something?" Ben asked.

"What could we say?" Sean said. " 'Sorry you married a jerk'?"

Mrs. Wortham had stopped crying by the time Sean and

Ben turned in. In the relative silence, Ben asked quietly, "Hey, have you ever heard of some people called the Tufa?"

"I think somebody mentioned it today. Is that the family name?"

"No, it's like, their tribe."

"So they're Indians?"

"No, they're . . . hell, I don't know exactly. Bartender was telling me about them this morning when I was hanging flyers."

"You went to a bar in the morning?"

"To hang up flyers. Don't be so judgmental."

"And?"

"And what?"

"There must be some reason you brought it up."

"They sound really strange and interesting. I don't know, I was just thinking that any people who other people talk about that way . . ."

"What way?"

"Like they're . . . magical, or something."

"Magical."

"I don't know another word to describe it. Anyway, if they're as strange as people say, maybe we want to put them in the picture."

"Well, sure. I mean, if any come in to the auditions. How would I know them if they did?"

"They all have perfect teeth."

"Perfect teeth?"

"That's what the man said."

Then they were silent. Ben drifted off to sleep, but Sean continued to stare at the ceiling, wondering about the coming day's auditions. He listened for Mrs. Wortham, but heard no more sobbing. Her husband had not returned home by the time Sean finally fell asleep.

# 12

As she refilled Sean's coffee cup, Mrs. Delaney said, "My goodness, you boys are popular."

Sean looked up from his plate. He was the first one up, and although he'd insisted she wait for the others, she was just as insistent that he have his breakfast now. She won. "How so?" he asked.

"There's a dozen people waiting outside to talk to you."

"I guess they saw our posters."

"Are you really going to put just regular people in your picture?"

"If they've got the right look."

"They'll have to be mighty handsome to appear with Mr. Arliss."

"He would agree with you," Sean said.

"I would indeed," Richard said as he entered, Ben right behind him. As always, the actor was dressed impeccably, and the part in his hair was straight and fixed with pomade. He placed his bowler on an empty chair and took the seat next to it.

"Mrs. Delaney says people are already lining up," Sean said.

"Then we shouldn't keep them waiting. A cup of coffee, my dear, and an apple, if you have one."

"It's early in the year for apples, I'm afraid. The biscuits are fresh from the oven, though."

"That sounds lovely," he said, and took one from the basket.

"So Mr. Lee," Mrs. Delaney said, "if you don't mind my asking, are you planning to pay these people to be in your picture?"

"We are. Fifty cents a day."

"American money, or company scrip?"

"American money. Silver quarters."

"That explains the turnout. I just hope you can handle them."

"What do you mean?" Richard asked.

"A lot of these people would knife their mothers for two cash dollars."

Ben finally spoke. "Including the Tufa?"

Mrs. Delaney started. Then she forced a laugh. "Lord a'mercy, Mr. Hubbard; who told you about them?"

"I heard about them yesterday, when I was putting up flyers."

"Well, you'd best give them a wide berth, although I can't imagine any of them wanting to be in a picture. They're a strange people, and they keep to themselves."

"Strange how?" Sean asked.

"Oh, they're supposedly thieves, cutthroats, and witches. They say a Tufa truth is worse than a Christian lie."

Sean nodded. "I see. Well, thanks for the warning." He looked at Ben, who shrugged.


Just before nine, Sean and Ben set up the front parlor for their auditions. Ben assembled the tripod and camera, although he loaded no film; Sean could pretend to film people, to see how they responded. If they froze up, he'd know they weren't suitable, no matter how perfect their faces might be.

Richard remained in the kitchen, sipping coffee and watching through the open door. He was naturally curious who his director would cast opposite him, but wouldn't offer an opinion unless asked. That way he could avoid any blame if things went as thoroughly wrong as he expected from this mingling of trained professionals and rank amateurs.

By the time they were ready, over thirty people waited outside the boardinghouse. They milled about in the tree-shaded yard and crowded onto the porch. They talked among themselves, smoked, and checked watches. A few played banjos or harmonicas, and the distinctive twang of a jaw harp joined in. Most were men, as freshly scrubbed as they were able to get, and clad in their best clothes. The women had the sharp, angular faces of the mountains, even the ones with matronly forms. None of them had that eager, innocent look Ben saw on big-city actors about to audition. These people never expected to get good news.

Ben said loudly, "All right, form a single line here. We'll talk to each of you individually."

They had a loose scenario for their film: two families battling over moonshine territories, with star-crossed lovers and interloping revenue agents. It was a plot that had been used a thousand times, but it had never been filmed in the actual mountains where it was set.

"Send in the first one," Sean called.

Ben opened the door for a man who looked to be in his forties, wearing a shirt and tie. He'd slicked down his hair, but a few greasy strands still tumbled into his face. He stopped in front of Sean, eyes cast to the floor.

"I'm Sean Lee. I'm a motion picture director from New Jersey. What's your name?"

"Hiram. Hiram Rusk."

"How old are you?"

"Twenty-six."

Sean knew hard work aged people, but this was extreme. "You ever seen a motion picture, Hiram?"

"Nossir."

"But you know what they are?"

"Well, if the name's right, it's a picture that moves, ain't it?"

"It's more than that. It's a way of telling a story. It's like a play."

"I seen a play once't. At Sunday school, back in Kentucky. All about the disciples finding Jesus's tomb opened up."

"If I tell you to pretend you feel something, can you do it?"

"I reckon."

"Okay, show me your sad face."

The corners of his mouth turned down a little.

"Now your happy face."

He smiled, revealing gaps in his teeth. The smile was entirely mechanical, a rictus rather than an actual expression. Sean felt a wave of pity for the man, but not such a big wave that he would hire him.

"Thank you, Hiram. We'll be in touch if we need you."

"Thank you, Mr. Lee."

He shuffled out. Sean called, "Next!"

It took most of the morning, but Sean eventually had a list of seven people who met his criteria, five men and two women. But he still needed an ingénue, the one who would appear opposite Richard. She had to be, he knew, the kind of girl that men want to love and women want to protect. It was a hard thing to find even in Manhattan.

And then she walked in.

She had the fresh beauty of a girl just past the bloom into womanhood. Jet-black hair fell past her shoulders and framed her sharp, perfect features. She wore a simple dress that hinted at an exquisite figure.

"Hello," Ben said, and stood. "Please come in."

"Oh, I ain't here for the show," the girl said. "I'm just picking up Miz Delaney's laundry."

Sean blinked. "You're not auditioning?"

"Naw." She laughed. "I don't even know what that means."

As she walked out of the parlor, Sean motioned Ben over. "Go get her."

"Why? She doesn't want—"

"I don't care. She looks perfect, and I want to talk to her some more."

Ben sighed, shook his head, and followed the girl.

He found her talking to Richard in the kitchen. She listened, rapt, as he finished one of his theater stories.

". . . so when she saw the mouse, she jumped up on the sink, still in just her towel. The sink pulled out of the wall, and water went everywhere. Her screaming brought the stage manager, who took one look at the scene and said, 'What have I told you actresses about peeing in the sink?' "

The girl giggled almost uncontrollably. Ben waited until she'd calmed down. She wiped the corners of her eyes and said, "That's pitiful. Is that true?"

"I swear on my mother's eventual grave." Then Richard turned to Ben. "Yes, Benjamin?"

"Sean would like to see the young lady for a moment."

"I told him I wasn't here to audy-ation," she said.

"He understands that, but he'd still like to talk to you."

She thought it over. "Well, for a minute. I have to get back to work."

She followed him into the parlor. Sean was already on his feet, and extended his hand to her. "Hello, I'm Sean Lee. I'm a film director."

"Sophronie Conlin," she said. "Pleasure to meet you."

" 'Sophronie.' That's an unusual name. Where did it come from?"

"My mama and papa. That's where they usually come from in these parts. They do it differently where you come from?"

Sean smiled. "The exact same way. Tell me, Sophronie, have you ever seen a motion picture?"

"No. But I've heard about them. A friend of mine told me about seeing one about Samson."

"Have you ever done any acting?"

She laughed a little, looked up as she mustered her thoughts, and finally said, "Only when I need to get shed of a boy."

"Does that happen a lot?"

"More'n it used to before they opened Sadieville."

Suddenly Sean realized that not only did the girl have all her teeth, but that they were white, straight, and perfect. After a morning filled with partial or missing teeth, it was like seeing the sun after a storm. "So you didn't come in with the mine, then?"

"Oh, no. We been here a long time. Look, if you don't mind, I have to pick up Mrs. Delaney's washing and take it back to—"

"I'm sorry, let me get right to the point, then. I think you'd be perfect for the picture we're making, but I'd like to see how you handle yourself in front of the camera."

"I already got a job."

"I'll pay you fifty cents a day. Real money, not scrip."

"Will you, now," she said thoughtfully, suddenly looking much older and shrewder than her years.

"I will. Does your job pay that much?"

"Not likely." She nodded at the tripod beside him. "Is that the camera?"

"It is." He make a show of adjusting the tripod head, focusing, and getting into position at the viewfinder. "Can you make a sad face?"

Nothing changed at first. Then her expression fell, and her eyes grew heavy with tears. Astonished, Sean forgot to turn the handle. But Sophronie didn't notice.

Then she sang, softly and with all the sadness in the world:

*Can't never go back, don't have the will*
*Can't never go back . . .*

"Cut," Sean gasped. He and Ben were speechless, and Richard stood in the kitchen doorway, his mouth open.

She looked up, and as if nothing had happened, said, "What does 'cut' mean?"

"It's what we say when we stop filming."

She smiled shyly. "So how did I do?"

"Oh, you did fine."

"That was magnificent," Richard said, striding into the room. "Absolutely astounding. And you say you've never acted before?"

"Nossir, I ain't."

"If you don't offer her the job," Richard said to Sean, "then I'll have lost all faith in you as a director."

"Wait a minute, now," she said. "I don't even know what this pitcher you're making is going to be about. I might not care to be involved."

"If you take the job," Sean said, "You'll be playing a young woman who's in love with a young man from a rival family."

"Sounds a little like 'Blackjack Davy.' "

"Is that a story?"

"Yes, but we tell it with a song. Who's going to be acting the young man?"

"I will," Richard said.

She smiled. "Well, that's plumb nice to hear. You seem like a gentleman."

"You try to run away together," Sean continued, "but a revenue man forces you to betray your families to him."

"Ooh, that sounds exciting. I've known me a couple of revenue men. When do we start?"

"The day after tomorrow at first light."

"I reckon I'll do it, then." With that, she turned and walked back toward the kitchen.

"Wait, where are you going?" Sean asked.

"I work for you the day after tomorrow. Until then, I work for Mrs. Scrimshaw. And she's expecting Mrs. Delaney's laundry."

"But . . . but how do I find you?"

Now she gave him a smile that carried not just amusement, but a mature, womanly knowledge that he totally didn't expect. "Don't you worry you little head about it. I'll be here."

# 13

The Worthams did not attend dinner that night. Mrs. Delaney said they were dining with the mine superintendent, at his big house on the mountainside overlooking the town. The two old miners were there, and Tucker Carding.

And there were two newcomers. Reverend Nashe, of the Black Creek Primitive Baptist Church, was red-faced, with a fringe of beard around his jaw and no mustache; his wife wore a dress up to the neck, and her hair was covered by a bonnet.

After Mrs. Delaney made the introductions, Reverend Nashe invited them all to bow their heads. He spoke in a guttural, unpleasant voice that sounded like fork tines against a plate.

"Dear Lord," he said, "look down upon us sinners as we partake of your bounty, and forgive us our heathen ways. May the devil never learn how truly his dominion has come over this earth, so that the few who follow you may witness the damnation of those who deny your glory."

From the corner of his eye, Sean caught Ben's shoulders shaking as he fought not to laugh.

"May we watch them slide into the brimstone-filled abyss begging for mercy," Nashe continued, "and may their screams mingle with our songs to become a chorus of your praise. Amen."

When they'd all said, "Amen," Mrs. Nashe began to loudly slurp her tomato soup. The noise sounded a lot like the distant rattle of coal down the tipple to the trains.

Revered Nashe tucked his napkin into his collar and said, "I understand you gentlemen make motion pictures."

"That's right," Sean said.

"Motion pictures are immoral," Mrs. Nashe said between slurps.

"Not the ones I make," Sean said. He'd run across religious objections to the very existence of pictures before, and he had a list of responses memorized.

"Any of them," the woman snapped, and slurped.

"What about *Judith of Bethulia*?" Ben said.

"Yes, that's a biblical story," Tucker Carding agreed. "It's about a woman who disguises herself and kills the king of an opposing army."

"It's part of the Apocrypha, so it is Satan's scripture," Mrs. Nashe said. "And any motion picture is pagan idolatry."

"We'll just have to agree to disagree, then, ma'am," Sean said.

"My wife is a woman of beliefs firmly rooted in the rock of our Lord," Reverend Nashe said. He gave her a smug nod, which she returned between slurps. "I understand you held auditions for parts here today."

"That's right," Sean said.

"Did you find the people you sought?"

"I did."

"Were any of them," Mrs. Nashe said, with such disdain she splattered the tablecloth with red spots, *"Tufa?"*

"'Tufa'?" Sean said innocently. "What's that?"

"They are trash," Reverend Nashe said venomously. "They are stupid like pigs, but cunning like serpents. They clearly have the blood of niggers in their veins; it's obvious in their hair and skin."

"That's true," one of the miners said. They all looked surprised; the two men had been so quiet, the rest had forgotten about them.

"What knowledge do you have of them?" Nashe asked, his eyes narrowed with suspicion.

"Well, I work with a couple on the first shift. Tough old birds, but they don't speak much. Spend most of their time singing. I asked 'em about it, and they said it was because they liked to sing the coal out. Makes it easier to dig, they claim."

"Witchcraft," Reverend Nashe said.

"Perhaps the White Caps should clear them out, once and for all," Mrs. Nashe said.

"Who are the 'White Caps'?" Richard asked. "Railroad porters?"

"The White Caps he means don't work for the railroad," Tucker said. "At least not officially."

"They are," Reverend Nashe said with great dignity, "good men of conscience who step in when the law cannot or will not."

"Vigilantes, you mean," Ben said.

"Men of conscience," Reverend Nashe repeated.

"Vigilantes," Tucker said with certainty.

"I guess you don't like the Tufa much," Ben said with faux innocence, then jumped as Sean kicked him beneath the table.

"I despise them," Reverend Nashe said. "As does every white Christian soul here, although there are precious few Christians in Sadieville, I'm sorry to say. When a Tufa sleeps, the devil rocks him, and if it were up to me, every last one would be dragged out and burned at the stake."

"I thought that was just for New England witches," Ben said. There was a loud thud as he pulled his leg away, and Sean's kick struck the chair leg. No one commented on it.

"They are well-known traffickers in spells and charms,"

Nashe continued. "Many a man has been led to his doom by a Tufa girl, even under this very roof."

"Tell him about the incident," Mrs. Nashe prompted.

"Six months ago," the minister said, "four men who lived in this very house died because of a Tufa woman."

Mrs. Delaney's cheeks flushed red, but Sean couldn't tell if it was due to shame or anger.

"She taunted them with her harlot's ways," Nashe continued. "There was a gunfight, and all four died. And yet she was adjudged innocent, because she wore beauty like a mask over her true nature."

" 'Look like the innocent flower,' " Richard quoted, " 'but be the serpent under it.' "

"I don't know that verse," Mrs. Nashe said.

"My wife can recite the Bible," Reverend Nashe said, "from Genesis to Revelations."

"That must make cold winter nights pass quickly," Richard said, hiding his sarcasm with a smile. "No, it was not a biblical quote. It was Shakespeare. *Macbeth,* to be precise. Act one, scene five."

"I don't know any 'Shakespeare,' " Mrs. Nashe said. If possible, her crone face grew even more repulsive.

"Hell, I knowed them boys you're talking about," the other miner said. "Get some liquor in 'em, they'd have fought over the sky being blue. If they did fight over a girl, it's because she just happened to be in the wrong place at the wrong time."

"Oh, yes, the poor innocent Tufa girl," Nashe said contemptuously. "A Jezebel who lured good men to their deaths. That's typical of her breed. They have resisted the presence of churches and men of God, and there can only be one reason for that."

"They're heathens," his wife said. "*Pagans.* They worship the devil in their own vile ceremonies, with music and dancing."

"You don't approve of music?" Richard asked with exaggerated politeness.

"The New Testament of our lord and savior Jesus Christ commands us to lift up our voices, not to hide them with noise-makers," Nashe said.

"My goodness, look at the time, we've been chatting here for so long, the soup's gotten cold," Mrs. Delaney said as she jumped to her feet. "I'll get dessert, and coffee for those who'd like some."

She scurried out, leaving the table awash in tension. Only Tucker Carding still seemed relaxed, as if the whole scene amused him.


Upstairs after dinner, Sean took off a shoe and threw it at Ben's head. The heel struck with a conk.

"Ow!" Ben said. "What was that for?"

"For trying to pick a fight with that preacher."

"Oh, come on, he deserved it."

"He sincerely believes what he says," Sean said.

"So did Benedict Arnold. Did you hear what Richard said about him?"

"Benedict Arnold?"

"No, that preacher." Imitating Richard's precise diction, Ben said, " 'He has an ego like a raging tooth.' "

"Well, I'm glad he and his wife found each other," Sean said. "That way there's only two miserable people, not four. I do wonder, though, why Mrs. Delaney invited them here."

"I got the feeling she didn't have a choice."

They both jumped as they heard a *thump*.

After exchanging a look, they both ran to the wall and pressed their ears to it. No noise came from the Worthams' room.

"Do you think he killed her?" Ben whispered.

"It doesn't sound like anyone's in there," Sean said. They heard another *thump*. This time, they saw the small rock as it rolled across the floor, followed by a third through the open window. Sean went over and looked out. He saw nothing except shadows in the yard outside.

"Mr. Lee," a voice said in a loud, feminine whisper. "I need to talk to you."

"Who are you?" Sean called back in the same tone.

"We met earlier. Please, it's important. It's about your picture."

"I'll be right down."

Ben grabbed his arm and yanked him away from the window. "Whoa, boss," he whispered. "You don't even know who that is."

"I think it's Sophronie," Sean said.

"Or it could be a setup. What if it's the White Caps? What if it's the Pinkertons?"

"I'll be careful." He couldn't believe how eager he was to see the beautiful Tufa girl.

Downstairs, one of the miners sat in the front parlor, smoking a pipe and staring into space. "Evening," he said without looking at Sean. "Some scene at dinner, weren't it?"

"It sure was," Sean agreed, and went out on the front porch. The street was busy, and the noise told him that a lot of people were cutting loose. He slipped around the edge of the boarding-house and into the darkness. "Hello?" he whisper-called.

"I'm here," a woman said quietly. She stepped from the shadows, but was visible only as a silhouette.

"Sophronie?" Sean said.

"What? No, I'm Basemath."

"I beg your pardon?"

"It's a biblical name. She was a wife of Esau."

The voice finally registered on him. "I met you in the church when I was hanging up flyers."

"Yes. And you had dinner with my parents tonight."

Instantly Sean tensed. "What do you want?"

"My parents are . . . not safe to know, Mr. Lee. Not unless you're willing to kowtow to them. They're furious because they haven't been able to finish building the church here, because something always seems to happen. Supplies disappear, a part of the building collapses, a whole list of things."

"Sounds like nobody wants them here."

"Yes, that's the sensible thought, but he only sees Satan at work. And if my father believes Satan is involved, he will do whatever it takes to stop him. *Whatever it takes,*" she repeated, leaning close.

He understood. "The White Caps."

"That was the first thing he did when we got here. He found a few people who felt as he did, and before long he had a dozen men willing to do whatever he said, as long as he claimed it was to battle Satan. Men and women have died because of him, Mr. Lee. He's a . . ." She struggled for the word.

"Hypocrite?" Sean said. "Liar?"

"Monster," Basemath said.

"Yeah, I knew a priest like that once."

"You're *Catholic*? Does my father know?"

"It didn't come up. And I don't consider myself anything."

"If he learns you were even raised Catholic, he'll consider you no better than the Tufa."

"So why do you stay with them? You're a grown woman."

She ignored the question. "Please, you seem like a good man, and even if you're not, you don't deserve to die by his command. Leave as soon as you can."

"We *are* leaving, at the end of the week, once we shoot our picture."

She looked off into the darkness, as if afraid something followed her. "I hope that's soon enough," she said, and with that, vanished back into the shadows.

Later, Sean lay awake listening to Ben snore and pondering the events of the day. But before long, only one thing went through his head: the brief song Sophronie Conlin had sung, the one that had helped her access the feelings of sadness that came across her lovely face during her audition:

*Can't go back, don't have the will*
*Can never go back . . .*

Back to *where*? he wondered.

# 14

"Are you sure there's decent scenery around here?" Ben asked, pausing to wipe his sweaty face with his handkerchief. He leaned against a tree, careful not to damage the camera on his back, and took a drink from his canteen. "Because me, I'm seeing nothing but pine trees. We have those in New Jersey."

Sean paused as well. "But those aren't on majestic hillsides, are they?"

Earlier that morning, when he heard their plans over breakfast to scout suitable locations, Tucker Carding had sketched them out a map, with several Xs marked. "Those spots are pretty as a Pingree potato patch," he'd promised. They hadn't yet reached any of the Xs, so they couldn't tell if he was accurate. But if the climb continued to be this hard, they might drop dead before they saw anything other than tree trunks.

The weather wasn't terribly warm, but the humidity had them both drenched. Mist also clouded the view, making the forests resemble the Gustave Doré drawings Sean had seen in his schoolbooks.

Ben drank some more from his canteen, and when

he pulled it away, water dripped from his mustache. "You know what really makes me happy about this?"

"What?"

"I have to do it all over again tomorrow, only this time carrying *all* the equipment."

"Afraid you're not up to it?"

"I'm a technician, not a pack mule. I lived in a sixth-floor walk-up when I was a kid, and it wasn't this hard a climb."

At last they reached the first X on the map, a bare ridge at the level of the valley's treetops. Here there was at least some wind, and the breeze felt amazing on their sweaty skin.

"Sean, I'm a city boy," Ben said between breaths. "I'm not built for . . ."

He trailed off, and it took a moment for Sean to notice. He followed Ben's gaze.

The sun shone just above the rolling mountains, burning away the mist to reveal a vista all around them of forested mountaintops and hillsides. They rolled away into the distance in every direction like waves frozen in time, bristling with trees. Behind them rose the acrid soot-filled fumes of Sadieville; ahead, not far away, homey smoke rose from a cabin. The whole vista was staggering in its primal beauty.

"Well," Ben said when he could finally speak again, "it sure ain't Jersey, I'll give you that."

"It sure ain't," Sean whispered. "Maybe you should shoot a few feet."

"I think you're right," Ben said. He wound up the spring-loaded drive, held the camera as still as he could, and did a slow horizontal pan. "I take back everything I said. This was all definitely worth it."

"Definitely worth what?" a new voice said.

They both jumped. Sophronie Conlin stood not twenty feet away. Instead of the prim dress she'd worn in town the day before, she was in men's trousers cut off halfway up her calf, and a plaid shirt with no sleeves. Her hair, rather than being pulled back in a neat ponytail, was loose and wild. She was barefoot, and seemed as much a part of the landscape as the trees and rocks around her.

"Miss Conlin," Sean said, hoping his voice didn't sound as high and startled as he feared. He'd seen his share of attractive women in the city, but everything about this girl put them all to shame, not least her willingness to put her body on display so publicly. "I didn't expect to see you today."

"Likewise, Mr. Lee," she said. He couldn't tell if she was mocking his politeness. "Yet here y'all are, practically in my back yard."

"We're scouting locations for filming tomorrow. The whole point of coming down here was to capture the natural beauty of this place."

"Then I hope you found what you're looking for."

"You better believe it," Ben whispered, blatantly looking the girl over. "Wow."

Sean gave him a warning scowl. To Sophronie he said, "What are you doing up here, if you don't mind my asking?"

"Oh, we live just over there." She pointed to the rising smoke. "My feet got itchy, so I decided to come out for a walk. Now I'm right glad I did."

"I'm 'right glad' you did, too, Miss Conlin."

"Oh, please. Call me Sophronie."

"Sophronie, then. And you can call me Sean."

"Sean," she said with a little mock curtsy.

"You know," Sean said, "I bet you could help us out. I'm sure you know all the best spots in this area."

"Best spots for what?" she said with a teasing little smile.

"Like this," he said, gesturing around them. "Places that we could never film back in New York or New Jersey. A friend in town gave us a map, but I'm sure a guide would be more useful."

"I suppose I could show you some places. But why don't you come meet my family first?"

Sean turned to Ben, who was about to speak. Before he could, Sean surreptitiously tucked a dollar bill into his shirt pocket. "Ben, you go on back and finish drawing up the schedule for tomorrow. I'll get the rest of our locations squared away."

Ben scowled. "Why didn't I think of that?" he said dryly.

"Now, you're welcome to come visit, too," Sophronie said to Ben.

"Nah, Sean's right. Work to do, you know? Pleasure seeing you again, Miss Conlin." He tipped his newsboy cap to her and walked away whistling back down the trail.

When he was out of sight around a bend, Sophronie said, "Did you send him away on purpose?"

"Would you be angry if I said yes?"

"I'd be surprised if you said no."

"I really was serious, though. I need to find locations."

She slipped her arm through his. "Don't you worry, I have plenty of things to show you."

The walk through the woods was positively lyrical. There was no trace of Sadieville's ugly industrialization, or any sign of civilization at all. The trail wound through the forest, around boulders and large trees, up and down hills and along ridges until at last the Conlin home was in sight.

For most of the way, Sophronie held Sean's hand. It was a loose grip, her fingers threaded through his, but she never let go and occasionally gave him a quick, affectionate squeeze.

For his part, he had to resist the urge to look at her, drinking in her clean, soft beauty and the sun-kissed skin she so blatantly exposed. He'd never met a woman so at ease in her own body; the women who flocked to the Jersey shore wore bathing suits that looked more like Puritan nightgowns, and while he'd met plenty of actresses willing to shed their clothing, some at a moment's notice, even they had not been as relaxed, as *free,* as this poor uneducated mountain girl.

When they reached her family's cabin, the front door opened and a friendly middle-aged woman smiled out at them. "Well, looky what y'all done caught in the woods," she said.

"This is Sean," Sophronie said eagerly. "He's the fella who offered me a job in his motion picture."

"Pleasure to meet you, Mrs. Conlin," Sean said.

"Oh, please, we don't stand on no politeness around here. You call me Viney. Short for 'Elvina.'"

"Pleasure to meet you, Viney," he said.

"And Sophronie, you go put on some decent clothes before your father sees you. He'll tan your hide good, young lady."

"Yes'm," Sophronie said. "I'll be right back. Y'all promise you ain't gonna run off?"

"I promise," Sean said.

She dashed into the house past her mother. He heard giggling, and other female voices. Viney called out, "You heathens leave your sister alone, she's got company!" Then she turned to Sean. "She's got two sisters and three brothers. They've been known to pick on each other."

"Brothers and sisters do that everywhere," Sean agreed.

"You missed breakfast and you're a mite early for lunch, but if you're hungry I reckon I can whip something up."

"Oh, don't do anything special on my account."

Before Viney could reply, two teenage boys ran around a corner of the house and skidded to a stop.

"Heard tell a Yankee was here," the older one said breathlessly.

"Is that you?" the younger one said, peering at Sean as if he was a zoo exhibit.

"Hodge, Randy, act like you been to town before," their mother said. "This is Mr. Sean."

They both stood up straight and stuck out their hands. Sean shook them firmly and said, "Pleasure to meet you, gentlemen."

"Are you really a Yankee?" the older one, Hodge, asked.

"I am."

"Where you from?"

"Fort Lee, New Jersey."

"A fort?" Randy said. "So you're a soldier?"

"No, I make moving pictures."

They both looked blank. "What's that?" Randy asked.

"Something neither of you need to bother him about," Viney said. "Git."

The boys dutifully turned and ran off the way they came.

Viney sighed wistfully. "What I wouldn't give for a fraction of that energy. But that ain't no matter, come out of the sun and have a seat." She gestured at a rocking chair on the porch.

From the chair, he could see out across the whole valley. The heavy smoke from Sadieville rose in multiple columns straight up, like prison bars against the blue sky. It was a harsh industrial stain on the otherwise bucolic scene.

"That all used to be ours," Viney said wistfully.

"I heard. I also heard you got cheated."

She snorted. "Yeah, I reckon we did, if you're measuring by money. Right now my husband Enoch's up in the mine, feedin' the beast that thinks it killed us."

"You don't feel cheated?"

"If I've learned one thing, it's that things balance out in time," she said. "And time don't work the same for everybody."

Sean didn't know what to make of that, so he just smiled and nodded.

He heard giggles, and turned toward the door. Two girls younger than Sophronie peeked out at him, then vanished when they saw him watching.

"Young 'uns," Viney said, and shook her head. "If I could

get 'em to wash their necks, I'd wring 'em. Would you like a drink of water, Mr. Sean? Or something harder?"

"I wouldn't mind some water," Sean said.

"Revonne!" Viney called. "Go down to the well and bring back a bucket of water."

"I don't want to be any trouble," Sean protested.

"Giving an idle child a task ain't no trouble, it's a blessing."

Yet another young man came around the corner of the house. He was older, almost grown, and carried a fiddle and bow. "I heard Sophronie brought in another stray," he said flatly. "Where'd she find this one?"

"Behave yourself to our company, Welton Conlin," Viney said. "You ain't yet too big for me to take a switch to."

Sean stood and extended his hand to the young man. "I'm Sean."

"A Yankee," the boy drawled, ignoring the hand. "Don't that beat all. You down here working with the coal company?"

"No, I make moving pictures."

The boy's eyes narrowed. "Like they show in town?"

"Yes."

"I thought there was only one of those. *Judith of* something-or-other."

"Bethulia."

"Yeah, maybe. So there's more?"

"Thousands."

The girl Revonne brought Sean a glass of water. She handed it to him without making eye contact, and as soon as he took it, she ran back inside.

The boy Welton tucked his fiddle under his chin and began playing "The Arkansas Traveler." Sean recognized it as one of the standard songs that often accompanied pictures in vaudeville shows. When Welton stopped after the first verse, Sean said, "You play that very well."

"You play anything?"

"No."

He smiled sarcastically. "Sophronie sure can pick 'em." He turned and walked off, continuing to play the same jaunty tune.

"You'll have to excuse him," Viney said. "He's got a chip on his shoulder 'bout us losing all that land. He'll warm up to you, if you give him a little time."

"I'm sure he's just . . ." Sean began, then trailed off.

Sophronie emerged from the cabin clad in a light blue dress that was clearly meant for a younger, and smaller, girl. Once it probably reached her calves, but now only came down to her knees. It was also tight in inappropriate places, and Sean could only imagine the scowling reverend's apoplectic reaction if she wore it to town. With her hair pulled back in a matching bow and her delicate bare feet, she looked both wild and innocent, and it took Sean a moment to find his voice.

"You're back," he said. "You look lovely."

"You're just full of Yankee charm, aren't you?" Sophronie said. Then to her mother, she added, "Did I hear Welton out here?"

"You did. That boy's got the manners of a hound dog with worms. I apologize, Sean."

"No offense taken," Sean assured her.

"Sean needs to look for pretty places to make his pictures, Mama," Sophronie said, "so I'm gonna take him on a walk. Don't know if we'll be back in time for lunch, so don't wait on us."

"Y'all be careful out there," Viney said. "Blackberries are blooming early this year, and it's drawing in the bears."

"We'll be fine," Sophronie said, and took Sean's hand.

"Pleasure meeting all of you," Sean said as she led him off. He still heard the strains of the violin threading through the silent morning, growing fainter as they got farther from the cabin.

# 15

"Should we really worry about bears?" Sean asked.

Sophronie laughed. "They ain't got bears in New Jersey?"

"Actually, they do. And in the Catskills, near where I grew up."

"Did you know that these mountains and the Catskills are all connected?"

"No, I didn't."

"Well, see?" she said with a playful nudge at his ribs. "You Yankees don't know everything, after all."

At the moment, Sean couldn't recall knowing anything. Sophronie filled his senses, his attention, and even blocked out his memories of anything and anyone else he'd ever known. As before, he had a difficult time not watching the way her body moved beneath the dress, imagining what that soft, smooth skin would feel like under his hands.

"So what sort of places do you need to find?" she asked as she stopped to pick some wildflowers.

"Places where I can stage the action, but still see the scenery in the background. That ridge where we met this morning was a perfect spot."

"Why not do the whole thing right there, then?" she asked, as she carefully arranged the flowers into a bouquet.

"Because I know there have to be other beautiful places around here."

She laughed. "You're right about that. This whole place is beautiful. We've been here for so long, sometimes we forget it. We just see the hard parts, and not the beauty."

"I think that's true of everybody. You get used to a place, and you don't really see it anymore."

Now they emerged into another small clearing. Ahead was a small cemetery inside a rusted knee-high fence. A half-dozen tombstones stood inside it.

"What's this?" Sean asked.

"The Conlin family plot," Sophronie said distantly. "Some of those stones go back further than you'd believe. And there's people buried without stones who go back even further."

She released his hand and walked to the fence. He followed uncertainly. She looked down at the newest stone, one with the name TUCKER CONLIN, and the date *January 19, 1914.*

"Tucker," Sean said. "Must be a popular name around here. The fellow who gave us that map I mentioned was named Tucker."

"That ain't a surprise," she said.

"Only one date," Sean observed.

"He never saw another," she said, her voice now soft and reverent.

"Stillborn?"

"No, he lived a few hours. But he was born too early, and he never really had a chance. We all knew it."

"Your brother?"

She shook her head.

"Cousin?"

She didn't look at him. "My son."

He felt the jolt in his chest. Eighteen months ago, this girl he'd thought of as innocent and unspoiled had suffered a loss he could barely comprehend. And if she'd had a baby, that meant . . .

"Your husband must've been very sad," he said.

She laughed, a cold and desolate sound. "There ain't no husband."

"I'm so sorry," he said, not knowing if he should try to comfort her or not. "It must've been awful."

"I appreciate that," she said. Then, in the saddest and purest voice he'd ever heard, she began to sing. It was the same melody she'd used during her audition, but the words were fuller, and the sorrow in them almost unbearable:

> *For it's there he lies buried,*
> *Within the sounds of the rill,*
> *And when it comes springtime,*
> *There're sweet daffodils,*
> *And they say if you listen,*
> *When the night starts to chill,*
> *They say how that old whip-poor-will,*
> *How he'll sing for him still . . .*

She bent over the fence and placed the bouquet on the little grave:

> *Lost my baby, lost my son,*
> *Lost my only, my only one,*
> *Can't go back, don't have the will,*
> *Can never go back to my Sadieville.*

So the father had been someone from Sadieville, Sean realized. And now this poor girl had to work in that town, no doubt reminded of her loss every day. Was the man still there, he wondered, or had he skipped out once his misdeed could not be denied?

She rose, smoothed down her dress, and turned to him. Her eyes were dry and clear; she'd expressed all her sadness in the song. "I'm sorry if this all makes you think less of me."

Sean was not so lucky, nor so strong. Tears ran down his cheeks. "Oh, Sophronie, you've got it all wrong." And he pulled her very gently into his arms and kissed her. She returned the kiss with equal tenderness.

She pulled away enough to look him in the eye. "Some men wouldn't want a girl who'd been through all that."

"Some men are idiots."

"Not you. You're a good man, Sean."

"I don't know about that," he said with a little smile.

"I do," she said with certainty. And she pulled him into another kiss.

When their lips parted, she said, "I should warn you, though. Fall in love with a mountain girl and you end up in love with the whole mountain."

"Both are incredibly beautiful," he said, and kissed her again.

"There's more you need to know," Sophronie said. "Especially since Tucker sent you here."

"What's he got to do with it?"

"That's what you need to know."

"I know all I need to know about you, Sophronie," he said seriously.

"No," she replied with certainty, "you don't."


The trees grew heavier and denser, darkening the forest and somehow making even this bright, sunny day seem a bit sinister. But Sean chose not to dwell on this, or even think about it.

Ahead the terrain broke into the open and rose up, a bare mountainside with a stand of thick hawthorn trees right at the base.

"That's what I brought you to see," Sophronie said.

When he looked more closely, Sean saw a cave hidden behind the trees. "The thorn trees, or the cave?"

"The cave."

"Is it a gold mine or something?"

"Not really. For people like me, it's the way home."

"Home?"

"My people originally came from a far place. A very far place. And we came through this cave." She turned to him, and when she spoke, she no longer sounded like a simple mountain girl. "Remember what I told you about these mountains and the Catskills? How they're connected?"

"Yes."

"Did you know that *all* the lands of the earth used to be connected? These mountains around us, your Catskills, and the Highlands of Scotland? They were once the same mountain range. They were all as tall and rough as the Rockies back then. Only as time passed, they drifted apart and wore down, like an old man's teeth."

Sean didn't quite know what to make of this. "Did they teach you that in church?"

She laughed. "The Tufa don't go to church. There's not a one in this county. Not even in Sadieville."

"I met a minister who was trying to build one. He seems to think the Tufa are responsible for its bad luck."

"I know the one you mean," she said, wrinkling her nose in disgust. "He tried to church me once. He wanted to show me the glory of the coming of his little bitty lord."

Sean was horrified, if not surprised. It was one more reason to hate the repulsive Reverend Nashe. "Christ, Sophronie. Did you tell anyone? The sheriff, or—"

"That wouldn't do no good. They're all secretly White Caps, so they help each other out." She put her arms around his neck and looked up into his face. "After all I done told you, deep down you still think I'm half a child, don't you?"

He'd never had a woman talk to him like this, not even actresses, and the sense of her body against his own pretty much short-circuited his brain. "Uh . . ."

"It's okay to admit it. I know what I look like. But I'm a lot older than you think I am."

He felt himself blush. "I didn't mean—"

"I don't mean because I've had a baby." She turned her head and looked up at the cave mouth. "On the day we came through that cave, my ancestor was the last one. And us, his descendants, are the only ones who know where it is. Can't none of the other Tufa even find it; it's hid by what you'd probably call a spell. If one was standing right here with us, she wouldn't even be able to see it."

He could think of nothing to say.

"My people are supposed to forever stay away from yours," she said, her voice growing distant. "We're likely to slip up and enchant you even when we don't mean to. And once we do, there's no release."

He gently turned her chin so that she faced him again. "Am I under your spell right now?"

"If you were under my spell, you wouldn't have to ask," she said with a laugh. Then she kissed him again.

"I want to tell you a story, Sean. I may have some of the details wrong, but it's mostly true. And I think it'll explain some things."

"Is it a story about where you said you come from?"

"No, it's a story about this place, this valley, when my people first arrived. Why we are like we are. It's one of our most sacred stories, one of our treasures. The thing my family is supposed to protect. That's one reason I still can't believe my daddy sold our land, *this* land we're standing on, to the coal company."

She leaned against a nearby tree, looking sexy and desirable and untouchable all at once. "So, a long time ago, the Tufa were exiled by our queen because of . . . well, that ain't important.

What *is* important is that the Tufa were sent into a cave back home, and came out of this cave, stark naked and with everything, even our names, taken away. But even like that, we all hoped the Queen might change her mind, and that it might turn out that we didn't have to stay here. For the time being, though, we *were* here, so we had to make the best of it."

She walked up to the cave. "And this story starts a little bit later, with the people who were here in this valley before us. A beautiful girl named Dahni and her little brother stood right where we're standing now, looking into this cave, not knowing what was about to come out of it, or what that would mean to them, their people, and their world . . ."

# III

# DAHNI AND
# THE DRUMMER

# 16

"Don't . . . wake . . . the bear," Yakon whispered to his older sister, Dahni.

"Shut up," Dahni shot back. "If there is a bear in there, you're the one who'll wake it up."

Dahni was nineteen suns old and a daughter of one of the Ta-Mihzo elders. She was tall for a woman, with a figure that had filled out so much over the last few seasons that she had to spend the winter making all new clothes.

Above them, the sun blasted its way through the pristine air and banished shadows across the valley floor. The jagged mountain slopes cut into the sky, rising so high that wisps of clouds clung to the sharp spires. Wide-winged birds navigated the swirling air currents, watching the ground below for anything small enough to kill, or dead enough to eat. The air was cool, and dry, and felt like the soft sigh of a contented lover.

Dahni and Yakon often hunted rock bird eggs in the foothills of the towering mountains. Today, they scrounged in the crevices around a narrow, vertical cave mouth. As Dahni resumed hunting for eggs, Yakon crept close and peered into the cave opening.

"What did I tell you?" she whisper-shouted.

"Come here!" Yakon said urgently. "You have to see this!"

"If you wake it up—"

"It's not a bear, idiot. Come see."

She put down her basket of eggs and joined him.

"Look on the ground," he said.

In the dust were the prints of bare human feet; not just one or two, but dozens, all overlapping and all headed out of the cave.

"Have the elders been meeting up here?" Yakon asked.

"No," Dahni said with certainty.

"Then who made these?"

"I don't know." She let her eyes follow the tracks out of the cave, but they vanished as soon as the ground grew rocky.

"A war band?" Yakon suggested.

"From where?" Dahni asked.

"Let's go find out," Yakon said, and started into the cave.

She grabbed him by his ponytail. "Not a chance. We have to go back and tell Papa and the other elders."

"What if they don't believe us?"

That made her laugh. "I guarantee they'll believe *me.*"

"What could you tell from the tracks?" asked Dahni's father, Kesak. They sat in the council lodge, and the other five elders waited for her response with serious faces. As she predicted, none of them had questioned her veracity. They knew she would take her father's place on the council when he died, and treated her accordingly.

"They seemed recent; the edges of the prints were still clear in the dust," she said carefully. "And I saw none going back in; I do not believe they have returned."

"Then where did they go?" Olonta, the most senior woman on the council, asked.

"I don't know," Dahni admitted.

"Thank you, daughter," Kesak said. "We'll discuss this in private now."

Dahni nodded and left the lodge. Yakon and their younger sister Mikka waited just outside and immediately flung questions at her.

"Did they believe you?"

"Are you going to be punished?"

"Is there going to be a war?"

"Where are you going?"

She answered that last one. "*We* are going back to the cave."

"We are?" Yakon said excitedly.

"Me, too?" asked Mikka, her seven-suns-old eyes glittering with anticipation.

"Yes, you, too. We're going to look around more closely, and see what else we might learn."

"And then maybe there will be a war?" Yakon asked, almost with delight.

"Maybe," Dahni had to admit.


Nothing had changed at the cave. The tracks remained, with no new ones going in or coming out. Nearby, she found the fresh print of a saber-toothed cat, but she saw no sign that it had entered.

She pointed it out to Yakon. "Keep your eyes open for that," she said.

He clutched his hunting spear for dear life. "I will."

Mikka stayed quiet, holding the hem of Dahni's dress with one hand and sucking the two middle fingers of the other.

Dahni peered into the cave. She squinted against the darkness and listened as hard as she could.

And suddenly, there he was, his face a finger's length from hers. His eyes were wide and bright blue, something Dahni had never seen before. He had black hair matted with dirt, a scraggly beard, and was totally naked.

He yelled.

She screamed.

Mikka and Yakon screamed.

The naked man squinted into the sunlight. His body was also filthy, covered with dirt and dried mud. He dropped to his knees with a cry of anguish, then fell forward and lay still.

"Get over here!" Dahni called to Yakon. She didn't expect help from him, but she wanted his spear a lot closer in case she needed it.

Yakon aimed the stone point at the man's spine and demanded, "Who is he?"

"You know as much as I do." She knelt beside him and said, "Hello? Are you all right?"

With great effort, he rolled onto his back. He was so skinny his hip bones and ribs were visible beneath his pale skin. He said something in a language she didn't recognize and that had a weird lilt to it that she'd never heard before. Then he pointed at the cave.

"He looks scary," Mikka said around her fingers.

"He's sick," Dahni said. "Yakon, give me a hand. We have to get him back to the village."

"I'm not touching him," the boy said. "Look at him; he's filthy."

"He's *sick*," Dahni repeated.

"Yeah, well, that's not my problem."

Dahni glared at him. "Get . . . over here . . . and help me," she growled.

"Will he hurt us?" Mikka asked.

"He won't right now," Dahni said. "Hopefully when he's well, he'll remember that we helped him."

———

They took him straight to the lodge of the medicine woman, Sixela. It stood at a distance from the rest of the village, so that the sick might not spread their maladies.

Sixela was almost as young as Dahni, and had taken over from her late mother Tomulza just eight moon cycles previously. She ordered the stranger brought into her lodge and placed near the opening, to benefit from fresh breezes. She knelt and ran her hands quickly over him, pressing and turning to check joints and organs. Then she opened his mouth and examined his gums.

"He's dying of thirst," she said. "Didn't you give him any water?"

"He wasn't awake," Dahni said, too ashamed to admit that the thought hadn't occurred to her.

Sixela, as usual, cut her no slack. "So you don't know how a mouth opens?"

"I didn't want him to drown," she mumbled defensively.

Sixela took a ladle from her water barrel, raised the man's head and put it to his lips. As soon as he tasted it he grabbed the ladle and pressed it against his face, moaning as he drank.

"Easy, calm down," Sixela said. "You're safe."

"He doesn't understand our language," Yakon offered.

"And you know this how?"

"Because he spoke just before he passed out, and we didn't understand what he said."

"Do you even know how to think, Yakon?" Sixela said. "That just proves *we* don't understand *him*. It tells us nothing about what he understands." She turned back to her patient, who had gulped down another ladle of water. She took it from his hands, then raised his chin so he faced her. She touched herself over her heart. "Sixela. Sixela." Then she touched his heart.

He looked blank.

She waved her hand in front of his face. His eyes didn't move.

"Is he dead?" Yakon asked.

"No, he's exhausted." She closed his eyes for him, and he began to lightly snore. Then she looked grimly at Dahni. "Tell your father about him. But also tell him he's in no condition to answer questions. I'll let them know when he is."

"So you think he'll live?" Dahni asked.

"I think he might."

"I'm sorry if I made his condition worse."

"You didn't run off and leave him, which an awful lot of our people would've done. That makes you one of the bravest people around."

Dahni nodded at the compliment, but inside she was still furious with herself. She needed some time alone, so she took her brother and sister to her uncle's lodge and left them with her aunt. Then she grabbed her hunting spear, longer and lighter than Yakon's, and headed into the woods.

## 17

Miles away, outside a different cave on the far side of the valley from the Ta-Mihzo village, a sound totally new to this world rang out: music.

An unseen drummer kept the rhythm, while a chorus of voices sang, so quietly it was almost a whisper:

> *See that bear, sleeping by*
> *See that bear, sleeping by*
> *If I wake that bear, I might die*
> *See that bear, sleeping by . . .*

There was no movement from the cave. The next verse was louder:

> *See that bear, waking up*
> *See that bear, waking up*
> *If I poke that bear, he'll rip me up*
> *See that bear, waking up . . .*

That did the trick. An enormous female cave bear emerged into the light, sleepy and pissed off. The drumming grew louder and more insistent, taunting her with its steady rhythms. She stepped out into the open and rose to her massive twelve-foot height. Popping her jaws and roaring her challenge, she swiped at the air. There was nothing, she knew, that could stand against her in a fair fight.

Unfortunately this fight was not fair at all. Free of the cave's protection, she was immediately pierced by a dozen arrows and spears, their stone tips burrowing deep into her body. One found her heart, and she fell onto her back, swiping at the shafts. Her roars grew weaker, until at last she lay still.

Only then did her killers emerge from their hiding places behind various boulders, gnarled trees, and stands of tall, dry grass. There were four of them, clad in animal hides. Instead of cheering or celebrating, they approached their quarry wearily, and warily, humming along with the drumbeat.

Finally one of the group, a man known as the Carpenter, stopped humming and said, " 'Tis a fair big beastie, she is."

"Now, now, lads, there's no hurry," a woman, the Healer, said. "Let's let her be for a bit. When our queen made time, she made plenty of it."

The mention of the Queen made them all do the same elaborate hand gesture of respect and fealty.

The drumming continued. Finally the Carpenter yelled, "Hold your bloody fingers, will you? They've done their job!"

The drumming ceased, and another man emerged from the trees. He carried no weapons, but only a drum made from a bit of hollow log and an animal skin. He was young, lean, and one of those people who radiated both confidence and irreverence. He tapped his fingers on the drumhead as he approached, calling out, "See? Gave the old hairy one a slap on the ear, didn't it?"

"Could've done the same thing with shouts or songs," one of the older men, the Jeweler, said.

"Aye, perhaps," the Drummer agreed smugly. "Never know, will we?"

The Jeweler narrowed his eyes. He didn't care for the Drummer in general, and his attitude in particular. "You're a chancer, my friend."

"Keep your breath to cool your porridge," the Healer said to the Jeweler. "We need to skin that bear and get whatever meat we want from it."

The hunting party drew their bone-handled stone knives and warily approached the bear. As they began their work, the Healer sang:

> *Where is the home for me?*
> *Inis Ealga, set in the sea,*
> *Fomorian's home in the soft sea-foam,*
> *Would I lend to thee;*
> *Where in the wings of the wind are furled,*
> *And faint the heart of the world . . .*

It was almost sundown by the time the hunting band returned to their village, a circular collection of primitive huts made from tree branches and animal skins, similar in concept to the Ta-Mihzo lodges. But near them, several half-built log cabins rose, permanent homes in place of the temporary ones. There were only grown men and women, no children, although a handful of women had large bellies.

Three moon cycles ago, they'd stumbled naked, nameless and disoriented, from a cave on the far side of the valley. It had been cold, and damp, and three of them were killed by animals before they even managed to reach the shelter of the trees. Now they'd begun, slowly, to acclimate.

Their leader's second in command, known as the Tall Woman, met them at the village center. She was, as her name implied, taller than most of the men, with the broad shoulders and narrow eyes of someone used to fighting, and winning. She asked the group, "How did it go?"

"The cave's all his," the Hunter said. "Or it will be, once we muck it out."

"So the drumming worked?" she asked the Drummer.

"Like a charm," he said. He was, of course, being sarcastic; it had worked like a charm because it was a charm. "The better the day, the better the deed."

"Aye, except when you're acting the maggot," the Jeweler muttered, scowling beneath his glaring eyes.

"Let's bring him the good news," the Tall Woman said.

There was only one completed wooden home in the village, a small cabin set away from the rest. They'd all pitched in to build it first, both out of respect for their leader, and to give him someplace to go so he wouldn't just wander around and stick his nose into their business. Survival in a strange place was hard enough without the boss looking over your shoulder.

A deerskin marked by a white handprint with six fingers hung over the cabin door. She knocked on the wooden frame.

" 'Tis me," she said. "The lads have returned with bounty."

After a moment, a six-fingered hand pushed the deerskin aside and their leader, the Six-Fingered Man, emerged and scowled into the bright sunlight. He was broad-shouldered, pot-bellied, and had the look of both immense strength and chastened arrogance. "What bounty?"

"That cave you wanted up in the foothills."

"The one with the bear?"

"Aye. 'Tis now an empty hole in the sullen rock."

"So you killed it?"

"Not me. They did," she said, and nodded back at the group.

The Six-Fingered Man looked over the hunters; his gaze stopped on the Drummer. "And what did you do?"

He smiled smugly. "Called her forth with a rhythm and a song."

"And it worked?"

" 'Tis true, it did," the Hunter said.

"And it went straight to his already swollen head," the Jeweler muttered.

"I wasn't talking to either of you," the Six-Fingered Man said. He continued to watch the Drummer for a long moment, then said, "Hmph," and turned to go back inside.

The Tall Woman was just about to sigh with relief when he stopped and turned back. "Wait. Were any other eyes cast your way?"

"No," the Hunter said. "We saw not a one besides ourselves."

The Six-Fingered Man frowned. "Did you look?"

"Not . . . so much, you know," the Hunter said, suddenly nervous. "As you do. We did have a fair big bear to worry about, you know."

"So they could've been watching?"

The Hunter looked at the Tall Woman, who shook her head microscopically.

"As the wind's own truth, I can't see how," the Hunter said.

The Six-Fingered Man looked up at the bright sky and the ring of peaks around them. "This is their world, you know. They could be anywhere. They could be watching us right now, waiting to pick us off."

"Now, there's nothing to make that true," the Tall Woman said.

"There's nothing to make anything true, for good or ill. And until there is, my rule stands: no contact with the others."

The Tall Woman made a weary gesture of respect and fealty. The Six-Fingered Man responded with one of his own, and went back inside.

"Now what do you suppose that was all about?" the Gardener asked softly.

"Maybe he feels guilty for getting us exiled," the Hunter said. "Guilt has quick ears for an accusation, after all."

"Perhaps," the Gardener said doubtfully. Then he looked around. "Wait—where'd the Drummer go?"

# 18

Deep in the forest at the center of the valley, the Drummer strode along the riverbank, sending out a steady rhythm of triumph. Birds rose from the trees and cawed their annoyance at him before settling back down in his wake. The trees overhead rippled with the winds, casting mottled shadows.

He reached the bend in the river where the current created a large, still pool. He climbed up onto a high rock overlooking it, and watched the fish swim lazily in the clear water. He wondered if there was a way to drum the fish into a net, or even onto the bank.

Then movement caught his eye. Something came through the forest on the other side of the river. And when it stepped into the open at the river's edge, his eyes opened wide.

It was a young woman.

Dahni emerged from the forest and stopped at the edge of the pool, lost in thought. Somewhere in the valley, a group of strangers might be preparing to assault the Ta-Mihzo. Despite her brother's enthusiasm, the idea of war terrified her. She had never seen anyone die by violence. She thrust her spear point-first into the soft ground and stared at the water for a long moment before something very obvious struck her.

The pool's surface showed a man watching her from atop the big rock on the opposite bank.

She hid her reaction. It was not one of the Ta-Mihzo; she knew everyone in her tribe, even at a distance, even in an uncertain upside-down reflection. So it must be one of . . . *them*.

She glanced surreptitiously at her spear. Could she pull it free, shoulder it, and hurl it with enough speed and accuracy to kill her watcher before he moved?

Then she mentally kicked herself. She was thinking like Yakon, not like a grown woman, certainly not like an elder. A Ta-Mihzo did not base decisions on fear. So she took a deep breath, raised her chin, and looked straight at him.

The young woman was certainly beautiful. He wondered how such a delicate creature survived in this savage land.

Then he nearly fell into the river when she looked up directly at him.

She laughed as he regained his balance.

"Oh, 'tis a real laugh," he said. "You see me as a blind cobbler's thumb, do you?"

She tilted her head. Clearly she didn't understand his language.

"You remind me of a braw girl in a song, did you know that?" He brought his drum into position, found the rhythm and sang:

*My beautiful girl, she thinks me a fool*
*She laughs at me all day long*
*But if I'm a fool, then I'm hers alone*
*And that's why I'm singing this song . . .*

If he'd suddenly sprouted an extra head on his shoulders, he doubted she could've looked more startled. It was his turn to laugh at her.

"Ah, no harm meant, lass, it's only a *gáire*," he said. He put down his drum and stood, keeping his hands above his head. "Look, no sword, no knife. I'll not hurt you. Stay there."

Without really thinking it through, he leaped from the rock into the river. He landed in the fastest part of the current, which quickly tore away his crude garments. He fought his way into the still backwater pool.

Treading water, he looked around, but the woman had vanished. "Hey," he called. "Come on out. I don't bite."

There was no reply, and no sign of movement. He swam to shallower water and stood up.

She emerged from the trees where she'd hidden and looked him over, her eyes traveling up and down his naked form. She said something he didn't understand.

"Don't judge me too harshly," the Drummer said with a grin. "That water is cold." She smiled back uncertainly, still not comprehending. "Ye don't ken me at all, do you? We need to find something in common." He closed his eyes and sang a single long, clear note.

Then he looked at her. She stared at him in surprise, but no fear. He gestured to his mouth, then pointed at hers, encouraging her to sing.

When he'd first emerged from the water, Dahni had been shocked, and a little frightened. Then she looked him up and down, and couldn't repress a snicker. "That water must be cold," she said.

He clearly didn't understand, but there was something unthreatening about him, a friendliness that cut through most of her fright. Besides, if he intended to either kill her or take advantage of her, he'd gone about it in the completely wrong way.

Then he opened his mouth and made . . . a sound. Something she'd never heard before. It wasn't a word, she was certain. It was more of a cry, like something an animal or bird might make, but there was no fear in it, no anger, just something that made her tingle all over.

Then he gestured at her to make the same sound.

She tensed, wanted to run, then forced herself to stand her ground. She took a deep breath, opened her mouth, and made a noise that approximated his cry.

He smiled, laughed, and clapped his hands in delight. Then he made the sound again, but added a second, different sound after it. She mimicked it as best she could.

He continued, adding sound after sound, building a chain of noises that were entirely different than anything Dahni had ever heard. She did her best to keep up.

Finally he gestured for her to make the noises alone. As she did, he made *other* noises, different from hers, yet blending with them in a way that thrilled her more than anything ever had. They made their noises several times in a row until finally they both had to laugh with delight at the sheer, joyous absurdity of it.

And then, as they sighed their way to silence, they looked deeply into each other's eyes. Then she stepped willingly into his embrace, and into the kiss that sealed their doom.


The next morning Dahni made her way to Sixela's lodge to visit the Stranger. Sixela was out, checking on a newborn in the village, so Dahni had the Stranger to herself.

He lay almost exactly where they'd left him yesterday. His face was now clean, and his hair brushed away from it to reveal handsome, ascetic features. She caressed his cheek, her fingertips scratching on his beard, but he didn't awaken.

She leaned close to his ear and, as best she could, made the string of sounds she'd learned from her new, secret lover. Then she waited to see if the sounds would penetrate his coma and bring him back to the world.

His eyelids fluttered, and beneath them his eyes worked back and forth.

She made the sounds again.

His eyes opened, and he turned to her. He stared at her blankly, trying to place her in his memory. When he failed, his brow creased in confusion.

She made the sounds a third time.

He looked at her with such sadness that she felt tears build in her own eyes. In a pitifully weak voice, he made the same string of sounds.

She smiled with encouragement.

He said something rapidly that she didn't understand. Then he passed out.

Dahni sat back on her heels. That settled one thing, at least: both strangers were from the same tribe. But was this man someone they valued and sought, or had he been cast into the caves as punishment, maybe even execution?

She could only learn more about this stranger by learning more from the one who'd taken her on the soft grass by the river.


"They don't sing," the Drummer said.

"Pull the other one, it's got bells on," the Tall Woman said in disbelief.

"I'm nae pulling anything. And when I sang to her, she looked at me like I'd grown a second head next to my first one."

They walked through the woods, far enough from their village so they knew they wouldn't be overheard. The Drummer had tried to keep things to himself, but he simply had to tell someone, and the Tall Woman was his closest confidante.

"So do you have a glad eye for her?" the Tall Woman asked.

"I do indeed," the Drummer admitted. "She's a fiddle in the moonlight, she is."

"The Man with Six Fingers will be mad as a box of frogs if he finds out."

"He won't find out unless you tell him."

"I should."

"Why?"

"Because it's against his orders." She paused, thinking. "Still, I suppose 'tis not hurting anyone."

"And it nary will," he insisted. "Not even me."

Many nights later Dahni and the Drummer, both naked, lay together on a woven blanket she'd brought to their tryst. Above them, the sky turned from blue to purple on its way to the starry black of night. "I can't believe," he said, "that you kenned our language so quickly."

"What can I say?" she said. "I'm smart."

"Are all your people so smart?" he asked.

"Oh, most are a lot smarter than me," she assured him.

"Mine, too," he agreed. "I'm the village idiot."

"You're my idiot," she said, and kissed him.

After that first day, they'd met in secret every chance they got. At first it had been at the pool, but later, at places where the river was easier to cross. Their intimacy was immediate, and powerful, like the point where lightning touched its target. It almost—almost—made the Drummer glad he'd been exiled.

And as much as she'd learned his spoken language, she'd also learned his language of what he called "music." They'd begun with simple children's songs, and he'd taught her rhythm, and harmony. Then he'd brought a second drum for her to play.

Now she kissed him passionately, and when she pulled away asked, "What are your people called?"

"The Tuatha—" he said without thinking, then looked surprised. "Wow. That's the first time I've been able to remember it. We're the Tuatha . . . something."

"The Two . . ." she said, struggling with the sounds.

"No, Tuatha."

"Two . . ."

"Say it with me: 'tu . . . a . . .'"

"Two fah?" she said with charming earnestness.

"Near enough," he agreed with a smile.

"So can you recall *your* name yet?"

He thought hard for a moment, then shook his head. "Not a clue."

"That's so *sad,*" she said, and kissed him again.

# 19

The Stranger opened his eyes as Dahni bent over him. "Hello," she said in his language. "How do you feel today?"

He stared at her, but didn't reply.

Sixela had been called away to attend a man who'd driven a broken stick through his foot. So as long as Dahni could hear the man's faint screams echoing from the fields, she knew the healer was occupied. She repeated, "How do you feel today?"

His eyes, clear for a moment, glazed over as he sank back into his pillow. His body had responded well to Sixela's treatment, but his mind remained addled, disconnected from the reality around him except for stray lucid moments, like the one that had evidently just passed.

"Can't go back," he said weakly. "Don't have the will . . ."

"Shhh, calm down," she said, and stroked his cheek. "You're safe here, I won't hurt you."

"I know the way," he murmured, "but she won't let them come back . . ."

"Do you want to find your people?" she asked as gently as she could.

"Yes," he said, his head twisting on his pillow. It was one of the few times he'd responded directly to a question.

"I can help you. But you have to talk to me."

"She won't let them come back," the Stranger continued, talking either to himself or to someone who existed only in his mind. "I know the way, but we don't have the will . . ." It wasn't the first time he'd mentioned this strange, powerful woman who inspired a soul-deep terror in him.

Suddenly he grabbed the front of her dress and pulled her close. His eyes, wide and shining, took in her face, her clothes, and the lodge. "You're not . . ."

"I'm a friend," she said, her voice calm despite her pounding heart. "A friend."

He released her, sank onto his sweaty pallet and drifted back into his troubled sleep. She had not yet mentioned him to the Drummer, and with each passing day that decision loomed larger, and harder to justify. She had to bring it up soon, maybe even risk bringing the Drummer to Sixela's lodge in secret so that he could meet the Stranger.

But she couldn't bring herself to do it now. Their time together was so perfect, she wasn't willing to do anything that might impinge on it. So she wiped the Stranger's face a final time and left him alone in the lodge.


One afternoon in a clearing deep inside the forest on his side of the river, the Drummer suddenly said, "I can't keep this up."

"Not many men could, after all we've done today," she teased.

He playfully yanked a strand of her hair. "That's not what I mean." He tapped his fingers on the drum, creating a soft, steady beat that hid beneath the natural sounds around them. "We each need to tell our people what's going on. That there's no need to fear each other anymore. We need to bring them together."

"My father thinks your people are eventually going to try to drive us from the valley. Then there will be war, and many on both sides will die."

"That's pure havering."

"Does that mean nonsense?"

"Aye, it does. We're not looking for a fight. We're not violent people."

"How do you know? You said you couldn't remember."

"More pieces have come back. I think I know the story."

"Tell me, then."

He settled into a comfortable position, the drum between his legs, and began to tap a new rhythm, statelier and somehow sad. "We lived in a village deep inside a great, ancient forest. This forest was ruled by a woodsman who was immensely strong, and had six fingers on each hand. One day he did something that angered our queen, and she exiled him."

"What did he do?" she asked.

He bit his lip in concentration. "I *think* . . . he made a bet he shouldn't have, and he lost. This embarrassed the Queen, so she drove him from his forest into a cave, and he emerged . . . here."

"That sounds," she said, trying to sound casual, "like a children's story."

"No," he said seriously, "that's *history*. And the rest of us, his subjects, had to follow him here. The Queen's magic took away our memories of our names, our families, everything. We're just now starting to get them back, in little pieces."

"Perhaps we were right to be afraid of you," she said at last.

That made him laugh. "That's funny. The idea that anyone would be scared of us."

"I'm not scared of you."

"Ah, but you terrify me, lass," he said as he stretched out beside her and kissed her.

———

The next day, Dahni stood alone at the entrance of the cave where the Stranger had emerged. The footprints had faded, erased by the wind or the passage of an animal seeking shelter.

A cold, damp breeze from the depths of the cave blew her hair back from her face. She leaned into it and called out, "Hello? Is anyone there?" Then she caught herself and repeated it, this time in the Drummer's language, adding, "I'm looking for the Queen."

Her voice echoed back into the cave, rebounding until it faded.

"So much for that," she murmured to herself, and turned to go.

Then another sound rose out of the wind. It grew louder and clearer until it became a musical sound, a woman's voice raised in a song more beautiful than anything Dahni had ever heard. It contained every possible feeling, from ecstasy to sadness, and swept over her the way a lover's caress might.

Then it changed. It grew harsh, offended, vengeful. No, that wasn't strong enough. It was *rage*. And no mere mortal rage; this was the rage of a furious god, one offended that some lesser being had dared to approach it in song. This was the voice, Dahni realized, of the great Queen that had sent the Drummer's people away, and was prepared to remind them of their exile should they ever try to return.

Dahni clapped her hands over her ears. It didn't help.

She turned and ran.

# 20

The Six-Fingered Man had finally moved into the bear's cave. It had been cleaned, swept, scoured, then painted with symbols and signs that marked its, and his, significance. The Artist had completed the task without help, despite her ancient and shaking fingers. She was likely to be the first natural-death casualty of this new world, and then someone would have to take her place. As a people, they simply couldn't be without her colors.

Now the Drummer and the Tall Woman stood outside the cave. Wind tore at them, chilled from its passage over the mountains. They huddled inside their fur cloaks.

"He calls himself the Man in the Rock House now," the Tall Woman said.

" 'Tis clever," the Drummer agreed, glad he could blame his trembling voice on the wind.

"Aye. Wait here." She entered slowly, waiting both for her eyes to adjust to the dimness, and for the Man in the Rock House to acknowledge her.

The cave no longer smelled of bear shit, at least. The coals from a dying fire glowed near the back, the smoke filtering up through cracks and channels in the ceiling. The Man in the Rock House sat beside it, his crude new lyra in his hands, staring into the embers as if the secret to his happiness lay within their faint glimmer.

"Beg your pardon," the Tall Woman said, and made a gesture of respect. "The Drummer would like to speak with you."

He did not respond or acknowledge her presence.

"He's made contact with the people across the river. He's learned some things you might find useful."

"Send him in," he said in a voice ragged from disuse. "And wait outside."

She made the same gesture of respect again, then bowed and left.

After a long moment the Drummer appeared, tense and uncertain. He cleared his throat. "Sir," he said respectfully. "I apologize for intruding on your solitude, but I need to speak with you. It's about the tribe across the river. Sir, I've gotten close to one of them. A woman."

The Man in the Rock House finally looked up. "A woman?" he repeated.

"Yes, sir."

"Sit."

The Drummer did, carefully placing his drum to one side. He desperately wanted to tap on it, to use it to calm his thundering heart, but no one dared play along with the Man in the Rock House without an invitation.

The Man in the Rock House also set aside his lyra. The Drummer was shocked to see the grime on his face streaked with tears, some of which still shone with wetness. "Do you recall our days in the Queen's forest?"

"Aye. Small bits of it have come back to me . . . sir."

"Those were bonnie good days," he said as casually as if speaking about a walk to the creek. "I was fair good at my job, and all respected me. Even the Queen."

After a long, uncomfortable moment, the Drummer said, "Sir, about the tribe across the river . . . ?"

Something changed in the older man's face; a hardness settled there, and his gaze cleared. The wistfulness was gone, replaced by iron certainty. "What about them?"

"They're peaceful. Friendly."

"How do you know?"

"Because I've met one of them. She's learned our language, and I've learned the tongue of the Ta-Mihzo. It's what they call themselves."

The last of the glaze left his eyes, and for the first time, he was really paying attention. "You've been keeping company with one of them?"

"Yes. A young woman. We're—"

"Don't say you're in love," he barked, all the hesitation gone. "That's just insipid. She's in love with you because of what we are, and whatever you feel for her can't be anything more than a passing breeze." He stood and shook himself, as if awakening his whole body. "We don't mix with anyone, do you understand? If we do, we can never go back. We have to stay pure."

"But sir, perhaps the Queen—"

"I know what the Queen said!" he roared. "I was there, remember? She said it to *me*!" He paced now, speaking mostly to himself. "I heard every word, saw every gesture, felt every bit of her magic. She exiled us with a *thought,* and just like that, here we are!"

"I understand," the Drummer said, knowing this had been a mistake, wishing he was anywhere else.

"Do you? Perhaps you do; you've always been different from the others, always followed your own way, even back in the Queen's forest." He ran his hands through his grimy hair, leaving it spiked and wild. "Do you truly see that she might regret what she did? That it was only a stupid bet, only a momentary mistake in a lifetime of faithful service? Maybe even right now, she's considering bringing us back, returning us to our homes and our names, ending our exile. If we start mixing with these others, loving them and having children with them, then we'll be tied to this land just as we were to our home."

The Drummer took a deep breath. "Sir, whatever happens in the future, we're here now. We don't need to fear the Ta-Mihzo. We could help them, they could help us."

"No. *No,*" he repeated more forcefully, as if hoping the word itself would carry back to the Queen. "They can't help us, and it's not our place to help them! We're just visitors here, we're waiting for our call to come back home."

The Drummer bit back his words. "Aye, then. Thank you." He stood, picked up his drum, and turned to go.

The Man in the Rock House sat back down and began to pick his lyra again. "Drummer."

He turned back. "Yes, sir?"

"I'm sorry I have to do this, but I have no choice. I *order* you to have no more contact with this woman. Not with her, not with her people. And if you disobey me . . . I'll sing your dying dirge."

The Drummer started to respond, but the words caught in his throat. He walked out of the cave, the view of the sun-drenched valley blurred by his tears. He pushed past the Tall Woman's attempt to stop him and ran for the shelter of the forest.

"Father," Dahni said, "you sound like an old woman. A *cranky* old woman."

"Don't speak to me that way," her father Kesak said as he stirred the stew. As a village elder, he was one of the most venerated men of the tribe, whose wisdom was often sought to settle disputes. He was respected and honored by all the Ta-Mihzo.

Except for his own children, of course. And especially his eldest.

"I don't make idle rules," he continued. "I let you run free, and don't demand an accounting of your time. So when I tell you something, I expect you to *listen*!" He didn't intend to shout the last word, or to slam the wooden spoon into the side of the simmering pot for emphasis, it just happened. It made both of them jump.

"Don't treat me like a child," she said through her teeth, her fists clenched at her sides.

"I'm not treating you like a child," he shot back. "I'm treating you as I would anyone in our tribe. You are no mere girl, you're a future leader, and that's why I expect you to keep the whole tribe's interests at heart over and above your own."

"They have no plans to drive us out."

"And how do you know this? Because of the boy you keep going off to meet? Did he teach you that noise you've been making lately?"

"Yes," she said, her chin high. "They call it 'music.' It lets out feelings that words can never express."

"Maybe those feelings are *supposed* to stay hidden. Did you ever think of that?"

"Father, please, just *talk* to them. We share this valley; why not share it in peace?"

Kesak put down the spoon and stood, his broad shoulders straight the way they were in the council lodge. "Dahni, I didn't want to have to do this, but—"

She fought the tears pushing at the corner of her eyes. "He's had many chances to kill me, or to capture me and drag me to their village. He's never even tried."

"The long-tooth cat is good and kind to its mate. Not so much to others of its kind who come near its territory."

"He's not an animal."

"No, but he's *different*. And I'm *telling* you: do not see this man again. And if their leader has any sort of sense, he's told your young man the same thing."

"My young man," she repeated bitterly. "No longer."

"I'm sorry." He reached out to hug her, but she shrugged out of his arms and ran out the door.

## 21

Sixela and Dahni sat in the healer's lodge. The Stranger slept, as he always did. They spoke as if he wasn't there, like he was no more than another pot or bundle of skins. "I love him, and now I can't see him," Dahni said, her voice flat and hopeless. "Sixela, what do I *do*?"

Before Sixela could answer, the flap of her lodge flew open, and a tall, gangly boy appeared. "Sixela, my mother is ready to have her baby," he gasped, out of breath. "Please come now."

"Go tell them I'm on my way," Sixela said, and got to her feet. She put a hand on Dahni's cheek. "We'll talk more tomorrow. Make no decisions until then, please."

When Sixela left, Dahni sat alone in the medicine lodge, staring into space and wishing for an end to the pain inside her. So she nearly screamed when a new voice said. "I'm sorry we've done this to you."

She slowly turned. The Stranger watched her from his pallet, clear-eyed.

And he'd spoken in Ta-Mihzo.

"Don't be afraid," he said. His voice was weak, but kind. "I won't hurt you."

Dahni swallowed hard. "You . . . speak our language."

"Yes. Learning new tongues is something our people do very easily. I'm sure you've noticed."

"So did you listen to the whole conversation?"

He smiled wryly. "I had nothing else to do."

"That's rude," she said, smiling back.

"I apologize. But I have a suggestion that might solve your problem. Would you like to hear it?"

She nodded.

"Our people have one particular weakness. I bet you can guess what it is."

"Music," she said without hesitation.

"Very good. So if you want to force a change, you have to *sing* it into existence."

"That doesn't make sense."

Again he smiled. "It will, I promise you."


It took the Drummer most of the morning to make the climb, his drum bouncing against his back. Finally, though, he reached a ledge that let him look out over the whole valley.

He sat and dangled his feet off the ledge. He situated his drum between his knees and began to play. His rough hands struck the skin with a fury that threatened to punch right through, and the sound rang through the still air.

The callused skin on the Drummer's hands began to split as he played, streaking the drumhead with blood. He wanted to scream, but his voice was nothing compared to what he channeled through his instrument.

In their village, the Tall Woman looked up. She knew who it was, and what he was saying, and it filled her with sadness and, when she looked off toward the Man in the Rock House's cave, a simmering fury. How long would they agree to be led by a man who made someone feel what the drum conveyed?

Then joining this came the high keening wail of a woman.

"Now who," the Tall Woman muttered to herself, "is *that*?" But of course she knew.

As the Stranger had advised, Dahni stood by the river, putting all her feelings into a pure, wordless wail that caught the wind and spread out across the sky. Birds rose from the trees around her, frightened by the sound. In the river, agitated fish jumped and churned against the water's surface.

The Tall Woman looked around. Everyone else had also paused to listen. The whole village was frozen by the pain in the music.

The Tall Woman said nothing. The Drummer and his native lover had earned this moment, this last comment on what they'd lost. A final release of their mutual pain would let them both move on, she thought.

Until the next day. When they blended their songs again, sending ripples of loss, loneliness, and aching pain across the valley.

And the next.

Finally, after many days, the Drummer returned from one of his climbs to find his entire tribe waiting for him at the village well.

"This has to stop," the Tall Woman said. The others murmured their assent.

He looked around at their grim faces. "What?"

"Your drumming, and her singing. You're depressing us all."

The Drummer looked more closely. Many of them had eyes red from crying. "Pull the other one," he said, but there was no humor in their faces.

" 'Tis no mockery. Lad, you've both made your point. The Messenger's on his way to their village to arrange a meeting."

It took the Drummer a moment to register this. "Wait . . . he's what?"

"Arranging a meeting between the Ta-Mihzo and us."

"Does the Man in the Rock House know about this?"

"The meeting was his idea."

# 22

The representatives of the two tribes met on a small island in the middle of the river, just after sunset. Treeless and flat, it was perfect for an intimate meeting, and the river's width and noise ensured privacy. A circle of torches provided illumination; on opposite banks, the newcomers and the Ta-Mihzo waited and watched.

Everyone assumed the Man in the Rock House would speak for his people, but he never emerged from his cave. The Tall Woman was forced to take his place, and now stood opposite Kesak, clad in the elaborate ceremonial attire that indicated his importance. The Tall Woman likewise wore a long fur cloak, the closest thing to a garment of status that her people had yet created.

Dahni stood beside her father, covered in the body paint that marked her as a leader of the next generation. The Drummer, standing beside the Tall Woman, was dressed no differently than the last time she'd seen him, and carried his drum before him, ready to play at a moment's notice. They were ostensibly there to translate for their representatives, but all they could do was stare at each other, aching for an end to the ritual so that they could finally touch each other again.

"Thank you for agreeing to this meeting," the Tall Woman said. The Drummer translated the words into the Ta-Mihzo language.

"Our children are the reason for this," Kesak said. "They suffer for our cowardice." Dahni repeated his words in the Drummer's language.

The Tall Woman laughed. "The Drummer is not my child. I sit here for our leader, who is in seclusion. I have his authority to make decisions, and to hopefully build a bridge where there has been only a wall. Or in this case, a river."

Kesak's expression after the Drummer translated showed that he was impressed with her eloquence. "Then we should be able to settle this peacefully for us both."

"I agree," the Tall Woman said.

"And as a symbol of this," Kesak said, "I present one of your own. He was discovered on the verge of death by my daughter, and healed by our medicine woman."

The Stranger stepped out of the shadows behind the torches. "Hello," he said to the Tall Woman. " 'Tis wonderful to see you again."

"It's you," the Tall Woman said, her voice trembling with emotion. To Kesak she added, "Thank you."

Kesak turned to his daughter. "You and your young man should perhaps try more . . . singing. Something happy now."

Dahni, with tears of joy in her eyes, looked at the Drummer. He nodded and picked up his drum.

And then a new voice roared, *"NO!"*

Before anyone could react, before either side even realized he was there in their midst, the Man in the Rock House suddenly struck with a pair of stone-tipped knives. He plunged one into Dahni's chest, and slit the Drummer's throat with the other.

"I won't let this happen!" the Man in the Rock House said, so loud that his voice seemed to roll around the valley. "We are not of this land, and we will not mix with its people!"

Kesak held his daughter as she died, the knife imbedded in her chest, her final sound a sigh. The Drummer stumbled past the Man in the Rock House and dropped to his knees, the last of his blood pulsing onto Dahni's face as he tried and failed to give her a final kiss. He fell at Kesak's feet, dead.

Kesak stared at his daughter's fur-clad slayer. How had he even gotten to the island without anyone noticing? Had he dropped out of the sky?

The crowds on both sides of the river stood immobile with shock, fear, and horror.

Then the Tall Woman wrenched the knife that killed the Drummer away from the Man in the Rock House and put it to his throat. "You *monster*!" she roared, right in his face. "You think you can rule us here the way you did in the Queen's forest?"

"I am your leader!" the Man from the Rock House shouted back.

"No more!" she said, and threw the knife into the river. "We've indulged your pitiful ego long enough! You're no different than we are here!"

She turned to Kesak, who sat on the ground holding Dahni's corpse. "He has killed my daughter," Kesak said flatly. "My child is dead."

Although there was no one to translate, the Tall Woman had no problem understanding him. Tears in her eyes, she turned to her people on the bank. "From this point on," she announced, "I am leader. Those who wish to follow me may do so. Those who still care to follow this traitorous, murderous pig may also do so. But he no longer has any authority over me."

She turned to say more to the Man in the Rock House, but he was gone.

The Stranger stepped around Kesak and Dahni. "I think we've done enough damage here," he said quietly to the Tall Woman.

"I agree," she said. "Bring the Drummer back to our village. Let us leave these people to attend to their dead in their way."

The Stranger wanted to comfort Kesak; Dahni had been his savior, and his friend. But he knew that all her father now wanted was to never see any of them again.

Soon after that day, Kesak led the Ta-Mihzo out of the valley, never to return. Many of his tribe counseled war, but he saw no point; it would not bring back his daughter. In time, the Ta-Mihzo died off, leaving no surviving mark on time and no one but their usurpers to even remember them.

As the Tall Woman had proclaimed, the tribe of the newcomers split that night. Her people retained the village, and those who followed the Man in the Rock House spread into the forest below his cave. Upon the Tall Woman's death in childbirth, it was discovered that she'd passed on her life's experience to her daughter, something that continued in her line, amassing more and more knowledge with each generation.

As the eons passed, the mountains wore down to smooth, rounded slopes, the river disappeared underground, and both groups of exiles learned to avoid the world as it changed around them. Their memories returned, a mixed blessing as they now remembered the paradise where they'd once lived. They discovered that they *could* leave the valley, as long as they truly intended to return. They were able to choose names, and some took wives or husbands from the later people who came into the mountains seeking game, fur, or minerals.

But the Stranger kept one secret to himself: the cave where

he'd been found. The Queen's magic hid it from the rest of their people, but not him. And he, and the family that descended from him, watched over it from then on, waiting for the day that the Queen might let them return.

# II

# SADIEVILLE

## (ONCE AGAIN)

# 23

"And the Stranger," Sophronie concluded, "was my ancestor." She did a little half-pirouette, her ponytail swinging behind her head. "And that's my secret."

"Is that all true?"

"Who's to say? It's the story I've heard all my life, passed down through the generations. My family's great secret. And this cave? We've kept it from the Man in the Rock House ever since. He hasn't got a clue, and neither do his people."

"He's still around?" he asked dubiously.

"Oh, yes. Go over to Needsville, look on the porch of the post office. You'll find him there picking his banjo, thinking of ways to make his people more miserable."

"How will I know it's him?"

She held up her hand and wiggled her fingers. "He's still got six of these on each hand."

"But if it's such an important secret for your family," he pressed, "why are you telling it to me?"

She gave him a look that he couldn't decipher. It mixed amusement, sadness, and a sense of something—antiquity?—into an enigmatic little smile. "You ever known something you wasn't supposed to share, and felt like you were about to bust if you didn't tell somebody?"

"Sure."

"Well, imagine that about a hundred times stronger, and you'll know how I felt."

"How do you feel now?"

She shivered with delight. "Like a big ol' weight just came off for a little while."

"Will you get in trouble?"

"Only if you tell somebody. Are you going to?"

"Who would I tell?"

"That nice boy Ben. Or your handsome friend Richard."

He put his right hand over his heart. "I swear. I won't tell a soul." He looked up at the cave, now a mysterious portal to another world if her story was true. "Have you ever tried to go back through?"

She shook her head. "A few of my ancestors tried over the years. They came back all messed up."

"Messed up how?"

She put her finger to her temple and twirled it, the universal symbol for insanity.

He walked up to it and peered through the medieval-looking spikes of the hawthorns. Then gave her a sly smile. "Want to try now?"

"Can't. I'm pretty limber, but I can't get past all them thorns."

He carefully reached through and grasped one of the bushes right at the ground. He grunted with effort, and then the hawthorn came loose. He tossed it aside and pulled another one out of the shallow dirt, leaving a passage large enough for a man to use. "Come on," he said.

She held back. "I don't know. Can you check first?"

"Should I call for the Queen?"

"I wouldn't," she said seriously.

He went a few feet into the dark opening, then stopped. He

closed his eyes to listen. At first he heard only the faint sounds from outside and the soft wind through cracks in the mountain.

But then he heard *it*.

The closest description he could think of was the music that might come from fragile, delicate glass instruments. But there was also a woman's voice, pure and high. He'd been to symphonies and minstrel shows, heard bar pianos and chamber music concerts, and none of them approached the beauty of this faint music.

"You hear anything?" Sophronie called.

"Oh, yes," he said, eyes still closed.

"That's the same thing Dahni heard all them years ago."

"It's beautiful." Without a conscious choice, he moved toward it, his feet sliding in the dirt and sand. "I'm going to go a little farther, okay?"

"Yeah," she said. If he hadn't been so distracted, he might have caught the worry and reluctance in her voice.

He felt along the rock walls as he moved. Ahead, the passage turned slightly, and once around it, he would be out of sight of the cave mouth.

"Sean!" Sophronie called, with an urgency that snapped him from his reverie. "That's enough, I reckon you better come on out of there."

He reluctantly rejoined her outside the cave. She took his hand and pulled him farther away, as if afraid the vengeful queen of her story might burst forth.

"That was fascinating," he said. "What was that noise?"

She took this so much more seriously than he did. "I told you already. It's what Dahni heard. The song of the Queen, a warning to all our people to go no farther."

"Right," he said patiently.

She seemed to make up her mind about something. "Look, Sean, now that I've told you that story, I need to show you something. It's so you'll know that the story is true, and what the Tufa really are, what *I* really am."

He recalled the viperish reverend's derogatory comments about the Tufa's racial origins. "I don't care, Sophronie."

"That's because you don't *know*. Close your eyes and don't open them until I tell you."

He did as she asked.

"Open your eyes now, Sean," Sophronie said.

He did. And couldn't move. He wasn't even sure he could breathe.

Sophronie now wore loose, shimmery garments that showed more than they covered. She was perfect, every curve and contour exquisite, her skin now pale, her black hair loose and wild.

But that wasn't all. Those qualities were minor compared to what overwhelmed him.

She had *wings*. Wide, diaphanous, sparkling wings.

"This is me," she said, her voice no longer that of a young, illiterate mountain girl. Something sang in it, a musical quality that permeated even these mundane words. Then she began to *truly* sing:

> *Oh, time makes men grow sad*
> *And rivers change their ways,*
> *But the night wind and her riders*
> *Will ever stay the same . . .*

If this was the enchantment she'd mentioned, then he would gladly fall under its spell. She danced in the air now, turning with a grace that he'd never imagined possible.

He reached a tentative hand toward her. "Is this the real you?" he asked softly, afraid to disturb the moment.

"I'm real no matter what," she said.

"I love you," he blurted, the words springing forth before he even realized he'd formed them.

Still touching his fingertips, still hovering in the air, she laughed. But it wasn't malicious; it was a sound of delight, of happiness. "You hardly know me," she said.

"What else do I need to know?" he said, and stepped closer.

She laughed again, pulled her hand away, and twirled in the air. The breeze from her wings blew against Sean's face, reminding him again that he wasn't dreaming, or hallucinating, or drunk.

He laughed as well, happier than he'd ever been, happier than he ever thought he *could* be.

Through the nearby undergrowth, hidden behind trees and a pile of rocks that used to be a boulder until a winter freeze shattered it, Ben Hubbard held his camera steady. The mechanism was so quiet that its mechanical clicking was lost in the wind.

He'd followed Sophronie and Sean on a whim, a little jealous of Sean's effortless success with the girl. He wanted to shoot some candid film of them so that when Sean watched it back in Fort Lee, he'd jump a mile. But now . . .

*Wings,* he thought. *She's got wings. She's a—*

And then the word sprang to his mind with no prompting. His younger sister had once owned paper dolls that looked like Sophronie did now, little sprites that danced around flowers just as the real girl now danced around trees and boulders.

He thought of his sister, now working in a silk garment factory in Paterson. What would she say if he told her that he'd seen an actual, real live *fairy* in the mountains of Tennessee?

Ben could only think of one thing to say. He mouthed it, afraid to voice it even as a whisper, lest he disturb the magic of what he was seeing.

*Wow.*

It was late afternoon before Sean and Sophronie returned to Sadieville. The streets were filled with people, but they barely registered on Sean. He had eyes only for the magical girl beside him, now back in her simple farm dress and hair bow.

As they approached the boardinghouse, Sophronie slipped her hand from his. When he looked at her, she said quietly, "It's better for everybody if we don't make it too obvious."

"I'm not ashamed of you," he said.

"And I'm not ashamed of you," she said with a knowing, mischievous wink. "It's just better."

He couldn't argue. About anything. He now believed all the warnings about being under a spell, because he was totally enchanted. From the first touch, the first kiss, he'd been entirely hers. He no longer cared about his career, his family, or anything except being with Sophronie.

As they passed the half-finished church, Reverend Nashe emerged and watched them from the steps. He said nothing, but the disgust and hate on his face was plain. Sean ignored him, but Sophronie suddenly walked faster until they reached the boardinghouse.

"I better get going," Sophronie said, suddenly serious. "I'd like to get home before full dark."

"Well, just be here tomorrow morning by eight," Sean said. "We've got a long day of filming ahead of us."

"I will."

He considered kissing her. He didn't care who saw him, but realized it might make things awkward for her. She squeezed his hand, then turned and walked away. She strolled off down the street, glancing back at him until she was out of sight.

# 24

Sean floated above the trees, held in Sophronie's slender but amazingly strong arms, kissing her with all the gentleness and love he could muster. The soft gust from each slow flap of her wings caressed his face, and the tinkling glass music from the cave filled his ears. All the cares, ambitions, and fears that defined his life were gone, replaced with an overwhelming warmth and peace. If this was love, then he'd never even come close to experiencing it before.

"Sean! *Sean!*"

Sean opened his eyes. Sunlight streamed through the window, the shafts illuminating the dust in the air. "Yeah," he muttered. "I'm awake."

Ben leaned over him. "Jesus, man, I thought you were dead. I couldn't wake you up."

"I'm awake," he repeated, annoyed.

"You better come downstairs."

"Are the actors here?"

"Yeah, but . . ."

"What?"

"It's better if you just come down."

Sean dressed quickly and combed his hair into place.

Ben nervously paced behind him. Sean asked, "What's wrong with you?"

"Just come down," Ben repeated, pushing him toward the door. They descended the stairs to the parlor.

Two men waited at the bottom of the stairs: Sheriff Bowden and Reverend Nashe. Perhaps the snide minister thought his civic prominence would get him a spot in front of the camera. But the sheriff hadn't brought his banjo.

"Gentlemen," Sean said. "Good morning."

"Good morning, Mr. Lee," Bowden said. He wouldn't meet Sean's eyes.

"Is there a problem?" Sean asked.

"I'm afraid so," the sheriff said. "Can we step outside?"

Sean and Ben followed the lawman and minister out onto the porch. It was a cool morning, and mist filled the street, creating a sense of loneliness and isolation. Bowden said, "I understand you were with Miss Sophronie Conlin yesterday?"

"That's right," Sean said guardedly. "I visited her family's home up in the hills, and she helped me scout out filming locations. Why?"

The sheriff finally looked directly at him. "I'm sorry to have to tell you, but Miss Conlin is dead."

Sean felt as if the world withdrew, leaving him alone in a desperate void. "What?"

"We found her body hanging from a tree down by the Reverend's church. She'd been lynched." He cut his eyes at the Reverend Nashe. "Most likely it was the White Caps. They never took too kindly to the Tufa, and I guess they caught her in town after dark."

Sean stood completely still, then without a word turned and bolted out the door and down the street toward the church.

———

It was her.

That had been his hope the whole way to the church. Another girl, slender and dark-haired, might have been mistaken for Sophronie. That would be tragic as well, but it would be someone else's tragedy.

But there was no doubt. Even with her purple, distorted face, bulging eyes, and swollen tongue, he could tell instantly that it was her. She wore the same dress, and her bare feet, stained black from a lifetime of running around the mountains, still swung in the slight breeze three feet off the ground. The rope around her neck went over a high branch and had been tied around the trunk.

Already, people gathered around the tree. Many pointed at him and whispered.

Sean's throat constricted, and he concentrated on breathing through his nose. He choked out, "The White Caps did this?"

"Men with white masks," Bowden said sheepishly. "That's all anybody saw."

"Men of conscience," Nashe said, "sometimes have to protect themselves from the unjust." His wife had joined him, and they both looked smug and triumphant.

Sean ignored the minister. "If you know who they are," he said to Bowden, "why don't you arrest them?"

"Ain't got no proof, and no witnesses," he said sadly.

Sean could only nod. He understood organized crime; it had begun to reach its tendrils into the motion picture industry, requiring kickbacks from exhibitors and extra consideration from film companies.

Bowden stepped close to Sean, and said quietly, "For what it's worth, I'm real sorry. She was a real sweet girl."

Basemath Nashe pushed her way through the crowd and stared up at Sophronie's corpse. She covered her mouth with her hands, and tears sprang to her eyes. She let out a single hard, harsh sob.

"Basemath," Reverend Nashe snapped. "Behave yourself."

She turned and looked at her father. "You did this," she said coldly. "Just as you did in Virginia. And Georgia before that."

"Basemath!" Mrs. Nashe said in a shrill, biting cry. "To your room this instant! On your knees and pray for forgiveness!"

Basemath walked right up to her father and looked him in the eye. Sean had never seen such cold, pure hatred. "You're a liar and a murderer, Father."

Nashe's face turned red with rage. "You will not—"

He got no farther. Basemath snatched Bowden's revolver from its holster and shot her father point-blank in the face. Then she shot her mother right in her twisted, venom-spewing mouth. She turned back to her father and fired three more times into his dead body.

The gunshots echoed in the morning mist. No one moved.

Then, before anyone could stop her, she put the gun to her temple and put the final bullet through her own brain.

At last, someone in the crowd screamed. People ran in all directions, leaving Sean and the sheriff alone among the dead bodies.

"Cut her down," Sean said quietly.

Bowden looked at him, then at the bodies on the ground, then back at him. He was totally unprepared for this. He retrieved his gun from Basemath's dead hand and said, "What?"

*"Cut her down!"* Sean screamed, louder than he'd ever screamed anything before in his life.

Bowden blinked, and the glassy look left his eyes. He produced a large pocket knife and cut the rope where it was tied. Sean caught Sophronie as she fell; she weighed hardly anything in his arms. He pulled her close; her body was stiff and cold.

Tucker Carding appeared at his side. He looked down at Sophronie for a long moment. "You poor little thing," he said to her, and lightly stroked her hair. "This is all my fault. You didn't deserve this."

"Come with me to the undertaker's," the sheriff said quietly. "We'll lay her out there."

"What about them?" Sean asked, nodding at the Nashes.

"They can rot right there for all I care."

"Who'll tell her family?" Sean croaked out around the sob stuck in his throat.

"I will," Tucker said.

"No, I'll head out there and do it this afternoon," Bowden said. "I've got a whole speech for this sort of thing."

"No, I'll do it," Sean said. "They deserve to hear it from someone . . ." He trailed off before he said aloud, *someone who loved their daughter as much as they did.* Because he couldn't explain how that was possible, after knowing her for slightly more than one day. But he also knew it was true.

Later that day, after Sophronie had been placed in the best coffin Sean's money could buy, he returned to her family's cabin. As he approached, he knew something was wrong. No smoke rose from the chimney, and the front door stood open. All the little homey touches, like rocking chairs, butter churns, and moonshine jugs that had been on the porch were gone. A look inside confirmed it: the Conlins weren't there.

That did it. He sat down on the porch and cried, his loneliness piercing the silence of the forest with his sobs. He put his head in his hands and expressed grief greater than he ever knew he could feel.

He didn't know how long he sat there, but he looked up when a sharp male voice said, "Sean. *Sean.*"

Tucker Carding stood in the yard. He was dressed in country work clothes instead of his dapper city duds, which emphasized how much he resembled the Conlins. Sean was amazed he hadn't noticed it before.

"What are you doing here?" Sean choked out.

Tucker sat beside him and put a hand on his shoulder. Gently he said, "You know, I bet you're even scaring the catamounts away with all that blubbering. And it won't bring Sophronie back."

"What's a catamount?" Sean choked out.

"You'll know when one grabs ahold of you."

"I don't think I'd care."

"Do you care about your friends, Ben and Richard?"

The warning in his words broke through Sean's agony. "What about them?"

"Y'all need to leave. Immediately. Tonight."

Sean took out a handkerchief and blew his nose. His head pounded. "Are you one of the White Caps, then?"

Tucker smiled. "Me? No. I'm just giving you a friendly warning. Has nothing to do with the White Caps."

"Back in town, you said this was all your fault. What did you mean by that?"

"I gave you the map that led you to Sophronie. And I sent her out to meet you yesterday."

"Did you plan for us to . . . ?"

"Ah, what does it matter now? Forget about Sophronie and the cave and what you think you know. And get out of here *tonight*. Or you'll never leave."


It was 10 P.M. before the last train of the day, the 9:15, belatedly pulled out of Sadieville station, slowly chuffing itself up to speed. Ben sat beside Sean, wanting to comfort his friend but afraid to try.

Richard sat across from them, impeccably dressed as always, watching the town move past the windows. "As the lady said, 'I make so many beginnings there never will be an end.'"

"What lady?" Ben asked.

"Louisa May Alcott in *Little Women*. I had the misfortune of playing Fritz in a rather dire stage adaptation."

Sean watched the lights of the town slide by, replaced by the flickering of trees as they passed through illumination shining from the train's windows. At last he turned to Ben. "You'll have to excuse me," he said numbly. "I have to visit the hopper."

Ben looked out the window; the town was completely gone now, left behind them as they picked up speed and headed north. And the only film they'd shot was hidden in his bag, because he never wanted Sean to find out about it.

A tremble went through the car, noticeably different from the rhythm of their passage. Richard looked up. It continued for a couple of minutes, then faded.

"What was that?" Ben asked.

At that moment a porter hurried by, and Richard grabbed him. "Excuse me, but what was that shaking?"

"I don't know, sir," the man said. "It wasn't anything to do with the locomotive, I'm certain. I know all the ways that the engine shakes."

Additional jolts hit the train, shaking it from side to side.

"Still not the engine?" Richard asked the porter.

The man was obviously scared. "No, sir. That's something coming through the tracks."

A third series of jolts rattled the train, but these were much less intense. Whatever it was, they seemed to have outrun it.


In the lavatory, Sean pushed open the small window. Unbidden, unwanted, Sophronie's voice came back to him from that day at her son's grave:

*Lost my baby, lost my son*
*Lost my only, my only one*
*Can't go back, don't have the will*
*Can never go back to my Sadieville.*

He took off his suspenders, tied one loose end around the lavatory's door handle, and the other around his own neck. He cinched both as tightly as he could. Then, already choking for breath, he squeezed through the window and let himself fall.

It was an hour before his friends realized he was missing, and nobody found his body, beaten to a pulp against the train car, until the next stop for coal and water.

# I

# THIS IS REAL
## (ONCE AGAIN)

## 25

*Can't go back, don't have the will,*
*Can never go back to my Sadieville.*

Azure's voice faded, and there was total silence. Then the normal sounds of the forest resumed, like a volume knob slowly turned up. The night winds returned as well, rustling the top branches high above.

The First Daughters, though, remained silent. The song had done its job, and the spell that hid the story of Sadieville and the tragedy of Sophronie Conlin was gone. The tale opened like a blossom in the First Daughters' minds, producing memories that slotted into mental files alongside the things they'd always known. It didn't happen all at once, or in the same way for everyone, so they looked at each other as much as they could in the dark, confused and overwhelmed.

Then, when it was all sorted, the same things ran through each of their minds:

Sadieville, a town they destroyed, and then decided to forget;

Tucker Carding, who'd been there and was here, yet whom they all only vaguely seemed to recall;

And finally, *the cave.* The passage back to . . .

None of them dared complete that thought.

At last Mandalay said, "Thank you, Azure." Her voice was shaky with the new knowledge. It might have been the first time the girl hadn't known part of Tufa history.

"That'd jerk a tear from a glass eye," Carnelia Rector said with a sniffle. Someone handed her a tissue.

"The song carries the magic," Azure said. "So only those who hear it will know what we now know."

"And if we sing it for someone else?" Bronwyn Chess asked.

"Then they'll know, too." She took a bottle of water from her bag and gratefully drank it.

"So we all agreed to forget all this?" Bronwyn's mother, Chloe Hyatt, said in disbelief.

"We did," Bliss said. She remembered it now, as plainly as anything: the meeting of the First Daughters after the Sadieville disaster, Viney Conlin tearfully announcing Sophronie's murder, the decision, the agreement of the Silent Sons, and the mass singing on Emania Knob that locked all the memories away.

And spearheading it all had been Tucker Carding. Hadn't he? Bliss sorted through the images bursting through her mind, looking for the reason. Tucker had always been there, always been involved . . . right?

"There's one more thing," Azure said. "Those students I mentioned, who are here to find Sadieville? Tucker Carding brought them to me, just like he made sure Sean Lee and Sophronie got together."

"I know Tucker," Adria Feldman said uncertainly. "I mean . . . I think I do. Right?"

"We all know Tucker," Mandalay said. "We know him when he's here, and we forget him when he leaves. That's how he's managed to slip around without anyone noticing."

"Leaves?" Berra Banks asked. "Where does he go?"

Mandalay held up her hands for silence. She stepped into the middle of the circle. "There's one question we don't have the answer to, and it's more important than I think any of you realize. *Why* did Tucker Carding want Sean to meet Sophronie in the woods?"

The women all looked at each other blankly. "Well, I mean . . ." someone started, then trailed off.

"Sean," Bronwyn said slowly, "was the canary."

"Right," Mandalay said. "Sophronie was supposed to get Sean to go through the passage. If he got through, then perhaps the Tufa could, as well. If he didn't, he was just a stray from this world, and nothing for the Queen to get upset about."

"But love got in the way," Chloe said sadly.

"As it tends to do," Mandalay agreed.

"That film's been around for a century," Chloe said. "Why did it turn up now?"

"Who brought your daughter back from the war?" Mandalay said, turning as she spoke so that she faced them all. "Who sent a vision of Rockhouse Hicks to Rob Quillen? Who let Bo-Kate Wisby find her way home? Who let Ray Parrish live long enough to complete *Chapel of Ease*? Who brought Duncan Gowen to justice?"

In the silence that followed, the trees around them shivered as a gust of wind tore through them.

"The night winds," Chloe said.

"But those poor kids," Azure said. "Is it fair for them to be used like this?"

"I don't know about 'fair,'" Mandalay said, "but maybe that's why the night winds sent two of them this time. So Tufa enchantments wouldn't get in the way."

"So what do we do?" someone asked. "Sit and wait?"

"For now, we spread the song. Let everyone know. And then, yes. We sit and wait."

# 26

Junior Damo's laugh filled the air. As always, it was thick with contempt, mockery, and venom.

He sat beside Mandalay in a rocking chair on the post office porch. This was where they held court, so that people who had problems or needed disagreements adjudicated could find them. This morning, the town was deserted, and no one came to them for wisdom. Which meant they could discuss the events of the previous night's meeting of the First Daughters.

Mandalay sighed as Junior continued to roar. She did that a lot around Junior, her opposite number who led the other half of the Tufa community. If the Tufa had an overall leader, Mandalay was it; but Junior had taken the place of Rockhouse Hicks, the six-fingered former leader who'd died (hopefully) three years earlier. While alive, he had been the undisputed leader; now neither of his successors had quite managed to fill the power vacuum.

"Are you finished?" Mandalay asked when he finally stopped long enough to draw a breath.

He wiped his eyes. "Just about."

"Good. Because this ain't funny."

"Oh, it's pretty fucking hysterical," Junior said. "You First Daughters plumb outsmarted yourselves, didn't you? Singing a huge part of our history away, and now having it come back to bite you in the ass."

"Your people were involved, too. Rockhouse agreed with us."

"I bet he did, but you know what? I bet that was because he knew someday it'd all end up like this. And he knew how damn funny it would be. Too bad the old SOB missed it."

*If* he missed it, Junior added, but only to himself. In the three years he'd been in charge of his half of the Tufa, in quiet moments when no one else was around, he swore he heard the voice of old Rockhouse whispering hints and instructions, as if he'd never left and Junior was just his puppet. Occasionally he even glimpsed shadowy forms that resembled Rockhouse, but they always vanished when he looked directly at them.

"The song is spreading," Mandalay said. "Your people are going to want answers. And more importantly, leadership."

"Where the hell am I supposed to lead them? Sadieville is fucking gone."

"The cave isn't."

He snorted. "The cave? Some crazy girl's story? I thought the Queen *threw* Rockhouse here, and he landed on Eskatole Mountain, or Emania Knob, depending on who you believe. So now you're saying he was sent crawling through a hole?"

"Stories change over time."

He looked directly into her eyes and said snidely, "But weren't you there? Ain't you the one who knows everything from all the way back?"

She'd never wanted to punch him so much. "I *know*, Junior, that some important decisions are coming up, and like it or not, your people will expect you to have both knowledge of it and an opinion about it."

"And if I tell them it's just nonsense, just a folk tale like Lorena's ghost up in Half Pea Hollow?"

"Then you better pray you're right. Because if you're wrong, your people may lynch you."

Then the two leaders of the Tufa both folded their arms and turned away from each other, like an old married couple at the end of a another pointless argument.

In the parsonage beside the Triple Springs Methodist Church in Unicorn, just past the Cloud County line, Bronwyn Chess and her minister husband, Craig, looked down at their sleeping daughter Kell on her first night in her new toddler bed.

Craig bent down and kissed her on the forehead, tucked the blanket under her chin, and watched her fingers, no longer tiny but still small, delicate, and beautiful, curl around the edge.

"She's got your chin," Bronwyn whispered.

"That's a terrible thing to say," he teased. "And she's got your eyes."

"Hope her personality has both of our good qualities, too."

He put an arm around his wife. "If she's got your courage and nerve, it won't matter what she got from me. She'll do just fine."

Bronwyn looked up at him. That first time she'd seen him, five years earlier when he'd come by her parents' house in his official capacity to see if she needed anything as she recovered from her war injuries, she'd known he was the one. It helped that he was handsome, and funny, and good-hearted almost beyond belief.

She had broken with the First Daughters over Craig. Even her mother wanted her to choose a Tufa husband, someone who would help keep the Tufa bloodlines pure. They'd tried to fix her up with Terry-Joe Gitterman, younger brother of her old boyfriend Dwayne, but he'd been only seventeen at the time. So she'd cut a deal, one that kept the Tufa lines true, yet let her make her future with Craig.

Even now, people whispered that Craig wasn't actually Kell's father. The little girl was too true, too magical, to be his. But Bronwyn knew that, in all the ways that counted, Kell *was* his. Kell was *theirs*.

And now she had to threaten all that certainty.

They carefully closed the bedroom door, then walked into the kitchen, her arm around his waist. She got a beer from the refrigerator and said, "Want one?"

"No, thanks."

Bronwyn opened her bottle. *Deep breath,* she thought. "I need to talk to you."

"About the First Daughters meeting?" Craig was no Tufa, but he knew a lot about them, including what they really were, and how highly Bronwyn ranked in their hierarchy. Being married to a First Daughter was, it turned out, a lot like being married to a minister. Both had responsibilities to their communities that took them away from home, often with no warning.

"Yeah. We found out something . . . amazing."

"Which is?"

"There may be a way for the Tufa to return home. To where we're really from."

"I thought you were all banished."

"We were. But that doesn't mean we still are."

"Wouldn't you have been . . . I don't know, notified somehow?"

"Beats me. I may be a pureblood Tufa, but I was born here. All I know about where we came from are the stories I've heard."

"Who told you those stories?"

"Mandalay and Bliss. They both remember it firsthand."

Craig nodded. After knowing them for years, he had no difficulty believing both Bliss and Mandalay were, at some level, old enough to recall things from prehistory. But he couldn't stop the way his stomach both tightened and dropped, leaving a huge hole inside him. He finally asked the only question that mattered.

"If it's true, will you go?"

Bronwyn took a long drink from her beer. "I don't know, Craig, I honestly don't. It's such a huge possibility." She burped lightly. "I've heard stories about it all my life: how beautiful it was, how beautiful *we* were when we were there. How much magic filled the air. How could I *not* want to go?"

He nodded toward their daughter's room. "And us? Do we get to come?"

"I honestly don't know that, either. Kell probably can, since she's got so much true Tufa in her. But mortals who wander in don't usually fare so well. If the stories are true," she added.

"I know some of those stories," Craig said. And he did; when he realized exactly what Bronwyn, and now his daughter, truly were, he'd read everything he could get about it. There were hundreds of stories telling how ordinary people often suffered if they so much as encountered the Good Folk; even the name "Good Folk" was a charm against their supposed indifferent malevolence. "If I go, is there any way you can protect me?"

She shrugged with the bottle. "Same answer."

He looked down at his own fingers on the tabletop. As a minister, he was used to counseling people facing tough decisions, and he tried to see Bronwyn that way, as just another parishioner needing his objectivity. "Bronwyn, we have a life here. We have a family. Whatever waits back there, it can't be *that*. So I guess the question is, which is more important to you?"

She didn't answer, but looked down at her own fingers wrapped around the beer bottle. The silence grew between them until it seemed to thicken and become a barrier separating her from her husband and daughter, possibly for good.

————

Deep in Cloud County, Bronwyn's parents, Deacon and Chloe Hyatt, also sat across their kitchen table from each other. They had no drinks, but both wished they had. Chloe had just sung "Sadieville" for Deacon, and now the heavy silence between them hummed with tension.

Both Deacon and Chloe were full-blood Tufas. Because of the Tufas' malleable relationship with time, they remembered those first years in this new world. Their memories of before that, of the glories of the Tufas' original home, were vague and indistinct, but overwhelmingly positive. So the thought of returning should have elated them. Instead they felt morose and uncertain.

"Everything we've worked for," Deacon said at last. "We'd have to leave all that. The house, the farm, the land. Aiden, unless he wanted to go. And Kell. *Our* Kell."

"Their" Kell was their oldest child and elder son, the namesake of Bronwyn's daughter, who'd died in a knife fight with a Tufa from the other group. He was buried on their land, and they visited the site regularly. Blood-soaked ground bound the Tufa to a spot more thoroughly than any charm, and the thought of leaving him behind was enough to have them both tied up in knots.

"Did you talk to Bronwyn?" Deacon added.

Chloe shook her head. "She left before I could. I'm sure she's talking it all over with Craig right now."

"He won't take it well."

"How do you know?"

"Because if you told me you might be leaving without me, and taking my kids with you to boot, I wouldn't take it well, either."

"At least we have Aiden," Chloe said. "He'll come with us."

"Will he? He's a teenager now. He might decide to stay. This is the only world he's ever known."

"He's also still a boy. We can make him."

"But we won't."

Chloe smiled sadly. "No, we won't."


In the dark hallway that led to their bedrooms, Aiden listened to his parents discuss the latest news. He'd overheard the Sadieville song, and felt both elated and terrified that they'd decided to leave such a monumental decision about his future up to him.

He went into his room and picked up his banjo. It had belonged to his big brother Kell, and he'd begun messing with it only in the last year, as he felt the true weight of Kell's absence.

Carrying it, he slipped out through the bedroom window, tangling loudly in the yew bush just beneath it. As he skulked across the yard, he saw his parents through the screen door, seated at the table and looking at each other intently. He didn't really think he'd slipped away unnoticed; but then, his misbehavior was a minor thing compared to what he'd overheard.

When he was out of sight, he used the flashlight app on his phone to find his way through the woods to the Hyatt family plot, a little cemetery deep in the forest, accessible only to those with either permission or right by blood. Any others simply wouldn't be able to find it, just like the hidden cave.

Kell's tombstone shone new in the faint starlight, its white marble a stark contrast to its faded, worn, and moss-covered neighbors. The old saying was that you could kill a Tufa but they didn't just die, so there were long gaps in the dates between the stones. Anyone trying to put a family tree together would be completely frustrated.

He began to slowly play the Cook Creek Girls' "White Oak Mountain," not singing but just expressing the melody as softly and cleanly as he could. And as he did, he pondered.

He thought about his friends. Many were Tufa, not purebloods like him but with enough of it that they could make the journey with no consequences. But some just couldn't, and would have to stay behind no matter what their friends did. They would have to face, and live with, the fact that they were simply not good enough, not *Tufa* enough, to make the trip to what was essentially their promised land.

And as always when he played the banjo, he thought about his big brother Kell, and wondered what he'd have to say about all this. He missed his brother's presence, that male energy that was in between his own adolescent angst and his father's rock-solid taciturnity. Kell was supposed to be here now, to help guide him through everything that was about to happen.

Of course, Kell's absence wasn't his own fault. He'd been stabbed by Dwayne Gitterman, his sister Bronwyn's old boyfriend. And Bronwyn had exacted revenge for herself, her family, and the Tufa. Bronwyn had even named her daughter Kell, in honor of her big brother. So in most ways, the case was closed. Everything had been settled years ago.

But not in Aiden's heart.

He didn't even feel the tears start, and didn't notice them until they reached his lips. His playing began to falter as sobs, locked away for fear they might embarrass him, began to break free.

He listened through the music, hoping to hear his brother's voice, the one that had teased and tormented and reassured him as a child. But there was only the melody, now a stuttering thing that sounded as raw and ragged as he felt. At last he stopped, sat down on the ground, and cried harder than he had since he was a small boy.

Then he felt fingers tousle his hair.

He looked up, but no one was around. He jumped to his feet.

He recognized that touch. It was the aggravating, infuriating way Kell used to condescend to him when Aiden was being annoying. He'd grown to hate that touch, and everything it implied about being the baby brother.

The winds sighed in the trees above him, and a gentler breeze blew against his face. Had it been merely the wind?

It didn't matter. Whatever its source, the brief touch had somehow calmed his heart. He breathed normally, and wiped his nose with his forearm.

He began to play again, the same song but in a more up-beat, positive way. The winds grew louder overhead, as if in approval.

# 27

Bliss Overbay cried out, uninhibited and wild with abandon, arching her back as she straddled Jack Cates in their bed. He also finished a moment later, hands around her slender waist, pulling her down atop him to get as deep as possible. Then, with a mutual sigh of mingled satisfaction and exhaustion, they relaxed.

Without climbing off him, Bliss reached for the bottle of ice water on the bedside table. "Glad you were here when I got home," she gasped between drinks.

"Me, too," he said, pushing his sweaty hair from his eyes.

She chuckled and held the bottle to his lips. He drank a long swallow. Then, biting her lip lasciviously, she poured some water onto her breasts, shivering as it trickled down to pool between them.

He sat up and licked the trailing droplets. She quivered with delight.

Then he fell back with a chuckle. "Is this ever going to get boring and routine?"

She crawled off and stretched out beside him. Her hand rested on the skin below his navel. "Not if I have anything to say about it."

He slid his arm under her neck and pulled her close. "That must've been some meeting you went to tonight."

She laughed. "The meeting had nothing to do with it," she said, but of course that was a lie. The whole way home, all she could think about was that a time might come when Jack *wouldn't* be there, when she couldn't touch him or kiss him or take him in her mouth or feel him fill her. So when she got home and saw his work truck in her driveway, she'd jumped him before he could even say hello. He hadn't put up much of a fight.

"Well, whatever the reason, that was fantastic," he said. She marveled again at how such a strong, masculine, normally tac-iturn man opened up to her when they were alone; he was to-tally unafraid to show his emotions, and cared as much for her responses as she did for his. Could she really walk away from this?

"So," he said, "what *was* the meeting about?"

"Just Tufa stuff."

"Big Tufa stuff?"

*Oh, brother.* "Maybe."

He shifted to look into her eyes. "I get the sense that you want to tell me more."

"I do."

"But you can't?"

"Not . . . yet." Jack, like Bronwyn's husband, knew the truth about the Tufa, but unlike Craig Chess, he didn't understand how the society operated. Bliss knew that as a law enforcement officer, Jack needed to treat everyone the same, and if he knew more of their secrets, he'd leave himself open to favoritism. After all, how can you write a ticket for not having a fishing license to someone who could reveal their wings and fly away?

"You know I can keep a secret," he pointed out.

"I know you can, honey. But I'm still figuring out how I feel about it, and I need to do that before I share it."

"Okay. But I'm here when you're ready."

She rolled onto her side and kissed him. "I know you are."

"And I always will be," he said with the kind of certainty that only comes when you don't know all the details.

She kissed him again, then giggled. "Well, *that* was fast," she said, her hand dropping lower. "Especially for a guy your age."

"I'm inspired," he said, and rolled over on top of her.

Later, after Jack had fallen asleep, Bliss walked naked out the back door and down the stone path to the little dock that protruded into her small lake. The thing that lived in the water, sensing her presence, let its broad finless back breach the surface before sliding down into the blackness that was deeper than any non-Tufa could imagine. Overhead the moonless night was clear, showing the belt of the Milky Way across the sky. There was no night wind.

"Oh, man," she said quietly, pushing her sweat-matted hair out of her face. "What the hell do I *do*?"

She waited to see if anyone would come. Sometimes Mandalay dropped out of the sky, summoned by her majordomo's uncertainty about something. But on this windless night, there was nothing. Bliss was naked and alone.

She sat down at the end of the dock, careful to avoid splinters, and dangled her feet in the water. The thing that lived there slid under them, letting her feet slide along its smooth, scaleless back. She was the only one who knew of it, the one who'd given it a safe place and watched it grow there until it could live nowhere else.

If she left, what would become of it, trapped and alone? Would Jack come and feed it, or would he kill it for the common good, the way he occasionally had to kill bears who grew too accustomed to a human presence? Would he simply refuse to believe it existed?

She lay back on the dock and stared up at the sky. The stars of home were different, a cosmos as removed from this world as the surface of a distant planet. Yet, if Azure was right, they were still connected to it *through* this world. She knew the mountains around her and the mountains of their home had once been part of the same range, before the continents drifted apart; a tunnel through them, suffused with the Queen's magic, might still remain connected. There was no way to know except by finding it, and going through.

She remembered the day Radella, daughter of the Tall Woman, had been born, her mother dying on animal skins soaked with blood. It had begun a tradition that was as cruel as it was essential: Radella had in turn died giving birth to her first daughter, and so on up to the death of Mandalay's mother.

She recalled the way Radella grew up in their village, and the wonder they all felt when they realized she had not only her own memories, but that of her mother as well. And with each generation those memories grew, until now there was a fifteen-year-old girl who could remember when the mountains around them were as tall as the Alps. Yet each generation also brought its own personality, some eager for the responsibility and some far less so, adding emotional wisdom to accumulated history.

And now the latest, Mandalay, faced a bigger decision than her whole line of ancestors had faced since that day.

And Bliss herself? She'd slid through time, never growing older, never truly connecting with anyone because of her duty to protect, guide, and ultimately serve the next young woman in Radella's line. Her glamour kept her secret, kept any non-Tufa people from noticing that she never changed, that she'd been there from the beginning.

But she *had* changed. She loved Jack with a ferocity that only eons of self-denial could unleash. He was a simple man, really; not stupid by any means, but not eaten up with anxiety or self-doubt. And that didn't matter; he was hers, and she loved him, and she'd hang on to him as long as she could.

Unless, of course, she returned home with the other Tufa.

"Fuck," she said, drawing out the word, draping her arm across her eyes. "Fuck, fuck, fuck."

"Your fly's open," a new voice said.

Without getting up, Bliss twisted to look behind her. "Hey. What are you doing here?"

"Hey," Curnen Overbay said to her big sister. She wore a sundress, hiking boots, and a leather jacket, and looked like any trendy undergraduate. The fact that she'd spent fifty feral years roaming the woods like some animal, and had barely avoided a curse that would've erased her from the world's memory as thoroughly as Sadieville, left no visible trace. She was calm now, and relaxed, and only a deep look into her eyes revealed the scars her experience had left. "How's the water horse?"

"Restless," Bliss said.

"Me, too," Curnen said. "I got the feeling something was going on." She stepped out of her boots and sat down beside Bliss, putting her feet in the water. "Something big. Am I right?"

"You are. Do you want to know what?"

"I do." She frowned. "Or do I?"

"You can't unlearn it."

"That's always the way." After a moment of silence, she added, "So tell me already."

"I have to sing you a song." And she did, softly repeating the tune Azure had sung to them.

When she finished, Curnen drew up her knees and wrapped her arms around them. "Wow," she said softly. "I never saw that coming."

"None of us did."

"Are you going to go? I mean, you remember it. You lived there. I only have your stories to go by."

"I don't know. A lot's happened. There's some pretty compelling reasons to stay."

"If you go, who gets the tapestry?"

In the cellar beneath Bliss's house, untouched by the fire

that destroyed the original home four years earlier, was a secret room where a special tapestry hung. It had been woven during the first years of the Tufa exile, and depicted the moment of their leader's supreme failure. The Overbay family had protected it ever since, even before they took the name Overbay.

"I assume," Bliss said, "that we'd take it with us."

"If you go."

"If I go. If I *can* go. What about you?"

"Oh, I can't. Rob and I have two kids."

Bliss sat up. "What? Already?"

She shrugged, and gave her sister a little smile. "What can I say? We like to fuck, and I've always wanted kids. You should see them: a four-year-old girl and a three-year-old boy. They're already musical."

"You're damn right I should see them. Why haven't you sent me any pictures? Why didn't you *tell* me?"

"I don't know, I just . . . lose track of time," she said with a shrug. They both laughed.

"So you wouldn't bring the kids? They're half-bloods, they'd do fine."

"No. I'm happy where I am. Rob teaches at a college and plays in a band on the weekends. The kids and I catch every show we can, and I've got my own studio where I paint." She held up her hand, spattered with tiny drops of different colors. "I can't imagine a better life, even there."

Bliss lay back and again stared up at the stars. "I can," she said quietly.

Curnen lay down beside her, their shoulders touching. "Then don't tell me," she said quietly. And she held her big sister's hand while Bliss cried.


"So what will we do?" Thorn Parrish asked her parents. Her mother and father said nothing.

Thorn sighed in annoyance. She'd just returned from six months in New York City, living with Cyrus "C.C." Crow's boyfriend Matt Johanssen and singularly failing to make a dent in the music scene. Now she was back home and trying desperately to get Janet Harper, a girl three years her junior, to let her join her group, Little Trouble Girls. Her pride was severely battered, so the thought of simply leaving this world had an undeniable appeal.

Ladonna Parrish finally said, "I don't see us going back. We've got our place here. We've got our world."

"*I* don't have this world," Thorn said. "This world has pretty thoroughly kicked my ass."

"Oh, settle down," Gerald Parrish said. He recalled the tales he'd heard of the place, and that he'd passed on to his children as bedtime stories. That's how they felt to him now, too; whatever reality they embodied paled beside the tangible world around him, the one he understood. "You're just pissed off because it didn't work out up north."

"So? People have relocated for worse reasons. And what if it didn't work because I'm *supposed* to go back?"

"It ain't just relocating," Ladonna said. "You go back, that's it. You stay there, you follow their rules, and you act like you like it. No trying out new things, no finding true love or being a big success in the music world. There, *everyone's* a great picker."

"But everyone's happy, too," Thorn insisted. "Isn't that right?" She thought of the line from the spoken intro of "Let's Go Crazy": *a world of never-ending happiness.*

"But when everyone's happy, is anybody really happy?" Gerald said. "Don't you need the unhappiness so you've got something to compare it to?"

"Oh, come on, that's just wordplay," Thorn said.

"Well, it's how I feel," her father said.

"What about all the sadness? The fear? You can't *want* that. You can't want Rayford to have died."

"Thorn!" Ladonna scolded.

Thorn's big brother Ray had also left for New York, and thoroughly conquered it with his now-famous musical *Chapel of Ease,* even if he did die tragically just before the premiere. Ray would understand her desire to leave this world, to find a place where everything wasn't such a goddamned *struggle.*

At any other time, Gerald would've reacted with anger, but tonight he just shook his head. "You know what? I'd rather live in a world with sadness and fear, because then I'd really *know* when I was happy."

"If you ever were," Thorn fired back, but it was weak and she knew it.

"Thorn Parrish, you apologize to your father right now," Ladonna said.

"I'm sorry, Daddy," she mumbled.

"And we'll decide as a family whether to go or not, *if* there's ever a real chance."

"I'm a full-grown woman," Thorn said. "I make my own decisions." But her cowed tone belied the defiance in her words. She left them, slamming her room's door the way she'd done as a teenager.

"That girl," Ladonna said, and shook her head.

"Maybe she's right," Gerald said.

## 28

Ginny Vipperman passed the joint to her best friend Janet Harper. They sat on a picnic table at a scenic overlook that gave them a panoramic view of the Needsville valley below, and the cloudless star-filled sky above. The two girls, both just turned eighteen, were already thoroughly stoned, and their conversation moved with the sluggish certainty their minds were used to.

"You going to let Thorn Parrish join the band, then?" Ginny asked. She opened the can of Pringles she'd brought.

"I don't know," Janet said, taking an offered chip. "She writes her own songs, and this band already has a songwriter. I ain't interested in us being Fleetwood Mac."

"But she's worked in New York," Ginny said as she chewed. "She might be useful."

"Then she should be our manager, not another guitarist."

"Well, *I* like her," Ginny said. They passed the joint another time, and Ginny added, "Wow. Going back home. For real."

"For real," Janet said tightly around the smoke she held in her lungs.

"I wonder what the boys there are like?" Ginny asked. "Are they all kind of . . ." She made a fluttering, flighty hand gesture.

"What the hell does that mean?" Janet asked. "You asking if they're all gay?"

"No, not gay, just . . . not overtly masculine. Sissies, but not in a gay way. I mean, look at all the art. Even the painting over in the Cricket library."

That painting, *The Fairy Feller's Master Stroke,* had been painted in an insane asylum by a man who'd killed his father. It was considered by most to be the delusional imagination of a damaged mind. Only the Tufa knew that Richard Dadd's insanity had allowed him to glimpse, and maybe even visit, the Tufa homeland at the exact moment before the Tufa were exiled. The original painting now sat quietly on the back end of a standing bookshelf in the Cricket library, exactly as it had been for 150 years, except for the vandalism committed by Bo-Kate Wisby four years earlier. She'd scratched away the face of the Fairy Feller, which resembled that of the late Rockhouse Hicks, and no one had made any attempt to restore it. Bringing back the image might accidentally bring back Rockhouse, and no one wanted that.

But Ginny was right, the people as depicted in that painting were not exactly paragons of masculine virtue. And Ginny liked boys. Janet, on the other hand, had no particular interest in either the opposite or the same sex, and was content to turn all her energies toward her music. It was one reason their friendship had endured; they didn't compete over anything.

"Are the kind of boys there important?" Janet asked.

"They are to me. I like it." She blew a smoke ring and smiled. "I like it a lot."

Janet was too fuzzed to take offense. "They say the music is in the air itself," she said dreamily. "Can you imagine that? Just walking along and passing through songs and melodies, feeling them blow around you like a summer breeze?"

"No," Ginny said honestly.

"I can. It sounds amazing."

"So you'd go?"

"I don't know. I don't even know if I can. I don't have that much Tufa in me."

"You've got it where it counts," Ginny said, and tapped her friend over her heart. "I've heard you play and sing. You're not just a talented musician, you're magic."

"Maybe," Janet said.

"'Maybe,' my skinny white ass. Don't humble-brag at me." Ginny was a good bassist, but she suspected that any heights of musical ability she reached was just riding on Janet's coattails. Her friend was a legitimate phenomenon, and everyone knew it. Ginny had no doubt that Janet would likewise dazzle their true community in their homeland.

She took another long toke on the joint. "I don't guess we have to worry about it just yet, until they tell us they've actually found the way."

"They'll find it," Janet said. "It's the kind of thing they always find."

"What do you mean?"

Janet waved her hand at the world around them. "The thing that fucks up everything good with a promise of something even better."

"Whoa," Ginny said. "That is seriously deep."

"I know."

"I mean, *seriously*. Seriously deep."

"I know."

They sat in silence, looking out at the stars and the lights on the road, the air around them still and quiet. If they noticed that the night winds were silent, they didn't comment on it. They were content to let their slowed awareness take in all the details that they were usually too busy to appreciate.

Saggory "Sag" Gowen sat with his grandson Kurt on his knee as his wife refilled his iced tea. His daughter-in-law Renny, the boy's mother and the widow of his deceased son, stood at the window looking out at the night.

"I can't believe it," Renny said at last. "It must be some kind of elaborate practical joke. I mean, if it was going to happen, wouldn't it be . . . I don't know, announced or something?"

"It has been," Sag said. "That's what that song was about."

"I guess." She took the refill that Sag's wife Bobbie handed her. Although she'd sworn she'd never darken the Gowen doorway after she'd learned that her late husband Duncan was responsible for her brother Adam's death, Renny had mellowed over the intervening months. Kurt deserved to know his grandparents, especially since they were just as appalled at their son's behavior.

"Anyway, it doesn't matter," Bobbie said. "We're not purebloods, or even half bloods. We've got just enough Tufa in us to cause trouble."

"What about Kurt?" Sag said.

"He's not going anywhere," Renny said with certainty. "And neither am I."

"What if they make us?" Sag asked.

Renny snorted. "I'd like to see 'em try."

"They could. Mandalay, she could do it. She's strong enough."

"Nobody's strong enough to make me leave my son or my home," Renny said firmly.

The Gowens fell silent, each of them mulling their own thoughts. Only Renny had the absolute certainty that she wouldn't go; Sag and Bobbie wondered first if they would, and then if they'd even get the choice.

———

Mandalay and Luke drew their lips apart. His hands were under her shirt, and her right hand stroked him between his legs, over his jeans. This was as far as they'd ever gone, and in calmer moments, both agreed it was a good stopping point. They were just kids, after all, and Mandalay especially was aware of the cliché of the knocked-up hillbilly girl. Plus there was the undeniable truth of who she was, and the fact that she was pretty much doomed to die in childbirth.

And yet the sense of hovering right on the edge, of only a few pieces of cloth keeping them from each other, made them both rethink that agreement. For Luke it was the thrill of new discovery, while for Mandalay it was a reminder of just *why* her predecessors risked agonizing death.

They were in her bedroom, alone in the dark, in the trailer she shared with her father and stepmother. The adults were away at the Pair-A-Dice roadhouse, drinking and dancing, and Mandalay was too old (*far* too old, if you thought about it) for a babysitter. Nothing stopped them but their own wills, and neither felt they could count on that much longer.

She knew what to do in this situation; having the memory of millennia of women, all of whom had had lovers, meant she would be very capable of guiding the inexperienced Luke to do exactly what she wanted. And she knew what to do to him, to make sure he enjoyed himself as well. But something held her back, and it wasn't morality; it was the sense that she needed to focus her energy elsewhere. No matter, she thought heatedly, how much other parts of her body felt differently. So she fought the memories of her past selves' sexual experiences and tried to remain a fifteen-year-old virgin.

She felt her bra come unsnapped. She said raggedly, "Move your hand up a little." He did, cupping her breast. "Oh," she said, her eyes closed.

He was shirtless, and she ran her left hand over his shoulder and back, feeling the lean muscles under his skin. If he grew up like his father, his shoulders would grow even broader, and his arms would develop whipcord muscles that stood out beneath his skin. His fingers would remain long and nimble, allowing the easy playing of guitars.

And other things. His long fingers trembled against her, and the sense of power it gave her made her stomach drop.

"Okay, stop for a minute," she managed to choke out, and Luke withdrew his hands. He tucked hair behind her ear and let his fingertips brush her cheeks, not ready to entirely quit touching her.

"Too far?" he asked.

"I just . . . I need to keep my head clear." She stood, pulled her bra free of her tank top, straightened her clothes, and took a long, deep breath.

He stayed on her bed, watching. They'd begun dating when they were both twelve; she was the leader of her people, and his family had always followed the group led first by Rockhouse Hicks, and now Junior Damo. It was not a true Romeo-and-Juliet situation, since no one tried to keep them apart, but there was tension whenever they appeared in public together. So they tended to keep their encounters private, which had brought its own set of issues. Especially now.

"Thinking about going back to . . . home?" he asked.

"Hard not to," she said. "I remember it."

"That must be strange."

"That's one word for it," she said with a chuckle too mature for her years.

"What was it like?"

She thought that over. How to describe a place that, for her and her people, was as much a part of them as a limb or an organ? "Everything was beautiful. I'm not just saying that, either. The people, the land, the air . . . it was all perfect. Everywhere you looked, there was something that should take your breath away. Except . . . nothing did. When all you see is beauty, you have nothing to compare it to. So none of us realized how beautiful it *truly* was, and how happy we were in it, until we came here, and saw how crude and ugly this world could be."

He came up behind her, brushed her hair from her neck and kissed it. "This world has its nice points."

She smiled and leaned back against him. "Yeah, it does."

"Are you going to look for it, then?"

"No. I think that's what those two strangers are here for. To find it for us. To give us time to decide what we'll do when they *do* find it."

"Is that what the night winds want?"

"I don't know. The night winds have done things like this before: brought in outsiders to do things that the Tufa can't or won't do." She turned to face him, astounded anew by the sheer youth of his face, the untested bravery in his eyes. Would his courage prove strong enough if it came down to it? Did she want to know?

"So the winds haven't spoken to you about it?"

"No. One thing I've never known is whether the night winds came with us, or were already here and just took us in when we arrived."

"So if they're native to this world, they may not want us to go back," he said, thinking aloud. "They may not *let* us go back."

"That's a possibility."

"It sounds like there's a lot of things you just don't know, and that you can't control."

She laughed. "That's totally true. Does it surprise you?"

"A little," he said, and put his hands on her waist. "Maybe you need something to take your mind off it."

She put her arms around his neck. "Have you got any ideas?"

"I do," he said, suddenly sounding confident and mature. She knew it was an act, since she felt his legs trembling, but she appreciated it more than she could say. The mere fact that he sensed what she needed and was trying to give it to her almost made her cry.

"You have to promise me something, though," he added.

"What?"

"No thinking about the future. Or the past. You stay in the moment, right now, with me."

"I'll do my best," she promised.

"And I'll do my best to keep you here."

Later, after Luke left and her parents came home, Mandalay lay awake staring at her ceiling. Everyone expected answers from her, from the one person they were sure knew what the night winds were thinking. Sometimes that was true. But not this time.

She began to sing, very quietly, the only song that mattered now:

> *As a girl I walked your hollers*
> *Down by the shallow, springtime creek*
> *But now where I walk, a shadow follows*
> *And I pray the Lord my soul will keep . . .*

As she sang, the wind picked up outside. She went to the window and opened it. The breeze was cool against her still-warm skin, and she closed her eyes to it. When she opened them, she jumped. Something now stood in her yard, silhouetted in the orange-pink glow of the sodium security light.

It was a deer, but almost as big as an elk, with broad antlers having a staggering thirty points between them. Beside the stag stood two coyotes, lean and still.

She swallowed hard. *The King of the Forest.* This was serious.

She dressed and slipped out of the trailer carefully, without waking her parents. She winced as the screen door squeaked shut.

By then the stag and coyotes were gone, replaced by a man nearly seven feet tall, with a broad chest and wearing only an animal-skin cloth tied around his waist. He still sported the antlers from his temples, though in this light, it could've been a headdress. If she didn't know better.

As she approached him, two young women with dreadlocks, also dressed with just animal-skin sashes around their waists, came out of the shadows and escorted her, one on each side. They smelled like outdoor dogs, and as they walked, one of them leaned forward and sniffed at the back of Mandalay's neck.

Mandalay only came up to the middle of the big man's broad, hairy chest, so she had to look up into his bearded face. The two coyote women circled them as they gazed at each other.

"So you've heard the news," she said.

His immense head nodded.

"Do *you* know where to find the passage?"

This time he shook his head.

"Will you try to stop us if we go?"

Again the head shake.

She had to swallow before asking the next question. "Do you *want* us to go?"

The winds were still in the darkness above them. The only sound was the soft padding of the coyote girls' bare feet. Then he slowly put one enormous hand on her shoulder. A shudder ran through her, overpowering and intimate, a primal response to the most masculine thing any woman might experience in this world. It wasn't invasive, or an invitation; it simply *was*, as he simply was.

Then he spoke. Not many encountered the King of the Forest; usually he was glimpsed, in his stag form, in the distance. There were stories of encounters, but usually those were warnings, and ended badly for those who met him. In no stories did he ever speak; he usually left that up to his escorts, the coyote women. But this time, he spoke as equal to equal.

"You have been kind to my forest for a very long time," he said in a voice so deep she felt it in her chest more than her ears. "If you depart, the ones who settle here after you will not be."

"And you've been kind to us as well," she said, her voice trembling. She put her hand over his. "I don't know what we'll decide. But when we do, I'll come find you."

He nodded and removed his hand. The tips of his enormous fingers lightly stroked her cheek, just as Luke's had done earlier. Then in two long strides he disappeared back into the darkened woods. His women companions had vanished, and now two coyotes followed him. The shadows between the trees swallowed them at once.

Mandalay let out a long breath. The encounter had shaken her, just as her only real confrontation with the spirits of the night winds had once done. That time, they had spoken to her directly, in a human voice, but she had lacked the courage to turn and see them. At least with the King of the Forest, she managed to look him in the eye.

She went back inside and tried futilely to sleep. But too many uncertainties battled for supremacy in her head, all boiling down to one issue: could they, or anyone, find the cave the Conlins once guarded? And if they did, would it still lead them home?

At the Catamount Corner bed-and-breakfast, in the little apartment behind the front desk, Cyrus Crow sat at his kitchen table and smiled at the face on the laptop screen. "Hey," he said, his heart filling with love in a way he'd never imagined possible.

"Hey," Matt Johanssen replied. He was exhausted but wired, as he always was after a performance on the road.

"How was the show tonight?"

"Okay. The board Jason was dancing on cracked halfway through the wedding scene. Sounded like a gun had gone off, and since I *had* a gun, everyone thought it was either part of the plot, or a mistimed sound effect."

"At least you got their attention," C.C. said.

"They were riveted," Matt agreed with a laugh. Then he rested his chin on his hand. "So what's wrong?"

"What makes you think anything's wrong?"

"Well, mainly I just had a feeling about it. But now that I see you, I see you've got that little furrow between your eyebrows. You only get that when you're worried."

C.C. smiled again. He understood that Matt had to honor his contract to the show *Chapel of Ease,* that his career was important to him, but he wanted nothing more than to hold Matt's hand as they walked through the woods and talked about the future. In his perfect future, Matt retired from the stage and helped him run the Catamount Corner; it may have been a gay couple cliché, but truthfully, it was C.C.'s fondest dream.

"I learned something new tonight," C.C. said.

"So you had a very special episode?"

"Ha."

"Okay, so what did you learn?"

"Remember how I told you that the Tufa came from . . . somewhere else?"

Matt's tired, relaxed face suddenly tightened, and his eyes flashed with wary alertness. He even sat up straighter. "Yes."

"Well, now there's talk that we might be able to go back. Some college kids who are doing some research project may have found the way." As he spoke, he looked up at the ceiling, imagining Justin and Veronica asleep in their room, excited to hunt up the ruins of Sadieville and having no idea what they might unleash by doing so.

Matt swallowed hard. His voice, though, was casual. "Do you want to go back?"

C.C. sighed and rubbed his eyes. "I don't know, Matt. All I know about that place are the stories I've heard. Yes, it sounds wonderful, but so does Florida until you find out about the palmetto bugs and the fire ants."

After a pause, Matt said, "I'm guessing I'm not invited?"

"It's a dangerous place for people who aren't Tufa."

"That's not an answer."

C.C. knew Matt deserved the truth. "No, you wouldn't be invited. It's only for the Tufa, and then only for those of us with enough true Tufa blood."

In the silence, the refrigerator compressor kicked on, making C.C. jump.

"Wow," Matt said finally. "I don't know what to say. I mean, we've made this long-distance relationship thing work, but that's *really* long distance."

"Yeah. I guess it sounds silly, doesn't it?"

"That's not for me to say. They're your people, not mine."

"I've always thought so." He touched the laptop's screen, caressing Matt's video cheek. "But you know what I realized the moment I saw your face tonight?"

"What?"

"That *you* are my people now. That nothing over there can possibly beat what I've got here."

"Seriously?"

"Seriously."

C.C. saw the relief in Matt's eyes, even as his actor's skill kept it off his face. He realized Matt had been genuinely, truly afraid that C.C. would choose the Tufa over him.

"I can't wait to see you, you know," Matt said.

"I know," C.C. agreed. And then they described what they'd do with each other the next time Matt visited.

———

Upstairs, sated by exhaustion and sex, Justin and Veronica slept in each other's arms. It was the kind of position long-term couples usually abandoned, but they clung to it, and each other.

Then Veronica's eyes suddenly popped open. She lay still, looking around in the darkness, wondering what had awoken her. Had she heard a sound? For an instant she was disoriented, wondering where they were, then she recalled the events of the past day.

Azure, the professor in the forest, had told them the story of Sadieville. They had only to go out tomorrow into the hills and find it. With the GPS coordinates and topographical maps, it should be possible. Then Justin's academic career would be back on track.

But what about her?

Lying there in the dark, with his steady breathing in one ear, she realized that she really served no purpose here other than being a supportive girlfriend. She often imagined stretches of her life as a movie, and in this one, she realized it wouldn't even be her story: she'd be the spunky love interest, the Manic Pixie Dream Girl, whitewashed of course so she could be played by the latest version of Katie Holmes or Rachel McAdams.

Was that okay? Was she somehow cheating herself by making Justin the priority right now?

And then there was the tarot reading Dr. Tully had given her. She would go on a journey that would end in acceptance and forgiveness. Acceptance of what? Forgiveness of whom?

She carefully got out of bed, took her bag into the bathroom, and closed the door. There, in the harsh fluorescent light, she got out her tarot deck, sat on the floor and draped her reading cloth over the closed toilet lid. *What am I doing here?* she silently asked the cards. *What's going to happen? Is this what I should be doing?*

She stopped shuffling and turned over the top card.

*Death.*

The image of an armored skeleton on horseback, carrying a flag with a white flower, dominated the card. Corpses littered the ground. A man in ecclesiastical garb reached out toward the rider in supplication.

Veronica knew this card didn't mean literal death. But it did represent change, the kind that resulted from life-altering decisions. Was this in her actual future, or was it just a symptom of her current self-doubt?

She could put other cards out to try to clarify, but it was late and she had a long day ahead. Well, that wasn't exactly true: Justin had a long day ahead. She was just tagging along. But the cards implied something significant in her future, too.

She crept back to bed and snuggled into Justin's embrace. He kissed her bare shoulder and said, "What's up?"

"Nothing. Go back to sleep."

"What did your cards tell you?"

She felt a momentary embarrassment at being caught, even though Justin never made fun of her. "You know how it works. They only tell me what I know that I already know."

"Oh, so they told you everything?"

She mock-jabbed him in the ribs, then they both laughed sleepily as they snuggled back down together.

## 29

Justin looked at the forest around him, drew a deep breath, and began, "Oh, I'm a lumberjack and I'm okay—"

*"No,"* Veronica quickly interrupted. "No you're not."

"Which?"

"Either."

He made an exaggerated pouty face.

She kissed his cheek. "Well, you're okay, I suppose."

The woods around them were vibrant and alive, sunlight shafting through the greenery to make pools on the forest floor. Birds sang and insects buzzed, including mosquitoes that seemed only mildly inconvenienced by their expensive organic bug repellent.

"Wait, I need a drink," Veronica said, and leaned against a tree. She took a long draught from her water bottle.

Justin checked his phone again. They worked from the GPS coordinates Veronica had figured out back at West Tennessee University, and the line from where they'd parked to their destination was straight and short. The phone, however, didn't factor in the rolling terrain, with steep hillsides and surprise gullies and hollows. Their one-hour hike was already two hours long, and they were barely a third of the way there.

She peered down at the phone in his hand. "So how far?"

"Looks like a little less than three miles, as the crow flies."

"Which crow, Russell or Cameron?"

"Duritz. It's a counting crow."

She stretched and yawned. "I didn't sleep too well last night."

"I slept like a rock."

"I know. That explains the gravel in the bed."

"Well, I *did* get my rocks off before we went to sleep."

"That's because you were my quarry."

"I think for the symbolism to work, hon, you'd have to be the quarry. I'd be the excavator."

She mock-thought it over. "I can dig it."

Laughing, they resumed their hike. Their packs grew heavier with each ascent of a hill, and the relief of a downslope was tempered with the sure knowledge that another upward slope awaited.

Finally they stumbled down a long incline to a stream, where they gratefully dropped their packs on the rocky bank and sat on the rocks at the edge of the water. "This," Justin said between deep breaths, "is Black Creek, if I'm reading the map correctly. That bridge you found crosses it."

Veronica took a fresh drink of water from her half-empty bottle. "How far away?"

Justin held his thumb and forefinger about an inch apart. "This far, according to the phone."

"I know the opening is right there waiting for me, but I'm too tired to make a joke about men and their dick lengths," she said. "Let's just pretend I did and move on."

She was about to take off her boots and cool her feet in the stream, when a new voice said, "Well, hello, you two."

They looked up. Tucker Carding stood on the opposite bank,

as nonchalantly as he might on a city street corner. He looked as puzzled as they were. "Y'all would be mighty far down on the list of people I would expect to see here."

"Tucker?" Justin said. "What are you doing here?"

Tucker indicated the rod and reel and tackle box at his feet. "Having second thoughts about fishing. It's hotter'n a burnt clutch out here, and these skeeters'll suck you dry. You?"

"Trying to get to Sadieville."

"Oh, that's right. Did Miss Azure give you directions?"

"No, we figured this out on our own," Justin said. "Why?"

He looked around them at the forest. "Seems like a strange place for a whole town to disappear is all."

"You know this area?" Veronica asked.

"Like the back of my hand."

Justin held up his phone. "According to this, it's three miles that way."

Tucker followed his gaze, which showed only more hills and woods. "Huh. Y'all mind if I tag along? See what's left?"

Justin was instantly on guard. After the weird experience yesterday, running into this guy here was just too big a coincidence to credit. Trying to sound casual, he said, "We're here to do research, not sightsee. It'd probably be pretty boring."

"I've been on these trips with him before," Veronica added, following his lead. "He's not kidding."

"Won't be boring to me. I ain't never seen real scientists at work."

"We're just trainees," Justin said.

"Hey, if you two just want to be alone in the woods, just say so."

Justin and Veronica exchanged a look. The last thing they wanted was to anger a local, who might then run off and round up some "friends" to teach them a "lesson." Veronica gave him a minute shrug and nod.

"Ah, sure, come along," Justin said.

"Well, that's mighty kind of you," Tucker said. He left his fishing gear near a tree trunk, and crossed the creek on protruding stones. "And to earn my keep, I'm gonna tell you a faster and easier way."

"What's that?" Justin asked.

He gestured at the creek. "This here's Black Creek, and I'm betting that if your missing town was anywhere around here, this was where it got its water."

"Makes sense."

"Well, instead of going up and down those hills and hollers, why not follow the creek? Should lead you right there, and since water always finds the easiest way, it's likely to be a whole lot more pleasant."

Justin's eyes opened wider. "Wow. Can't believe we didn't think of that."

"Ah, that's all right. Glad to help."

As it turned out, he was right. There were some tricky passages with slippery rocks and overhanging brush that forced them briefly back on land, but for the most part it was considerably less trouble than the way they'd been going. And it kept their feet cool, which in turn made the heat far less bothersome.

"So what's so special about this town you're trying to find?" Tucker asked casually. They walked single file, and he'd worked his way in between Justin and Veronica.

Justin wasn't about to reveal the whole truth, but if Tucker had already spoken to Azure, then he'd know. "When you're trying to get a master's degree, you have to study something that hasn't been done to death. I don't know of any other towns that have vanished without a trace, that don't also appear in all sorts of books. It's almost like something came along and erased all mention of this one."

"And people care about that?"

"Academic people do."

Tucker whistled. "Who'd think you could make a living at that?"

"Oh, I won't make a living," Justin said. "It'll just keep me from having to pay back my student loans a little longer."

An hour later they spotted something ahead and above them. As they got closer, it resolved into a flat piece of concrete that crossed from one side of the creek to the other, supported by worn and rotted wooden struts. The trio stopped, and for a long moment the only sound was their labored breathing, and the bubbling creek.

"Well, what do you know?" Tucker said at last. "Dang if there ain't a bridge out here in the middle of nowhere. Would you look at that?"

"If it's the one we want," Justin said, "it was meant to lead to a road that never got built."

"So you think that's it?" Veronica asked.

Justin took out his phone; they'd indeed reached the spot indicated on their map. "The phone says so."

"The phone wouldn't lie," Veronica said.

"Only when it comes to billing." He looked at her, trying mightily to control his excitement. "I suppose we won't know for certain until we climb up and look around."

"Then what are we waiting for?"

They easily climbed the bank and emerged at the edge of a weedy clearing. Before them, the open space extended two miles to the base of a nearby mountain, and halfway up that slope was an old pile of boulders out of character for the rest of the vista.

"The Great Sadie mine," Veronica said, pointing. "It must've caved in when the town did."

Justin reached into his pack and pulled out an image captured from the movie's first scene. He held it up; in the background, the mine opening appeared at the same spot as the debris. All the other broad contours were identical.

"I think so," Justin said.

She looked around at the clearing. "Then this open space here . . ."

Justin took a deep, calming breath that didn't really calm him at all. "I think that we're looking at Sadieville." He turned to Veronica, and she leaped into his arms and gave him a long, triumphant kiss.

"Y'all sure you don't want to be alone?" Tucker said after a moment, deliberately looking away.

They broke apart, and Justin spent a moment just looking around, taking in the view in which he'd invested so much of his future. Then he took out his phone and began snapping pictures.

"Look there," he said, pointing. "See how the ground has sunken in all the way around? The hole's been filled in over time, but the town is still under there."

"Y'all ain't planning to excavate, are you?" Tucker asked.

"No, just document. Although someone might want to, once word gets out." He looked up at Tucker. "Do you think the rest of the Tufa would mind?"

"Depends on who wants to do it," he said, "and how politely they ask."

Justin couldn't repress his huge grin. "Hopefully, I'll be involved in some capacity. And I'll make sure they're *very* polite."

He switched from pictures to video and made a slow pan of the area to take it all in. In his mind, he filled in the gaps based on the image captured from the film. To his left would've been a row of shops and businesses, and behind that the railroad tracks and the rows of identical miners' houses. To his right were more shops and essential services such as cobblers, barbers, and dentists, including the five-star hotel that served the company men.

Tucker broke his reverie. "Hey, you two, get out on that bridge. I'll get a picture of you. Perfect for the author photo on your book."

The concrete bridge was remarkably intact, although of course the wooden covering had long since rotted away. Justin and Veronica walked a few feet from the edge, not wanting to chance the very middle.

"Do you suppose," Veronica said quietly, "that he's deleting all your pictures and video?"

"That's paranoid," Justin said the same way.

"Only if I'm wrong. You're not paranoid if your clock is right twice a day."

"Even a broken clock might be out to get you."

Justin put his arm around Veronica's shoulders, and she leaned close. He made sure to stand up straight, because he wanted to look powerful and assured, two qualities he did not normally project.

"Perfect," Tucker said, and took several pictures.

"He's taking them vertically," Veronica muttered through her smile. It was a pet peeve of hers that people took vertical videos and photographs when horizontal was always better.

"He's doing us a favor," Justin said the same way. "Be gracious."

"Honey, any more gracious and I'd be a minister."

"We definitely don't want that," he said, and turned to kiss her.

"Aw, sweet one!" Tucker called. "Beautiful."

They began a slow, methodical walking tour of the field, searching for any other trace of the vanished town. But except for the bridge, they found nothing man-made. Justin shot hundreds of pictures and lots of additional video, but there was really nothing to indicate a thriving industrial town once stood here. The disaster that destroyed it appeared to be total.

Tucker and Veronica stood off a ways as Justin made notes. "Is he all right?" Tucker asked quietly.

"He'd hoped to find more evidence. But that bridge is pretty conclusive: it's in the right spot, it looks exactly like the one in the picture, and the mine is there, too."

"Then he's pretty sure."

"Are you missing another town?"

He laughed. "No, ma'am. This is the only one we've misplaced."

"There's one thing we haven't looked for," Justin called out to them. "The railroad. Even if the tracks in the town were destroyed, there ought to be some remains out in the woods. Come on."

He was right; at the edge of the woods they found a straight path, overgrown now with small trees and weeds, extending into the distance. In a few minutes Justin found a section of rusted rail beneath the leaves and dirt. He exposed several feet of it, then took more pictures.

"That clinches it," he said. "That fucking clinches it." Then he wrapped Veronica in a hug and happily spun her around.

Which meant that neither of them heard Tucker singing low under his breath, or noticed the quick, subtle hand gesture he made in their direction.

Justin stopped in mid-spin. "Hey. Look at that."

"What?" Veronica said.

He pointed. "Right there. That ridge, up above the trees. See it? That patch of bare rock?"

She squinted. "I see the trees."

"Remember that spot in the movie where the girl—" He stopped, remembering Tucker's presence.

Veronica understood. "Yeah, I suppose it does look like . . . that. But so do a lot of places around here, I bet."

"Like what?" Tucker asked innocently.

"Something else we saw in that old movie," Justin said evasively. "They shot some stuff on a bare ridge above the town, and from here that looks like it might be it."

Tucker stood beside him, shielded his eyes and stared. "That a fact?"

"It is," Justin agreed.

"That ridge might've been bare back then, but do you think it still would be?"

"I don't know," Justin said honestly.

"Well, I reckon we better go check it out," Tucker said. "Hate for y'all to come all this way and leave a stone unturned. That's the kind of thing you might kick yourself over in a week when you're back home."

Justin and Veronica exchanged a look. Something in the man's eagerness seemed suddenly false, and they both wondered what his agenda might be. Was he trying to keep them from going, or make sure they did? "It's already going to be late when we get back," Justin said evasively. "Besides, I've got enough for my thesis."

"Oh, come on, we're this close," Tucker said, and patted him on the shoulder. "And remember, we can go back to your car along the creek, which is a lot faster."

"Okay," Justin said uncertainly. "I guess."

"That settles it, then. I bet there's even a trail that leads up there. Let's go look for it."

Just as Tucker predicted, they found a trail that did indeed lead them in the right direction. It was narrow but well traveled, supporting Tucker's assertion that it was a game trail used by deer and elk, not a remnant of the human presence.

The woods around them were now thick, heavy trees blotting out the sky in several places. Oddly, there were none of the gnats and mosquitoes that had tormented them earlier, possibly because they'd climbed out of their range or moved away from the water.

Then the forest changed again, growing sparser and less deciduous. The ground went from stony soil to just stone.

The air was different as well, but in ways that were hard to quantify. Cooler, yes, and breezier, but also filled with a tension that, Justin thought, actually seemed to resist their presence. It was like a gentle push back, a slight but firm touch trying to guide them in a different direction.

"Maybe this was a mistake," Justin gasped, his knees aching from the effort.

"I'm never walking upstairs again," Veronica said, hoping she didn't sound as worried as she felt. She couldn't shake the memory of the Death card in her reading last night.

"Don't give up now, we're almost there," Tucker said. He was barely breathing hard.

The trail opened up at the top of the hill, and the blue sky raised all their spirits. The area was relatively flat, and a mountainside rose into the misty clouds beside them.

"Look," Veronica said.

A small cave gaped in the side of the mountain, a black orifice set in the rocky hillside. It was about as wide as a man with his arms spread, and a little shorter than Justin. In front of it, three twisted hawthorn trees, their spiked branches entwined, grew in the rocky soil.

"See?" Tucker said. "There is a cave here."

Justin wanted to pull out another frame capture, one that might confirm their location, but since it also showed the fairy girl, he was reluctant. "It sure looks like it. Doesn't it?"

"It does to me," Veronica said seriously, trying to watch every direction at once. Even in the bright, cheery sunlight, the place instantly and insidiously gave her the creeps.

"So, y'all gonna go in?"

"Why would we?" Justin asked.

He shrugged. "No reason. Just thought you might want to."

"I don't even know how we'd get in there," Veronica said.

"Carefully," Tucker said with a laugh. "Here, let me give y'all a hand." He pulled out a Gerber minitool, snapped the pruning blade into place, and began to saw at the hawthorn branches. In minutes he'd made an opening big enough for a person to pass through.

Justin stuck his head inside the dark opening, then backed up with a frown. He motioned for Veronica to join him. "Do you hear that?"

"Hear what?" Tucker said.

"Yeah," Veronica said. "It's . . . music of some kind. I can't make out the melody, but it's music."

"Yeah," Justin agreed. He stepped over the cave's threshold, listening intently. "I can't quite catch the tune either, but I think it's something I've heard before."

"Ah, up here it's probably just the wind," Tucker said, "or a bird, or—"

"Shh!" Justin snapped, then added apologetically, "Sorry, man, I'm just trying to hear."

He listened as intently as he ever had in his life. What he heard was impossible to describe: it had no melody, but there were harmonies, and no words, though there was a sense of a story being told through the sounds. He'd never even conceived of music like this, both abstract and tangible, both airy and somehow grounded. It felt like a tune he should know by heart, but he couldn't quite place it.

But he knew he had to get closer to it.

"Justin!" Veronica cried.

Justin turned, and suddenly realized he was ten feet inside the cave. He blinked in surprise; he had no memory of dropping his pack and entering, but he had. Tucker and Veronica were silhouetted against the blue sky behind him. He said, "Just a little farther. I can almost make it out."

"Son, I'm telling you, it's just the wind," Tucker insisted. "One time I had a crack in my chimney that sounded like the horn part of '25 or 6 to 4' when the wind blew out of the north."

"No," Justin said with certainty. "This isn't wind."

"Wait, I'm coming with you," Veronica said. She quickly dropped her pack beside his and joined him in the cave.

"Y'all don't even have a flashlight," Tucker said.

Justin held up his phone and turned on the flashlight app. "Yes we do."

"We'll be back in five minutes," Veronica said. "We won't go far. Keep an eye on our stuff, okay?"

And then they were gone.

For a long silent moment, Tucker Carding stood at the cave mouth, staring into the darkness. Eventually their footsteps faded, and the only sound was the song Tucker knew so well.

But then he laughed, a wry sound that conveyed amusement and irony, but oddly very little concern. He took the camp chair from Veronica's pack, snapped it open and put it in the shade. And he sat down to wait.

## 30

The blue-white glow from the app cast steady illumination. Justin and Veronica had done some amateur spelunking, so they weren't put off by the bugs and sleeping bats all around them. The floor was reasonably level, the few narrow spots easily passable, and it wasn't long until there was darkness behind them as well as ahead.

The music grew no louder. It still hovered just beyond their hearing, drawing them on without change.

"Do you think Tucker will steal our gear?" Veronica asked quietly. Something about the music made her want to whisper.

"Oh, I don't think so," Justin said. "He seems like a decent guy."

"They say serial killers are really good at that. Seeming like decent guys."

"They say the same about Republicans."

"And they're not wrong. You don't think there's something weird about him showing up in the middle of the woods just where we happened to be?"

"And your first instinct is to jump to 'serial killer'?"

"Or Republican." She shivered. "It's just spooky. And it's cold in here."

"It's a cave. And don't change the subject."

Suddenly she grabbed his arm. "Hey, look."

"Where?"

"On the ground."

He shone the light where she pointed. In the dust on the floor of the cave were many bare human footprints. They over-lapped, and all went toward the cave entrance where Tucker waited.

"Look at that," Veronica said. "How many are there?"

"Too many to count."

"And they're all heading toward the entrance. None of them are going back in."

"So I guess we know this tunnel opens out somewhere at the other end."

Veronica ran her fingertip over a rock surface, disturbing the dust. "Wonder how long they've been here? They wouldn't get disturbed much, this far back. And who goes caving barefooted?"

"Probably just kids messing around. Someone probably dared them to come back in here, they got spooked and ran out."

He was about to start walking when Veronica said suddenly, "Wait."

"What? Did you hear something?"

"No, turn off your light."

He did, and the darkness settled around them. Then, as their eyes adjusted, they saw a faint glow ahead.

"We can't already be through," Justin said, looking into the darkness behind them. He usually had a good sense of direc-tion, and he felt as though they should still be deep inside the mountain. "Did we get turned around somewhere? Is that where we came in?"

"No," Veronica said with certainty.

"Then what is that?"

"I think it's the other end of the tunnel, and we just went farther than we realized. Or it's a balrog."

He took her hand. "Then let's go see."

"If it's a balrog, you owe me a drink."

"If it's a balrog, it means we'll come out in New Zealand. Win-win."

The light grew brighter as they approached, brighter than it should have even with their eyes adjusted to the cave's darkness. "Fucking hell," Justin whispered, shading his eyes and squinting. "Where *are* we?"

Tucker looked out over the Sadieville valley, remembering the view before the coal company built the town: nothing but trees as far as the eye could see. When it had been cleared, it had been the ugliest thing he'd ever seen, at least until he witnessed mountaintop-removal mining.

He looked up in surprise as Veronica stumbled from the cave, sweaty and covered in streaks of dirt. "Tucker," she said, out of breath. "Please help me."

Tucker jumped out of the camp chair and guided her to sit in it. "What happened? Where's Justin?"

"He . . . ran . . . off," she said, gasping between words.

"Ran off where? In the cave?"

She shook her head, almost hyperventilating. "With . . . the fairies."

"With the what? Calm down and tell me what happened." He handed her the aluminum water bottle from her pack.

Veronica drank until she choked. She took several deep breaths, calming down and putting her panicked thoughts in order. "We found another valley. On the other side of this mountain."

"There is no valley on the other side of this mountain. There's a hollow, but it's little-bitty and nobody lives there."

"I know that!" she snapped between gulps. "But that's what we found. A huge valley, that we could see for miles, and there were no other mountains."

"That don't make no sense."

She swung the water bottle at him, and it clanged when it hit the side of his head. He cried out and stumbled away, both hands to his temple. "OW! What the hell?"

Veronica got to her feet, bottle cocked for another blow. "You may be used to dealing with stupid people, my friend, but you aren't now. You knew exactly what we'd find over there. It was Tír na nÓg, wasn't it?"

"What is that?" he said.

She drew back to hit him again.

"All right, all right!" he said, holding up one hand. "Tell me exactly what happened."

"We saw a troupe of people playing music and dancing. I didn't leave the cave, but Justin ran out to talk to them. The next thing I knew, he was dancing off with them."

Tucker shook his still-ringing head. "So you got all the way through."

"We did. And now I need you to go back with me, to help me find him."

Tucker was silent for a long moment, then said at last, "That wouldn't help."

"Why not?"

"Because it wouldn't."

"Then call the police!"

"That really wouldn't help."

She threw the bottle at him in a rage. "I can't just leave him there! Please, you have to help me!"

"Listen, I can't."

"Fine, then I'll go back myself." She turned toward the cave.

He jumped in front of her to block the way. "Whoa, hold on."

"Get out of my way," she said coldly.

"No, no, wait. I can't help you, but I know who might. If anyone can."

"Then take me to him," Veronica said. "Now. Which way is your truck?"

"I'm not talking about the truck," he said, and put his arms around her.

Her eyes widened, and at first she thought he was going to kiss her. As she drew back a knee to slam into his groin, he lifted her off her feet. "I know this may not be a total surprise at this point, but it's still probably better if you close your eyes."

They began to move upward. And she closed her eyes tight.

# 31

When her feet again touched the ground, Tucker said, "Okay, you can look now."

For a moment Veronica was as speechless as she'd been at the other end of the cave. Then she blurted, "Somebody *here* can help us?"

"Like the song says," Tucker said with an irony Veronica didn't yet understand, "what you see ain't always what you get."

The double-wide house trailer was on a bare lot in the middle of nowhere, surrounded by woods on three sides and a paved two-lane road in front. A swing set, truck, and car took up the yard. A satellite dish was mounted in the side yard.

She had no idea how far they'd traveled from the ridge above Sadieville. The sun had dipped in the west, and now almost touched the treetops. She turned to Tucker. "Whatever you've got in mind here, we have to hurry, it'll be dark soon."

Tucker climbed the cinder-block steps to the trailer's front door and knocked on the metal.

A handsome middle-aged man peered out through the screen. "Tucker?"

"Yeah, it's me, Darnell. I need to see Mandalay."

"Now?"

"Yeah. It's important." He made a quick, complex hand gesture. "Real important."

Darnell thought it over, then said, "All right, wait here."

"You're not gonna invite us in?"

"Not till I find out if you're welcome," he said, and closed the door.

"Who's 'Mandalay'?" Veronica asked.

"She's in charge."

"Of what?"

"Of the Tufa."

"Like a mayor?"

"Sorta."

The door opened again, and Mandalay Harris emerged. She came down the cinder-block steps and stood before Tucker and Veronica. "I hear there's a problem."

"Wait, wait, *wait*," Veronica said. "This is a *kid*."

"I know," Tucker said. "But—"

"I don't know exactly what's happened," Mandalay said to her, "but if there's anyone in this valley who can help you, it's me. I know what I look like. And I really am a fifteen-year-old girl. You'll just have to accept that what you see ain't always what you get."

Something in the girl's voice, something heavy and ancient, stopped Veronica's next comment. Those eyes belonged in a much older face, one that bore the signs and marks of hard-earned wisdom. "I'm sorry," Veronica said. "I'm a little upset."

"I can tell. What happened?"

"You really don't know?" Tucker said.

"I know everything, but not all at once," she said with a little smile. "Tell me."

Tucker nodded at Veronica.

"My boyfriend and I went into a cave in the hills above

Sadieville," Veronica said. "We came out the other end and . . ." She stopped, unable to find the words that wouldn't make her sound like a lunatic.

"What?" Mandalay prompted.

Tucker stepped up. "You remember that thing the Conlins guarded for so long?"

She looked hard at him. "Yes."

"Well, her and her boyfriend found it."

Mandalay's eyebrows went up. "With your help?"

"Maybe. Kinda."

The girl's eyes turned hard as granite. "So just like Sophronie Conlin, you've lost another canary."

He took the heat of her gaze without flinching. "I deserve that. But Sophronie was my family; the baby she lost was even named after me, and losing her hurt more than I can say. And I'm doing all this for the Tufa."

"Excuse me, but what are you two talking about?" Veronica said. "Who is 'Sophronie'?"

"I'm sorry," Mandalay said. "There are things involved in this that you don't know about."

"Or care about," Veronica said. "Tucker says you can help me, and I'm willing to listen. But not if all you're going to do is gossip. I'll just go back and—"

"No," Mandalay said firmly, "you won't. Now tell me what happened when you got to the other end of the cave."

She gave a short version of the day's events. "I don't care where it was, or what it was," Veronica said, "just that my boyfriend ran off into it. He wasn't himself, he'd never do that. It's just like in the old folk tales, when people stumble onto fairy dances."

"They are old folks, that's for sure," Mandalay murmured. "Come on inside where it's cooler."

The trailer was cramped but neat. Darnell stood in the kitchen sipping a beer. Mandalay gestured for Veronica to sit on the couch, and Tucker took the seat beside her.

Mandalay's stepmother Leshell came out of the bedroom, picking lint from her black pants. "These things'll pick up anything except men and money," she muttered, then jumped when she saw the others. "Lord a'mercy, I didn't know we had company."

"They're here for me," Mandalay said.

"I hope so, 'cause I'm on my way out. Picking up a late shift stocking at the grocery store over in Bristol. If y'all will excuse me?"

"I'll drive you over there," Darnell said with the weariness of someone used to this sort of thing. "I imagine Mandalay will want to speak to these folks in private."

"Thank you, Daddy," the girl said.

When her parents had gone, Mandalay sat down on the coffee table, knee to knee with her guests. "Tell me again exactly what you saw in that other place," she said to Veronica. "Don't leave out anything, any detail. I need to know everything that happened, if I'm going to help you."

Veronica looked questioningly at Tucker. "Is this girl for real?"

"She is," he assured her.

"I am," Mandalay said.

Veronica swallowed, took a deep breath, and poured out the story in all the detail she could muster.

When she was finished, Mandalay said, "So Justin just ran out to talk to these people?"

"Yes."

"Why didn't you?"

The image of the Death card flashed in her mind, just as it had in the cave. "Because I realized where we were," she said, which wasn't technically a lie.

Mandalay got up and paced as much as the tiny room allowed. "Could it really be true?" she asked aloud, not really expecting an answer.

"Wait," Veronica said, "you don't *believe* me?"

Mandalay gave her an impatient scowl. "I know you're worried about your boyfriend, and you're right to be," she said as calmly as she could. "But there are some other considerations here, and they have serious ramifications for the Tufa."

"*Are* you people fairy folk?" Veronica asked bluntly.

"Yes, we are," Mandalay said just as plainly. "Eons ago—and that's not an exaggeration—we were exiled here. The only way back home for us was through that passage you may have found, but it's been hidden from us by glamour. Until now."

"So what do we do?" Tucker asked.

Mandalay finally stopped pacing. "Tucker," she said, "bring Veronica to the Pair-A-Dice at six."

"Will do."

Veronica immediately glanced at the clock on the wall; it was a little after five. "Wait, what's the 'paradise'?" She immediately thought of that wondrous world where Justin had disappeared.

"No, it's 'Pair *of* Dice,' Pair-A-Dice," Tucker said. "It's a road-house."

"How will that help us find Justin?" Veronica said, and looked up into the girl's eyes. She saw what lurked there, and even though she couldn't put a name to it, she felt its weight and power. It was not the gaze of a teenage girl, but something older, more primal, more fierce. She was glad, she realized, that it wasn't focused on her with anger.

Mandalay put a hand gently on Veronica's arm. "I know you're scared. I promise you, we'll do everything to help bring your friend back."

And in that moment, Veronica believed her.

Veronica stared up at the two huge flat, wooden cutouts atop the building's roof. They had once been painted to resemble dice, one with a five showing and the other with a two. Now, though, the paint had faded and peeled, and bird droppings streaked down the image.

"Pair of dice," she murmured. "Now I get it."

The Pair-A-Dice was a rectangular cinder-block building, windowless and with only one visible door, set back from the highway in the center of a gravel parking lot. The cutouts of dice on the roof were the only signage. Like many things to do with the Tufa, the place could be found only by those meant to find it.

They'd driven there in Tucker's pickup, which was inexplicably waiting at Mandalay's trailer when they came outside. It was sundown by the time they parked among the many other vehicles present.

"So exactly how will coming to a bar help?" she asked Tucker, who'd said virtually nothing since they left Mandalay's trailer.

In a Harrison Ford accent, Tucker said, "She may not look like much, but she's got it where it counts, kid." At Veronica's blank look, he added, "That's from *Star Wars*. The first one," he added helpfully.

"Oh. I only saw that once, when I was a kid."

"Come on, they're waiting."

Inside the roadhouse the atmosphere was warm and close. A haze hung in the air from cigarettes, and people sat in clumps around the tables. Most nursed beer, although a few had sodas. Like a ripple, people noticed Tucker and Veronica, but no one said anything.

Tucker looked around, then saw Mandalay's wave. He nodded and let Veronica precede him to the table.

In addition to Mandalay, two women and a white-haired man sat there. "Thank you for coming," Mandalay said. "This is Bliss Overbay, Bronwyn Chess, and Snowy Rainfield."

Veronica realized the white-haired man was actually only in his thirties. "Nice to meet you all," she said quietly. To Bronwyn she added, "I saw your picture on the wall at the cafe."

"Long time ago," Bronwyn said. "Now I'm just a mom and a preacher's wife."

"Let's get down to business," Mandalay said quietly. She waved her hand in the air, and instantly it was as if they were under an invisible cone of silence; all the other voices in the room were muffled and indistinct, and Veronica got the feeling they could neither be seen nor heard by anyone except those at the table. "This young woman and her boyfriend have found the cave the Conlins guarded. The one above Sadieville."

She paused to let that sink in.

"So it *does* exist," Bronwyn finally said. "I never really believed it."

"I've seen it," Tucker added. "It's no longer hidden."

"Why not?" Bliss asked.

"There's two possibilities," Mandalay said. "Either the glamour that hid it has just faded with time, or . . . *she* isn't hiding it from us anymore."

"Or it's a trick," Bronwyn said, looking hard at Tucker.

"Okay, I deserve that. But as soon as I knew someone was looking for Sadieville, I had Azure bring you the song. I wasn't trying to hide it, at least not anymore."

"Excuse me, but how does this help find Justin?" Veronica asked, feeling more alien than she ever had before. She fought the urge to run screaming into the twilight. "We're running out of time here."

"Time doesn't work the same for everybody," Mandalay said. "And we've got plenty of it right now."

"Excuse me, but who *is* this?" Snowy asked, with a nod at Veronica.

"She and her boyfriend went through," Tucker said, pointing at Veronica. "*All* the way through."

"What," Bronwyn asked with quiet intensity, "did you see?"

"Is this important?" Veronica asked. "Right now? I already told her," she said with a nod at Mandalay.

"Yes, it's important," Bliss said seriously. "Right now."

The others leaned closer, as if every word might contain some secret. "It was like a storybook world," Veronica said at last. "Or a Maxfield Parrish painting. Everything was beautiful, and vivid, and alive. It was like seeing everything in incredible detail all at once."

"And you saw people, right?" Bliss asked.

Veronica nodded. "It looked like a group of musicians and dancers, like something you'd see at a Renaissance fair. Justin went to join them, even though I tried to hold him back. It was like he was under—" She stopped, about to say "a spell." "The influence of something," she finished instead.

The white-haired man, Snowy, finally spoke. "He was."

Veronica wiped at tears she didn't even know had started. "I've read all about what happens to people when they go off with the fairies. I'm so scared for him right now."

Mandalay put her hand atop Veronica's. "I know, and I'm sorry. I'd like to say you were wrong to be scared, but that's not true." She turned to the others. "Bliss, Bronwyn, Snowy: I've asked big things of you in the past, and you've never let me down. Now I'm going to ask you the biggest thing ever: go find this boy Justin and bring him back."

It took a moment for that to sink in. At last Bronwyn said, "You want us to go . . . there?"

"And come back," Mandalay said.

"Why us?" Snowy asked.

"Bliss remembers the place, and knows its dangers. Bronwyn, you and Snowy have firm ties to this world, so you'll be less tempted to stay. Plus, you've all proven many times that I can depend on you."

"I'm going, too," Veronica said.

"No," Mandalay said, in a way that brooked no argument. "You were lucky once; it'd be foolish to push it."

"You do realize you're asking us to go back to the place all the Tufa want to return to," Snowy said, "find somebody dumb enough to run off to it—no offense, I'm sure he's a nice guy—and then drag him back here?"

"Yeah," Mandalay agreed. "That's exactly what I'm asking you to do."

"I don't know if I'm up to that," Snowy said. He looked at Bronwyn. "I mean, you've got a husband and child here, that'll bring you back."

"You've got Tain," Bronwyn pointed out.

"Yeah," Snowy agreed. His live-in girlfriend, Tain Wisby, was part *glaistig*, which meant she craved men's attention; Snowy understood and didn't judge her for it. But when he saw other couples, exclusive ones, he often wondered how strong a bond he really had with Tain. *I guess,* he thought, *this'll settle that.* "When do we go?"

"Right now," Veronica said. "It's not that late, and—"

"No," Bliss said. "First thing in the morning. I'm sorry, but we're taking a lot of risks already."

Veronica swallowed her protest, and nodded.

"Keep this to yourselves," Mandalay said. "If word gets around, it'll be difficult to stop others from following you."

They nodded. Mandalay waved her hand again. The muffled effect faded, and the noise of the crowded bar filled Veronica's ears. She put her hands over them and closed her eyes, exhausted and terrified.


Veronica couldn't bear the thought of going back to the Catamount Corner and facing all of Justin's belongings, so she went home with Bronwyn. Snowy went home to Tain, and Tucker just went wherever he went, leaving Mandalay and Bliss at the Pair-A-Dice. They sat in silence for a long time.

"What do you think will happen?" Bliss asked.

"I don't know."

"You don't really care about that girl's boyfriend, do you?"

"I've only got so much space for caring. Most of it's taken up by the Tufa."

"So if we actually *can* go there?"

"Then we—the Tufa—have a lot to think about. And I do care very much about that." She paused, frowned, then continued, "Have you ever thought that we've been here so long, we might no longer *be* true Tuatha de Danaan? Even those of us with pure Tufa blood? That's crossed my mind a lot over time."

"So by sending the three of us back—" Bliss stopped at a sudden realization. "Son of a bitch. Now I get it."

"Get what?"

"Why you told that girl she couldn't go with us. You're not sending us to rescue her boyfriend. You're using us as bait. We're your canaries, just like they were Tucker's."

"Yeah," Mandalay said, eyes downcast. "I'm not proud of it, but that's exactly what I'm doing."

"And if we don't come back?"

"Then we'll know. *I'll* know. If the Queen welcomes us back, she'll send word with you, and let you bring that boy back with you. If she doesn't . . ."

"If she doesn't, we'll likely be dead."

Mandalay had no response to that. Bliss wanted to get angry at the thought that she could be so easily sacrificed, but she understood Mandalay's point. This might be the only way they would know if their deep desire to return home was as truly hopeless as they all believed.

# 32

"Can I get you anything?" Craig Chess asked Veronica.

She sat on the edge of the bed in their guest room, staring at nothing. He'd seen people zone out from stress many times, and knew he could do nothing but make her feel safe and comfortable until she came out of it.

"Well," he added, "Bronwyn and I are right across the hall. Our daughter's next door, but she's pretty good about sleeping through the night. You should be okay."

Veronica finally looked up at him. "I met you at the cafe yesterday, didn't I? You and your daughter."

"That was us."

"You're not a Tufa, are you?"

"No, I'm not."

"But your wife is."

"Yes."

Veronica swallowed hard; her throat burned from choked-down sobs. "So you know what the Tufa are, then."

"Yes."

She laughed a little, a hysterical chuckle that almost got away from her. She crudely wiped her nose and said,

"Last week this time, I was teaching a lab section. It was all about logic, and science. Cause and effect, you know? And now, I'm making decisions based on the reality of . . . of . . ."

She collapsed into tears and threw herself sideways on the bed.

Bronwyn came in and stood beside Craig. She knew that there was no one better in situations like this, and didn't want to break any rapport. "Can I do anything?" she asked softly.

"Get her a beer from the fridge?"

"Sure."

Bronwyn slipped back out. Careful to leave the door open, Craig sat down beside Veronica.

"You love Justin very much, don't you?"

Veronica sat up and looked around for a tissue. He handed her a box from the nightstand. She blew her nose and said, "Yes. I honestly didn't realize how much until I saw him d-dance off with those people." She looked up at him. "Do you know the story?"

"Bronwyn told me, yes."

She took out her phone and stared at it. "I didn't even think to take any pictures. You know what my major is? Parapsychology. I literally stood there on the threshold of the other world and didn't think to take a picture."

"I don't mean to ask the obvious, but have you tried calling Justin?"

"Yes. It went straight to voice mail."

"Under the circumstances, that's not a surprise."

Veronica took several deep breaths. "So did she catch you the same way those people did Justin?"

He smiled, but didn't laugh. "I don't know, honestly. I *think* I fell for her of my own free will, but if I didn't, would I know it?"

"That's not reassuring."

"I know. I'm sorry. Are you religious?"

"My family is Catholic. I'm . . . undeclared."

"I'm a Methodist minister. Same school, different major, you might say. I can pray with you if you'd like."

She stared at him. After the last two days of strangeness, odd events, and unbelievable people, this was so normal and down-to-earth she could scarcely comprehend it. Craig radiated the simple piety of a man who didn't hide behind the ceremony and Mafia-like intimidation of her Catholic Church, who merely tried to do what he thought God wanted. At the moment, she realized, he thought God wanted him to keep a total stranger from having a full breakdown.

"Or," he continued, "I can just sit here with you. Or leave. It's up to you. But you don't have to go through this alone, unless you want to."

She nodded. "I think I would like to be alone right now."

He stood. "Of course. Like I said, we'll be right across the hall."

She looked up sharply. "But—"

"What?"

She swallowed again. "Will you pray for Justin?"

"I will."

Bronwyn came into the room then and handed Veronica a beer. "That'll feel good on your throat. I'll see you in the morning."

Across the hall, Bronwyn closed the door to their bedroom and faced her husband. Quietly, she said, "You amaze me, you know that?"

He sat on the bed and kicked off his tennis shoes. "How so?"

"When I was driving her here, I had no idea what to say to her."

"I didn't really say much."

"But it was the *right* 'not much.'"

"I hope so."

Bronwyn sat down beside him. "Tomorrow's going to be an interesting day."

"I'd be lying if I said the idea of it didn't scare me to death right now."

"But you haven't asked me not to go."

"No, and I won't."

"We'll be fine, hon. And we'll come back."

She kissed him, and it turned passionate. They fell back on the bed together.

"I heard what she asked you," Bronwyn said softly. "For the record, I didn't put a spell on you. It's true love, fair and square."

"I never really doubted that."

They kissed again. And that led to more. Quietly.


In her darkened room, Veronica lay on the bed in her underwear and stared at the ceiling. She could hardly breathe from the weight of recent events, and would cry some more if she only had the energy. But she didn't, and instead she studied the plaster swirls above her, visible in the faint glow from the nightlight.

At last she swung her feet off the bed, sat up and reached for her pack, which had somehow gotten from the ridge outside the cave into Bronwyn's truck. She took out her tarot cards, and with shaking fingers managed to shuffle them and cut the deck three times. She wondered if it was some kind of sin to use the tarot in a minister's house. She stared at the deck, took a deep breath, and turned over the top card.

*The Tower.*

The last time, she'd drawn Death, which did not really represent death. But the Tower *was* the card of death, of disaster, of the worst possible outcome.

She stared at the card in her hand, then let it fall to the bed. She curled up and clutched a pillow to her chest.

———

In the middle of the night, unable to sleep, Veronica cupped her hands over her cell phone as it rang on the other end. A sleepy male voice said, "Hello?"

As quietly as she could without actually whispering, she said, "Mr. Tully? This is Veronica Lopez. I'm sorry for calling so late, but may I speak to Tanna?"

"Sure, Veronica," he said. She heard the phone get passed and the man say, "It's Veronica Lopez."

Tanna Tully's voice came on the line, clear and wide awake. "Veronica? Is something wrong?"

Unable to control her shaking voice, she blurted out what had happened, and what card she'd pulled from the tarot. When she finished, she lay there gasping, trying not to sob. It all sounded so ludicrous.

"That's awful," Tanna said with real sympathy.

Veronica asked the only question that mattered. "What d-do I do, Tanna?"

"Have you called the police?"

"I've been told that wouldn't do any good. That they wouldn't come, and even if they did, there's nothing they can do."

"Do you think that's true?"

"I don't know."

"If you're right about what happened, the longer he's there, the more danger he's in."

"S-some of the locals . . . some Tufa locals are going in at first light. They don't want me to go with them."

"Do you trust them?"

Even though she didn't know Bronwyn well, she trusted Craig, and *he* trusted Bronwyn. "One of them."

"Then you'll have to follow your instincts."

Veronica found herself chuckling. "You want to know the worst part? I stood there on the edge of Fairyland and didn't even think to take a picture. Now I have no proof at all."

"That should give you more sympathy for those people who never get a clear picture of Bigfoot."

Despite it all, Veronica laughed.

"Do you want me to come there?" Tanna asked.

"What?"

"If we leave now, we can be there in five or six hours."

Veronica looked at the clock. "No. By then, I'll know." *Know whether or not he's coming back to me.*

"Call me, then, and let me know. All good thoughts your way, Veronica."

"Thanks."

They said good night. Veronica felt stronger, as she always did after speaking to Tanna. She turned on the bedside lamp and picked up her tarot deck. Without reshuffling, which kept the Tower card on the bottom of the deck, she put down the first card of a basic past-present-future reading.

It was the World, in an upside-down position. It meant feeling the weight of everything, which was certainly accurate. But it was in the position of the past; had she been weighed down all along, and not realized it? By what?

The next card, for the present, was the Devil, right side up. That represented feeling trapped, which again was certainly accurate.

And finally, for the future, the Hanged Man, upright. That card meant that, in matters of the heart, it might be time to let go.

To let go of Justin.

She carefully put away her cards, turned out the bedside lamp, and lay staring up at the ceiling again.

Then, in the stark silence that had her thoughts racing, she heard the unmistakable glass-rattle noise of someone opening the refrigerator. She got up, pulled on her jeans, and stuck her head out the door.

Bronwyn stood illuminated by the light from the open fridge

door. Veronica walked quietly down the hall and said in a whisper, "I hope I'm not bothering you."

"Nah, not at all," Bronwyn said. "I just couldn't sleep, thinking about tomorrow morning."

"It's actually this morning," Veronica said after a glance at the clock on the microwave.

"Yeah. You want some yogurt?"

"No, thank you."

Bronwyn grabbed the tub of yogurt, closed the door, and motioned for Veronica to join her at the table. After a few moments of awkward silence, Brownyn asked, "So where are you from?"

"My family's Puerto Rican," she said. "My grandparents on both sides came to Chicago, but I grew up in Mississippi."

"Went to Mississippi once when I was in the service. Well, *through* it, at any rate."

"What did you think?"

"It was at night. I didn't see much."

"That's about what you'd see during the day."

"You go to school at West Tennessee State over in Weakleyville?"

"Yes. I'm going for my masters in psychology. Justin and I live in . . ." She trailed off and put a trembling finger to her lip so she could bite it to keep from crying.

"I'm sorry. We don't have to talk about it."

She took a few deep breaths. "No, it's okay. The worst part is, my mother and both my grandmothers think I'm *loca* for taking up with a black guy. If he doesn't come back, I'll never hear the end of it."

"That's the first time I've heard you use Spanish. You don't have much of an accent."

"No, I speak it, but my field already has a bunch of strikes against it in the credibility department, so I figured I'd better as least sound like I've been to school."

"Psychology?"

"*Para*psychology."

Bronwyn's eyebrows went up.

"Yeah, I know. I've seen those same TV shows, too. But there is legitimate science being done, and I want to be part of it." She paused, then asked, "How did you meet Craig?"

Bronwyn smiled. "That's a story, all right." She told Veronica about meeting Craig after returning from Iraq, and how he'd been so steady and strong when her brother Kell died. It was Craig's idea that they name their daughter for him.

"Your daughter is beautiful," Veronica said. "I saw her yesterday at the cafe."

"Thank you."

Veronica looked away, mustered courage that was only available in the wee hours of the morning, and said, "I know you're fairy folk. Is she?"

"Yes," Bronwyn said without hesitation.

Veronica shook her head. "I know what I've seen, but it's still . . . I mean, here we are in a kitchen. That's a stove, that's a refrigerator, this is a table. All those things I know are real. And then there's you. Just as real as the other things. How did Craig take it when he learned?"

"Like you. It took him a while to figure out how we fit into his idea of the world."

The women were silent. The refrigerator compressor kicked on, making them both jump. They laughed.

From her bedroom, Kell began to half talk, half cry. "Excuse me," Bronwyn said. A moment later she returned with her daughter in her arms. The girl rubbed her eyes and pushed sleep-tangled hair out of her face. She snuggled close to her mother and watched Veronica closely.

"She knows when things are happening," Bronwyn said as she sat. "She hates to miss anything. Ain't that right, punkin?" She kissed the top of the girl's head.

"I've been thinking," Veronica said. "What if I was totally wrong? What if we just saw another valley, and those were just hippies from a commune or something? What if I've been freaking out over nothing, and Justin just ran off because he's an asshole, not because he was under a . . . a spell."

"Is that what you really think?"

"Not really. I mean, it would *have* to be magic to turn him away from me so easily. Wouldn't it?"

"Do you believe in magic?"

"I don't know. I think I'll just fall back on that as my go-to answer from now on. 'I don't know.'"

Now Bronwyn looked away into the dark house, thinking hard before saying, "Close your eyes, Veronica."

She remembered Tucker's identical admonition. "Why?"

"Because you deserve to at least know you're not out of your mind."

Veronica closed her eyes. She heard Bronwyn's chair scrape back as the other woman stood. Then her voice, somehow musical even though she wasn't singing, said, "Open your eyes."

Veronica did.

A beautiful dark-haired fairy stood in the kitchen, with wide wings that brushed the walls on either side. She wore a shimmering togalike wrap, and her head almost touched the ceiling. Veronica looked down and saw that the woman's delicate bare feet hovered above the floor.

In her arms, the fairy woman held a little girl who also had wings, and looked at Veronica with a wisdom and compassion that seemed to both reach into her heart, and connect her back with the original spiritual source of kindness.

"Oh, my God," she whispered.

"No God," Bronwyn said, and while it was the same voice, it now gave a magical lilt to even these mundane words. "Just people different from you."

And then they were gone, and two normal people stood

before her: a weary young mother and a sleepy little girl. "So you see, you weren't imagining things."

"Yeats was right," Veronica said. "He said, 'The world is full of magic things, patiently waiting for our senses to grow sharper.'"

"Who is Yeats?"

"A famous poet." She almost giggled. "Who believed in fairies."

# 33

At sunrise, the group from the Pair-A-Dice stood outside the cave. Bliss, Bronwyn, and Snowy carried backpacks of basic camping gear, including plenty of fresh water; drinking something at the other end of that tunnel, even for the Tufa, might prove disastrous.

Bronwyn carried her Hoyt Spyder Turbo compound bow. She knew firearms would probably be useless, but at the same time, she wasn't about to go off without at least one weapon. The quiver held eight arrows, all with fixed blade broadhead points.

Bliss and Snowy were unarmed. Snowy simply felt uncomfortable carrying a weapon into this situation, while Bliss understood the utter futility of thinking one would make a difference. But she didn't say so to Bronwyn.

They'd cleared away the hawthorn trees, and Mandalay now gazed into the cave's darkness. The music from the day before was gone, and she sensed nothing untoward about it, no sense that glamour lurked unseen to protect it. When they had been exiled, the cave had been hidden from them by the Queen's magic, but that seemed to be over now. How long, she wondered, had it been waiting to be rediscovered?

Tucker stood beside Veronica. The girl's eyes were red and swollen, and she slumped wearily, but she still stepped forward and said to Mandalay, "Please let me go with them. He'll listen to me."

"He didn't before," Mandalay said curtly.

Veronica bit off her reply and turned away. Tucker put a comforting hand on her shoulder. *That was mean,* he mouthed silently at Mandalay.

Mandalay ignored him and turned to Bliss. "I doubt you'll be gone long. Or at least, it won't seem like it here." Mandalay stood on tiptoe and kissed the other woman's cheek. "Be careful. Come back."

"I will," she promised.

"*We* will," Snowy said.

Bliss had dim, confused memories of the way the cave had first looked all those eons ago, as she and the other first Tufa stumbled out naked, nameless, and confused, lost in this new world. Where it was once an opening at the foot of an enormous mountain, it now protruded into the side of a rounded hill, all that was left of that ancient peak. Now she stood on its threshold, about to return to a place that, through rivers of time, she still recalled with an ache in her heart.

"I'm a little nervous," Bronwyn said quietly just behind her.

Bliss smiled. "You? You're a war hero."

"Doesn't take a hero to get shot up, then blown up," Bronwyn said, distilling her service down to its most dramatic events. "Walking into that cave . . . that needs real nerve."

"So you have it?"

Bronwyn grinned. "Oh, hell, no. All I have is enough nerve to follow you."

Bliss turned to Snowy. "Ready?"

"No, but why let that stop us?"

"We'll be here waiting," Mandalay said.

"Good luck," Tucker added.

"Please," Veronica said, "bring him back. He's a good man, and I love him."

"We'll do our absolute best," Bliss assured her.

She stepped up to the threshold. This was it. Closing her eyes, she sang a line from a song by the Old Crow Medicine Show: "I was born to be a fiddler in an old-time string band." It was, she hoped, an anchor that would draw them back if things got out of hand.

Then she turned on her flashlight, shone it into the cave, and led the other two down into the darkness.


The passage had taken, Veronica told them, barely a quarter of an hour. But sixty minutes later they were still going, picking their way through narrow passages and carefully checking for sudden drops. It didn't surprise any of them, especially Bliss: if these rocks were still infused with *her* magic, they stood a real chance of never seeing daylight again.

Every few feet, Bliss stopped and reached into a cloth pouch tied to her hip. She pulled out a large iron nut with a strip of white silk tied to it. She tossed it ahead, listening to make sure it landed on something solid.

It was more than just a way to check for drop-offs, though it did that well enough. Iron was something that fairies disliked, much as vampires retreated from garlic. It didn't affect the Tufa, who lived in a society laced with iron, but then, they'd existed through the human Iron Age, and had had generations to acclimate. Those who hadn't, who remained in their homeland, would lack this adaptation, and be unable to interfere with this trail of metallic bread crumbs. Hopefully.

As she readied another throw, from behind her Snowy said, "Hey, I just realized something."

"What's that?" Bliss said, her eyes locked to the circle of light before her. She watched the white silk ribbon ripple off into the darkness.

"Turns out I'm a Buddhist."

"What?"

"I'm a Buddhist," he repeated.

"How do you figure that?" Bronwyn asked.

"I'm following my Bliss."

The tension had ratcheted them up so much that they all burst out laughing, so hard they had to sit down until the urge passed. The cavern filled with the sound of their amusement, dispelling all thoughts of strange beings lurking in the shadows. Eventually they wound down, until all three were gasping to catch their breath.

Then a new voice, one they all instantly recognized, said softly, "Well, ain't this a sight."

The laughter choked off at once, their throats locking in mid-breath. Bliss and Snowy froze in place. Bronwyn slipped an arrow from her quiver, ready to use it as a knife.

Barely moving, Bliss turned on her flashlight and slowly shone it around the floor until it illuminated a pair of legs, in denim pants and old work boots. The circle of light trembled as her hand shook. She didn't have the nerve to raise it to the figure's face.

"What the hell do y'all think you're doing?" the voice of Rockhouse Hicks, once the Man in the Rock House, once the Six-Fingered Man, demanded in a voice that was simultaneously distant and immediate, like a phone call from another country.

Since their arrival in this world, up until a cold winter night three years earlier, he had been the final arbiter of the Tufa world. While Mandalay was the latest in a chain of avatars, Rockhouse had never abdicated to a younger man, even one of his own descendants who might have carried his memories. The overwhelming magic in his powerful songs had ensured that his longevity and omnipresence never raised suspicion, and his isolation made him bitter and mean.

And yet Rockhouse Hicks was dead, full dead, *truly* dead; he'd had his throat torn out by his incest-born daughter, Bliss's half-sister Curnen, and his extra fingers cut off by Bo-Kate Wisby as part of her plan to take over the Tufa. He'd finally died of exposure, and been buried only after his blood had been drained and disposed of somewhere else. Songs had been sung, the night winds invoked, all to keep him quiet and gone. Yet it looked as though he *still* wouldn't stay in his grave.

"What's the matter?" he said in his distinctive smug, taunting way. "Cats got all y'all's tongues?"

"I still remember your dying dirge, old man," Bliss said, hoping her voice didn't shake. "Go back where you belong."

His sharp, hateful laugh echoed around them. "I'm afraid that don't matter no more, Bliss Overbay."

"What do you want?" Snowy demanded.

"If it ain't the white-haired freak who took up with that *glaistig*. Well, you Charlie Rich–looking bastard, I'm here to make sure nobody goes where they ain't supposed to."

"He's lying," Bronwyn said. She stood up, brandishing the arrow. "Tell the truth, old man. Tell us that this is the punishment the night winds gave you when you oozed up out of your grave and tried to interfere in the Tufa again. They put you here, stuck between where you came from and where you went to."

There was no response, and the shoes in the circle of light didn't move.

"We've all heard the rumors that you've been whispering to Junior Damo," Bronwyn continued, her voice growing louder, firmer, and drawlier as she spoke. "You do that because it's all you *can* do." She grinned almost hatefully. "This is your own personal hell, old man. Welcome to it, enjoy it, and get the fuck out of our way." With that, she threw the arrow directly at what should have been the center of his chest.

The feet stepped out of the light. The arrow struck the rock wall and fell to the ground. When Bliss tried to find him again, there was no sign.

The three got to their feet. "Was that real?" Snowy asked.

"Real enough," Bliss said, and shone the light on her own trembling fingers. "Had me shaking like a leaf on the Widow's Tree."

"He's gone," Bronwyn said with certainty. "He was always a bully, and there's no reason death would make him different."

Bliss shone the light around them. "Does anything look different?"

They followed the light as it traveled over the cave walls and ceiling. "No," Snowy said. "Why?"

"I'd just swear this was different," Bliss said. "Like it changed while we were talking to . . ." She trailed off, afraid to say his name lest she invoke him again.

"It'd be just like the old peckerhead," Bronwyn said. "Distracting us with his bullshit while fucking with us when we weren't looking."

"There's still only one way forward," Bliss said, shining the light ahead.

"Unless we're actually going back."

" 'The awful solemnity of its dismal grandeur,' " Snowy said. When the women looked at him, he added, "Something I read about a cave once. Seemed applicable."

"Well, if Rockhouse has flipped us around and we come back out where we started, we just try again. Agreed?"

"Yes," Snowy said.

"You bet," Bronwyn agreed.

They headed in the direction they believed was forward, still thoroughly rattled by their encounter.

# 34

Tucker dozed in Veronica's camp chair outside the cave. He snapped awake as he heard feet crunching through the forest. He sat all the way up as Tain Wisby, Snowy Rainfield's girlfriend, emerged.

Tain was sexy even among a people who had the knack of using glamour to appear as all things to all people. Whatever she wore seemed to cling to her in just the right way, and the light always seemed to cast shadows on her that emphasized her curves. Clad as she was now, in high cutoffs and a tight tank top, she could've reduced any normal man she met to a blubbering pile of tumescent need. Even Tucker found it difficult to concentrate at first.

"Hey, Tucker," Tain said wearily. "Mandalay." She made a gesture of respect to the girl, who sat with her back to a nearby tree. She turned to Veronica, who paced in front of the cave. "Hi, we haven't met. I'm Tain."

"Veronica Lopez."

"It's your boyfriend that my boyfriend has gone to rescue, then."

"Yes."

Mandalay said, "What brings you out here?"

"Sitting around waiting isn't my best skill. Figured that here, I'd at least have some company."

"Well, they haven't been gone that long, just so you know. Nothing to get worried about yet."

Tain peered into the cave. "So that leads home, huh?"

"It's the way back," Mandalay corrected. "Whether it's still home . . ."

Tain sighed and dropped gracefully into a cross-legged position beside the girl. "So we wait?"

"We wait," Mandalay agreed. She looked up at the sky, bright blue above the treetops, the sun only now high enough to fully strike the uppermost branches. "Nice weather for it, at least."

Tain picked up a stick and dug idly at the dirt with it. It was in her nature to charge forward, making everything happen as quickly as possible; it was one reason why, before Snowy, she had burned through so many men. *Why waste time on courtship that was only going to end in fucking?* she often said. *Let's just get to the fucking and enjoy it.* But she understood that right now, there was nothing else to do, and even fucking someone else wouldn't make things happen any faster.

"Can we wait with y'all, too?" a new voice said.

Janet Harper and Ginny Vipperman emerged from the woods. When Janet had heard the song about Sadieville, she'd immediately sung it for Ginny. And when they heard about the expedition, they couldn't help wondering whether the stories they'd always heard about the Tufa's original, beautiful home were true. And if they'd live to see it for themselves.

Like Tain, they walked up to the cave and stared into its darkness, looking for answers that they imagined were hidden there.

"Doesn't look like much," Ginny observed.

"What did you expect?" Janet asked.

"I dunno, something more . . . epic."

"If it was epic, it would've been found before now."

"I'm still a little disappointed."

"You might as well find a spot in the shade," Tucker said. "This could be a while."

"Come on," Ginny said with a wink. "I got something to help us pass the time."

"Don't tell me," Janet said. "it starts with a *g*."

"'Goint'?"

*"Grass."*

"Oh. No, it's a joint." Ginny turned to the others. "Y'all are cool, right? You won't tell our folks or anything."

"They won't hear it from us," Mandalay promised, knowing full well their parents were totally aware of what their girls did, and were just glad they usually stayed at home to do it.

Janet and Ginny went a few yards away and found a mossy rock, in the shadow of a cedar tree, that gave them an unobstructed view of the cave. Ginny lit up the joint and passed it to Janet. As Janet drew in the smoke, Ginny said, "Think they have weed over there?"

"Never thought about it," Janet said through her smoky exhalation. She caught Veronica's eye and made an offering motion with the joint. Veronica shook her head.

"But you can have everything you want there, right?"

"You're thinking of heaven."

"But that *is* Tufa heaven. *Our* heaven."

"No it's not. It's just the place where we came from."

"You don't sound very excited."

Janet took another toke and looked up at the cave. Veronica still paced, Tain and Mandalay still sat, and Tucker settled back into his camp chair.

"I'll get excited," Janet said at last, "when I hear their music."

————

The air in the cave was now almost cold. The only sounds were their mixed breathing, grunts of effort, and boots crunching gravel. The circle of flashlight illumination ahead showed the same sort of terrain over and over: rocks, stalactites and stalagmites, a reflection where water splashed down from the ceiling. In a couple of places they'd had to crouch, and in one crawl on their bellies, pushing their gear ahead of them.

"All right, ten-minute break," Bliss said. "Everyone sit down and drink some water. I'm turning off the light to save the battery."

They dumped their packs and slumped to the ground. The exertion hit Snowy, the most out of shape, the hardest. He said between gasps, "I think . . . we might want to . . . reconsider our strategy here."

"I second that motion," Bronwyn said.

"We keep going," Bliss said firmly.

"Is that for the boy," Bronwyn said, annoyed, "or for you?"

Then there was silence. Bliss did not answer. After a moment Bronwyn mumbled, "Sorry."

As they sat in total darkness, they began to see spots of light in their peripheral vision that vanished when they looked at them directly. None of them wanted to be the first to mention it, in case it was just something generated by their brains to fill in the darkness. But before long they resolved into spots of soft blue glow from lichen on some of the rocks.

"Foxfire," Bronwyn said.

"Somewhere two foxes are getting married," Bliss said, verbalizing the legend behind the glow.

"Wait," Bronwyn said. "That doesn't make sense."

"It's simple," Snowy deadpanned. "When two foxes love each other very much—"

"Not that." She crawled to one of the glowing spots. Her fingers encountered a pile of soft and crumbly sticks, the glowing fungus growing from the decaying surface.

"That's what I thought," she said. "This stuff only grows on decaying wood. Give me the light, Bliss."

Bliss turned on the flashlight and shone it at Bronwyn's feet. There was a stack of partially burned sticks nestled in an alcove just off the passage.

"That looks like a fire," Snowy said. "A real one, not a fox one."

"An *old* one," Bronwyn said, "but not too old. The wood's still damp enough for the foxfire to grow. If it had been here a long time, it would've dried out."

"So what does that tell us?" Snowy asked.

"That maybe we're closer than farther," Bliss said. "Let's get going."

They'd gone another hundred yards when Bliss stopped suddenly and whispered, "Listen!"

Beyond the soft drip drip of moisture, over the soft sigh of barely moving air, they all heard it. And recognized it.

*Fairy music.*

It touched each of them differently, but all of them at the same core level. For Bliss it reminded her of childhood, of running through fields of flowers or soaring above thick forests. There had been nothing but joy then, a happiness that she'd never even remotely reached since she was forced to leave. Yet now, hearing those lilting notes, it all came back, reminding her of the crudity of the human world, and the sheer delicate nirvana of her real home.

Bronwyn felt an ache in her heart, but it wasn't for the land ahead. Of course she'd heard stories of it, and fantasized about it. But she'd seen more of the human world than most Tufa, and she understood that most places were neither entirely good nor bad. Their ancestral home might be more suited to the Tufa in some ways, but there had to be flaws, and problems, and aspects that left some of its denizens unsatisfied. After all, it was ruled by a queen who would banish a whole population for the failure of its leader to win her a stupid bet. How perfect could it be?

No, the ache in Bronwyn's heart was for her daughter and husband, her anchors and quiet sources of strength. What was she doing here, risking her life for a stranger, leaving them alone and possibly never coming back to them?

But she knew the answer. She did it because someone had to, and she had the necessary skills and experience. If she hadn't come, she wouldn't be the woman she wanted her daughter to see.

Snowy's response was more primal. After all the time spent with Tain and her intense sexuality, he responded to this music with arousal and excitement. The idea of a whole world of women like Tain, all of them willing and glad to have him, almost had him vapor locked. He had to really struggle to keep his attention on the task at hand.

Bliss said, "Deep breaths, everybody. We knew it would affect us. Just stay focused."

"No problem," Bronwyn said.

"I'm fine," Snowy said, his voice a little ragged.

They resumed their trek. The passage twisted and turned as they crept along, and soon they were thoroughly disoriented, unsure if they'd gone up or down, forward or back.

"We must be close," Bliss said. "This is all designed to confuse us."

"You mean it's not real?" Snowy said.

"No, it's real. It's just not natural; it's deliberate."

"Turn off your flashlight," Bronwyn whispered.

Bliss did so. Again they waited for their eyes to adjust.

They saw a faint glow ahead, made of white sunlight instead of the foxfire's soft blue. And the music came from the same direction.

"Holy shit," Snowy breathed. "There it is."

"Deep breaths, people," Bliss said. "Are we ready?"

"Damn skippy," Snowy replied.

"As ready as we're likely to be," Bronwyn said.

Bliss turned the flashlight back on, since the faint sunlight didn't yet provide enough illumination. They headed toward the light, and the music.

They reached the mouth of the cave and squinted into the light. Through her fingers, Bliss saw not the Tír na nÓg of her oldest memories, but a village of low, square buildings on either side of a wide street that started at the cave and stretched to the other end of the town.

Bronwyn finally asked, "Is that . . . ?"

Bliss slowly nodded. "It's Sadieville."

## 35

"Looks like quite the party," Craig Chess said as he emerged from the woods. Kell followed, holding his hand while serious eyes peeked out through her unruly bangs.

"Who's that?" Tain whispered to Mandalay.

"Bronwyn's husband." She stood up and brushed off her jeans. "What brings you here, Reverend?"

"Seemed like a good day for a walk in the woods. Figured I'd find some of you around here." To Kell he said, "Want to go see Mandalay?"

"Come here, munchkin," Mandalay said, reaching out. The girl jumped into her arms.

"Is Mommy here?" Kell asked.

"She will be soon," Mandalay said, with a certainty she didn't feel.

The girl looked at the cave. "I don't like that place," she said seriously.

"Don't worry, we're not going in there," Mandalay assured her. "We're just going to stay out here and wait."

"Is that where Mommy went?"

"Yes. But you know how tough she is. And she wasn't alone. Your aunt Bliss went with her."

The girl seemed satisfied with that, but she continued to stare into the opening while Mandalay held her.

Craig also gazed into the dark cave mouth. He said quietly, "I know how tough Bronwyn is, believe me. But I've also heard the stories about that place." He sighed, then added, "Is there anything I can do to help?"

Craig accepted the Tufa with no judgment, and had once helped Mandalay through a spiritual crisis. He'd never insisted that Bronwyn convert to his religion, or that she abandon her Tufa family if she wanted to be with him. He simply did the things that made both her and the Tufa first appreciate him: he helped where he could, listened when he needed to, and stayed out of things that weren't his concern. She could imagine how hard that could be, especially now that he had a Tufa daughter.

Yet here he was, asking if he could help.

"Craig," Mandalay said, "you believe prayer can influence the way things come out, don't you?"

"I do."

"Then I hope you're praying right now."

"I am," he said. "I surely am."

He felt a hand on his arm. "Craig?"

He turned to Veronica. "Hey, Veronica," he said easily. "How are you holding up?"

"Okay, I guess. It's nerve-racking just sitting here and waiting."

"I can imagine. Can I get you anything?"

"No, I'm okay. Do you really think they can bring him back?"

"If anyone can," he said with absolute certainty, "it's my wife. In all the time I've known her, she's never failed at anything she decides to do."

Veronica nodded, wanting desperately to believe him. "It's just all this *waiting*."

"Like Tom Petty says, it's the hardest part," Craig agreed.

She looked at him blankly. "I don't know that song. It is a song, right?"

"Yes. Before your time. Is there anything else I can do for you?"

She struggled for words. "This will sound weird, I know it, I just . . . I'm used to seeing priests as some sort of minor deities, you know? As a child, they terrified me. They still do, actually. But . . ."

"But what?"

"I overheard you say you were praying. For your wife?"

"Yes. And for you. And for Justin, like you asked."

"Thanks, Craig. I mean, *Reverend,*" she corrected.

"Craig is fine."

She nodded and walked back down the hill. When she reached the shade, she began to pace again, eyes downcast. Craig wanted to do more, but he knew there was nothing for him at the moment. Like her, he could only wait.

He walked up to the cave and peered inside again. He saw nothing but rock, stretching back into blackness. He listened, but heard only the soft sigh of the wind.

"Spooky, isn't it?"

He looked down at Tain Wisby, seated with her back to the exposed rock. He blinked a little as she had the same effect on him that she did on any man, Tufa or otherwise.

"I'm Tain," she said. "You must be Bronwyn's husband."

"Yes," he said uncomfortably. "Craig."

"Tain!" Mandalay said warningly.

She sighed and stood. "Fine. Nice to meet you." She walked down the hill toward Veronica, and it took all of Craig's strength of character not to watch her as she did so.

He wrenched his attention to his daughter, who now happily played pattycake with Mandalay. He knew that in many ways,

Mandalay had more in common with her than he did. They shared the same fairy blood, after all.

But he also knew whom she called out to when she had a bad dream or an owie. And that made him smile.

He just hoped her next bad dream wouldn't be wondering why her mother never came back.


"What the hell?" Snowy demanded for them all.

There was no denying it, if only from the signage: Sadieville Tavern, Sadieville Dry Goods, Sadieville Barbershop. At the far end of the street, on the mountainside that rose above it, was the opening of the Great Sadie mine, its machinery all present and ready to go. Only one thing seemed off: above the mountain rose the towers of a distant, impossibly large castle, its minarets barely visible through the haze.

And it was deserted: no miners worked, no families strolled, no children scampered. There were no horses, carts, or primitive automobiles. The dusty street bore their traces, but the sources were nowhere in sight. The buildings were still, and quiet, like a museum exhibit or an abandoned ghost town. The only sound was the soft whistling of the wind.

"Well, we won't find out anything standing here," Bliss said at last. "Come on."

Knowing full well the cave might vanish behind them and trap them here, they stepped from it onto the street. The faint music faded as soon as they did.

Now the only sound, besides the wind, was the crunch of their feet on the dirt road. To their right stood the half-built church, and the tree where Sophronie Conlin was lynched. Ahead they saw the boardinghouse where Sean Lee had stayed.

"This is creepy," Snowy said softly. The silence felt heavy and oddly sacrosanct.

"Why are we seeing Sadieville?" Bronwyn asked. "It's not what Veronica described at all. Is it what you remember?"

"No," Bliss said. Even more than with the ghost of Rockhouse Hicks, she felt the chill of vague, uncertain terror. "I do know this place can appear as anything it wants to non-Tufa, but we should see it as it really is."

"Is it a trap?" Bronwyn asked quietly.

"I have no idea," Bliss replied honestly.

Snowy nodded at the distant castle. "What about that? Is that really where *she* lives?"

"She lives anywhere she wants to in this world," Bliss answered. "But yes, that's her castle."

"Too bad we can't just call Justin and have him meet us here," Snowy said.

Impulsively, Bronwyn pulled out her phone and punched in a number.

"What are you doing?" Snowy asked.

"Calling Justin. I got his number from Veronica."

"That's crazy! You actually get a signal?"

"It's ringing. Hello? Is this Justin? Justin, I'm a friend of Veronica's. She's worried to death about you. You need to come back to the cave now. We'll take you back to her."

She listened, then growled impatiently. "The little bastard hung up on me."

Snowy was still flummoxed. "But . . . that's a cell phone. There are no cell towers here. I mean . . . are there?"

Bronwyn ignored him. To Bliss, she said, "He sounded drunk. And I heard a girl giggling."

"Do neither of you think it's weird that a cell phone works here?" Snowy almost shouted.

"I'm not worried about it," Bliss said. "You know how time doesn't work the same for everybody? Well, here, neither do the laws of physics."

"Great," Snowy snarked. "Sitting in my own driveway? Nothing. But a supernatural fairy realm? Five fucking bars."

Then, loud in the almost silence, two fiddles began scraping out a tune. All three jumped.

On the porch of the nearest building, which had appeared empty moments before, two red-capped fiddlers now sat in rocking chairs, sawing away at a sprightly melody. Bliss recognized it as "The Devil Went Down to Georgia."

Suddenly the fiddlers stopped and, in spooky unison, turned to look at the newcomers. Their faces were weathered, with long gray beards, and their eyes lacked anything like kindness.

Snowy waved nervously. "Hi . . . y'all."

They jumped to their feet and scurried out of sight down the nearest alley between the buildings.

"Hey, wait!" Snowy called.

"Don't waste your time," Bliss said. "Those were just sentries."

"For *her?*"

The steady thumping of a drum, a *big* drum, reached them.

"Now what is that?" Bronwyn said, and nodded up the street.

A band of people emerged from an alley on the opposite side, far up the way. They were dressed in the style of Sadieville's era, all stiff suits and long dresses, bonnets and bowler hats. Some of the women fluttered fans in front of their faces. Except for the marching bass drum at the front of the train, carried and played by a small old man who could barely keep it off the ground, they were silent. They looked like an old-fashioned temperance parade, except they carried no signs.

"Think they know where Justin is?" Snowy asked.

"Wait," Bliss said.

"Why?" Bronwyn asked.

"Something's wrong." A dark shiver crawled at the edge of her consciousness, an impending sense of . . . something. It certainly wasn't the way she remembered this place feeling.

Bronwyn immediately raised her bow and reached for an arrow from the quiver. "How wrong?"

"Not that wrong, at least not yet. Just . . . stand still and let me talk."

By then the troupe had turned in their direction. Bliss held her ground, but kept glancing up at the spires of the distant castle, wondering if it was the reason the hairs on the back of her neck were tingling. Was *she* watching them right now?

# 36

By mid-morning, Tufa from all over Cloud County filled the little ridge outside the cave and spread into the forest around it. No one had organized it; much like the way the "Sadieville" song had spread, word about the rescue expedition into the cave, and what it might mean for them all, spiraled out to everyone.

People from both bands of the Tufa milled about under an unspoken flag of truce, just as they did at the Pair-A-Dice. This was bigger than any petty differences, and even Junior Damo seemed to know that. Many brought instruments, and played softly in hushed little groups throughout the nearby woods. Others hauled in camp grills to cook burgers and hot dogs. A troupe of four-wheelers brought cases of beer, distributed at no charge.

To Veronica, this carnival atmosphere was both perplexing and insulting. Justin was in serious danger, and so were the three sent to rescue him; yet these people were throwing a damn *hootenanny*. Finally she went up to Mandalay, who had returned Kell to Craig and now stood alone.

"What are all these people doing here?" she said, softly but urgently.

"Waiting, just like we are," Mandalay said, watching the growing crowd.

"But it's a cookout. And listen to all the music. It's like Bonnaroo or something."

"It's how we express ourselves."

"By having a party while Justin *and* your friends might be dying?"

Mandalay gave Veronica her full attention. "This isn't a party, Veronica. It's not even a celebration. The music is the way we put our thoughts and feelings out there, so they don't burn us up inside."

Veronica looked at the people in their little camps and circles in the woods. "What do they hope will happen?" she asked bitterly. "Is this like the way people at Nascar hope for wrecks?"

"You're being too harsh," Mandalay said. "They want good news just as much as you do."

"They don't even care about Justin."

"That's not true. But they, and that includes me, have other concerns as well."

"Like what?"

The girl smiled sadly. It was the oldest, heaviest expression Veronica had ever seen, all the more severe because it was on such a young, unlined face. "Whether or not we can go home."

A lone plaintive fiddle note rang through the air. It came from a young woman in a sundress and wide-brimmed straw hat, coming up the trail toward them.

From the woods came the strumming of guitars and the plaintive plink of a mandolin. It joined with the fiddle to make the saddest music Veronica had ever heard. The girl in the straw hat joined a group of old men seated with their instruments on a log. She swayed before them, her body as musical as the sounds that poured from the fiddle strings, and they provided expert accompaniment to her leads.

"You inconsiderate bastards," Veronica fumed, clenching her fists.

"Hey, like Mandalay said, don't be so harsh," Tucker said.

She looked up suddenly; where had *he* come from? And where did Mandalay go?

"Let's go down and listen to the songs," he continued. "You might be surprised."

"Yeah? Surprised how?"

"Just give it a try. Come on." He offered her his arm, and she took it, because what else could she do?

Tucker led Veronica down the hill, to stand in the shade and watch the girl in the straw hat play her mournful tune. Veronica crossed her arms, determined to resist, but the music *did* start to get to her. She felt the great knot in her chest loosen ever so slightly, and it no longer hurt so much to breathe.

She glanced up at Tucker's rapt face. He reminded her of a music teacher she'd once had, who clearly got more from classical music than he was ever able to convey to his blockheaded junior high students. When he played Rachmaninoff's Piano Concerto no. 2 in C Minor, he'd cried unabashedly in front of the class, to the eternal mockery of most of the students—including, she was now ashamed to say, herself.

"What do you think?" Tucker asked quietly.

"Yeah, sure, it's beautiful," she said, knowing how petulant she sounded.

"That's the thing about music: it says things words never can."

Veronica did not respond. She just let herself get lost in the music, her own pain merging with the song's.

Junior Damo sauntered up to Mandalay, who stood in the forest shadows away from the group. "Quite a show you've got."

"It's not my show," she said. "It's everybody's. Even yours."

"How the hell long is this going to take?" he complained. "I got things to do today."

"As long as it does. I don't know any more than you do right now."

"Really?" He couldn't keep the snide, taunting tone from his voice. "So the great Mandalay Harris don't know everything about everything?"

"Are you just here to bitch, Junior?"

He gestured at the cave. "What if they're dead in there? What if there was, like, a cave-in or something? Or they fell down a hole?"

"Veronica and her boyfriend made it with no trouble."

" 'Veronica and her boyfriend made it with no trouble,' " he mocked. "That's because they had no history with . . . *her*. What if *she's* at the other end and don't take kindly to having our sort show up?"

"What are you trying to say, Junior?"

"I just want to know if we're going to send more people in if these don't come back."

"I don't know. I'll decide when and if it comes to that."

"Oh, *you'll* decide?"

"Yes."

"That we have to risk our lives?"

"You're not risking anything, Junior," Mandalay pointed out. "You don't even have to be here."

He ignored this, and nodded at the crowd dispersed through the forest. "Look at them. Most of them only know about the place from stories. I could count on one hand the people who actually remember it."

"I do," Mandalay said.

"Well, I don't. I was born here, and my parents died here. There's nothing there for me." He looked at the cave, and then back at her. She was surprised by the desperation in his expression, the complete opposite of his defiance. His eyes pleaded desperately, *Tell me I'm wrong.*

She smiled cruelly and said, "You might be right about that, Junior."

He stared at her, stopped dead by the cold matter-of-factness in her voice. "Fine," he choked out. "That's fine."

He marched petulantly away. Mandalay knew she should feel bad, but she didn't. There was something about cruelty that was, in fact, enjoyable, and she'd have to really watch that she didn't indulge in that.

Veronica realized with a start that Tucker had gone. She looked around for him, but with all the black-haired people, she couldn't single him out. Folks nodded at her, and a few said hello, but most just watched her sideways the way you might the survivor of a car crash pacing the side of the road.

A clearing had been hastily carved out of the undergrowth, and two children, a little boy and Kell Chess, sat in the sunlit center and played with plastic toys. They could have been brother and sister, if not fraternal twins: both sported the same Tufa hair and skin. They were so young they played near each other, but not really together, each keeping up a monologue that did not involve the other. Craig stood nearby, a case of bottled water under his arm, watching the children along with a large woman Veronica assumed was the boy's mother.

Craig offered a bottle of water. "Cyrus Crow brought some of these, Loretta. Thought you and Trey might want one."

"Thank you," Loretta Damo said, and quickly added, "Reverend." She liked Craig, but was always nervous around him, afraid he would judge her as inadequate somehow. She and Junior fought constantly over how to raise Trey, with Loretta usually winning because Junior would give up and run off with his friends. That didn't make her any more certain that she was right, though; in fact, she second-guessed so many things that it was hard for her to even decide what to have for breakfast.

"Your little girl is so sweet," she said.

"Trey seems like a fine boy, too."

"I hope so. I try really hard, but I don't have a lot of good role models. Most of my family's so dumb, they sit on the TV and watch the couch." She looked back at the cave, where Junior stood talking to Mandalay. "What will you do if they come back and we can all . . ." She trailed off, suddenly unsure if she should even be talking about this to Craig.

"First, I'll talk it over with Bronwyn," Craig said calmly. "Then I'll pray about it. Then, I'll hopefully make the right decision."

"So you believe the stories about what those people saw?"

"Bronwyn believed it. And if she did, then I do."

"You trust her that much?"

"Yes."

"I don't trust that piss-ant husband of mine any farther than I could throw him," Loretta said bitterly.

"That must be tough."

Loretta started to agree with him, but something about his tone stopped her. She realized that he was offering her genuine, sincere *sympathy,* something she got from none of her friends and family. Not even Junior's ascendancy to the role vacated by Rockhouse Hicks had made people any kinder to her.

"It is," she said, choking with emotion.


Veronica felt uncomfortable listening to any more, so she slipped quietly away. She came around a tree and found herself directly behind two big, sloppy men, one in overalls and the other in *very* ill-advised black athletic shorts with a neon-green stripe.

Like the minister and the large woman, they didn't notice her and continued their conversation unawares.

"Y'all reckon Junior might tell us what's what?" Snad Wisby, the one in overalls, asked his brother Canton. He passed over a mason jar of moonshine. "Just saw him talking to Mandalay."

"Hell, Junior don't know shit," Canton said, then took a drink.

"Mandalay musta tole him something," Snad said, and spit tobacco juice at the ground.

"I reckon it has something to do 'bout going back to that place they say we come from," Canton said.

"Hell, we ain't never gonna go back there. You know how long ago that's been?"

"Time don't work the same for everybody," Canton said. "Think about that ol' rockabilly singer, sitting up in a bubble for sixty years. He come back like it was the next day."

"Sixty years is one thing. We're talking *gazillions* of years." Snad spit again. "And we ain't in no bubble."

"Still could happen. Ain't that why everyone's up here? To be the first in line?"

"Hell, I just come up here to see what all the fuss was. All that shit happened so long ago, I couldn't give a new shit about it now."

"So you wouldn't go back?"

"Back? I ain't from there. I was born here, just like you was. Ain't nothing for us to go back to. You just want to flit around like Tain does in the moonlight?"

Canton took another drink from the jar. "I wouldn't mind living in a place where nothing was ugly," he said thoughtfully. "Wouldn't mind that at all."

"Have you looked in the mirror lately?" Snad joked. "If that's how they judge you, they ain't gonna let neither of us in. Nor most of the people in this county."

Canton passed the jar to his brother and muttered, "You got a mean streak, you know that?"

Snad realized that he'd hurt his brother's feelings, and more, that Canton really *did* hope they could relocate to their legendary homeland. He looked down at his own big, bare feet and punched his brother lightly in the shoulder. It was the closest he ever got to apologizing to Canton, and they both recognized it for what it was.

"Ain't gonna happen nohow," Canton said. "Nothing that good ever happens. I don't know about that other world, but *this* world don't work that way."

Veronica left the Wisby brothers to their moonshine, again feeling slightly dirty for eavesdropping. She moved through the forest, looking in each little knot of people for Tucker. She did not see him anywhere.

Then she almost stepped on a pair of black-haired girls seated on the ground, each with a guitar across their laps. "Oh! I'm sorry!"

"Nah, don't worry about it," one girl said. "Pull up some moss and have a seat. I'm Janet."

"Ginny," the other girl said.

"Yes, we sort of met earlier, when you first got here. I'm Veronica."

Janet's bloodshot eyes narrowed as she looked Veronica over. "Oh, yeah."

Veronica sat down cross-legged and asked, "Are you two sisters?"

"What?" Janet said. "No!"

"She means the hair," Ginny said to her friend. "And the teeth. And the skin."

"Oh!" Janet giggled. "No, it's just that we all look kinda similar. It can be a little weird, I guess."

Veronica realized they were stoned, if not out of their minds, then at least beyond meaningful conversation. She almost laughed, not with disapproval but delight. "I'm sorry for interrupting," she said, and started to rise.

"No, wait," Janet said. "Don't run away. We don't bite, or take your money. And we have a song for you."

"We do?" Ginny asked.

"We *do*," Janet said emphatically.

"She does this to me all the time," Ginny asided to Veronica. "Pulls songs out of the air."

"And occasionally out of my ass," Janet added with a grin. She strummed quietly and expertly, her skill apparently not damaged by her altered consciousness. Ginny listened once through, then added harmonies and flourishes. They were so good that almost at once, without even realizing it, all her worries vanished, and Veronica was riveted.

Janet began to sing quietly:

*I wouldn't leave you in the darkest night*
*I wouldn't leave you on the brightest day*
*I wouldn't leave you when everything failed*
*Nothing can make me go away*
*We call it love when we're having fun*
*But if that's love, then what is this*
*That keeps me fighting to see your smile*
*And determined to feel another kiss*

*I don't have a word for what I feel,*
*Nothing covers it all*
*If it's just love, then the word is all wrong*
*It's weak and it's stupid, like a bad theme song*
*Yet it's the word that stands by*
*It's my heart's battle cry*
*As I stand here awaiting your call.*

When they finished, Janet looked at Veronica. "What did you think? I mean, I was making it up as I went, so it needs some work, some of the rhymes are pretty bad, but—"

"I thought it was beautiful, Ginny," Veronica said. "Thank you."

"I'm Janet. She's Ginny." Both girls giggled.

"Sorry. And you made that up right now, on the spot?"

"She's like that," Ginny said.

"It's not as hard as it looks," Janet said.

"Not for you," Ginny pointed out.

They both burst into giggles again.

Somehow the impromptu song had eased Veronica's heart, taking away the worst of the worry and apprehension. "So what do you think will happen?" Veronica said, amazed at how casual she sounded.

"You mean up there?" Ginny asked.

Veronica nodded.

Janet exhaled, and frowned with the effort to think clearly. "Well . . . obviously we hope everyone comes back."

"Obviously," Ginny said.

"And we hope we'll at least be able to see what it's like over there. We've all heard the stories."

Wanting to give something back to these two silly, wonderful girls, she said, "You know I've seen it, right?"

It took a moment, but both of them finally registered astonishment. "Really?" Ginny cried.

"What was it like?" Janet asked eagerly.

Veronica gave an answer so clearheaded that it astonished even her. "It was like what this world would be if you took away all the human evil."

Janet and Ginny both nodded in slow unison, such a stoner cliché that Veronica expected them to say together, *Whoa.*

"I hope I get to see it someday," Ginny said.

"I hope you do, too," Veronica said sincerely.

Janet produced a fresh joint. "Want a hit?"

"I better not. I might need a clear head later." Veronica stood and wiped moss and leaves from her behind. "And thank you both. I feel a lot better now." And she did.

## 37

The girls' song left Veronica inexplicably lighthearted, and she forgot the urgency of her search for Tucker. Instead she wandered through the forest, stopping to listen to more songs and eavesdrop on different stories. Occasionally she glanced back up at the cave, but nothing seemed to change: Mandalay still stood nearby, like a guard at a castle gate, while various people came up and spoke to her.

No one paid any attention to Veronica, or if they did, they just smiled and went on with what they were doing. Now it felt more like a big family-reunion picnic than an in-denial death watch. She thought about finding Craig again and asking if he felt the same, but decided not to; in the jargon of her new stoner friends, she didn't want to harsh the buzz. Anything was better than the throat-constricting panic she'd felt before now.

She stopped outside another group of musicians, this one all men. She listened as one of them, a tall man with a great, powerful voice, sang over the music:

*Goin' home, goin' home, I'm a-goin' home;*
*Quiet-like, some still day, I'm just goin' home.*

*It's not far, just close by,*
*Through an open door;*
*Work all done, care laid by,*
*Goin' to fear no more.*

With a sudden rush of comprehension and sympathy, Veronica fully understood what the possibility of going "home" meant to the Tufa. Although they had been here seemingly forever, it wasn't and never would be "home." She imagined what it must be like to know there was a place you belonged, yet to which you could never return. She knew her family was originally from Puerto Rico, but that had been three generations ago, and she'd thought herself fully anglicized. But of course, she could go to Puerto Rico whenever she wanted, and had visited twice in her life. These people could not, *had* not.

The singer finished the song with a long, sustained note, which the instruments supported for as long as he could hold it. When the song ended, the others applauded, and the big man smiled and nodded in gratitude.

The group began to disperse. One bearded man with a fiddle bumped into Veronica and said, "'Scuse me, ma'am." When she looked back only two musicians remained, a teenage boy with a guitar and another with a harmonica. They showed no sign they noticed her.

Logan Durant looked up the hill at Mandalay and said, "Still nothing, I reckon. How long did your sister say this would take?" He patted his harmonica against his palm to clean out the loose moisture.

"She didn't," Aiden Hyatt said. "So I reckon it'll take as long as it takes."

"Your sister's tough, ain't she?"

"She is that," Aiden agreed, a hint of pride in his voice.

"I wish someone in my family was tough. They're all just bullies. They don't do a thing if they have to look somebody in the eye, but they'll sure as shit shoot 'em in the back when no one's watching."

Aiden knew the basics of how Logan's brothers, led by Billy Durant, shot Gerald Parrish two years earlier. He also knew that Cyrus Crow's boyfriend, a New York dancer, had publicly kicked Billy's ass for it. That had kept the worst of the family back on their own land ever since.

Logan, though, was different; as the youngest and smallest, he got even worse bullying than outsiders did. The time was coming, everyone knew, when Logan would bring a day of reckoning to the Durants.

Logan looked around. "My brothers are all here somewhere, too. Surprised they ain't tried to muscle in."

"They want to go back?"

"Fuck, no. They know they'd never get away with anything back there. My grandaddy's told us all about it. He was one of them first ones to come here."

Aiden nodded. "My grandpa, too. On both sides."

"So you think you'll go?" Logan asked seriously.

"Hell, I don't know. I suppose I will if the rest of my family does. It ain't like things are great here."

Suddenly they both realized Veronica was there. "Howdy," Aiden said with a big grin, one he clearly thought was all sorts of charming. "You must be the girlfriend."

Veronica's eyes narrowed. She hated being defined by her relationships to men, and being worried about Justin didn't change that. "I'm Justin's girlfriend, yes. But I'm also a human being. And I have a name. It's Veronica."

"Wow, dang," Aiden said, blushing. "Didn't mean nothing by it."

Veronica forced herself to calm down. Having a feminist hissy fit in the middle of the woods wouldn't help anyone, including her or Justin. It just felt so good to have something tangible, something she understood, to get angry about. "Women are people, too," she told the boys. "You should remember that, if you ever want girlfriends of your own." Then she walked away.

Aiden looked down, embarrassed. "I didn't mean anything by it," he repeated.

"Ah, don't let it get to you," Logan said. "I hear the girls over there—" He jerked his head toward the cave. "Are all eager and willing."

"Who told you that?"

"My grandaddy."

"What did your grand*mother* say about that?"

Logan laughed. "She just slapped him in the back of his head with a flyswatter, and said she wouldn't pee in his ear if his brain was on fire."

They both laughed. Then they started picking a fast, rocking version of the old tune "Forked Deer."

Veronica started back up the hill toward the cave, wanting to check in with Mandalay to see if there had been any word. She knew there hadn't, but she had to feel like she was doing *something*. She thought anew about simply rushing past Mandalay and the others and going through the cave herself; it hadn't been any trouble the day before, and whatever the rescue party had accomplished, she knew Justin would pay more attention to her than a stranger.

Yet she stopped halfway there, behind two middle-aged men in lawn chairs. An open cooler of beer rested between them, and they sat looking up at the cave, blank and patient like her father watching a soccer match.

———

"This is a hell of a thing," Sam Roberts said. "Hell of a thing."

"Sure enough," Gerald Parrish agreed.

Each of the men had lost children in the last few years, and their urge to comfort each other manifested in a kind of herd instinct, where they simply stayed in each other's company and never talked about their pain. Sam's daughter had been killed by a wild boar, while Gerald's son died from an unde-tected cerebral aneurysm while in New York City.

Sam nodded at the cave. "I remember hearing tales 'bout that place when I was a boy. Well, *over*hearing 'em; if my daddy had caught me listening, he'd have tanned my hide, that's for sure. He didn't put up with no kids who didn't know their place. He was so damn country that when he opened his mouth, sticks fell out."

The two men laughed. Then Gerald said heavily, "Just a shame all of our kids won't be here with us."

"Sure is," agreed Sam. "Surely is that."

Gerald began to sing. Veronica recognized it as a song from the play *Chapel of Ease,* but of course didn't realize that the man singing it was the father of the man who wrote it:

> *The stones were set to last forever*
> *But the mortar crumbles away*
> *The trees may stand for centuries*
> *But eventually fall to decay*
>
> *And me, I'm a blink of the great oak's eye*
> *My time so pitiful and short*
> *So why does this pain cut me so to the quick*
> *And leave a hole in my chest for my heart?*

This was too much, so again she slipped away before they noticed her.

———

While Veronica had been moving from group to group, a long table spread with paper plates and fixings was set up under a bright orange awning. People stood in line to get burgers and hot dogs from the steam table behind it. The cooking odor was heavenly, and Veronica realized she hadn't eaten since yesterday. She got in line and picked up a plate.

The man behind the table glanced up and saw her. "Oh! Hello. We met back at my cafe a couple of days ago, remember? I'm C.C."

"I remember," Veronica said. "How much for the burgers?"

"Oh, nothing, this is all for family. But . . ." He looked around to make sure no one watched them. "Do this."

He made a simple hand gesture.

She repeated it. "Why?" Before he could answer, she added, "It's because it's dangerous to drink something offered by the fairy folk, isn't it?"

He shrugged with a little smile. "It's just an old wives' tale. And believe me, around here we've got more than our share of old wives."

She held out her plate and accepted a burger. "Thank you."

"My pleasure. No word about your boyfriend . . . Jerry?"

"Justin. And no." She looked over at Mandalay and Junior, once again talking earnestly in front of the cave. "Exactly who *are* those two?"

C.C. said carefully, "The Tufa are one people, but two . . . tribes, I guess you'd say. Those two lead them."

"Mandalay is just a kid."

"A kid on the outside. There's a lot more to her than what you see. Junior, though . . . he's pretty much *exactly* what you see."

Veronica shook her head. Her own studies now dovetailed with her life experience in a way she never would have expected. "So it's like the Seelie and Unseelie Courts."

C.C. smiled knowingly. "Pretty damn close."

"So which one is which?"

He shrugged. "Not sure it matters."

While Veronica talked to C.C., Junior said to Mandalay, "This is fucking ridiculous. Did you call them all here?"

"No," Mandalay said.

"Then what are they all *doing* here?"

"They just know. Their blood knows. Doesn't yours?"

"But that damn Vipperman girl is here. My dog's got more true Tufa blood than she does. Her mama's family married all kinds of other people."

"You know as well as I do that it ain't always about the amount. It's about how well you listen to the song in it."

Junior took out his phone and checked the time. "Where the fuck *are* they? How far did they have to go?"

"All the way," Mandalay said. She closed her eyes and tried to find that quiet center where she could hear the night winds and the voices of all her prior incarnations, but it eluded her. Here on this mountain, before this cave, she was no different than the rest of her people: she could only wait, and try not to go mad.

"Now that faggot C.C.'s got a damn restaurant set up," Junior continued. "What's next, a bunch of dancing girls?"

"Take it easy," Mandalay warned.

"I *am* taking it easy. You're lucky I ain't taking my people and going home."

Mandalay laughed. The idea that Junior's presence had any real value was the kind of ridiculous claim he always made. "Junior, I'd love to see you try. Go ahead, make an announcement. See how many listen to you."

"You think I won't?" he said, his defiance paper-thin.

"I know," the girl said, and turned away.

Mandalay joined Veronica in front of the cave. Veronica stared into the darkness as she ate the hamburger, willing something to move, to emerge from the shadow. Nothing did.

"I'm glad you're eating," Mandalay said. "It won't be long now."

"You said that this morning," Veronica said around a mouthful of burger.

"And I meant it. It's all in the scale. A year is nothing to a redwood."

"I'm not a tree."

"Those are three of the strongest, most trustworthy people I know," Mandalay said seriously. "Bliss has been my good right arm all my life, and Bronwyn . . . well, let's just say she does what's necessary without hesitation."

"And the one with white hair?"

"He's a good man, and he keeps his word."

Veronica finished the last of the burger. "What do you suppose they're doing right now?"

"Looking for Justin."

"Are you sure?"

Mandalay did not answer.

# 38

Now that the parade was closer, Bliss and the others could see the individuals more clearly. The women wore the sour, thin-lipped expression of prudes determined to stop anyone from having fun. The men were uniformly tall and thin, severely clothed in black suits, and scowled with disdain.

"Wow, who died?" Snowy asked quietly.

"It's not a funeral," Bliss said. "There are no funerals here."

"Then what is it?"

Bronwyn nocked an arrow. "A warning?"

Bliss nodded.

The parade came toward them slowly, and finally stopped about twenty feet away. The final beat of the drum echoed for a moment, and then there was only the sound of the wind.

One of the old women stepped forward. She had the sunken face of a dried-apple doll, and the cold eyes of a woman dedicated to hate. "What are you-uns a-doing here?" she demanded in an exaggerated mountain accent.

"We're looking for a friend of ours," Bliss said.

"Your kind got no friends here."

"And what kind is that?"

"Tufa *trash*."

Bronwyn and Snowy exchanged a look. Bliss kept her gaze on the woman and said, "I was born right here."

A tall, hatchet-faced man with an equally hateful glare moved up beside the woman. "You have been banished, for good and for all time. You have no rights here."

"We don't want any trouble from y'all," Bronwyn said. "We're here to find a friend. Tell us where he is, and we'll take him and leave."

"You have the blood of our kind on your hands," the man said.

Bronwyn turned to Snowy. "Think he means Dwayne?"

"Have you killed anyone else?"

"Not lately." She turned back to the man. "If you mean Dwayne Gitterman, then you're right, and I can live with that. And with yours, for that matter."

"No true blood will be spilled here," Bliss said. "None ever has. We won't be the first."

"Then turn and go!" the woman ordered, pointing one sharp, withered finger at the cave opening behind them. "While you can."

"Not without our friend," Bliss said.

"Look," Snowy said quietly.

In the middle of the crowd, dressed in the same old-fashioned way, stood Justin. He appeared as serious and pissed off as the others, and showed no sign that he understood who these newcomers were.

"I thought he was off gallivanting with the sexy fairy girls," Snowy said.

"He's doing whatever they're doing," Bliss said. "He's got no say-so." She called out, "Justin, you need to come with us."

"He came here of his own volition," the man said. "And just like any who do, he will stay."

Again Snowy and Bronwyn exchanged a look. Bronwyn stepped forward, raised her bow and said, "Nobody move. I have an itchy bow hand and a bad case of PMS, I'll take all of you *down*."

"Bronwyn!" Bliss exclaimed.

Snowy rushed forward and pushed through the crowd to Justin. The boy's face retained its scowl as Snowy grabbed him by the shoulders and said, "Dude, remember Veronica? That hot girl who follows you around? She sent us here. She's waiting for you. Now come on."

Several of the men stepped from the line, drew revolvers and pointed them at Snowy.

"Well, shit," muttered Bronwyn, and lowered her bow.

Snowy released Justin, raised his hands, and stepped away. "Okay, okay, I'm going." He backed up until he was behind Bronwyn and Bliss.

Then the men all pointed their guns at the three would-be rescuers.

"You'd spill *our* blood here?" Bliss challenged.

The man at the front doffed his hat and put it over his heart. "Our gracious Queen," he said, "look down upon us, so that those who follow you may witness the damnation of those who deny your will." The other men took off their hats, the women lowered their eyes, and in unison they all said, *"Sláinte."*

"Is he praying?" Snowy asked quietly.

"Near as," Bliss said. Louder, she added, "We're not leaving without our friend. So let's talk."

Something boomed in the sky, and they all looked up. Above the mountain, a huge, roiling thunderhead drifted toward them. It obscured the distant castle and drained all color beneath it, leaving the landscape in darkness.

"That ain't no April shower," Snowy said.

"No," Bliss said.

It moved too fast for any normal cloud, and thunderbolts

skittered around inside it. It settled atop the mountain, and began rolling down it, like a slow avalanche.

"Uh, Bliss," Bronwyn said uncertainly. "What do we do?"

"Run!" Bliss cried. Without waiting for the others, she took off back down the street, toward the cave. Bronwyn and Snowy followed at her heels.

"What is it?" Bronwyn yelled at Bliss.

"Oh, shit," Snowy said. "Look."

They skidded to a stop and looked back. The cloud began to roll over the top of the mountain. Inside the billows, momentarily silhouetted by each flash of lightning, appeared to be a horde of mounted riders. One instant they seemed to be solid entities, and the next they were shapes made up of cloud's vapor.

At the front, leading the way, was a pair of horses pulling a chariot.

And in that chariot stood an unmistakably feminine figure, with one hand raised to hold the whip that drove the horses. Each sweep of the lash sent out streaks of lightning and peals of thunder.

The sight, so simultaneously awe-inspiring and frightening, transfixed the three interlopers where they stood.

"Run," Bliss repeated softly, then louder. *"Run!"*

"But what is it?" Snowy demanded as they raced for the passage back home.

Bliss cried out in utter terror, *"It's the Queen!"*

## 39

Although Mandalay and Junior both stood beside the cave, it was Annie May Pritchard, pregnant with her first child, who initially noticed. She stood at C.C.'s tent, putting far too much mustard on her hot dog, when she suddenly cried, "Look!"

At first it was just a breeze that stirred the dirt and dust inside the opening. But soon that wind grew harder and rougher, and quickly became a gale that roared from the cave as if the mountain itself were blowing to scare away the annoying parasites crawling all over it.

C.C. quickly grabbed some plastic sheeting and covered his food. His tent went down almost at once, and many of the people seated in camp or folding chairs were blown over. Young people rushed to help the older ones, and even Junior ran to make sure Loretta and Trey were safe. Veronica caught Mandalay as she almost tumbled down the slight hill.

"What was that?" someone shouted.

Veronica put Mandalay back on her feet and looked around. Although she'd seen no guns before this, suddenly they were everywhere, and all pointed at the cave.

"Someone's coming out," another voice cried.

Figures emerged from the cave, struggling against the wind so that they weren't blown out like leaves before a twister. At first the rush of dirt and dust hid both their identities and their number. Was this the return of the rescuers, or the first wave of a vanguard riding the hurricane-force winds into this world?

"We should get out of the way," Veronica said to Mandalay, who still coughed dust from her lungs.

"Wait," Mandalay called out. "Don't shoot."

The wind subsided, revealing three sweaty, bedraggled figures, two black-haired women and one man with white hair.

The scattered Tufa put away their weapons. A few approached the cave. But Veronica got there first.

"Where is he?" she cried, grabbing first Snowy and then Bronwyn. "Did you see him? Is he all right?"

She was about to grab Bliss, but stopped when she saw how the woman was crying. They were big, full-body sobs, and her face was wrenched into a mask of anguish, the dirt and dust streaked by tears.

"No," Veronica said, assuming this meant Justin was dead. *"No!"*

She fell to the ground, too numb to cry, as Craig ran to Bronwyn and Tain Wisby rushed to Snowy. No one approached Bliss; she was left in a grief no one could understand.

Finally Mandalay came up to her. "What happened?" the girl asked quietly.

Bliss wiped her nose on her sleeve. "W-we found it . . . We got through. It was really there. But it was all wrong, too."

Mandalay kept her own voice steady. "That must've been hard for you."

Bliss nodded.

Mandalay glanced at Veronica, to ensure she wasn't listening. Quietly she asked, "Did you find him?"

Bliss nodded. "Yes, but he was too far gone. And then . . . and then . . . ." She just couldn't get the words out.

At that moment, a cloud drifted across the sun, casting the whole area in shadow. Bliss looked up and *screamed,* a sound no one who knew her could ever imagine hearing. It brought all conversation and activity to a stop.

Then the cloud drifted on, and sunlight returned.

Bliss continued to stare into the sky. "Sorry," she said. "I thought it was . . . ."

"The Queen," Mandalay said in a small, quiet voice. It was the only name that could render her *meek.*

Bliss looked down, wiped her nose again, and nodded.

"So you saw her?" Mandalay continued.

"We saw her approaching."

"Did she say anything?"

"We didn't stick around after she rode in."

"Rode in?"

"On clouds. Like that one. I thought for a minute she'd followed us here."

"So you ran?"

Bliss nodded.

"Probably the sensible thing to do."

This calm response made Bliss laugh, which quickly turned into hysterics. Mandalay put her arms around the woman and let her cry it out.

Bronwyn, holding tightly to Craig's hand, said to him, "Apparently we're still banished."

"I'm sorry," he said.

"Seriously?" she said with a wry smile.

"Yes. I know how important it was to everyone."

"You're not secretly a little glad?"

"I'm relieved. And that's not a secret. But no, I'm not happy for other people's disappointment."

She kissed him as if no one was around them, then said, "You're going to be one lucky man later on."

"Luckier than I am right now?"

"Ohhhh, yeah."

Nearby, Tain pressed herself against Snowy. "I'm really glad you're back."

"I can tell," he said.

"Mmmm, and you seem glad to see me, too. Was it awful?"

"It wasn't like the stories, that's for sure," he said, and patted her behind.

No one paid any attention to Veronica, who sat on the ground where she'd fallen. She looked around at the people all talking and whispering, and made a decision. She jumped up, snatched a pistol from the belt of a nearby man, and ran for the cave.

C.C. was closest, and caught her around the waist. He pushed her arm up, and the gun fired into the sky. The loud crack got everyone's attention, and when C.C. took the weapon from her hand, Craig Chess was there to catch her as she again collapsed in tears.

"Come on now," Craig told her with gentle firmness. "There's no way that running off with a gun is the right thing to do."

"They didn't try," Veronica sobbed. "They didn't even *try*."

"They did the best they could," he said.

"He wouldn't leave me," she said, "I know he wouldn't, he loves me . . ."

Tucker took her from C.C.'s arms. "I'll make sure she gets back to the Catamount Corner," he said.

Mandalay faced the assembled Tufa. "That's all, people," she said loudly. "Time for everyone to go home. Hug your families tonight. Sing all your favorite songs."

At first no one moved. Then a few wandered off, followed by more. Before long, everyone had picked up whatever they'd brought and packed it for the hike out. People fired up their four-wheelers, and the loud engines faded as they departed.

Junior appeared beside Mandalay. "That's it?"

"That's it," Mandalay said.

He looked back at the cave. "Wasn't much to it."

"No."

"Are you disappointed?" He wasn't snide when he said this, just genuinely curious.

"I'm tired, Junior," Mandalay said honestly. "I want some dinner, and a shower, and some sleep. Take Loretta and Trey home."

"Yeah," Junior said sadly. "I think we can all use a drink and a nap. See ya around."

Thirty minutes later, the hillside was empty; only a few missed beer bottles and crushed undergrowth remained to show how many people had been there. In the distance, the four-wheelers could still be heard, along with the sound of other vehicles starting.

Once the ridge was empty and silent, Tucker led Veronica out of the woods. He'd pulled her out of sight behind a large tree, and put a finger to her lips. She understood he wanted them to hide, but had no idea why. Still, she was too physically and emotionally beat to resist.

Now he looked at the cave, and then back at her. "They really did try, you know. You ever tried to pull a kid away from a video game he loves? Imagine that about a thousand times worse. That's what they were up against."

Veronica was numb. "So he's gone," she said simply.

Tucker's face drew tight as he struggled with his conscience. "I guess I can tell you this now, Veronica. Nobody else here knows. I'm kind of a . . . secret agent."

She sniffled. "A what?"

"The Queen banished the Tufa. But the King wanted to keep tabs on them. I'm the tab."

"Why?"

"Why me, or why tabs?"

"Both."

"Tabs because he sincerely believes one day the Queen will change her mind. Me because . . . well, nobody would notice if I was gone."

"So what now?"

He took a deep breath. "Now, I do it myself."

"Isn't it dangerous?"

"Very."

"Then why?"

"You're just full of that question, aren't you?" he said with a grin. "I was with them when the Tufa first came to this world. I started a family line back then that continues to this day. You met one of my descendants, Miss Azure."

Veronica just nodded. Nothing could surprise her now.

"And every so often, I'd point people toward this cave, to see if they could go through. No one ever did."

"Until me and Justin."

"Right. About a hundred years ago, my little manipulation resulted in the brutal death of another of my descendants, a sweet girl who'd already lost more than anybody should. That was her in *The Fairies of Sadieville.*"

"What was her name?"

"Sophronie. I'm the reason Sadieville vanished. I helped the Tufa sing it into that hole, and out of history, to avenge her death."

"You weren't quite thorough enough," she observed dryly.

"Nobody ever is with something like that. There's always a loose end, something you missed. Like a print of a lost film sitting in someone's office."

"So does the fact that we got through, and so did Bronwyn and her friends, mean that the Queen isn't mad anymore?"

"Apparently not. She wouldn't come riding out of the clouds just to put down the welcome mat."

"So how *did* we manage it?"

"I don't know. But I do know, to get Justin back, I need to hurry before the Queen redoes her magic."

"You still haven't told me why."

"The real truth?"

"Why not, for a change?"

He chuckled. "Fair enough. You know the story, right? About how the Queen banished the Tufa here after their leader caused her to lose a bet?"

"I do now." She hadn't thought to ask Bronwyn *why* the Tufa were in Appalachia. "I assume you mean the Queen of Fairyland?"

"That's her. And the bet she made was with me. The Feller, who became the Tufa leader here, bet he could split a chestnut with his ax. The Queen backed him. I bet that he couldn't."

"So you won."

"Yeah. Except I greased the chestnut before he tried so his blade would slip."

It took her a moment to process that. "So you *cheated*."

"Yes."

"The Tufa were exiled because of *you,* not the Queen."

"Technically, yes. She still kinda overreacted."

"Does she *know* you cheated?"

"No."

"Does anyone here?"

"I do. You do."

She thought that over. "Should I be worried I won't come down off this mountain?"

"Nah. It's time for it to come out. A gazillion years is long enough to keep any secret."

"Is that how long it's been?"

"Give or take a bazillion." He turned to look at the cave, still waiting as it had for so long, a dark passage to his bright land. He took a deep breath, hitched up his pants, and said, "I suppose I should get going. Justin's clearly not going to rescue himself."

"I'm coming with you," she said.

"I never doubted that."

## 40

"What's that?" Veronica asked, pointing at the ground.

Tucker picked up one of the iron nuts Bliss had thrown. "It's iron. Fairies don't care for iron."

"It doesn't seem to bother you."

"I've had a very long time to get used to it."

Veronica picked it up. "So they're like garlic is to vampires?"

He barked a laugh, and it echoed through the cave. "More like citronella candles to mosquitoes. They make the air unpleasant for us. They also keep this passage from changing if we leave and come back."

She didn't doubt him. The underground passage was completely different from her and Justin's earlier journey, but with Tucker leading the way it was still a fairly quick trip. In no time at all, they saw illumination ahead.

"Do we have a plan?" she asked.

"I've always done better making it up as I go."

"Not if what you told me before is true."

"You've got me there."

They crept toward the light. As the land beyond the cave became visible, Veronica said in confusion,

"Everything looks different. Did we come out somewhere else?"

"No, that's just how it works."

"It must be difficult to find your way around."

"For some. Not for me."

This time there was no open plain, like she and Justin saw, or mysterious town, as the rescue party discovered. Instead trees grew right up to the mouth of the cave, thick branches looming over it and trapping it in perpetual shadow. A narrow trail led away into the forest. She heard birdsong and faint wind, but otherwise nothing moved.

Veronica stepped right to the edge of the cave mouth. There was a line, a difference in texture between the cave floor and the dirt of the trail.

"Don't cross that threshold," Tucker warned.

"Why?"

"If you do, *she* will know you're here."

"Who is 'she?'"

"The Queen."

"Of what?"

"Of everything across that line."

"Ah. The one you made the bet with."

"That's her."

"Will she be mad at you?"

"Not if I stay on my toes."

"So what's the plan?"

"I go get him. You stay here."

"Not a chance."

He looked at her seriously. "Veronica, I'm not kidding when I say you got lucky before. It would take very little to get you dancing off into oblivion, just like Justin."

"I think I'm insulted."

"Don't be. Stronger men, and women, than you have been lost to the fairy folk."

"So I just wait here in the cave?"

"Yes. Don't go outside. Don't talk to anyone who might happen by. Don't eat or drink anything, but I shouldn't have to tell you that. And above all, follow Lloyd Cole's advice."

"I have no idea what that means."

"It's one of his album titles."

"Which is?"

*"Don't Get Weird on Me, Babe."*

"Well, in that case, you follow the advice of Barb Wire."

"Who is that?"

"The hero of my dad's favorite movie."

"And what's her advice?"

" 'Don't call me babe.' "

Veronica watched Tucker head down a trail that led into the forest. When he was out of sight, she looked up at the rock of the cave roof, damp with moisture. She caught a drop on her fingertip as it fell from a stalactite tip, almost touched it to her tongue, then remembered.

"Clever," she said to the fairy world in general, as she wiped her finger on her leg. "But you'll have to be sharper than *that.*"

Time passed. Or at least, to her it seemed to; she couldn't be sure about anything, even that. At least when she'd waited at the other end of the cave, she'd been distracted by all the Tufa playing and singing. Now, though, she had only her thoughts for company. She'd used up her despair and sorrow, which meant that she was now filled with simmering rage.

"You're gonna pay for this, Justin Johnson," she said as she paced inside the cave, careful not to cross the threshold. "How dare you just run off with the fairies and leave me standing there? I've put too much into this relationship to just throw it away like that. I guess you don't feel the same way, do you?"

She kicked at what she thought was a loose stone, which

turned out to be a protrusion from a rock solidly buried beneath the surface. She bit back her cry of anger, waited until her toe stopped throbbing, then planted herself cross-legged on the ground. Wincing and seething, she stared down the trail into the shadowy forest, wondering what this queen who'd exiled the Tufa was really like.

Movement caught her eye just before she dozed all the way off. She realized with a start that it was now almost dark outside; she'd missed the afternoon, and the dusk. Had she really been asleep, or was it just that in this place, hidden beneath the heavy trees, there was no twilight?

Someone approached the cave. He walked as fast as he could without blatantly running, and kept glancing behind him as if he were being followed. He was almost on top of her before she recognized him.

"Tucker!" she cried, and started to rush forward to meet him. She skidded to a stop just in time.

He also stopped, just outside the cave. He looked at her with no recognition.

"Tucker? Are you all right?"

He said nothing. He folded his arms and turned to look back down the trail.

Veronica was thoroughly puzzled. Then she remembered glamour. By the rules of this place, this guy might not be Tucker at all. She pulled out the iron nut she'd picked up earlier.

"Hey," she said. "Catch."

The maybe-not-Tucker turned, and she tossed it to him. Reflexively he caught it, then dropped it as if it scalded him. "Hey!" he cried in outrage.

"Don't ignore me, then. Who are you?"

"Right now, I'm Tucker."

"Oh, yeah? And who is Tucker right now, then?"

But he didn't answer, and resumed watching down the moonlit trail. He ignored all Veronica's subsequent attempts to engage him.

She heard the horse approach before she saw it appear down the trail. In the clear moonlight, two figures rode on its back. The one in front wore strange pointed headgear, and as they drew nearer, she saw that he was dressed in very elaborate, medieval-style clothes, including a cape.

But that registered on a secondary level. Because behind him on the saddle rode Justin.

She started to shriek and rush forward, but once again caught herself. Like the fake Tucker, she had no proof this was the real Justin. *Damn,* she thought, *this place* will *try anything.*

But this actually was Justin, and he slid from the saddle and came into the cave. He looked tired and worried, but she wrapped him in a hug at once.

"You're back," she whispered, wanting to believe it but afraid this was some new trick.

"I'm sorry, Veronica," he said. The weariness in his voice overwhelmed her.

"It's all right," she said, and kissed him. He smelled of flowers, sweat, and turned earth. "It's all right, as long as you're back."

She turned to the man in the headgear, who'd also dismounted. His cape was edged with fur and his elaborate clothing glittered with gold and jewels.

"I suppose," she said, "I should thank you."

"It's always smart to thank the Good Folk," he said, in Tucker Carding's voice. He took off the strange headgear, which she now realized was a crown.

"So which one is the real you?" Veronica asked. "Or does *everybody* here look like you?"

"I'm the real one," the royal Tucker said.

"He is," the other Tucker agreed.

"Excuse me a moment," royal Tucker said. "You two get re-acquainted." He began to undo the clasps on the big, heavy cloak. "Pay no attention to this man wearing the curtain."

He handed first the cape, then the crown to the "other" Tucker. Then both men quickly undressed, passing clothes back and forth. In moments the "other" was now dressed like a king, and the "real" Tucker was back to normal.

"King" Tucker climbed onto the horse, gave a jaunty wave, and rode off into the night. "Their" Tucker joined them in the cave, clearly proud of himself.

"Well, that was easier than I expected," he said. "Shall we go?"

"Who was that?" Veronica said.

"My twin. Not brother, but we're identical. In appearance, at least."

"You're an identical twin of the King of Fairyland?" Veronica said in wry disbelief.

"No," Tucker said. "He is."

He waited for that to register on her. A moment later, her eyes widened.

"I told you nobody would miss me," he said.

"Shit," Veronica said.

"Pithy but accurate. But we should go. If the Queen notices I'm gone before my double gets back—"

"Don't let the stalactite hit you on the way out," Veronica said, and pulled Justin into the dark passageway, switching on her phone's flashlight. With a last look behind him, Tucker followed.

Veronica wasn't sure how far they'd gone before she noticed the rumble behind them. An instant later, she felt the tremors under her feet.

She stopped. "What's that?"

"Something we don't want to catch up with us," Tucker said, his flippant tone underlaid with concern. "Come on, we're burning daylight."

"It was dark back there."

"Back there, yes. Can we discuss it later, please?"

He shoved them forward as dust shook free from the roof. No matter how fast they traveled, the rumbling drew closer. Veronica began to fear that the collapse, or flooding, or *whatever* was behind them would catch up before they got out, and this all would've been for nothing.

And then she saw light ahead. At the other end, it was still blessed daylight.

She coughed; the air was now filled with dust, and she felt wind behind them, building with every moment. They practically ran the last few yards, and as they burst onto the ridge outside the cave, Veronica glanced back.

She couldn't swear to what she saw. It was an impression, really, more than a memory. But it seemed like, inside the dust, possible even *made* from the dust, stood an unmistakably feminine silhouette, one that radiated fury and power and terrible, terrible beauty.

And then the tunnel collapsed in a tumble of rocks, gravel, and dust.

They didn't have to throw themselves ahead, like action stars before an explosion. They simply stepped to either side of the cave, out of the path of debris. Rocks and gravel burst out like buckshot from a giant's gun, propelled by the ferocious wind that had almost overtaken them. When it finished, when all that remained moving was the dust that filled the air, the three of them regrouped in front of the now-closed passage.

From the dust rolled a shiny, round metal object that landed at Tucker's feet. He picked it up; it was the crown he'd given to his double, only instead of gold, it now appeared to be made of old, rusted pieces of metal crudely welded together, a thing that might exist in this world, not the other.

"I think," he said slowly, "I've just been divorced."

## 41

The next morning, Veronica and Justin left Cloud County and headed west. She stared straight ahead and tightly gripped the steering wheel, her arms straight and her elbows locked. She barely glanced at the forest on either side of the highway, and took the curves faster than was probably prudent. She was more than ready to be gone.

After their narrow escape, Tucker drove Justin and Veronica back to the Catamount Corner. If everything they'd seen was true, if their experiences weren't some hallucination or dream, then he took his separation from the Queen of Fairyland with surprising equanimity.

"Too bad he's dead," Tucker mused as he drove. "Jerry Reed would plumb be tickled about the way things turned out."

"How so?" Veronica asked.

"He wrote this divorce song called 'She Got the Gold Mine, I Got the Shaft.' And damned if that wasn't literally what I just got."

After he left them at the motel, Veronica wanted to do anything except talk about what happened. She began to pack at once, but before she got very far, Justin pulled her into a kiss. Despite her anger at him, or maybe because of it, she melted with desire, and they spent the afternoon reuniting in the most intimate way.

Later, simultaneously exhausted and wired, twined around each other in the motel bed, Justin said, "Are we agreeing not to talk about what happened?"

"Would you say anything that would make it better?"

"Probably not."

"Then yes, we're agreeing to that."

"I should probably not mention it in my thesis, either."

"That seems sensible."

They fell silent. Outside, birds sang in the trees, audible over the subtle hum of the air conditioner. Veronica recalled the tarot reading she got from Dr. Tully before the trip, just days ago. The reverse five of cups meant forgiveness and moving on. Could she do that, after all this? She was too tired and sated to say.

Now, though, as she drove, she had time to really think it over. As they merged onto I-40, she finally asked the only question that mattered. "Justin?"

"Yeah?" he said, staring out the passenger window.

"Can I ask you something?"

"Sure."

Her mouth grew dry, and her words ragged. "Do you even remember what happened to you?"

"No, not really. I remember music, and dancing, but the rest is all a little . . . blurry."

She waited to see if he would continue. When he didn't, she asked, "Is that true?"

He sighed. "No. I *do* remember it all, Veronica. I can't explain why I ran off, or why I didn't want to go back with the first people who came to get me. I was just . . ." He sought the right word. "Happy."

Veronica said nothing. The lump in her throat threatened to choke her.

But then he put his hand on her leg. "But you know what? I mean this sincerely: I'm happier now. Right here."

A wave of relief she'd never thought possible swept over her, and for the first time in what seemed like years, she felt hope. She dropped one hand from the steering wheel and threaded her fingers through his. "Me, too," she said. "And your thesis will be awesome."

"That it will," he agreed. He still sounded distant, but she knew he was closer than he had been, and eventually he'd come all the way back.

Just before they left the motel, as she'd waited for the air conditioner to cool off the car while Justin settled the bill, Veronica drew one card from her tarot deck. Her question was simple: *What will happen between Justin and me?*

It was the three of pentacles, drawn upright, which showed an apprentice directing the actions of two architects.

That had puzzled her; was she the apprentice, or was Justin? And if so, who were the two architects in this situation? She'd worked it over in her mind, pairing off the people they'd met, standing them up in front of both herself and Justin, but none of the combinations made any sense. She considered calling Tanna for advice, but knew that would grow into a long conversation she might not want to have with Justin around.

Then suddenly, as they threaded through the traffic that grew thicker the closer they got to Nashville, she understood: she and Justin were the architects. And the apprentice, the one who directed everything, including themselves, was . . . .

"You know what I just realized, Justin?"

"What?"

"We thought this was all about us. I mean, we found the film, we found Sadieville, we found the cave. But we were wrong. This wasn't our story at all."

"No?"

"No."

"Then whose was it?"

"The man," she said wryly, "who once was King."

"I thought I'd find you here," Mandalay said, walking down the little pier outside Bliss's house. "Have you been here all night?"

Bliss gestured with the wine bottle in her hand, at the empties around her. A few had fallen into the lake and floated against the pilings. "Figured why the fuck not," Bliss said, her words slurred from alcohol. "It's not like I'll be going home . . . ever."

Mandalay sat beside her. "Was it that bad, being back there?"

"No, it was perfect," Bliss said sarcastically. "If it'd been bad, then I wouldn't feel like this right now."

"Like what?"

"Like that first day when we were exiled, when we came out into this world without anything, even our names."

"I'm sorry, I should've gone myself. Honestly, I was afraid to go. I worried that I wasn't strong enough to come back."

"We saw her. Well, kind of glimpsed her. In the clouds."

"And she was angry?"

"She was *furious*."

"Even after all this time." Mandalay shook her head. "How can anyone stay so angry, for so long?"

"Time doesn't work the same for everybody," Bliss said, and they both burst into giggles. But it didn't last, and soon they were back in morose silence.

"Word will get around," the girl said. "People will know. A lot of them might . . ."

"What?"

"A lot of the old-timers might not be able to stand it, knowing there's no hope."

"You can count *this* old-timer with them. What's the point of going on? Why struggle, and fight, and claw with all your strength at a hope that doesn't exist?"

" 'I was living in a world of childish dreams,' " Mandalay quoted.

"What's that?"

"A line from a Springsteen song. 'Two Hearts.' "

"Two hearts?"

"Are better than one."

"I don't get it."

"Oh, that's just the chorus. In the second verse, though, he says something like, he used to have childish dreams, and they never came true, but now it's time to grow up and have new dreams. Maybe that's us. We need to let go of that old hope, grow up and find something new."

"Like what?"

Mandalay said nothing. They looked out at the lake, and the mountains beyond, and the sunrise beyond that.

Tucker stood before the now-sealed cave. The landslide had been thorough in the way only a guided event could be. Its finality should have angered him, or at least upset him, but like Veronica, he just felt numb. He hadn't felt like fully a part of either world in a very long time, and knew someday there would be a reckoning. He just assumed it would be a choice, not a decree.

Still, it could be worse. There was still the music.

He was so distracted that he didn't hear the other person approach until a voice said, "Kinda figured I'd find you here."

He turned. Bronwyn Chess came out of the woods and into the open.

"Oh. Hey, Bronwyn."

She nodded at the now-blocked cave. "Your doing?"

"No. I was just the inspiration."

"It looks pretty final."

"It is that."

She patted the rock and dirt that sealed the cave. "So, Tucker. I've been doing some figuring. When Miss Azure sang us that Sadieville song, we all got back memories, even ones like me who weren't even born yet. And I think since I wasn't there when the Sadieville disaster happened, I might've noticed some things the rest of 'em missed."

He was both worried and intrigued. "That a fact?"

"Oh, that's a fact. Now, tell me how close I am to the truth. You've always known about this cave, and you've been able to use it to go back and forth between this world and the other one, haven't you?"

He did his best to sound neutral. "Yes."

"And the reason no one's noticed is that when you go, you take all the memories of your time here with you. And when you come back, *they* come back, and it's like you never left."

"Yeah."

"And *that's* why you knew how to take away the memory of Sadieville."

"It's where I got the idea, yes."

She narrowed her eyes at him. "Have to be a mighty powerful, important gentleman to be able to do that. You're not that here. Are you over there?"

"I was," he admitted. "Now I'm just what you see."

She studied him, and finally said, "Well. Ain't that a thing."

"It's a thing," he agreed. "Is that what you came here to ask me?"

"Partly. But after I finished thinking about you, I started thinking about Sadieville."

"What about it?"

"The Queen lost her temper when she sent us here. You did the same thing with Sadieville, didn't you?"

"That's harsh."

"Only if it's true."

He gazed into her calm, intelligent eyes. This girl had seen horrors, possibly perpetuated a few, and was content with herself and her place. She understood exactly who she faced, and yet she was neither afraid nor defiant. She stood before him, he realized, as an equal.

Which, now, she was. He was certainly no king.

"Yeah," he agreed. "I did. I buried Sadieville without giving anybody a chance to explain or ask for mercy. Good people died along with the bad because I was blinded by rage. Just like *she* was." He shook his head. "Guess I'm no better than her, am I?"

"Are you seriously asking me?"

"Yes. *Yes,*" he added with an emphasis that surprised even him.

"Sorry. That's way above my pay grade. You might try Mandalay."

His laugh echoed off the slopes around them, and prompted an irate call from a disturbed crow. Then he realized something he'd overlooked. "You said you figured you'd find me here. Why were you looking for me?"

She kicked at the gravel outside the cave. "You know, this time yesterday, I was standing in Tír na nÓg. The place where all the Tufa want to return. I've been hearing about it since I was born, about how magical and amazing it is, how the Tufa are part of that world in a way they never will be here, no matter how many generations go by. But you know what?"

"What?"

"I didn't feel it. I'm a pureblood, on both sides all the way back, so basically I'm the same as you. I think Bliss felt it, and even Snowy, but me? Nothing. So why is that?"

"Are you seriously asking me?" he said, imitating her earlier tone.

"If you have an answer."

"Now that you mention it, I might. I've been here from the beginning. I fathered an entire clan, the Conlins, Miss Azure's people." He gestured at the Sadieville valley below them. "It was one of them, in fact, who sold all this land to the coal company during one of those times I was back *there*." He nodded at the cave.

"Bad timing," she observed.

"When I heard about it, and especially when Sophronie was killed, I realized how much this world, this *place* meant to me. I was no longer a tourist here, or even a guest. After all that time, I had at least one foot in both worlds. But that's a balancing act, and it can't last. Sooner or later, you have to put both feet down in the same place."

"I'm not following."

"It's like this: if someone like me, free to go back and forth, realizes he's as tied to this place as the *other* one, then what must it be like for the Tufa, who have been here forever? *Of course* you didn't feel at home there. No matter what your blood, what your family or heritage, *this* is your home. Not just this town, or this valley. This *world*."

"So we've been wrong all this time," she said. It wasn't a question.

"Yeah, well, join the club."

The winds stirred the trees around them. Even though it was broad daylight, Bronwyn felt the unmistakable hum of the night winds, and the shiver of the spirits that gave them their guidance and wisdom. "That explains why we can ride the night winds, then."

"Exactly. They didn't come with the Tufa from over there; they were already here, and embraced you when you arrived.

I mean, hell, Bronwyn, you have your own *gods* here now; how much more at home can you be?"

She smiled wryly. "Don't you mean 'we' have our own gods here?"

"Point taken."

She thought over all he'd said. "It'll take a while for that idea to take hold. And some likely won't ever accept it."

"I know."

She looked out at the valley. "And there's one question none of this really answers." She paused. *"Why?"*

" 'Why?' " he repeated.

"Yes. Why did you make that stupid bet? Why did we end up here, of all places? Why did any of this happen?"

He moved to stand beside her, the two of them embodying the past and future of the Tufa. They gazed out at the treetops and meadows, and the blue rolling mountains beyond. He swore he almost heard Sophronie's voice in the wind, with the echo of the Drummer playing along:

*Can never go back, don't have the will . . .*

"Did you ever see *Chinatown?*" he asked.

"The Jack Nicholson movie?" Bronwyn said.

"Yeah. Remember the last line?"

" 'Forget it, Jake, it's Chinatown'?"

"Yeah. In the movie, it means that some things just happen, and that we can't dwell on wondering why, because we'll never find out anyway."

Bronwyn said, "I understand that, actually."

"You do?"

"Yeah." She smiled, then chuckled a little. She wasn't so much amused as she was *awed* by the scale of what she'd learned, and what it meant for the future. Nothing had changed, and everything had; laughter was the only possible response. "And I guess there's only one thing to say to it."

"Which is?"

She looked up at him and winked.

"'Forget it, Tuck. It's Sadieville.'"

All song lyrics are original, except as indicated here.

CHAPTER 7 (AND THROUGHOUT)
"Sadieville" by Jennifer Goree,
© 1998 Jennifer Goree
Used by permission

CHAPTER 17
revision of lines 467–472 of *The Bacchae* by Euripides (480– or
    485–406 B.C.)
http://www.bartleby.com/8/8/2.html

CHAPTER 37
"Goin' Home" by William Ames Fisher
Composed 1922; public domain
https://en.wikisource.org/wiki/Goin%27_Home